MILLIONAIRES ROW

NORMAN KATKOV

MILLIONAIRES ROW

A DUTTON BOOK

DUTTON

Published by the Penguin Group
Penguin Books USA Inc., 375 Hudson Street, New York, New York 10014, U.S.A.
Penguin Books Ltd, 27 Wrights Lane, London W8 5TZ, England
Penguin Books Australia Ltd, Ringwood, Victoria, Australia
Penguin Books Canada Ltd, 10 Alcorn Avenue, Toronto, Ontario, Canada M4V 3B2
Penguin Books (N. Z.) Ltd, 182–190 Wairau Road, Auckland 10, New Zealand

Penguin Books Ltd, Registered Offices:
Harmondsworth, Middlesex, England

First published by Dutton, an imprint of Dutton Signet,
a division of Penguin Books USA Inc.
Distributed in Canada by McClelland & Stewart Inc.

First Printing, January, 1996
1   3   5   7   9   10   8   6   4   2

REGISTERED TRADEMARK—MARCA REGISTRADA

LIBRARY OF CONGRESS CATALOGING-IN-PUBLICATION DATA:
Katkov, Norman.
Millionaires row / by Norman Katkov.
p.   cm.
ISBN 0-525-93843-5
1. Tobacco industry—North Carolina—History—20th century—Fiction.   2. Sheriffs—
North Carolina—Fiction.   3. Family—North Carolina—Fiction.   I. Title
PS3521.A654M55   1996
813'.54—dc20   95-21790
                                                                                        CIP

Printed in the United States of America
Set in Transitional 551

Designed by Steven N. Stathakis

For My Grandchildren
Amelia and Nick

MILLIONAIRES ROW

COMING BACK TO THE LABOR DAY PICNIC in 1932 after seven years, Wyn Ainsley felt as if he had not been away. The heat, the dust, the armies of kids yelling and scurrying around between the old tobacco drying sheds, the mothers trying to hold on to their kids, the closed circles of men sharing a bottle of Prohibition moonshine, the older men and women hugging the rare patches of shade were all familiar. Wyn Ainsley could not go ten feet without recognizing someone.

The company had been giving a Labor Day Picnic for as long as Wyn Ainsley could remember. The tobacco sheds were hung with red, white, and blue banners, and when night fell and the band began its concert of marching songs, the massive sign spelling KING-CASTLETON within a circle of cigarettes, all in electric lights, brightened the entire plant.

Although the Fourth of July Parade and the Harvest Festival late in October, the other company blowouts, attracted children as well as their parents, at those events the kids were spectators. The parade began only after a long series of speeches from a speaker stand in front of company headquarters downtown. And the Harvest Festival at Castleton Farms bored the youngsters. People filled their cars and wagons with the harvested crops. They brought their children to help carry home the free food, the Castleton largess.

The Labor Day Picnic belonged to the kids. The company

aimed the food at the kids: hot dogs with sauerkraut and mustard and pickles and onions; potato chips, and all the Coke anyone could drink, all the lemonade and root beer anyone could drink. And later, after the foot races, candied apples and endless pyramids of candy bars.

As Wyn Ainsley made his way to the children's races, he had to snake through the crowd, which seemed bigger than he remembered. The crowds around the food stands seemed bigger.

Wyn decided the Depression had swollen the attendance. People came for the free food. Hitchhiking home from Hollywood the year before, Wyn had seen hungry people along the road, seen them in town after town, city after city. He had seen long lines around soup kitchens, had seen children begging.

"Sheriff!" A food attendant in a high, floppy white chef's hat speared a hot dog from a tub of boiling water and slipped it into a damp, steamy roll, holding the roll aloft. Wyn grinned and shook his head. "Come back, y'hear?" Wyn nodded, still grinning.

Wyn Ainsley was a new deputy sheriff in a new tan gabardine uniform, shirt and trousers, which itched under the hot sun. He wanted to open his shirt collar and loosen his tie. Wyn removed his campaign hat and fanned himself. Except for a baseball cap, Wyn—Wyngard, his mother's maiden name—had been bareheaded all twenty-five years of his life.

Shading his eyes with the campaign hat, Wyn squinted, looking up into the sky. The weather had changed during the night. The heat had slipped in, and the day had dawned hot and sticky with not a trace of wind, not a breath of a breeze anywhere. North Carolina can be awfully hot in the fall, and this year the heat wave had come early, arriving with Labor Day.

The races were staged between the tobacco sheds and the railroad tracks, where the empty freight cars were filled with millions of cigarettes each day. Wyn remembered running in each race, even the sack race, teaming up with whoever would join him. He had grown up running, playing with every team in the neighborhood.

He stopped at the starting line, where a row of kids, some barefoot, elbowed one another for room. Somewhere nearby a woman said, "Hello," and Wyn found Kay beside him, close enough to touch.

"Hi . . . I didn't even see you," Wyn said. "Where did you come from?"

"Here," Kay said. "We've been here awhile, and you said you would be here . . . be working. I've been looking for you, and—" She broke off, a shy young woman, hesitant and soft-spoken. "Are you stationed here at the races?"

"Nope. I'm supposed to roam around in case there's trouble. So far everyone is happy," Wyn said. "You look smashing." He had read the word somewhere and thought it sounded worldly and sophisticated. "You really do, Kay."

"Thank you," Kay said. She found his hand and held on. Katherine Lefferts was taller than the girls of her generation, and slender, with sand-colored hair. She wore a dirndl and a loose blouse cut low. She spent many hours of her days in the sun, and her face and arms and legs were golden. Kay Lefferts had been a freshman at Washington High School when Wyn began his senior year, a child whom he barely noticed and did not remember.

Wyn went away after high school and stayed away for years, and when he returned and saw her again, Kay Lefferts had turned into a knockout, tall and sleek and smooth.

They met first at Edith and Jim Anderson's house. Wyn drove Kay home that night, and the next week he called her and they went to a movie. The following week they drove out into the country and had chicken in a roadhouse. And they had been seeing each other ever since.

The few weeks since meeting Wyn had turned Kay inside out. She became someone different, someone new. She lived in a kind of turmoil that raged on with no sign of ending. She became a prisoner of the conflict, no longer able to control her thoughts.

Kay did not recognize herself, her secret self. She lived a secret life that began anytime after she woke and continued all through the day and night. At any moment, anywhere, without warning, she would see herself with Wyn, alone with Wyn. She thought of them in bed together, in the woods together; she thought of them together on the bank of the creek, and in the creek and without clothes, everywhere without clothes. She thought of them together in his car, thought of them in her mother's car as she drove her mother to one appointment or another. She could not stop thinking of Wyn, could not dismiss him. He would not stay away. And daily her restless imagination became more daring, more explicit. Sometimes she would shut her eyes, but still, Wyn appeared, in the bus, in the market, and once in the dentist's chair as the dentist had leaned over her. The dentist had become Wyn, and he slipped into the chair atop her and they . . . oh, God!

Girls didn't do what she and Wyn—they didn't. Girls didn't go all the way. Kay didn't know a single girl who had gone all the way, had not even heard of one. Sometime during high school, starting with good-night kisses, girls began necking. And many girls reported necking, really heavy necking. But a girl didn't do . . . everything. Kay lived a life of daily, unremitting torment. "Wyn!"

Jim Anderson waved as he and Edith, Kay's sister, approached. Kay removed her hand from Wyn's, and he grinned. "Hey, you're a big girl now," he said, and the color rose in her face.

"We've had enough," said Jim, a trim, solid man with wide shoulders and a boy's waist.

Jim Anderson had come home from college and returned to Washington High, from which he had graduated. When he began, he coached the track team and doubled as an assistant coach for both football and baseball. He had remained an assistant for football, but by the time Wyn appeared, trying out for the baseball team, Jim had been named manager. Wyn liked Jim immediately, making him something of an older brother. Jim was an emotional man who gave the climactic speech at all school rallies in the assembly hall. He always made some students cry, and he himself often felt teary as he exhorted the kids to rally around their team.

Edith and Jim were alike. They were bighearted, genuinely decent people who believed in and lived by the eternal verities. Their home had long ago turned into a kind of campground of the students at Washington High, girls as well as boys.

"Too hot out here," Edith said as they joined Kay and Wyn. "We want to leave."

"If Kay can tear herself away," Jim said.

Wyn grimaced. "You're funny."

"Wyn, come for dinner," Edith said. "Jim brought home a bushel of corn. A bushel!"

"Wish I could," Wyn said. "Everyone in the department is on duty today. All day. All day and half the night, I guess."

"How's your father?" asked Jim.

"Okay, I guess," Wyn said, and grinned. "Mad as usual. He's around here somewhere." Wyn looked at Kay. "See you tomorrow night, okay?"

Kay said, "Yes. Wyn, would you—" and could no longer be heard as a roar like a clap of thunder ripped across the sky. An airplane dived directly at the crowd.

Women shrieked, and some put their hands over their eyes. Children burrowed into the legs and bellies of their mothers and fathers, and men raised their arms instinctively, as though to protect themselves from the aircraft.

The plane hurtled toward the ground, closer, closer. As the crowd stood helplessly, the pilot pulled back the stick, and the aircraft rose, climbing vertically, climbing to the sun, up and up and up. It seemed to stop in midair and hang motionless for an instant before falling over on its back, beginning a graceful loop, an Immelmann, turning slowly until it flew parallel to the ground. The crowd, which had been terrified seconds before, burst into a spontaneous cry of enchantment.

Now the aircraft could be seen clearly, a single-engine Waco biplane, a two-seater painted bright orange, with white spears on the leading edges of the wings and white spears on the tail. Everyone could identify the plane and the pilot, and all through the crowd men and women turned to one another, saying "Kyle Castleton" or "That's Kyle."

High above them, in the biplane, the pilot and his passenger wore identical leather flying jackets and leather helmets with goggles, and each had a long white silk scarf around his neck. Each wore gray suede gloves. When the pilot completed two consecutive loops and the plane leveled off, his passenger, Boyd Fredericks, looked back, jabbing his forefinger at the ground. "Let's land!" he shouted, although he could not be heard above the engine. He pushed up his goggles. "Set it down! I'm getting sick!"

Behind him Kyle Castleton nodded and turned the airplane on its side, beginning a barrel roll, turning over and over and over.

On Millionaires Row to the west, at the Castle, the redbrick palace Sam Castleton had built, three other spectators watched the aerial acrobatics from a terrace where Kyle had stationed them.

Coleman, a big elderly black man in a white jacket, stood behind the other two: Russell Vance, the estate manager of the Castle and Castleton Farms, and the pilot's wife. Faith Venable and Kyle King Castleton were newlyweds, married the previous November.

Faith, a slender young woman dressed all in white, wore a tennis skirt and a shift. She wore a white band over her long black hair, coiled and pinned at the back of her neck. She had especially large eyes, the color of slate, and her skin was white and almost luminous. In the sun she seemed angelic.

The black man, a servant since he could remember, chuckled as the orange aircraft twisted and spun through the sky. "Now Mist' Kyle is going for the sun again," Coleman said as the biplane climbed. "Now he'll quit. See? He quit. Now he'll start to roll. Now he's rolling." Coleman anticipated each move in Kyle's repertoire, laughing as the biplane streaked through the blue sky. "Makes me dizzy watching him."

Faith caught her breath. "I can't watch him." She turned sharply, her white skirt flaring as she left the terrace.

Russell Vance followed her. "Kyle is a good pilot," he said. "Even the professionals agree. It's something . . . he's proud of his flying."

"I've asked him to stop the stunts," Faith said, stepping inside the house. In the cool, high-ceilinged library she paused beside a long reading table. "I've pleaded with him."

━━━◦《◉》◦━━━

Hours later, as the waning day's first shadows fell across the courthouse parking lot, Dan Cohen left his car, where his son waited, to walk toward Sheriff's Headquarters in the basement.

Inside, Dan walked along a narrow corridor toward open double doors. Stark lights inside brightened the narrow corridor. He removed his hat, a white Panama, thirty years old, a gift from his mother when he had left for the University of North Carolina at Chapel Hill.

He entered a large room filled with lamps hanging from a low ceiling. Lights burned day and night in Sheriff's Headquarters. To his left a high counter running from wall to wall dominated the room. Three rows of desks were set behind the counter. Deputies in uniform sat at some of the desks, and two bent over typewriters, pecking out arrest reports. The sheriff, Earl Ainsley, Wyn's father, stood against one end of the counter reading a newspaper.

Dan Cohen went to the counter, where he stopped in front of Arver Long, a deputy with a mustache modeled after Clark Gable's. Using a primitive schoolroom pen that he constantly dipped into an inkwell, Arver Long wrote slowly in the charge book, a ledger with leather tooling. Dan Cohen waited for a time, but Long ignored him. "Excuse me."

Long continued writing. "My name is Cohen. Daniel Cohen. I represent Willy Floyd."

Long stopped writing. He set the pen in a trough beside the ledger. He looked up, grinning at the Jew. "Represent?"

"I'm an attorney," Dan said. At the far end of the counter Earl Ainsley closed the newspaper.

Earl tried to hide his pouch by wearing a uniform shirt too big for him. A dumpy little man with graying hair cut short, Earl Ainsley looked like a janitor or a night watchman. He heard Dan say, "I'm his counsel. You're holding Willy Floyd."

Earl said, "Ain't you got nothing better to do?" He moved slowly along the counter, hitching up his gabardine pants. He looked sleepy, but the sheriff saw everything. "Today's Labor Day," Earl said. "Today's a holiday."

Although he and Dan had grown up in different parts of the city and had different backgrounds, they had known each other most of their lives.

The first Cohen had established himself in the city long before the first Ainsley appeared. He emigrated from Warburg in Germany and settled in Knoxville, Tennessee. His uncle, a merchant, put Emanuel Cohen to work in his store. The lad worked hard and saved his money, and eleven years later, when he married, he began to think of owning his own store.

A drummer told him the widow of a customer in North Carolina had put up the store for sale. Emanuel Cohen boarded a train carrying his checkbook.

He was not a religious man, but when his first son was born, Emanuel headed the group that established the first—and for fifty years the only—synagogue in the city.

Earl stopped beside Arver Long and looked across the counter. He faced a slim, spotlessly neat man of middle height. Dan wore a poplin suit and a white shirt and a tie. "You got all dressed up in this heat," Earl said. "You come all the way into town for a nigger?"

"The Reverend Fitch telephoned me," Dan said. "Willy Floyd's wife can't take care of her children alone. She's sick, Sheriff."

"She's sick because Willy Floyd beat her up," Earl said. "And if I let him out now, he'll go right back to the Flats and beat her up again. And he'll get drunk again. So there'll be a knife fight out there, and I can't spare the men. Goddammit, I don't want my men in the Flats."

"What is the charge?" Dan asked.

"You know better," Earl said. He kept any black arrested in the Flats, the black ghetto, in a cell for a few days before releasing him, saving the county the expense of a court appearance and a possible workhouse sentence. "Willy Floyd stays right here until he—" Earl stopped as Dan took a long white envelope from the inside pocket of his jacket. "You've got a writ," Earl said.

"Habeas corpus," Dan said. "Abner Fletcher signed it." Judge Fletcher presided over the municipal court. Dan opened the envelope and removed a document, which he set atop the open ledger.

"On Labor Day?" Earl said. "You went to Abner Fletcher's house on a holiday for a nigger?" His arm shot out, startling his deputy, who sprang back as Earl snatched the writ from the ledger. "I'll bet a month's pay you don't even know the nigger. Do you know him?"

"The reverend called," Dan said.

Earl glanced at the document and tossed it aside. "Get Willy Floyd!"

"I was posted here at the charge ledger," Long said.

Earl shouted, "Get him! Get him now!" Long walked around Earl and near the wall raised a hinged section of the counter. Earl pushed his campaign hat down over his eyes. "I'm heading home," he said in disgust. As he passed, he added to Dan, "When are you going to grow up?" He turned and made his way between the desks to a door at the rear.

Dan went to a row of wooden folding chairs against the wall and sat down. A few minutes later the deputy returned with a tall, slender, very handsome young black man. Dan rose. "Willy Floyd, I'm Dan Cohen."

"Yes, sir, Mist' Cohen," Willy Floyd said. "Yes, sir."

"You're coming with me," Dan said.

"Yes, sir, I'm comin'," said Willy Floyd. "I'm comin', yes, sir."

In the parking lot Dan's older son, David, leaned against the fender of an Essex sedan, waiting for his father. The boy, who had graduated from high school the past June, wore a skivvy shirt and dungarees, and his bare feet were in worn, shapeless sneakers. He wore glasses to correct serious nearsightedness. In stature David resembled his father, but while Dan Cohen was unmistakably Levantine, his son had matured into a classic Anglo-Saxon with blond hair and blue eyes. David Cohen ignored his myopia and had been, from childhood, a ferocious competitor on the playing field. When he saw his father come out of the courthouse, he waved and spun around the hood of the car to the driver's side. He flung himself behind the wheel and started the car, anxious to get home for dinner.

So he didn't see the black man following his father until the two reached the car. "Get in, Willy Floyd," Dan said.

"Yes, sir, thank you, sir," Willy Floyd said. "I get in, yes, sir," he said, opening the front door of the car, holding it, and waiting for Dan to settle in beside his son.

"I'm sorry you had to wait so long, David," Dan said.

"You weren't gone that long," his son replied. Behind him Willy Floyd got into the backseat of the old Essex.

Dan turned into the seat so he could see both David and the black man. "Willy Floyd, this is my son David."

David said, "Hello," as he shifted gears and backed away from the courthouse.

"Hello, Mist' David," said Willy Floyd. "Your daddy saved me," he said. "Yes, sir, saved Willy Floyd."

David touched the brake pedal, and when the car stopped, he shifted into first gear but did not move forward. He looked at his father. "Did you have any trouble? Are you okay?"

The boy's concern annoyed Dan, and his face twisted for an instant. "Yes, yes. I'm okay." He waved his hand at the windshield, ordering his son to proceed. "I'm okay," he repeated. His family handled Dan Cohen as though he were a defective.

He had been physically awkward from childhood, without grace, and he lacked the natural coordination of his two sons. He had neither mechanical ability nor comprehension; he could not use a hammer or a screwdriver without creating a disaster. His wife, Sarah, had discovered these flaws immediately. It endeared him to her. She loved him even more fiercely because she could mother him. She magnified his shortcomings, and his sons, like their mother, watched over him protectively. Unlike Sarah, his sons really believed Dan needed their constant vigilance. Occasionally Dan revolted, but his rebellions were short-lived, ending abruptly since he worried about offending the boys or Sarah. "Drive on, please."

David turned right at the corner of the courthouse and right again, toward the street. "You made the wrong turn," Dan said.

"Wrong?" David pointed. "There's the bus stop, three blocks down."

"We'll drive Willy Floyd home," Dan said. "His wife needs him."

"You mean the Flats?" David said, sore at his father. David was ready to eat a horse. But he could count on his dad to dig up someone he could help. David spun the wheel and the car lurched to the left, throwing Dan against his son.

"Did you find that necessary?" Dan asked.

"I'm sorry," David said, his anger evaporating. He wanted to find a hole and jump into it.

IN THE CASTLE that evening Faith sang some of the popular songs of the day. She sat with Boyd Fredericks on the piano bench before the concert grand on which he accompanied her. Both had changed for dinner. Faith wore a dress cut low front and back. Her arms were bare, and a black lace shawl lay across her shoulders. Beside her Boyd was giddy, almost as though he was floating. The most beautiful woman in the world sat at his side, and when she turned, singing to him, the young man thought he would topple from the bench.

Faith's voice, low and seductive, offered promises of endless pleasure. In a chair near the piano Russell Vance sat motionless, caught up in the lyrics, and nearby, beside the coffee service, Coleman closed his eyes, remembering other summers and other summer nights.

Behind everyone, Kyle Castleton moved slowly through the music room, his hand passing over chairs, sofas, tables, seemingly alone.

Faith liked to sing, liked the innocent exuberance of letting go, letting her voice take over. Her voice could capture the listener, capture an entire audience. On Broadway five years earlier, she had created a sensation playing an ingenue and stopping the show in her debut. Eight months later she had the lead in a musical written for her, and she became a star.

The year before, 1931, Faith had opened in *All's Fair*, her biggest hit, to rave reviews. She was a smash. It was a season of memorable Broadway shows: *Of Thee I Sing*, the Gershwin musical at the Music Box; *Reunion in Vienna*, the Robert Sherwood play, at the Martin Beck; *Counsellor-at-Law*, by Elmer Rice, with Paul Muni in the lead, at the Plymouth. Yet no name had burned more brightly than that of Faith Venable.

As Faith finished, Boyd sat back, raising his hands and applauding fiercely. "You're wonderful!" Russell joined in the applause, and Coleman, clapping, made great smacks, his big, muscular arms extended.

Faith hugged Boyd, holding him close before releasing him. *"You're* wonderful," she said. "You are, Boyd. I wish I'd had you with me all those years in New York." She kissed him, and when she pulled away, he stared at her, his eyes wide. His lips parted but he did not speak, nervously running his hands over the keyboard. "What's next, Faith?"

"You choose," Faith said.

"I love everything you've ever done," Boyd said.

She put her hand against his cheek. "You're spoiling me." Just then she saw Kyle stop beneath a tapestry on the far side of the music room, glancing at the delicately woven, elongated figures in the shadows.

Faith's hand fell. Boyd played a brief, melodic introduction. "What will it be? Faith?"

She did not reply, watching Kyle proceed slowly like someone who has wandered aimlessly into a museum. "Kyle?"

She saw him pause and look across the room at the piano. "You choose, Kyle," she said more loudly. "What shall I sing for you?"

"Whatever," Kyle said negligently, leaving the tapestry and running his hand across a large console containing a powerful radio. He wore his flying jacket, and his white scarf lay across his shoulders and fell to his knees. The scarf had become spattered with food droppings: a glob of mustard, traces of piccalilli, and, just above one tassled end, an irregular island of catsup.

At Russell's suggestion dinner that night had been brought from the Labor Day Picnic. And Kyle, who normally pecked at his food and often ignored it completely, ate like a glutton when the hot dogs were served, layering each roll with mounds of relish. He ate enough for two people.

"Kyle?"

He reached a table filled with photographs of Kings and Castletons—and everywhere of Sam Castleton. He caressed a sterling frame, touched another. "Kyle?"

"Present," he said, moving past the table, holding the ends of his scarf with both hands, and waving them slowly as he circled the music room.

"I want you to choose a song," Faith said, but he did not respond. His silence signaled danger, which everyone around him could sense. Russell came out of his chair and stood beside it as though waiting for orders, and Coleman left the coffee service and went to the door, where he stopped like a sentry at his post.

Faith could see Kyle drawing into himself, blocking her out. After their marriage she had learned quickly that she could not penetrate the isolation in which he lived so much of the time.

She could see Russell standing erectly, like someone afraid even to blink, and Coleman at the door staring straight ahead. She could feel Boyd, rigid, beside her. She felt responsible for the nameless dread that now filled the oversize room. "Kyle, let me sing for you," Faith said. He turned as though he intended to leave, and Faith bumped into Boyd, hard. "Make room," she said. "Kyle? Kyle? Come and sit beside me."

He did not pause, did not look back. Faith made herself smile. "Come now or I'll come after you," she said.

He stopped and turned, and everyone waited until he took a

step toward the piano. Like Boyd, Kyle was twenty-two years old and slight and fair. Kyle cared nothing for clothes, but Boyd dressed daily like an eastern collegian, even though he had never been out of North Carolina. That night he wore a tan beer jacket of linen and a red-and-black-striped bow tie with his white shirt. Boyd seemed younger than Kyle, and he acted younger. He became excited easily, and then he would often clap his hands rapidly like a child, like Eddie Cantor.

When Kyle reached the piano, Faith patted the bench. She said, "Sit here." He stood over her, immobile until she raised her head. "Please."

Kyle threw one end of the scarf over his shoulder and sat down beside her. As Boyd played a fanfare, Faith put her arm through Kyle's. "Darling? Tell me what to sing for you."

Kyle didn't reply. The room fell silent. The faint ticking of a clock somewhere in the Castle crept through the open doors. An eternity passed until Kyle said, "You choose, darling, from your years of experience on the Great White Way."

He faced her, smiling slightly, completely at ease. No matter what he did, standing or sitting, he seemed to be posing. And he switched from one pose to another. Faith had learned to recognize his changing moods. He could be amused, then in a flash become annoyed, or impatient, or patronizing, or sullen and baleful. He could appear impassive and in the next instant threatening, even deadly. And his pale blue eyes always remained open, as though he were looking into the far, far distance which no other human being could penetrate.

Faith said, almost inaudibly, "Don't. . . . please," and then, nodding and forcing a smile, "I'll choose."

As she spoke, Kyle rose from the piano bench. "Time for me to turn into a toad," he said.

"Don't go," Faith said. "It's early and we're having a party."

He waved the ends of his scarf. "Happy party."

"You asked for it," Faith said. "You wanted a party tonight."

"Have fun," Kyle said.

Boyd slid off the piano bench. "If you're really going to bed, Kyle, drive me home first."

Kyle moved one of the family photographs on the table. "Can't leave. You're Faith's accompanist."

"Cut it out, Kyle," Boyd said. "If you won't drive me, give me the keys to your car or any car."

"Stay over."

"I told Mother I'd be home," Boyd said. "She expects me."

"Call Mother," Kyle said absently, moving on. At the doors he said, "Sleep well, Russell."

"After I put out the cat," Russell said. He did not join Kyle, waiting for the younger man to go ahead, with Coleman following. Russell gave Kyle plenty of room that Labor Day night. Since Kyle had decided the evening had ended, Russell hoped it would end quickly. He could not be certain where one of Kyle's moods would lead anyone around him.

At the door Kyle wagged the ends of his scarf at Coleman. "Stay away from the girls."

The big, elderly black man grinned. "Yes, sir, Mist' Kyle," he said. "Stay away from the girls, yes, sir."

Behind them Faith pulled her shawl close around her. She looked back at Boyd, who stood behind the piano as though he were in physical danger and needed protection. "You mustn't blame yourself," Faith said.

"I don't care about me," Boyd said. "I just hate to see him hurting you."

She tried to smile. "I'm a big girl," Faith said.

"We were having too much fun," Boyd said. He recognized all the signs: first Kyle's silence, then his withdrawal. Ennui followed, and this inevitably grew into disapproval, ending with abrupt departure. "We're being punished for having too much fun."

Faith rose and moved around the piano bench to join him, her hands extended. "Boyd," she said softly, so only he could hear, "I'm glad you're staying."

He took her hand, wrapping his fingers tightly around hers. "Now I want to stay."

They left the music room and walked to the Castle entrance. "I've got to call Mother," Boyd said. "She'll stay up worrying, especially since she knows I'm with Kyle."

They stopped at the foot of the broad staircase. Faith raised their hands and kissed his hand. "Sweet dreams," she whispered, her lips moving across his knuckles.

"Faith . . ."

She removed her hand. "Not now," she murmured. "Not here." She faced him, sending him away, waiting until he turned and walked down the hall to call his mother.

Faith looked up at the beams of the soaring prison to which Kyle had brought her. She remained at the foot of the staircase for a moment, her hand on the cold balustrade making her feel cold inside, and then, slowly, she started up the stairs to the boy she had married.

KYLE HAD SEEN HER FIRST ONSTAGE, the day after he reached twenty-one, giving himself New York for a birthday present, paying a scalper an exorbitant fee for a ticket.

Kyle had remained at the Castle for his birthday because he would not disappoint Coleman, who had ordered a huge cake from the cook. Coleman always made Kyle's birthday an event for the boy he had raised and adored.

Kyle told Coleman to invite all the servants into the banquet hall, and there he cut the cake and the black man served the others. Since no one sat, Kyle stood with them, happy in their midst. The black men and women were his family, his real family, and the lonely young man did not feel lonely that afternoon. He kept the servants with him in the banquet hall, talking a mile a minute until Lucius Peete arrived.

The aged retired general counsel of the company continued to represent each member of the family. Lucius Peete could not be replaced. Sam Castleton had made him the sole trustee of the Castleton Family Foundation. Peete countersigned every check.

"You had an appointment," Lucius said. "Any day last week."

"I've been flying," Kyle said.

"You did not keep your appointment," Lucius said. "You're twenty-one years old, Kyle. You're an adult. I need to talk with you."

"After your cake," Kyle said.

The old man saw all the servants backing away toward the walls, trying to hide. Kyle stopped at the head of the table and moved back the chair. Lucius Peete remembered how sickly the boy had been in his early years. Lucius believed the boy's illness had affected his mind permanently. Kyle stood behind the chair, and Coleman brought the plate with the cake and a fork. "Lucius."

Kyle sat down beside him and said, "I suppose you've come about money."

"You are very rich now," Lucius said. He said Kyle had inherited hundreds of millions of dollars. Kyle forgot how many millions. He didn't care. He already had his airplane. Lucius said he had many documents that needed Kyle's signature. "You must come to the office tomorrow."

"I can't tomorrow," Kyle said. He had to get away from the Castle. He felt imprisoned in the huge stone house. Kyle left for New York on a morning train.

Kyle chose *All's Fair* because he saw Faith's picture everywhere: in the newspapers; in the hotel lobby; in shopwindows; on billboards atop buildings in Times Square.

In the theater Kyle watched the audience greet Faith's appearance with an explosion of applause, and every song she sang triggered another explosion. When the curtain fell, the entire audience rose in homage, demanding more of Faith. Kyle saw men pleading for another glimpse of her. When she slipped through the curtain to bow once more, she galvanized the audience. Her presence became a gift that she shared with everyone.

Kyle went back the next night, and the next and the next, and he went to the matinees on Wednesday and Saturday. He chose a different seat for every performance and watched everyone around him. Every man wanted Faith, so Kyle wanted her even more. He bribed the doorman at the stage door and waited beside her dressing room after each performance. He bribed Malcolm, the doorman at Faith's apartment, and kept a taxi waiting on Fifth Avenue while he sat in the lobby so he could escort her to the theater, and everywhere, every day, he asked her to marry him.

When the Broadway run of *All's Fair* ended and the show went on the road, Kyle joined the tour. After every performance he proposed. And in Chicago, after a Saturday night performance, she said, "Yes. Yes, yes, yes. I will marry you."

"Now," Kyle said, "tonight."

"Tonight? We can't be married tonight," Faith said. "It's Saturday night. Everything is closed. Everything is closed tomorrow. We'll need to fill out forms. It takes time."

"Let's try anyway," Kyle said. He had stuffed his pockets with money in large and small denominations. They drove to northern Michigan that night, and whenever Kyle asked a question, he raised a hand thick with money.

Faith stayed with the show, and Kyle stayed with her. The tour ended in Los Angeles in December, and after the final performance Faith announced her retirement. "I've been a full-time performer, and starting tonight, I intend to be a full-time wife."

Kyle took her from California directly to the Castle. Faith belonged to him now, him alone, like the orange aircraft he owned, and he expected her, like the aircraft, to wait quietly until he had the time or the inclination to be with her. Faith discovered she had married a ghost.

———◦《◦》◦———

IN THE CASTLE THAT LABOR DAY NIGHT Faith stopped at the head of the staircase. The corridors above were shaped like a giant I. When Faith entered the long leg of the I, she caught a glimpse of Coleman at the far end, disappearing to begin his nightly ritual of turning off lamps. She walked slowly, wearily, until she saw a narrow band of light from an open bedroom door crossing the corridor floor ahead of her.

Faith transformed herself. She let the shawl drop to her shoulders and held her head high, walking toward the lane of light as though making her way onstage, and when she opened the bedroom door, smiling and radiant, no woman anywhere could have seemed happier. "Kyle . . ." she said, letting her voice linger on his name, "I'm glad we're alone."

She removed the scarf slowly, letting it slide from her shoulders, letting it fall to the floor as though she were disrobing for him. "I was so tired of playing hostess," she said. "You rescued me, darling." Faith began to remove the pins from her hair, gathered at the nape of her neck. She went past the bed to the vanity, where she set down the pins in her hands. "I hoped you would be in bed waiting."

"Been waiting," Kyle said. He watched her shaking her head to loosen her hair as it fell below her shoulders. A large mirror with mirrored wings rose from the vanity. So Kyle saw Faith and three more Faiths. She filled the room, crowding him out, crowding out everyone and everything as she had on the stage when he had first seen her. "There are four of you," Kyle said.

She looked into the large mirror, smiling at him. "We're all yours."

"Mine alone," he said, keeping himself in check. "Until death do us part."

"Until *my* death do us part," Faith said. She stepped forward, but Kyle retreated, and Faith stopped and stopped smiling. But she could not allow the evening to disintegrate into another disaster, and she said lightly, "Remember, I go ahead of you."

They had made their ages a joke. Faith warned Kyle, early, she was four years older than he. But in their bedroom that night she looked even younger than when Kyle first saw her.

When Kyle did not respond, Faith began to undo her dress. "Come to bed, darling. I'm absolutely worn out."

"Another sign," Kyle said. "Like morning sickness."

Faith said, "Morning—" and broke off, staring at Kyle on the other side of the bed as the bedroom filled with danger. Faith could feel it, as though the air had thickened.

"You might escape," Kyle said. "Not everyone has morning sickness. You might be one of the lucky ones. Here's hoping you're one of the lucky ones."

She knew he lied. He did not wish her well. "How did you . . ." she began, and stopped. "I've told no one."

Kyle raised his hand, and she saw the brassiere dangling from his fingers. "Mother Nature," he said, moving his hand from side to side, swinging the brassiere. "Your breasts must be swelling. You've sent for bigger bras."

She loathed him. "And you're spying again," Faith said. "Now it's my lingerie."

He tossed the bra into the air, startling her. Faith leaped aside, throwing her arm around her belly instinctively, fingers spread across her navel. The bra floated down, crumpling on the bed. Faith's arm fell, and she sank into the chair in front of the vanity. "I haven't seen a doctor," she said. "I'm not sure. I want to be sure. So

I didn't tell you." She raised her head, looking up at Kyle as though she faced a jailer. "Our first child," Faith said.

"Our?" He made a small smile. "Our?"

She stared at him, her eyes wide. He frightened her, but she fought the fear. "Yes," she said, and sprung up from the chair. She came straight at him. "Yes, ours! Yours and mine."

"Liar," he said. "You're lying to me! You're both lying! Do you think I'm blind? I see perfectly, see everything perfectly!"

Jealousy consumed him. She was treating him like a fool, as though he hadn't watched her, night after night, in city after city, hypnotizing every man in the audience. "I can see the signs!" Kyle said, his voice rising to a shout.

He put his hand against his face. "Dear Boyd," he said. "Pretty Boyd." His hand fell, and his face twisted in hatred. "You did it in front of me tonight, in my house, my own house, in front of everyone, even my nigger!" He swung around to leave the bedroom, the ends of the scarf swinging through the air as he turned.

Faith lunged forward and grabbed his arm to stop him.

He pushed her aside, freeing himself. "Get away! Stay away!" He opened the door and slammed it back against the wall. "Fair warning, whore. Starting tonight, we're not together." He gestured."Tell Boyd about *our* baby."

As he strode into the corridor, Faith followed him. "So you've added Boyd Fredericks to your list," Faith said. "Boyd Fredericks. I'm surprised he can dress himself. Maybe he doesn't. Maybe his mother does that for him too!"

Kyle opened the door of the sleeping porch that faced their bedroom. He closed the door behind him, but Faith opened it and followed him. "First it was that silly old man in Dallas," she said. "Because he smiled at me. Then that fool in Los Angeles, trying to be Douglas Fairbanks. And the hairdresser at the Mark Hopkins in San Francisco. The *hairdresser!*"

———◦◉◦———

BELOW, on the far side of the Castle, Russell Vance closed the doors to the terrace where he and Faith had watched Kyle's stunts that day. Before he went to bed each night, Russell went through the Castle like a housekeeper. He carried a small leather notebook, and he often made notes of anything he saw that needed attention.

He crossed the library and closed the doors. He walked down the long main corridor to the entrance. He locked the front doors, slipping the oversize key into his pocket. He liked to test the lock, and each night he tried to turn the big doorknobs. Russell turned away, on his way to bed. As he passed the staircase, he heard the sharp, ringing crack of a gunshot. He stopped and said, "Oh, God . . ." and then, as though he had been released, he spun around and raced up the stairs.

Climbing two steps at a time, Russell heard Coleman say, "Mist' Kyle?" and louder: "Mist' Kyle?" As Russell reached the top, he saw Coleman plunge into the sleeping porch, and he saw Faith, in her stocking feet, with Boyd.

Faith raised her arm like someone trying not to fall, and Boyd held on to her. "Mist' Kyl-l-l-l-l-l-e!" Coleman's voice tore through the Castle in a long moan of horror and pain. Russell ran once more.

Ahead of him Faith and Boyd crossed the corridor together, holding on to each other as they followed the black man into the sleeping porch.

Kyle lay across the foot of the bed, his eyes open and blank, like buttons. His clean, smooth young face was no longer real, and the ash gray of death crept across his brow. Only the brilliant red blood that poured from the wound above his right ear seemed alive, trickling across his face and falling into the flying jacket.

All three heard the rapid pounding of footsteps, heard Russell shout, "Coleman? Coleman?" but none of them looked up at him as he ran into the sleeping porch. He said, "Holy—" and stopped at the door, but only for an instant. He strode past them to get to the telephone. "We need an ambulance!"

"He's dead," Boyd said.

"Not dead!" Coleman said. He bent over the bed, put his arms under the body, and came erect, holding Kyle against his white jacket as though he were carrying a bundle of kindling. "He's not dead!"

Russell said, "Hurry, man, hurry!" into the telephone, and whirled around. When he saw the black man, Russell said, "You're right. We can't wait. Put him in one of the big cars, Coleman. Put him in the Stutz." Russell stopped beside Faith. "Do you want to come, Mrs. Castleton? You don't have to come."

"My shoes," Faith said, and left the sleeping porch as though she were alone.

TEN MILES FROM THE CASTLE, at the courthouse, Wyn and Len Egan, another deputy, a few years older, were playing handball against the wall above Sheriff's Headquarters. Behind the players two black-and-white sheriff's patrol cars faced the wall, the headlights lighting up the playing area. Wyn and Len Egan were stripped to the waist. Wyn held a sponge ball of the kind favored by girls for playing jacks.

"Eighteen to four," Wyn said. He had won the first two games and held the serve. He let the ball drop and bounce, and as he bent over the ball to drive it into the wall, another deputy came out of the building. "Wyn! Holy mackerel! There's been a shooting at the Castle!"

Nobody saw the ball hit the wall and fly out in an ascending arc to disappear in the darkness. "Sheriff called," said the deputy. "Says for you to meet him at the hospital. Where the hell's your shirt?"

Wyn pointed at the patrol cars. "A *shooting?*"

"You heard me," said the deputy. "Len, move your goddamn car so he can get out!"

They ran to the patrol cars. Their clothes lay against the windshields. Wyn set his campaign hat on his head and reached for his shirt. Len Egan scooped up his clothing, threw it into his car, and dropped into the driver's seat. As Wyn pulled on his shirt, Len shifted into reverse and shot straight back.

In his car Wyn turned the wheel hard. Len yelled, "Wyn! Hold it!"

Wyn jammed the brake pedal into the floorboard, and as the patrol car rocked, he saw Len, still half naked, out of his car. "Your gun belt!" Len said. Len pulled the gun belt with the gun in the holster off the hood of Wyn's car and shoved it into his chest.

Wyn drove into the street. He turned left at the intersection, skipping second gear to move into high. His campaign hat slipped over his eyes, and as Wyn pushed it up, he remembered his siren. Pawing at the dashboard, he turned up the heater, then turned it off before he found the siren switch. The shrill scream filled the patrol car. Wyn rolled up his window, but the car became unbearably hot. He turned off the siren and lowered the window. "Not chasing anyone," he said aloud. At that moment he remembered the orange aircraft rolling over and over and over in the sunlight.

Except for newspaper photographs, Wyn had never seen any of the Castletons. Like almost everyone else, he had never been in the Castle, never seen the lake house, which was supposed to be the size of a small hotel. Except for the newspaper stories, covering a wedding or funeral or someone famous visiting, the Castletons could have been on another planet.

A gust of wind caught Wyn's tie, throwing it over his shoulder. Wyn pushed the tie into his shirt. He had to knot it before he saw his father, and he had to remember his gun belt. Wyn took it from the seat beside him and dropped it across his thighs. Somewhere ahead of him Wyn heard a siren: his father, coming from home at the other end of the county. Wyn picked up speed.

The hospital, like the Castle, was redbrick. The large metal C in the entrance was a copy of the C in the gates of the Castle. Sam Castleton had built the hospital for the city and named it for himself. Wyn could hear the siren, closer now, as he turned into the hospital driveway and saw a pale green Stutz phaeton beside the emergency entrance.

Wyn parked in the shadows and got out of the patrol car, buckling his gun belt around him. He was knotting his tie in a rush when the siren stopped abruptly. Wyn grabbed his campaign hat, and as the sheriff's car slid in beside the Stutz with the canvas top, Wyn came into the light from the hospital. "Hi, Pop."

His father said, "Yeah, hi." Earl Ainsley wore an old fishing jacket over his skivvy shirt, and on his feet the romeos he favored at home. He looked smaller out of uniform, and older. Wyn watched his father approach. The little man in the ragged fishing jacket seemed frail and even unsteady, but Wyn knew he was about as vulnerable as a rattlesnake.

Earl came closer, squinting as he looked up at his son. "What did you do, run all the way?"

He made Wyn feel guilty for batting the handball around. "It's hot out."

"It's gonna be a hell of a lot hotter from now on," Earl said. "What did they tell you at headquarters?"

"A shooting at the Castle."

"Short and sweet," Earl said. "Shooting at the Castle. The *Castle*. Couldn't be worse. Come on."

Wyn followed him into a large white admitting area with several doors leading to examining rooms. A heavy, acrid smell of detergent and antiseptic hung in the air. Beside an open door Wyn saw an elderly black man with the shoulders of a fullback in a white jacket. The man sat with his head down, his shoulders slumped, his hands in his lap and his legs crooked, like those of a discarded doll. As Wyn and Earl approached, he looked up, his face wet with tears. " 'S Mist' Kyle," Coleman said. "Mist' Kyle."

Earl stopped as if he had been roped, and Wyn had to swerve to avoid him. "Kyle," Earl said. "Kyle Castleton. Oh, Jesus. Jesus H. Christ. All the way over I kept telling myself some nigger had got hold of a gun and had shot up some other nigger. *Castleton*."

Wyn stood by, wanting to help, cursing himself for being tongue-tied. Someone came out of the examining room, and Earl said, "It's Sheriff Ainsley, Mr. Vance. This here's my son, Wyn. He's a new deputy."

"Sorry to meet like this," Russell said, and turned to Earl. "It's Kyle Castleton, Sheriff."

"I heard," Earl said.

"He's dead."

"Dead?" Wyn didn't know he had spoken, didn't know he'd removed his hat.

"Wow." Earl could barely be heard. Then his voice rose. "Kyle Castleton has been shot and he's dead?"

"He's in there," Russell said, gesturing. "You can see him, Sheriff."

"Before we do that," Earl said, "what happened, Mr. Vance? You were there."

"We had a small party," Russell said. "I brought back food from the Labor Day Picnic. Afterward Boyd—Boyd Fredericks, Kyle's friend—played and Faith—Mrs. Castleton—sang."

Russell stopped, and Earl said, "What else?"

"Well . . . Kyle said he was going to bed. Of course that ended the evening. I began to lock up. Then I heard a shot and then Coleman . . ." Russell said, gesturing at the black man.

"Heard what?"

"He cried out, 'Mist' Kyle,' " Russell said. "I heard him from below. And I . . . ran. When I got to the sleeping porch, Kyle was lying across the bed with blood—" Russell broke off, indicating his forehead with his forefinger.

"Where was the nigger?"

"In the sleeping porch," Russell said, "with Mrs. Castleton and Boyd. They got there ahead of me."

"Got there ahead of you from where?"

"Boyd had gone to telephone his mother to say he was spending the night in the Castle. And Mrs. Castleton had been in the bedroom across the hall when she heard the shot."

"She said."

"Yes . . ." Russell said. "Yes, of course. She said."

"Tell me about the ambulance," Earl said, since the Sheriff's Department responded to all county requests for an ambulance.

"I called for it," Russell said. "While I was using the telephone, Coleman picked Kyle up from the bed. So I decided not to wait, and we—I drove here."

"Any sign of a weapon?"

"Weapon?"

"A gun," Earl said. "A man's been shot dead. Did you see a gun?"

"No. No, I didn't, Sheriff," Russell said. "It all happened so fast. It was so unbelievable."

"Yeah, well, thanks, Mr. Vance," Earl said. "C'mon, Wyn."

He went into the examining room and Russell and Wyn followed. Wyn could see the figure on the table. A young doctor in a white linen coat stood beside the table.

Wyn had never seen a dead person. He forced himself to look. Earl said, "You're Dr.—" and broke off, pointing at the nameplate pinned to the white coat. "Dr. A. Widseth. A for what?"

"Arthur," said Arthur Widseth. "I'm the intern on call tonight. I examined the body."

"Tell me about that," Earl said.

"He was DOA," said the intern, "dead on arrival. He'd been dead for a while when he got here. My guess is that death was instantaneous from a self-inflicted wound."

"Your guess?" Earl said.

"No . . . *no*," said the intern. "It's my medical opinion."

"Self-inflicted," Earl said. "You mean suicide, is that what you mean?"

Widseth nodded. "Yes, correct."

"You mean Kyle Castleton killed himself."

"That's right," said Widseth.

Earl looked at Wyn. "Hear that? How would you like to have the doc here for a witness, Wyn? He takes one look at the body and gives you a verdict, bang."

Wyn had learned quickly in his short career to play the foil for his father, listening without comment, or nodding, or shaking his head if his father nodded or shook *his* head. He had also learned to hide his surprise or shock at anything his father said or did.

Earl turned back to the intern. "You were right here in this hospital, and whatever happened happened twelve some miles from this hospital, and you decided Kyle Castleton killed himself."

"Decided after I examined the body," Widseth said. He took a slender flashlight from the breast pocket of his white coat and pointed it at the wound. "You can see it for yourself," the intern said. "The site of the wound. The angle of penetration. You can see the powder burns. He must have put the gun against his head."

"Yeah." Earl's right hand went down and came up, pushing the muzzle of his revolver into the doctor's temple.

Wyn almost dived across the table to grab the gun, and Russell cried, "No! No!"

The intern stepped back, but Earl stayed with him. "You can get powder burns without killing yourself, Doc," Earl said. "Here's one way." He lowered the gun, glancing at Wyn, who wanted to cheer. His father continued to astonish him. The little man with the belly showed Wyn a new surprise almost every day. From the day he had put on the deputy's uniform for the first time, Wyn began discovering a new Earl Ainsley, a new father. A kind of magician who had an inexhaustible repertoire, Earl amazed Wyn daily.

The intern rubbed his eyes. "I said it was my opinion."

"That's all you've got, Doc, your opinion," Earl said. "Nobody told you he killed himself." Earl looked across the table. "Mr. Vance, did you tell the doc here Kyle Castleton killed himself?"

"Certainly not."

"Certainly not," Earl said. "And, Doc, you didn't *see* Kyle Castleton raise a gun and kill himself. Where *is* the gun? The murder weapon? The only gun I've seen around here is mine," Earl said, raising the revolver, a .38-caliber Police Positive. He pushed it into the waistband of his trousers. "Being an intern, you're new around here, aren't you, Doc?"

"Four months."

"Are you from around here?"

"I'm from Raleigh," said Arthur Widseth. "I went to medical school at Duke."

"Close enough," Earl said. "Doc, this is Kyle Castleton. Maybe you saw him this morning, saw his orange plane. Kyle Castleton was thousands of feet in the air this morning, flying loop-the-loops. Do you think he went up there figuring to kill himself tonight? If he wanted to kill himself, he could've done that in his airplane." Earl bent over the table until his head was inches from the matted hair and the wound. He came erect, rubbing his hands as though they were dirty. "Give me a sheet, huh?"

The intern went to the instrument case and squatted to pull out a drawer. He removed a folded white sheet and brought it to the table. Earl opened the sheet and dropped it over the body. "You're through with him, Doc. He's the coroner's property now. You put him somewhere for the coroner, hear? Lock him up tight, can you do that?"

"Lock him up?"

"Thanks." Earl turned away, finished with the intern for the night. "Wyn."

"Sheriff?" Russell joined them as they went back out to the large waiting room. "Do you think there was foul play?"

Earl buttoned the flaps of the breast pockets on his hunting jacket. "Do you, Mr. Vance?"

"I . . . uh . . ."

"That's one answer," Earl said. "Maybe the nigger . . . what's the nigger's name?"

"Coleman."

"Maybe Coleman can tell us," Earl said. "If he ever stops crying. Maybe Mrs. Castleton can tell us, or the friend Boyd Something."

"Fredericks," Russell said. "They're here, Sheriff."

"Here?" Earl frowned. "She's here?"

"They were—" Russell said, and broke off, looking around the waiting room.

"Probably out in the car," Earl said. "Wyn, you check around. I got some questions I want answered."

———

TWENTY FEET AWAY, in one of the examining rooms, Boyd leaned against the wall. "Just look at us," he said in a low monotone. "We're standing here as though nothing had happened. As though in a little while Kyle will come back and say, 'All set, everything is copacetic, we're rolling, or chop-chop,' like he used to say."

Faith sat in a chair near the door staring at the orderly rows of instruments in the instrument case, trying not to hear the stupid little fool. The little fool would not stop, talking without a break since they left the Castle, talking in the Stutz all the way to the hospital while Coleman held Kyle, rocking from side to side and moaning and sobbing.

"I can't believe he's dead," Boyd said. "I can't. I suppose that's why I haven't cried. I can't think of Kyle dead, so how can I cry? I'm not even tired. It must be late but—"

Faith wanted to cover her ears. She wanted to gag the idiot. "Boyd," she said sharply.

He broke off, startled, looking across the narrow room. Faith said, "Come and sit beside me." She had to keep him from coming apart, had to prop him up so he would not collapse.

"I'm all right, honest," Boyd said. "I really am, Faith." He hated worrying her, hated himself for behaving like a baby when he should be doing everything he could to help her. She had to understand she could count on him. He would do anything for her. And she needed his help now. "Faith? There's something I want you to remember," Boyd said. "I'll do anything for you. Anything."

He infuriated Faith. The weak, babbling little fool, the toady who had followed Kyle around, grateful for handouts, sickened her. "Dear, darling Boyd," she said, "come and sit beside me."

He shook his head. He could not appear weak in front of her. "You mustn't . . ." he said, and crumpled, sliding down along the wall to the floor.

"Boyd!" Faith leaped up, catching the heel of her shoe on the chair leg. She lost the shoe, and the chair toppled as she went around the examining table. She dropped to her knees beside the still figure on the floor. "Boyd!" For a second she thought he was dead, believed she would be found with him dead here on the floor. Faith raised her head, thinking only of escape, and then, furious with herself for giving way to panic, forced herself to think, to think. She put her arm under his shoulders and raised his head, cradling him in her arms. "Boyd. Boyd." She patted his face with her fingers.

His eyes opened. He whispered, "What happened?"

"You fainted." Faith put her hand against his face, holding him close. "Rest for a minute," she said, as though to an infant. "You'll be all right. I'll help you."

Behind them Wyn entered. He heard a woman say, "We'll help each other." Then Wyn saw her, down on the floor with a man, their arms around each other. A chair lay on its side near the examining table, and under it, tilted against the seat, Wyn saw one of the woman's shoes. The man stared at Wyn as though he were facing an executioner.

When the woman looked up, Wyn stopped breathing. Her luminous face and arms, her hair, her eyes, big and dark, were mesmerizing, isolating her with Wyn, apart from all the world. "He fainted," Faith said.

Wyn stepped into the room. "I'll give you a hand," he said. She raised her arms, and Wyn brought Faith to her feet as Boyd pushed himself up from the floor. "Your shoe," Wyn said, bending. Her arm brushed against his, and he stopped breathing again.

Faith said, "Thank you," then held the table and raised her foot to slip on the shoe.

In the parking lot Earl saw Wyn at the door of the emergency entrance. "They're not in the car," Earl said. Wyn stepped aside so Faith and Boyd could precede him. Earl had seen newspaper photographs of Kyle Castleton's wife, but the pictures looked like someone else. This dame was a knockout.

Russell said, "We were worried about you, Mrs. Castleton." He joined her. "Coleman is in the car. We should leave now."

Wyn watched her. She seemed to be alone. She said, "All right." She headed for the green phaeton, and when Boyd followed, he found Earl in his way.

"We'll take my car," Earl said. He looked over his shoulder. "Got a minute, Mr. Vance?"

As Russell turned back, Boyd said, "My mother is waiting."

"Sure," Earl said, and to Wyn: "Help this young fellow to my car. He can sit up front with me."

Russell waited beside the Stutz, where Earl joined him. "I'm sending my deputy with you, Mr. Vance," Earl said.

"To the Castle? You're sending a police officer to the Castle?"

"I'm the sheriff," Earl said. "I'm sending a deputy sheriff."

"Good God, man, I'd think after what has happened tonight, you'd leave us in peace."

"That's my job," Earl said. "That's what I'm sworn to do in this county, Mr. Vance. Keep the peace."

"We're in no danger."

Earl opened the door of the Stutz. "You just go on back to the Castle, Mr. Vance."

Gesturing at Wyn, he left Russell and stopped behind his own car.

Wyn pointed at Boyd, in the front seat. "I'll take him home, and you can go home."

"I left a dead man with a bullet in his head in this hospital," Earl said. "I need something to show for that. Boyd Fredericks isn't going home. Neither are you. Go on over to the Castle."

"The Castle?" Wyn looked over his shoulder at the Stutz and turned back to Earl.

"Stay there," Earl said.

"*Stay* there?"

Earl leaned back against his car. He had a long night ahead of him. He pushed the visor of his hunting cap up from his forehead, looking at Wyn. "You're pretty young to be losing your hearing," Earl said. He always forgot Wyn's size, even now, seeing him every day. And he forgot what a good-looking stud the kid had turned out to be. Wyn sure as hell didn't look like his old man. He took after Peggy's side of the family. They were big in Peggy's family, women as well as men. They had raised a nice kid, he and Peggy. Too goddamn nice for anyone wearing a badge. "Hey, listen. They stand up to the piss pot over at the Castle, same as you." It was the best advice he could give the kid. "Just go over there and hang around. Don't do anything. Just be there."

Earl got into his car and waited until Wyn had driven out of the emergency entrance before following. He drove through the downtown streets, dimly lit and almost deserted. "This isn't the way to my house," Boyd said.

"I'm taking the long way around."

Boyd looked out of the car window, watching telephone poles, buildings, street signs, trying to block out the sleeping porch, block out Kyle.

He could not remember a time without Kyle. Olive Fredericks, who had given piano lessons to the Castleton children, brought Boyd along one day, hoping her child's presence would make Kyle more tractable for the hour on the piano stool.

Her gambit succeeded. Kyle would have welcomed an orang-utan for those sixty minutes of purgatory each week. And when Kyle learned the teacher's son also took lessons, he invited Boyd to practice in the Castle.

Kyle had been alone most of his life. His brother, Holt, was eight years older, a lifetime removed. And Gaby was not only older but a girl. Kyle had been the runt all his life, and when Boyd appeared, Kyle made him the runt.

Being chosen as Kyle's friend changed Boyd Frederick's life. He was welcome at the Castle. Kyle invited him constantly. Cars came to fetch him. He became unique among his peers in and out of school. Boyd reveled in the limelight Kyle Castleton focused on him. Boyd's mother did not share her son's delight in his status. Olive Fredericks came to regret the impulse that had brought Boyd to the Castle. Boyd had a gift for the piano. His mother urged him to practice, to concentrate, to devote himself to the instrument. But Kyle beckoned, the Castle beckoned, the Stutz, and the Pierce-Arrow, and the Marmon two-seater beckoned. And when no invitation came, Boyd sought Kyle out, a compliant confederate in all Kyle's harebrained schemes and adventures. Boyd was always available. As the years passed and Kyle left the Castle for other states and other countries, Boyd stayed behind, waiting patiently for him to return.

Beside Earl in the sheriff's car, Boyd sat up in the seat. "You're not taking me home! Take me home!"

"Hey, you!" Earl's right arm swung straight out and across Boyd's chest. Earl's elbow rammed into Boyd's neck. "Shut up, you!" Boyd began to gag. Earl let him gag. "We got a dead man here. You were there at the time. Now, I been nice to you. That can end too."

Moments later Boyd said, "Millionaires Row! You're taking me back to the Castle! Why are you taking me back to the Castle?"

"Yeah, shut up." Earl drove more slowly. He pressed the switch of the searchlight, which protruded from the door at an angle to the windshield. "Yeah . . ." Earl turned left into a long drive.

He stopped facing the entrance of a redbrick house and came out of the car. He locked his door, and that locked all four doors. "Christ!" The searchlight beam illuminated the heavy, studded door of the house. Earl unlocked the car, turned off the searchlight, and locked the car once more.

When he pressed the buzzer, Earl heard chimes. As he again raised his hand toward the buzzer, the door opened. Earl faced a slim, stately young woman in her thirties with café au lait skin and straight black hair cut in a pageboy bob. Her lips were full but not Negroid, and she had the facial bones of ancient Egyptian royalty. She wore a simple, elegant dress with long sleeves and white French cuffs. Her name was Honeychild, and Earl had heard of her. Workmen and delivery boys all over the county fought for the chance to be dispatched to the redbrick mansion.

"I'm the sheriff," Earl said. "I'm here for Mrs. Castleton . . . Mrs. Burris. I'm here to see Mrs. Burris."

Honeychild said, "Mrs. Burris has retired. She is in bed." She stood in the center of the doorway, directly in front of the runt who had disturbed her reading.

"You tell her it's the sheriff," Earl said. "It's important."

"Mrs. Burris cannot be disturbed now," Honeychild said.

Earl wanted to put his fist into her face. But he didn't have time to waste with the snotty black bitch who talked as if she had memorized a speech. "Listen, you . . . do you tell her, right now, or do I?" Honeychild closed the door in his face.

Earl turned from side to side, fists clenched, as though he could somehow rid himself of his anger. He found his gun sticking out of his waistband, grabbed it, and shoved the weapon into his pocket as the door opened, creaking, and he saw Frank Burris.

Burris wore white flannels and a pale blue shirt. He had heard the chimes in his study, a room he had furnished himself, with glass cases for his tennis trophies and, on the walls, framed photographs of himself and his opponents, in action on the court, or at the net before a match, or posing together after the match. In his last two years at Duke and for three years after he had been graduated, Frank Burris had been tenth in the national tennis rankings. He still played almost every day when there was good weather. He was older than Earl but looked younger, looked like a Viking. "Who in the hell . . ." he began, and broke off as he saw the sheriff's car and the dumpy man in the entrance. "Sheriff? Is that you, Sheriff?"

"It's me again," Earl said. He and Burris had been together most of the day at the Labor Day Picnic. Burris headed the company's department of promotion and special events. He supervised the preparations for the picnic, the Fourth of July Parade, and the Harvest Festival.

Burris hated to see the sheriff. The picnic had been a hit. People had stopped Burris all day, telling him how much fun they were having, their kids were having. "Get it over with," Burris said. "What's wrong out there?"

"Not out there," Earl said. "It's Kyle, Mr. Burris. He's dead."

"Kyle?" Burris winced as though he had been physically struck. "Kyle's dead?"

"He's been shot."

"Jesus and Mary," Burris said. "Holy Jesus and Mary. I guess you'd better come in."

By this time Honeychild had climbed the stairs and crossed the corridor to her mistress's door. She knocked once, lightly, and opened the door slightly. "Miss Serena? Ma'am?"

Serena Castleton Burris, Kyle's aunt, lay in bed, high up against the headboard. She lowered her book as Honeychild came into the bedroom. Serena looked at the stunning young woman whose entire life was her creation. "I said you could go to bed."

"The heat is . . . stifling," Honeychild said, finding the word she sought. "I've been reading. There is a man at the door. The sheriff."

"Now? Where is Mr. Burris?"

"At the door," Honeychild said. "He is with the sheriff."

"All right," Serena said. She threw back the sheer covers and came out of the bed. "All right," she repeated as Honeychild left the bedroom.

Serena was wearing a nightgown. She pulled it over her head and went, naked, to the closet. Serena was in her fifties, tall like her husband and slim as a knife. She swam every day until late in the fall, swam long distances wearing as little as possible, and her body remained a girl's body. She had thick hair, the russet of autumn leaves, and a nose like a scythe, which dominated her face. Nevertheless, she combed her hair straight back from her forehead as though to call attention to her nose. Serena was a singularly unattractive woman who lived her life demanding the world's homage for her great beauty.

In a gloomy room below Burris said, "I can't believe it. Just this morning—" Burris pointed at the ceiling, twirling his finger— "flying around up there."

"Dirty shame," Earl said.

Burris turned to him. "How old—" he began, and broke off. "Listen to me, asking you how old Kyle is. I ought to know. Twenty, twenty-one, around there," Burris said. "Just a kid, just a kid." Burris stopped beside a table, beating a tattoo on the surface with his fingers until Serena entered. He came forward. "Serena, this is Sheriff Ainsley. Something awful has happened."

Earl saw her veer to avoid Burris, saw Burris's lips tighten as Serena walked around the table to stand apart.

"Mrs. Burris," Earl said, "it's your nephew, ma'am. It's Kyle Castleton. He's dead, ma'am."

Burris started for his wife, arms extended, but she backed away and he stopped. "Dead," Serena said flatly. "Dead. In his airplane. In that orange deathtrap."

"No, ma'am, not in the airplane," Earl said. "He's been shot."

"Shot?" Serena said. "Who shot him?"

In the silence, thick and oozy, Earl heard her again and again. He could see the words plastered to his face. From his first glimpse of Kyle Castleton on the table in the hospital, from the time he saw Kyle dead, Earl had known he would have to face Serena that night, had to protect himself by facing her fast, because not facing her would make his life worse the next day. But he had kept himself in a kind of vacuum, kept himself insulated, clear of the confrontation until it happened. Well, it had happened. He wanted to sit down.

"If Kyle is dead, someone shot him," Serena said. "Who shot him?"

"I can tell you what I know, ma'am. Mrs. Burris," Earl said. "What I know so far." In his account he did not include the intern or the intern's verdict of suicide.

"I'll get you some brandy, Serena," Burris said.

She said, "No," and said to Earl, "Go on. Kyle is dead. Poor, silly Kyle. Do you have anything else to tell me?"

"I'm holding the body for the coroner, ma'am, for Porter Manship," Earl said. "He'll get into the case now."

"The case . . ." Serena said.

"Yes, ma'am," Earl said. "We know the cause of death. Gunshot. That's all we know so far. How but not who. So the coroner holds an inquest."

"Does he delay the funeral?" Burris asked.

"He's got to release the body," Earl said.

"Gaby and Holt need to be told," Burris said. "In the morning I'll get in touch with them."

"No," Serena said. "Let Lucius do it."

Burris said, "I only thought . . ." He shook his head, looking down at the floor. Frank Burris was an openhearted man who liked people and wanted people to like him. He could not escape now. He had to be in attendance, in attendance on her, until the end. "Nothing," he said. "Nothing."

"Now the circus begins," Serena said. "Another feast for the newspapers."

"Just like Branch and Celeste," Burris said.

"You are wrong," Serena said. "This is not like Branch and Celeste."

Earl remembered that day ten years ago. He had still been deputy. Kyle's father and mother, Branch Castleton and his wife, the Frenchwoman he had brought back from Europe, were killed when the foreign speedster he liked to race left the road on a bad curve.

Everyone knew Branch Castleton had fought with his father that day, another fight. Branch hated the company, hated working in the plants or in headquarters downtown. People said he hated to be away from the Frenchwoman and his children. People said he liked the farms, and spent more time in the fields, down in the dirt with the niggers, than he did in the Castle, especially when Sam Castleton was home.

Everyone knew after Branch died, Serena expected Sam Castleton to change his will to make her the heir to the Castle and Frank Burris the head of the company. Sam Castleton fooled her as he fooled everyone. After Branch, his only son, died, Sam Castleton got old awfully fast. He began staying close to the Castle more and more of the time. People said Branch's three kids became more important to him than the company. So did the farms. Sam Castleton hadn't known a hoe from a rake, but after Branch died, he learned awfully fast. He had the niggers over at the farms hopping, raising crops for the Harvest Festival. He had his grandchildren hopping too, even Gaby. People said the older boy, Holt, hated the farms the way his father had hated the company. But Sam Castleton had Holt out there with the black men same as Gaby and little Kyle.

Serena said, "Branch and Celeste were not shot, or have you forgotten? They were killed in an accident."

Earl saw the tall, handsome man rub his mouth. "I'm only talking about the newspapers," Burris said. "There are going to be reporters hounding us morning, noon, and night. Maybe I'll have a whiskey."

Serena said sharply, "Wait!" She took a step toward Earl. "Is there anything else?"

Earl ran his hand along the leather sweatband inside his cap. "I'm sorry about this, ma'am, sorrier than I can say," he said. "Sorry to bust in on you with news like the kind I brought. I came by because I thought I could make it easier—not easier but better— hearing about this from me instead of reading about it in the newspaper tomorrow."

"You're correct, Sheriff," Burris said. "One hundred percent. This couldn't have been easy for you either."

Earl said, "Well . . . good night. Good night, ma'am."

Burris went out to the car with Earl. "If I can help, I'm ready, Sheriff."

"Your saying that helps."

"Call me," Burris said. "I'm downtown most days, at the company. Call me. You've got my private number."

"I'm much obliged, Mr. Burris."

Burris waited until Earl got into the car before turning back to the house. As he walked in the open door, he saw Serena reach the head of the stairs. She stopped, looking down at him. "You're thinking what I'm thinking."

"Don't be too sure of that, Serena."

"Nothing will change," she said. "They had half the B Stock, and they will still have half. Kyle's stock will go to Gaby and Holt. You won't control the company."

Although the company was publicly held and its shares were traded daily in New York, control of the vast operation remained with the Castletons. Sam Castleton had not intended to leave his Castleton Company to strangers. The Castleton Family Foundation explicitly ceded 51 percent of the outstanding stock to his heirs and their heirs into perpetuity.

"Speak plainly, Serena," Burris said. "*You* won't run the company."

Serena crossed the corridor to her bedroom. "I stand corrected," she said. "Come to bed."

Burris closed the door and started up the stairs. "I didn't kill Kyle," he said. "I didn't send for the sheriff to bring you this terrible news about that fool kid. I didn't count on the kind of show you put on for the sheriff, showing him how you handle your husband. 'Come to bed,' " Burris said. "Not your bed. I'll come to your bed when I'm ready. I'm not ready, and I'm not your nigger either."

"Oh, stop sniveling," she said.

Burris climbed the stairs slowly. He passed Serena's open door on the way to his bedroom.

Below, Honeychild heard his footsteps. "Home sweet home," the black woman murmured, walking through the house to Burris's study. She went to the small bar Burris kept beside the fireplace and took a bottle of thirty-year-old brandy. Honeychild poured some brandy into a snifter, one of Sam Castleton's wedding gifts, and carried it to Burris's chair near the windows. She sat down in the chair, reaching for the afternoon newspaper.

Coleman had brought Honeychild to Serena when the beautiful girl was twelve years old and almost fully developed physically. "Honeychild belongs here with you, Miss Serena," Coleman said. "She's clean, and she's smart. She'll be good for you."

Coleman had taken Honeychild out of the Flats that day. The girl's rounded figure, her firm breasts, her delicate mouth, the inheritance of a Caucasian ancestor, made the place dangerous for her.

The girl standing silently beside Coleman had caught Serena's attention immediately. The following morning Serena took her downtown and bought the girl a wardrobe. Serena did not want her in a uniform, and ever afterward Honeychild wore simple, elegant dresses.

From Hartley Hall, the girls' day school Serena had attended, she brought Honeychild a tutor. "She must be taught to speak clearly, speak like you and me," Serena said.

So Honeychild entered still another new world. Miss St. Clair, her tutor, brought textbooks and pencils and writing tablets. And she discovered her beautiful young student was highly intelligent. Honeychild was also insatiable. She could learn anything. Within months, in addition to her textbooks, Honeychild was reading everything on Serena's bookshelves.

In Burris's study that night Honeychild sipped the last of the brandy in the snifter and finished the newspaper. She rose, letting the paper fall to the floor for the kitchen niggers to clean in the morning.

———◄◎►———

O N THE WAY BACK TO THE CASTLE in the Stutz, Russell sat stiffly, steering carefully, as though he were driving in a parade. He found a kind of exhaustion, an impulse to quit. He could not quit. He excoriated himself for the thought.

Kyle lay wrapped in a sheet in the hospital, dead. Kyle had a bullet in his head. Russell had men coming in the morning early to replace many of the rain gutters on the Castle. He had specified copper gutters, the specialty of a foundry in New Hampshire. The gutters, wrapped, lay stacked below the ballroom windows on the east side of the Castle. Russell supervised all work at the Castle. And now he had to arrange Kyle's funeral.

He had to prepare the Castle for Holt's and Gaby's arrival. Gaby and her husband. Russell's hands shifted on the steering wheel. He felt he should tell Gaby, but if he woke her, she would be awake all night. And forever afterward she would associate Kyle's death with Russell. He couldn't bear the thought.

Russell Vance had discovered very soon after his arrival at the Castle that he was not to fraternize with Branch's children. As Sam Castleton said when Russell arrived, "The young man is a hired hand." Russell would have preferred a more genteel phrase, but Sam Castleton's earthy locution did not offend him. Russell did not easily take offense. Coming to the Castle directly from college, he had been admitted to a center of enormous wealth and power. His work kept him in that center, and he even shared in the company's strength. He spoke daily with one or another company executive, and his title, his influence, his authority, at the farms and in the Castle, were unchallenged. He had arrived untried and unproved, and he had risen to formidable heights.

The Castle had become his home. Russell never spoke of his youthful years, and he tried not to think of his past. His father had been a bookkeeper for an insurance company, one of twenty or thirty little men who seemed to resemble one another, each coming to work in his only suit, carrying his lunch to save a quarter. Russell's father had made his lunches because his mother couldn't. For as long as Russell could remember, his mother was drunk.

His father would come home from work and cook supper for Russell and his brother. Then he would feed Russell's mother if she wasn't too drunk to eat. He would get his sons ready for bed, and when they were down, he would help his drunken wife into bed. He loved her.

Like all drunks, Russell's mother would stop now and then. She would line up her men, her two sons and her husband, and take an oath never to touch another drop of whiskey. And while she remained sober, a few days or a few weeks, she would embark on a buying spree, furniture, clothes, whatever caught her eye, running up bills all over the city. Russell's father returned what he could, but his wife wore many of the clothes she purchased, so he had to pay for those. He could not keep up with her spending, could not cover her bills. So he began to steal from the insurance company that employed him. Like all amateurs, he was not a successful thief, and he was soon caught and sent to prison.

Driving back to the Castle, Russell forced himself to dismiss the past and concentrate on the following day. He had no experience with funerals. He could call a mortuary in the morning, telephone Lucius Peete to ask for the name of the ranking mortician, and take the man down to the family plot behind the lake house. Russell had planned to bring in painters for the wooden trim on the lake house after the Labor Day Picnic. In his office in the Castle, which had been Sam Castleton's office, a calendar lined with huge squares for each day of the month covered most of Russell's desk. An identical calendar lay across the desk at Castleton Farms. These calendars were Russell's lifeline. The huge squares were crammed with notes that controlled his daily schedule. He kept his schedule sacrosanct. And tonight, in the crack of a gunshot, Russell's schedule had been shattered, perhaps irremediably.

The Sheriff's Department car remained close behind. Russell could see the bright glare of the headlights in the rearview mirror. He reached up to tilt it and saw Faith behind Coleman in a corner in the rear. She looked straight ahead, like someone alone on a train or a bus, not like a woman whose husband had just died. Russell had been waiting for her to cry ever since seeing her in the corridor with Boyd.

In his black-and-white trailing the Stutz, Wyn could not forget the startlingly beautiful woman he had helped to her feet in the hospital. Wyn thought of her alone in the backseat of the phaeton. Alone. She had started the day with her husband and was ending it without him. Wyn thought of her alone in the Castle, in that . . . stadium.

When Russell drove through the open Castle gates, he could see the headlights of the car following, as could Faith. When she left the Stutz, she saw the young man in uniform emerge. Faith stopped in front of him. "Why are you here? Why did you follow us?"

"I'm—" Wyn said before she interrupted.

"Are you arresting me? Is that why you're here, Sheriff? To arrest me for murder? Of my *husband?*" She glared at Wyn. "I gave up everything I worked to get. I left my career to go with Kyle. I said, 'Whither thou goest . . .' and I did. I came here to this"—Faith gestured wildly—"this . . . prison."

Wyn wanted to put his arms around her. "Ma'am, I'm not—" he said, before she interrupted once more.

"Kyle's dead!" she cried. "My sad, scared young husband is dead!" she said as Russell reached her.

"Let me handle this, Mrs. Castleton."

She looked directly at Wyn. "They are handling this," Faith said. "They're here to make it even dirtier." She turned to follow Coleman into the Castle.

Russell said, "I'll tell you what I told the sheriff. This is an insult."

"Hey, you!" Wyn had been awake since dawn, in his new, itchy uniform since daybreak. He wanted to shower and get between clean sheets and didn't know when he would do one or the other. Wyn pushed his finger into Russell's chest. "I've got my orders so—" he said, and stopped. He wasn't angry at this guy. "Let's go. Inside."

In the cavernous entrance, Wyn stopped. He looked up and turned slowly, awed by the grandeur, by the confidence of the man who had demanded this monument to himself.

Sam Castleton had started at the King Tobacco Company seventy years after it began making cigars. The King farm in the southern end of the county covered thousands of acres. So Elias King had all the space he needed to expand the company. He refused to tear down the old tobacco drying sheds, and after he had died, Sam

Castleton kept them as a kind of monument. He spent a lot of money having the barns repaired so they remained looking old.

Sam Castleton made the company famous, and he became famous as well. He made the cigarettes, Kings and Castletons, household names. He spent millions of dollars a year advertising the company's products. Crisps and Frosts, the company's mentholated cigarettes, were identified with two unique jingles, which Sam Castleton perpetuated by paying the country's dance bands to play and sing the tunes.

The company's advertisements filled the newspapers, filled the pages of weekly and monthly magazines. In the ads beautiful women smoked Kings or Castletons; handsome men smoked the company's cigarettes. Billboards across the country urged the pedestrian and the motorist to join the crowd. Radio announcers invited the listener to try a King or Castleton, a Crisp or Frost. A succession of songwriters, composers and lyricists, delivered zippy tunes with catchy jingles, telling Americans to light up.

The company flourished because of a single, irrefutable phenomenon: People smoked. Men and women and teenagers, young teenagers, smoked. They couldn't wait to start smoking. The country puffed away, all day and all night. The nonsmoker was an oddity, a thin minority.

While the Depression devastated the United States, leaving millions of men and women without jobs, King-Castleton, like other tobacco titans, flourished, grew.

Because of the Depression, cigarettes were cheaper than before. In drugstores across the country the smoker could buy a cigarette for a penny. Smokers didn't stop smoking. Those without steady supplies of pennies bought tobacco in tins or sacks, bought cigarette paper, and rolled their own. The company sold the tobacco and the paper.

Sam Castleton could not count his wealth, yet money did not really interest him. Sam Castleton had a single, abiding goal: He wanted to succeed.

He shared the wealth. Those around him in the company, the men who accomplished the tasks he assigned, were rewarded beyond their wildest hopes. They were given enormous bonuses. And a few were deeded huge plots of land near the Castle to build their own castles. This long avenue of splendid houses came to be known as Millionaires Row.

Russell broke in on Wyn. "Powerful, isn't it?"

"It's something."

"Can we get you anything?" Russell asked. "Coffee? Whiskey?" The Castle remained unaffected by more than ten years of Prohibition.

"I'm okay," Wyn said. "Where is the sleeping porch?" He couldn't just "be there," as his father had said.

"This way," Russell said, turning to the stairs.

Wyn stopped him. "Tell me. I'll find it," Wyn said. He didn't want any witnesses.

"When you get to the top, stay in the long corridor," Russell said. "It's on your left, the fourth or fifth door; you can use either one."

"Okay." Wyn walked to the staircase, listening to the sharp, hollow sound of his footsteps on the slate floor. He came up the stairs slowly and in the corridor, passing closed doors, could see her behind each door. To his left, the fourth door was open. On edge and apprehensive, Wyn pushed the door with his shoulder and stepped across the threshold to begin his first murder investigation.

Screens covered three sides of the porch, and the bed faced the lake and, in the far distance, Castleton Farms. Large lamps flanked the bed, and a copper chandelier hung from the ceiling in the center of the room.

All the lights were aglow. The drapes flanking the screened walls swayed in the faint night breeze, making crazy figures on the floor. Wyn moved into the sleeping porch slowly, slowly, remembering his training, looking everywhere. The size of the porch, bigger than any room Wyn had seen anywhere, even in movies, the huge bed, the lamps towering over the bed like sentries, the garish panoply of wealth offended Wyn. He expected a bedroom to be a bedroom.

In the bright light he could see a dull brown trail of dried blood on the bedcovers. Wyn knelt beside the bed and lifted the covers to examine the floor. He rose, went to the other side, and looked under the bed there. Then he walked slowly around the sleeping porch, looking everywhere, feeling everything, bending to push his hands under the chair cushions. Wyn went back to the door but remained facing the sleeping porch. "You're investigating," he told himself.

Wyn circled the room once more. "Okay," he said, stopping in front of the bed. He had a last look at the sleeping porch and took a step toward the open door. His left foot struck the thick folds of the bedcovers and something else, something solid. Wyn bent, grabbing the bedcovers. Something gleamed on the thick carpet. Wyn dropped to his knees and found himself looking at a gun with a nickel-plated barrel. He said, "Yeah," sounding exactly like Earl, and reached for his handkerchief, which he opened and dropped over the gun. He wrapped the gun in the handkerchief before rising to his feet. Wyn said softly, "Just be there." He could hardly wait to see his father.

Hiding the gun, Wyn left the Castle and got into his car. He put the gun in the handkerchief in the glove compartment. Then he opened the passenger door and swung his legs up on the seat. He could see the lights on the first floor of the Castle and above, through a cleft in the drapes, the soft glow of a lamp, and he knew it was her lamp.

<hr />

VERY EARLY THE NEXT MORNING Earl drove through the Castle gates. He stopped beside Wyn's black-and-white. Earl saw the tip of Wyn's head above the seat. "Christ!" Earl shook him awake. "What the hell are you doing out here?"

Wyn pushed Earl's hand aside. "Lay off." Wyn rubbed his face with both hands. He had been awake most of the night, turning and twisting, trying to get comfortable in the damp, cramped seat.

"You're not a watchman; you're an officer of the law," Earl said. He wore a fresh uniform. "You're on duty here inside, not outside."

"I'll try to remember," Wyn said. "Where's my relief?"

"You're not getting relieved," Earl said.

"Not— I've been working twenty-four hours, more than twenty-four hours," Wyn said. He followed Earl to the rear of the sheriff's car.

"I brought you some clean stuff," Earl said. He took Wyn's suitcase from the trunk.

"Where did you get that?"

"From your place," Earl said. "I'm the sheriff, remember? Don't you think I know how to pick a lock?"

"What's going on?" Wyn was half awake and groggy with weariness.

"You're staying here," Earl said, slamming down the trunk lid. "You're on duty here in the Castle. *In* the Castle," he said.

Earl looked up at the good-looking kid, the clean, straight kid. "Kyle Castleton shot dead is the biggest thing to happen in this county, in North Carolina, since his folks went off the road in that scooter Branch Castleton liked to race around. Bigger. 'Cause of Kyle Castleton's wife . . . widow. Faith Venable is from Broadway, Broadway in New York. There's going to be hell to pay for Kyle." Earl slapped Wyn's shoulder. "And you're going to be right in the middle of it. By the time this is settled, Wyngard Ainsley will be the best-known peace officer in the state, maybe in the U.S.A."

Wyn made a face. "What're you *talking* about?"

Earl pushed the campaign hat back on his head. "You saw Orville Clement at the picnic yesterday. *Senator* Clement. There isn't a bigger horse's ass this side of the river Styx. One of these days that could be you up there."

"Another horse's ass," Wyn said. He couldn't stop smiling. "I'm not a politician."

"Nobody is until he decides to be," Earl said. "You listen to me, Wyn. Soon there'll be an invasion here. You'll have reporters and photographers like locusts. And they'll stay awhile. This thing won't be over tomorrow, and it won't be over the day after tomorrow." Earl shook Wyn's arm. "And you'll be right in the middle of it where I put you. Every time one of them aims a camera he'll see you. So will millions of people, right there on the front pages of their newspapers. And every time a reporter asks a question, you'll be there to answer it. And when this is finally finished, when folks think about Kyle Castleton, they'll remember how you handled this, kept things in order, law and order. Then the next time someone needs a good man, he'll remember Wyn Ainsley."

"Me? A politician?" Wyn shook his head. "Uh-uh." Wyn Ainsley had been a big, robust, good-natured lad who grew up to be a big,

robust man. After college and after trying to play professional baseball, Wyn had hitchhiked to Norfolk with a classmate. Both went to
sea, deck hands who quickly became disillusioned by the coarseness
and vulgarity of their shipmates and the monotony of the long days
and nights. They left the ship in San Francisco and, eager and curious, made their way to Hollywood, ready for movie careers.

By the time their money ran out in 1930, the Depression had
devastated the entire country. Wyn's companion opted for California. "It's prettier than anywhere else I've ever been." So Wyn hitchhiked home alone. A year later, late in 1931, two vacancies appeared
in the Sheriff's Department, and Earl made Wyn a deputy.

"I'm happy where I am," Wyn said.

He turned away, but Earl grabbed him. "You listen to me," said
the little man. "You could do it. You could do it."

"Before I leave for Washington," Wyn said, raising his father's
hand and freeing himself, "I've got something for you."

He leaned into the car and took the gun from the glove compartment. "I found this." He came erect, facing Earl and raising one
corner of the handkerchief.

Earl wanted to give Wyn a swift kick in the butt. "I thought I
told you—" Earl said, and stopped. He couldn't bawl out the kid for
finding the goddamn gun. Earl hated looking at the goddamn gun.
He covered it with the handkerchief.

"You did," Wyn said. "You didn't want me doing anything.
Pop, I couldn't just *be* there, like you said."

"Right, you're right," Earl said. He took the gun in the handkerchief and set it down on the passenger seat in his car. "Where did
you find it?"

"In the sleeping porch," Wyn said. "I almost missed it, Pop. I
went through the place inch by inch, no fooling. And just before I
left . . ."

Earl stopped listening. He blamed himself. He should have
been the first one in the Castle, should have been alone. Goddamn!
"Let's have a look at the sleeping porch," he said, playing the sheriff
for the kid.

As they circled the cars, Earl stopped, stopping Wyn. "Get your
suitcase," Earl said. "Russell Vance or someone needs to find you a
bed in there."

———◦◉◦———

JUST OVER AN HOUR LATER and less than a mile from the Castle, Earl turned off Millionaires Row and stopped. He did not see a car coming and, in the rearview mirror, saw the road behind him deserted. He turned and looked through the rear window to double-check before reaching for the gun wrapped in Wyn's handkerchief on the seat beside him. Earl began to wipe the gun with the handkerchief, using both hands, rubbing the weapon from the muzzle down the pistol grip to the butt. He found the trigger guard within the handkerchief, pointed the gun at the floorboard, and carefully pushed the handkerchief through the guard and over the trigger, watching the road ahead and behind him. He had all the trouble he could handle already. Earl didn't want to know how Kyle Castleton died. He didn't want any clues. If a Castleton had killed a Castleton, Earl Ainsley wasn't sending the killer to the electric chair.

———◦◉◦———

AN HOUR LATER, on the other side of the county, Sarah Cohen heard the screen door on the front porch slam, heard it slam again. "Animals," she said, grimacing, as her sons, David and Joe, raced out into Fairview Avenue where Artie Strauss waited in his convertible. They were off for a day on the river.

Dan Cohen and his family lived in the house his grandfather had built out near Hartley Hall, where Serena had been a student. Dan's grandfather built the house of brick because he owned a brick-yard among other enterprises. Although the house was expansive, with an entire wing for servants beyond the kitchen, and three large bedrooms on the second floor, the contractor's blueprints specified only one family bathroom, the custom of the day.

While Dan's father and mother had been alive, he and Sarah lived on the upper floor of a two-family house downtown, just beyond the business district. David, their first child, was born while they lived downtown. That same year Dan's father died, and his mother came to Dan's office. "Now the house belongs to me alone," said Naomi Cohen. "Draw up a paper for me to sign so it will belong to you."

When Dan objected, his mother said, "If you won't, I'll find a lawyer who will. And if Sarah feels she can't live under one roof with me, I'll move. Maybe I'll move to Florida for my declining years. I hate where you live, Daniel. I've always hated it," said Naomi Cohen, one of whose ancestors helped write the North Carolina Constitution. "You're my son; you're not white trash."

Naomi Cohen didn't leave the brick house. On the night she died, two years later, Sarah lay in Castleton Community Hospital, in labor. She delivered her second child, Joseph, just after sunrise.

On the morning after Kyle's death Sarah stood on the porch watching David and Joe jump into the convertible. She watched the boys ride off and turned back into the house. She said, aloud, "Ben Strauss shouldn't have bought his son that car. An eighteen-year-old with a brand-new car! In this Depression. It's sinful." She pulled down the bay window shades against the coming day's heat. "Dan?" She turned and discovered she was alone.

Sarah went into the dining room and sat down. As she poured more coffee for herself, Dan came out of the kitchen. He wore a white shirt and a tie, and his jacket lay folded neatly over a chair flanking the sideboard. "Where have you been?" Sarah said, and before he could answer, told him, "Finish your breakfast."

Dan took his napkin from the chair where he had left it and sat down. He spread the napkin over his lap, and as he moved the chair closer to the table, an aged black woman appeared. "There's a black man out back won't go away. I told him but he won't."

Dan said, "Thank you, Ella."

The black woman did not move. "He says he's working, Mist' Dan."

Sarah came out of her chair. "Working?"

Ella said, "Yard work. Says you hired him for yard work, Mist' Dan."

Dan looked up at her. "Thank you, Ella. You can go now."

Sarah stared at Dan, raising her left arm to point at Ella. "You wait right there," she said, and to Dan: "Will you be kind enough to tell me what is going on in this house?"

Ella swung around, trying to hurry as she started for the kitchen. Sarah said, "You *hired* someone? For *yard* work? *What* yard work? Dan?" Sarah lowered her left arm and raised her right hand to point at the bay window in the living room. "We send those two boys off to play all day and you *hired* someone? We'll see about—" she said, and broke off to follow Ella. Dan leaped up from his chair.

As Sarah reached the kitchen, Corinne, the other black domestic, younger than Ella, put her hands over her ears and lowered her head, running to the servants' room.

"Sarah." Dan stopped beside his mother's large ancient stove, and as Sarah flung open the back door, he said quietly, "Please."

Sarah didn't move. "Please," Dan said. "Let me explain." He reached her, took her arm, and led her out of the kitchen.

In the dining room, when they were seated, he said, "The man is almost sixty. He is alone, Sarah, and he is indigent. He came to my office."

She said wearily, "Just like that out of nowhere. Dan, your office is now the downtown branch of the Resurrection Baptist Church. For God's sake, Reverend Millard Fitch is not our spiritual leader. Rabbi Sidney Levin is our spiritual leader."

"It's one day, Sarah. I offered Clarence"—Dan paused, gesturing toward the rear—"money, but he would not take it from me. He's too proud."

She sank back in her chair, her shoulders sagging in defeat. "We have a son leaving for college. We barely scraped together the first semester's fees."

Dan extended his hand, and she took it. Sarah adored Dan Cohen, had loved him almost from the night of their first date. When they met, both were juniors at the university in Chapel Hill. Sarah Weinberg had come to North Carolina from Scarsdale High School near New York to get away from her family. She had intended to go to law school at the University of Chicago. Then she discovered Dan planned to be a lawyer, and she abandoned Chicago forever.

They were married in Scarsdale and left the next morning. Sarah worked for three years supporting them while Dan went to law school. He brought her home and, after he passed the bar examination, opened his law office in one of his mother's buildings. His mother left Dan all three buildings she owned. Sarah collected the rents, or they wouldn't have been collected, and it wasn't easy after 1929, when the Depression began. But Sarah could be inventive and resourceful. She stalked the tenants; they could not evade her forever. She became relentless.

Sarah refused to be a housekeeper. She ignored her clothes. She cared only for her two sons and her husband, looking after him like a third son. She was proud of her husband, proud of his deeds. He was a prominent Zionist, a delegate to the World Jewish Congress, the president of the local B'nai B'rith, and the former president of his synagogue, the synagogue his great-great-grandfather had built. And he had been, from the first days of his career, the only white man in the city on whom a black, in trouble, could rely.

At the table in the dining room Sarah raised his hand and kissed it, and Dan kissed hers. "I should go."

Dan rose, taking his jacket and dropping it over his arm. He stopped beside her and ran his hand over her hair. "Finish your breakfast," he said, smiling.

———◦◉◦———

AROUND NOON THAT DAY Boyd's mother, Olive Fredericks, drove through the open Castle gates in her Ford Model T coupe, bouncing and swaying in the tinny black car, almost suffocating from the heat. She had started the day on her usual rounds, going from piano student to piano student, standing or sitting beside each boy or girl, her right hand moving for most of the hour, keeping the beat.

Olive Fredericks finished her ten o'clock lesson, and driving to her eleven o'clock, she saw a newsboy running down the middle of the street holding a newspaper in the air, yelling, "Extra! Extra!"

She thought the United States had declared war and they would take Boyd away from her for the army, or the newsboy was yelling because somebody had shot President Hoover. Olive drove slowly to see the headline.

TRAGEDY AT CASTLE
KYLE CASTLETON DIES

The newspaper lay on the seat of the Model T as Olive Fredericks stopped behind Wyn's black-and-white at the Castle. She got out of the Ford, leaving the door open, hoping it would not be as hot when she returned. Olive lowered her head against the sun.

In the Castle Wyn sat on a hard wooden chair beside a suit of armor in the entrance. When Coleman opened the door, Wyn saw a woman wiping her face with a handkerchief. "I'm Boyd's mother," she said. "Boyd Fredericks. You know me, Coleman. The piano teacher. Where is Boyd?"

"He's okay," Wyn said, rising.

Olive watched the officer approach.

"Coleman, tell Boyd I've come for him," Olive said.

Wyn said, "He isn't here, ma'am. Boyd . . . your son, isn't here."

"Isn't—where is he?" She charged at Wyn and stopped directly in front of him. "Where is Boyd?"

"He's okay," Wyn said. "He's . . . in jail, ma'am."

"Jail?" Olive's voice became a shriek. "You put him in jail?"

"Well, I . . . that's where he is," Wyn said. "In jail downtown."

"Are you trying to say he killed Kyle? Boyd Fredericks killed his best friend?" Olive pushed her purse under her arm. "I'll settle this lunacy," she said.

In the Model T, in the heat, Olive drove back into the city to the courthouse. When she stopped in the parking area, she needed to rest, to sit somewhere cool and quiet, but she didn't have a minute. Boyd was in jail!

Inside, Olive went to the booking counter, passing Len Egan, Wyn's handball partner, bent over the water fountain. Arver Long saw her coming and left his desk. "Help you?"

"Is Boyd Fredericks here? He's here," Olive said. "I'm his mother. I've come for him." Len Egan lifted the hinged section of the counter and went to his desk.

"Come— He's in custody," said Long.

"Custody? He didn't kill Kyle Castleton," Olive said. "Boyd couldn't hurt a fly. He's innocent. Go get him. Bring him out here to me."

"Ma'am, I can't do that," Long said.

"Let me see him!" Olive said. She held on to the counter. "I demand you let me see my son!"

Long said, "Ma'am, I haven't any orders allowing me to accommodate you."

"I have a right see my own son," Olive said. "You," she said, including Len Egan, "you're keeping my son. Boyd Fredericks. I demand to see Boyd Fredericks!"

"Deputy Long here is in charge," Len said. "He's the duty officer in charge right now."

"Ma'am, I already explained to you," Long said. "I haven't got any orders relating to your son, to Boyd Fredericks. The sheriff's in charge of your son, personally in charge."

"Then get him," Olive said. "Or take me to him." Directly ahead of her, Earl came through the door, returning from the cafeteria. "I demand to see the sheriff!"

"You see him," Earl said, making his way between the desks. "What's the problem?"

"You've got my son," Olive said. "Boyd Fredericks is my son. He didn't kill Kyle Castleton. Kyle Castleton was Boyd's best friend on earth."

Earl stopped at the counter. "Your son is a suspect, ma'am."

"I want to see him!" Olive said. She picked up the charge book and threw the heavy ledger at the wall. She swung around and ran across the room to the folding chair, which she threw at the counter. She threw another.

"Hey, you . . ." Long shouted. He reached for the hinged section of the counter so he could go after the loony but found Earl in his way.

Olive threw another chair. Panting, she stood facing the three apes in uniform, the enemy. Then she ran to the water fountain. She turned the handle all the way until water rose in a column high above her.

Earl came after her. "Guess you want to see your boy. Egan."

Len Egan followed Earl. Olive released the handle of the water fountain. "Bring him to my office, Len," Earl said. "This way, ma'am." He opened the door. Olive went past him, and Earl looked back at Long. "How about the gun Wyn found?"

"On the way to Raleigh, Sheriff, to the Highway Patrol to check for fingerprints," Long said. "I mailed it myself, like you told me."

"Yeah." Earl waved. "Clean up the place. Use a mop," he said, and followed Olive.

In his office Earl said, "Your boy will be here pretty quick, ma'am. I'd better get some air in the place." He opened the transom.

They heard footsteps, and Olive moved aside to stand in the center of the office. In the corridor Len Egan said, "In there," and Boyd Fredericks entered.

He looked as though he had been wandering in the wilderness. His beer jacket and trousers were crumpled and soiled. The jacket bore smudges of dirt. His bow tie dangled from the breast pocket of his jacket. His face was red and puffy from the heat. His saddle shoes were scuffed, and his eyes were wide open and wild, like a trapped animal's. "Mother!" He turned to Earl. "Can I go now?"

"Not just yet, son," Earl said, then said to Olive: "Nobody will bother you in here."

Stepping into the corridor, Earl waved off Len Egan and leaned against the wall, beneath the open transom.

In Earl's office, Olive said, "The way you look. Your *clothes.*" She raised the hem of Boyd's beer jacket, brushing it with her other hand. "We'd better pray this comes off," she said. "And your pants. This pigsty. Did they hurt you? Did anyone hurt you?"

"They didn't come near me," Boyd said. "They put me in a cell and left me there." His face twisted in revulsion. "The filth, Mother. I feel like I'll never be clean again."

"Tell me what happened last night."

"You know what happened," he said. "Kyle's dead. God . . ." He choked back a sob. *"Kyle* is dead . . ."

"Boyd!" Olive took Boyd's chin firmly, holding on as their eyes met. "Boyd Fredericks, you tell me what happened."

He swung out, hitting her hand and pushing it aside. Boyd sat back in his chair, looking directly at his mother as though he intended to leap at her. "I don't know!"

"You don't *know?*"

"Will you please, please stop repeating every single word I say?"

Olive took a deep breath. She stepped back, pawing behind her for the chair, and, finding it, sat down. "Go on," she said. "Continue." Boyd shut his eyes so he wouldn't see her. "Open your eyes and talk to me!"

He stared at his mother, his mouth closed tightly, defying her. All through the night Boyd had heard the gunshot in the Castle, again and again and again. He did not remember reaching the top of the stairs, remembered nothing until he started down the corridor for the sleeping porch and saw Faith slowly emerge, backing away from Kyle, dead on the bed inside.

"Boyd!"

He didn't care if his mother started screaming, didn't care what she did. Nothing and no one would ever make him tell what he had seen in front of the sleeping porch before Coleman came running, before Russell came running. He couldn't betray Faith.

"Boyd!" Olive stood over him. "Why are you torturing me?"

He rose slowly, stoically, unafraid. "We had a party," he said. "Hot dogs and root beer and the rest, from the Labor Day Picnic at the plant. Kyle ended the party early. After I called you, I heard a shot. I ran upstairs. I saw Faith in the hall and we . . . I guess we were afraid to go in. Coleman went in, and we followed. And then Russell came."

Olive watched him. He didn't seem to see her, seemed to be alone. "Sit down, Boyd, before you have a stroke in this heat."

"I will not sit," he said. "I *can't* sit. I've been sitting, all day, all night and all day."

Olive rubbed her face with her sodden handkerchief. "You could have made something of yourself," she said. "You had talent. You could have been a fine pianist. I begged you to practice. To work. To devote yourself."

"God, not today," Boyd said.

"But you were too busy flying through the air with your friend Kyle Castleton."

"For your information I hated the plane," Boyd said. "Can we go now?" He walked to the door, his head high, as though Faith were watching him. He had not failed her. At the door he waited for Olive, and as she joined him, he opened it and faced Earl.

"You were spying on us!" Olive said.

Earl stepped into his office, ignoring her. "You can't go yet, son," Earl said. He went to his chair behind the desk, and Boyd sprang forward, following him.

"You think I did it!" Boyd said. "I didn't!"

"He couldn't shoot a gun!" Olive cried. "He's never fired a gun in his life!"

"Sure hope that's true," Earl said. "Young man like you with his whole life ahead of him."

Olive joined Boyd. She pushed him away from the desk and behind her, shielding him with her body, looking down at Earl. "You mean little man," she said. "Little bully. You can't bully me, little man. You can't arrest someone and . . . keep him. He has rights. Every citizen has rights in this country."

Earl looked at the scarecrow with her cake-eater son, dressed like someone in vaudeville over at the Orpheum. "Right," Earl said, remembering Dan Cohen with his goddamn writ. This biddy didn't have Willy Floyd's luck. "I'll tell you his rights, your boy's rights," Earl said. "He's a suspect in a murder case. So I'm holding him until the coroner's inquest. If your boy is innocent, like you say, you'll have him home soon as the coroner is finished." When Olive did not respond, Earl curled his arm around the upright telephone on his desk and raised the receiver. "Send Len Egan in here for Fredericks."

EARLY THE FOLLOWING MORNING Russell found Wyn having breakfast in the kitchen of the Castle. "Kyle's sister and her husband are on their way from New York," Russell said. "I'm picking them up later. The reporters will probably be there. They find out everything. They're fierce, Wyn. Will you come?"

"Sure." Wyn would have walked to get away from the Castle for a while.

When they reached Union Station and Wyn saw the gang of newspapermen, he grabbed the cop on duty. "I need help."

"*We* need help," the cop said. He sent for two railroad detectives, and the four made a ring around Kyle's sister, Gaby—Gabrielle—and her husband, Colin Inscott, hurrying them out to the Stutz. They had to wait for the redcaps with the luggage. Wyn and the cop stood guard beside the open trunk of the phaeton.

Wyn yelled, "Come on, come on," as he waved at the redcaps.

"One side or a leg off," the cop said, pushing back the reporters. "I'm warning you."

When they got away, Russell looked back at Gaby with Colin Inscott in the rear. She seemed tiny in the roomy backseat. "I'm sorry, Mrs. Inscott. I wish I could have spared you."

"They're not important," Gaby said.

"Are you all right?" Russell frowned. "What a stupid question."

She tried to smile. "I'm all right," Gaby said. From Russell's first days in the Castle she had been the kindest of the Castletons.

Colin said, "I say, trooper, good show, old sport."

"Very good show," Russell said. He glanced at Wyn. "You saved us from disaster."

Wyn felt ill at ease, shoved in among all the Castletons with all their money. "It's my job," he said.

———※◉※———

LUCIUS PEETE HAD CALLED GABY the day before, early, as she sat on the piazza of her home in East Hampton, on Long Island. She liked to start the day there, facing the Atlantic. After she spoke with Lucius, Gaby remained alone, a petite woman of no physical distinction, who seemed swathed in her peignoir. She repeated to herself everything Lucius had told her, but she could not imagine Kyle dead.

For almost as long as Gaby could remember, she had depended on Kyle. He had been her refuge, making no demands on her. Kyle had let Gaby run free.

From the time Gaby's mother and father were killed, her grandfather had taken control of her life. Sam Castleton imprisoned the child. He had her watched constantly, as though she were incompetent, physically and mentally. The servants surrounded her from the time she woke. She was never alone. She was driven to and from Hartley Hall, and the chauffeur remained throughout the school day in the event an emergency arose. When she could, Gaby began to run away from the Castle, hiding in the loft above the garage, or in the trees that surrounded the lake, or in the lake house, free for a little while. Then she began to follow Kyle around, and he, enjoying the authority she bestowed on him, allowed her to join him in his escapades. And until Kyle met Boyd Fredericks, her brother was her only escape from the cordon in which Sam Castleton imprisoned her.

On the piazza in East Hampton Gaby discovered the telephone in her lap and set it down on the table at her side with the tea service. She remained unmoving for a long time before taking up the telephone once more to call the Castle. She recognized Coleman's voice and tried to disguise hers. "Mr. Vance, please. Russell Vance."

Coleman said, "Mist' Russell, yes, ma'am. I'll fetch him."

As she waited, Gaby suddenly remembered running through the fields at the farms with Kyle, remembered hiding in the tall rows of corn. She dropped the receiver into the cradle and began to weep. She wept convulsively, in deep, choking sobs, making no effort to stem the tears. She bent far forward, a tiny person made bereft by sorrow, weeping for Kyle, for her lost dead parents, who had forsaken her by dying, weeping for herself.

When she stopped, patting her eyes with the linen napkin in her lap, Gaby left the piazza and summoned Bliss, the English butler her husband had chosen. "You'll be driving us to New York, Bliss. To Pennsylvania Station."

She climbed the stairs and moved through their bedroom without a sound so as not to wake Colin. They had hours before the train left.

He had gone off to a horsemen's dinner in Montauk the night before. "You'd find it awfully dull, old girl," Colin said. "I may be late. Don't wait up." When he returned, stumbling around and waking her, Gaby could see gray daylight seeping through the windows.

In her dressing room Gaby chose the clothes she would take before she showered and dressed for the journey. She stole out of the bedroom and, below, returned to the piazza for the newspaper she had left behind.

She took the paper inside and tried to read but could not, and when she heard Colin ring for Bliss, she went into the kitchen. "I'll take Mr. Inscott's tray up for him."

Gaby waited while Bliss prepared the tray. "It's rather heavy, madame," the butler said. "Let me carry it up the stairs."

"I can manage," she said firmly.

In their bedroom Colin Inscott sat high up in bed, the covers smooth across his knees. "Gaby! This is a surprise, old girl. Where's Bliss?"

"I told Bliss I'd bring your tray," she said.

Colin took it from her. "Not a moment too soon," he said, pouring coffee into his cup. "Afraid I've got a bit of a head." He grimaced. "I *do* have a bit of a head. Damn Hugh Gannett. Bloke wouldn't stop filling my glass. Turned out he got absolutely blotto. Had to drive the poor chap home, don't you know. Kept me out till all hours." He sipped his coffee. "You're all prettied up, old girl. Where are you bound for?"

"Kyle is dead."

"Dead?" He set down his cup. "Kyle? I say—" Colin broke off. He raised the tray and set it on Gaby's bed so he could get out of his. He wore white pajamas with red piping. "Kyle dead? I *am* sorry, darling." He came to her, extending his hands and taking her arms. "Dreadfully sorry." He kissed Gaby's cheek and stepped back, releasing her. "I say . . . the plane? In the plane?"

"No," Gaby said. "Not in the plane." She could not repeat what she had learned from Lucius. She would tell him later.

"You should have wakened me, old girl," he said. He unbuttoned his pajama top. "Be with you in two shakes, darling," he said on his way to the bathroom.

Despite his English idiom, Colin Inscott had in fact never set foot in Great Britain. His locutions were adopted, like his name. His father, born Carlo Inasmora in a Calabrian village in Italy, had come alone to the United States at sixteen. He found a job as a custodian's apprentice in Wall Street. Within six months he was an office boy in a brokerage firm.

Carlo was clever, and he dressed carefully, keeping himself neat and clean. And he could add and subtract, fast, without pencil or paper. He changed his name to Inscott. He rose in the firm. Carlo married an Episcopalian, and when his first child, a son, was born, named him Colin.

Colin Inscott started life as a rich man's son. Colin liked the outdoors, liked horses. He did not like his father's business or any business.

In October 1929 Colin's pampered life ended. The stock market crash made his father a bankrupt. In New York, on the day before Thanksgiving, Colin's father told his wife he would be home early. His family never saw him again.

Colin stopped in the bathroom doorway, looking back at Gaby. "I say, old dear, if we're going to the Castle, I'd better reserve some space for us. A drawing room should do. And ring for Bliss, that's a good chap. He'll need to pack for me."

Colin closed the bathroom door, and Gaby turned to pull back the drapes, filling the bedroom with sunlight. She left the windows to call for Bliss and saw Colin's clothing in a heap on the floor, as usual. Gaby's grief turned into fury at her husband. She lashed out with her foot, scattering the pile of clothing. His white shorts, the only underwear he wore, sailed into the air. Gaby saw a flash of pink as the shorts floated slowly to the floor. She stood over the shorts and saw the unmistakable imprint of lipstick on the white fly.

———————

IN THE STUTZ BESIDE GABY, Colin said, "Still leading the stag lines, are you, Russell?"

"Afraid I am," Russell said.

"See here, Gaby, we must marry off this old buck," Colin said. He wore a houndstooth sport jacket and had knotted a blue kerchief around his neck beneath the open collar of his shirt.

"Russell's standards must be very high," Gaby said.

"Thank you, Mrs. Inscott," Russell said. "Actually my standards *are* very high."

"We'll keep a sharp eye peeled, old sport," Colin said. He raised his arm to look at his wristwatch. "I say, the sun is over the yardarm. I could use a dram. Bar still well stocked, Russell?"

"It's the same old place," Russell said. "Nothing has changed."

"Except Kyle is gone," Gaby said. "It's so hard to believe."

"I know," Russell said. "I expect to see him whenever I turn a corner."

"Kyle was always so . . . fragile," Gaby said. She looked out the window once more. "When we were young, I had to tiptoe past his room. Mother built the sleeping porch for Kyle, for hot summer nights. I remember Kyle always being sick. He had asthma and hay fever from the time he was born. And later mumps and measles, and scarlet fever and diphtheria. He had everything. For weeks and weeks Holt and I were kept away from Kyle. Twice my mother thought Kyle would die. She believed one night he *did* die. And returned. She heard him die and fainted across his body, and when Daddy and Coleman revived her, she saw Kyle come back to life." Gaby began to cry.

"I say . . ." Colin reached for her, but she moved aside, turned her back, and pushed her face into the leather seat. "Gaby. I say, old girl—" Colin broke off.

Wyn could hear her crying, and despite himself, he looked into the rearview mirror. He glanced at Russell, who drove as though he were alone. Behind him Gaby said, "I'm sorry. I can't seem to stop. I think I'm cried out, and then I begin again."

"Hardly needs explaining," Colin said. "You've had a blow."

"Another blow," Gaby said, and then added, "I hate coming back to the Castle. Everything always goes wrong here."

Wyn felt trapped in the Stutz, listening to the woman's secrets. She made him uncomfortable, spilling everything in front of strangers. She didn't know him, yet she kept blabbing, saying anything that came into her head. All his life, even with pals, in and out of school, Wyn had not shared any part of his life. And if a friend began to unburden himself, Wyn found a way to cut the confession short, even if he had to run.

Behind him Colin said, "Journey's end." He gestured at a sign. "Millionaires Row."

Russell said, "The reporters are right behind us."

"They won't bother you," Wyn said. He could barely wait to get out, to get away. As Russell drove through the Castle gates, Wyn opened the door of the Stutz. "Drop me, and keep going."

When Russell stopped, Wyn came out fast and headed back toward the gates. He walked directly into the newspapermen, arms spread wide. "I've told you before, you're on private property," Wyn said. "You don't belong inside the gates. I'm tired of telling you guys. I can send for the wagon. I can fill the tank downtown with you guys."

Behind him, Coleman came out of the Castle, lumbering forward. "Miss Gaby!"

She said, "It's Coleman!" and hurried toward the black man, arms out.

At the phaeton Russell opened the trunk. Beside him Colin said, "Belay, Russell." Colin reached into the trunk for a pair of brown leather riding boots, highly polished, with a wooden shoe tree in each. "My pride and joy, old sport," Colin said. He pulled a riding crop out of one boot.

Coleman began taking the suitcases from the trunk, setting the luggage on the ground. "Hold on, Russell," Colin said. He flicked the riding crop, slapping a suitcase. "Coleman can't handle all this."

As Russell said "I'll send someone out," Colin saw Wyn on his way to the Castle.

"I say, trooper!" Colin raised his riding crop. "Trooper!"

Russell said, "No, Colin! No!"

Colin said, "Nonsense." He waved Wyn forward and said, "He's a big, sturdy lad." He told Wyn: "Give the darky a hand with the bags, that's a good chap."

Colin's order stopped Wyn in his tracks. Nothing in Wyn's life had prepared him for Colin's peremptory command. The posturing toff enraged Wyn. Only Russell's distress saved Colin.

As Coleman, loaded with luggage, passed him, Colin said, "Right you are, lad," and gestured with the riding crop. Wyn yanked it out of his hand, threw it aside, and turned toward the Castle. Ahead, at the entrance, he saw Faith and Gaby embracing. He stopped, all alone in the bright sunlight. He didn't belong in the Castle, didn't belong with these people who carried riding boots a thousand miles on a train. He could see the windows of the bedroom to which Russell had escorted him, with a bathroom bigger than his entire apartment and towels like tents. He remembered his pop's exhortation, here at the Castle gates, promising him fame and fortune, promising Wyn the moon. He felt as though the entire world were staring at him, laughing. And when Gaby and Faith moved aside so Coleman could pass, then arm in arm followed the black man into the Castle, Wyn went the other way, toward the smokehouse behind the kitchen to use the kitchen entrance into the Castle, where his father kept him imprisoned. When he came abreast of the smokehouse, Wyn began to run.

He took the steps to the kitchen two and three at a time, holding on to the railing. Wyn burst into the kitchen and raced through it, frightening the black women preparing dinner. He strode through the corridors and into Russell's office, where he bent over the desk and scooped up the telephone to call the courthouse. Wyn could not identify the deputy who said, "Sheriff."

"Let me talk to him. It's Wyn Ainsley."

"Hey, Wyn. Len Egan," said the deputy. "Wyn, he's busy right now."

"Tell him it's an emergency," Wyn said. He didn't give a damn.
"Another emergency?"

"Tell him—" Wyn sat down on the desk with the telephone.
He could feel the sweat on his back and on his face and forehead. He
lifted the telephone and rubbed his forehead with his left arm.

He had to get away from Faith, had to stop worrying about running into her. Whenever he saw her, he became a kind of tin soldier
in his uniform, standing at attention like some dopey kid in the au-
ditorium in a school play. Wyn couldn't think straight around her.
Even if they only said hello, he felt like a big, retarded goof. For
hours after seeing her, Wyn would go over the encounter, remembering every instant. And the night before, turning down the light,
he had thought of Kay, but she quickly became Faith. And Kay
melted away into the inky night.

Earl came on the line. "Wyn? Christ, now what?"

"Send someone over here," Wyn said. "I want a relief over
here."

"You said emergency."

"Goddamn right," Wyn said, getting angrier as he continued.
"I'm the emergency. I've been cooped up here long enough. And
don't start your fairy tale about being mayor or senator. You send
someone over here by tomorrow morning or I leave, Pop. And you
can fire me or suspend me or do anything you want." He had to get
away from her.

In his office Earl sat far back in his chair, pushing one shoe off
with the other. His feet hurt. His head hurt too. Thinking of the
next day gave him a headache. Wyn gave him a headache too. He
didn't understand his son. Hell, if someone had put him in the Castle when he was Wyn's age, they would have needed a tractor to get
him out.

"Pop." In Russell's office Wyn stepped away from the desk, facing the open windows and hoping for a breeze. "Did you hear anything I said?"

"Every word," Earl said. "You want to get out of the Castle.
Well, you can go but not until tomorrow afternoon. The coroner
holds his inquest over there in the morning."

"Here? In the Castle?"

"I'll see you tomorrow," Earl said.

Wyn said sharply, "Wait! Pop? How about the gun? Did the gun come back from Raleigh?"

Earl leaned forward, moving his chair against the desk, looking at the small carton with isinglass sides that lay on his large blotter. Inside, Earl could see Kyle Castleton's gun, its nickel-plated barrel gleaming. "It's here."

"How about fingerprints?"

"No fingerprints," Earl said.

"No—" In Russell's office Wyn lowered the phone, staring ahead, as though he were in a crowd and needed corroboration to accept what he had heard. He raised the telephone. "No *fingerprints?* Pop, Kyle Castleton didn't wear gloves that night."

Earl caressed the isinglass container. "Somebody did."

—————=◈=—————

JUST BEFORE MIDNIGHT THAT NIGHT Gaby slipped out of her bedroom. She closed the door slowly, silently, and remained listening. She wore a robe over her nightgown. After a while she moved out into the corridor, passing the sleeping porch on her way to the staircase.

Below, a single dimmed lamp illuminated the entrance. Gaby skirted the circle of light, moved confidently into the shadows, and made her way through the darkened house. In the music room a slender shaft of moonlight made a path to the open terrace doors.

The still night, the cool flagstone floor of the terrace against her bare feet revived Gaby.

Comforted somehow by the rough surface of the bricks against her body, she leaned into the terrace wall. Although she could not see beyond the smokehouse, she knew every foot of the Castle grounds. She remembered exploring them with Kyle, remembered excursions to the lake with Kyle, running ahead of the blacks, the strong swimmers who accompanied them. She remembered an afternoon when Kyle's spontaneous nosebleed covered them both with blood, and Coleman carried him back to the Castle while she cried and tried to hide, believing she would be blamed. She wanted to forget and could not. Gaby could forget nothing, old or new, and she recalled again, after telling Colin of Kyle's death, finding her husband's clothing on the bedroom floor with the latest evidence of his adultery. The episode revolted her. As she tried to dismiss Colin from her mind, tried to retrieve the melancholy comfort of solitude, she heard footsteps.

Certain it was Colin, she whirled around in a rage. "Must you follow—" she said, and stopped as Russell came out of the music room. He too wore a robe.

Both said, "I'm sorry," and he backed away. "I'll— Excuse me."

"Wait!" She extended her hand as though to keep him from leaving. "I didn't mean . . . I expected . . . thought you were—" She broke off, trying to smile, all the while hating herself for behaving like a silly schoolgirl. She looked away and said quietly, "Don't go."

She turned back, out of the light, welcoming the safety of the darkness. Her heart pounded, and in the humid, clammy night her hands were cold. Gaby wanted to disappear, yet she hoped the night would never end.

Russell came closer to her. "I couldn't sleep," he said. Gaby seemed far, far away, but he knew he could reach out and touch her.

"Nor could I," she said.

They both were silent, looking out into the darkness until Russell turned his head to glance at Gaby. She had not changed. She seemed even younger than he remembered, and more beautiful. And she seemed completely alone.

"I'd forgotten the heat," Gaby said.

"Doesn't it get hot in New York?"

"In East Hampton," Gaby said, "we're far out on Long Island. It gets very hot, but we're on the ocean."

"So you have the sea breeze," Russell said. "It must be very beautiful there, facing the Atlantic."

"Yes," she said. "Beautiful."

"Do you like living there?"

"It's . . . my home," she said.

Russell said, "Of course. Your home." He had to end this inane, meaningless exchange, had to go, had to resume his solitary life. But he could not leave. "This has always been my favorite corner of the Castle," he said.

"And mine," Gaby said.

"Yes . . . I remember."

"Do you?" Without warning, she swung around to face him squarely, looking directly into his eyes. Nothing and no one could have moved him aside. "Do you?" she repeated fiercely.

"Everything," he said. "I remember everything."

"Except my name," she said. "You've forgotten my name."

"Gaby," he said. "Gaby, Gaby . . ."

She said, "I've been waiting," before Russell spread his arms and swept her up.

"Gaby, oh, Gaby," he said, bending his head to kiss her. "Gaby, Gaby, Gaby . . ."

STANDING IN FRONT of the Castle the following morning with some of the deputies Earl had sent ahead, Wyn heard one of them say "Here he comes," as the sheriff's car turned off Million-aires Row. Other deputies kept the newspapermen back beyond the gates.

Len Egan was driving Earl's black-and-white, and Boyd Freder-icks sat behind them. Wearing the fresh clothes his mother had de-livered to the courthouse the previous evening, Boyd sat on the edge of the seat, his feet and knees together and his clenched fists on his thighs. His body was rigid, ready for the most important day of his life, the day he made sure Faith was cleared.

Boyd squeezed his fists hard, hurting himself, so he wouldn't forget what he would say in the Castle and, more important, what he would not say. As long as he lived, he would never admit to anyone that he had seen Faith backing out of the sleeping porch that night, like someone in a trance, a step at a time.

Boyd rehearsed the answers he would give when his turn came. "I heard the shot," he said to himself. "When I got to the top of the stairs, I saw Mrs. Castleton standing in the hall. I went to stand there with her. And that's all I can tell you."

Boyd wanted to see Faith and reassure her, but he couldn't say anything to her in public. When he saw her inside, he could only say hello in passing. He couldn't give any kind of sign that he was pro-tecting her. As the car rolled to a stop in front of the Castle, Boyd opened his fists and rubbed his hands on his thighs. He had woken that morning scared stiff, more scared than he had ever been, but Boyd didn't care. Being scared wouldn't stop him.

Wyn opened the car door, standing back to give Earl room. His father came out carrying a brown paper bag. "You sounded a whole lot worse yesterday than you look," Earl said. He turned and tilted the seat forward, gesturing to Boyd. "All right, son. You go on inside with Deputy Egan here. You're with him, Len."

Len said, "Got you, Sheriff. Let's go, Boyd, okay?"

Earl nudged Wyn. "You too. Let's go." They followed Len Egan and Boyd. "Everyone here?"

"We're all set," Wyn said. "This is pretty cute, holding the inquest in the Castle. Who had that bright idea?"

"Who had that bright idea? Who do you think?" Earl asked, and after a moment he said, "Your mother. I couldn't keep the reporters out of the courthouse. It's a public building. This isn't. Your mother said move the inquest here. I got Russell Vance to help me."

Inside, Coleman led them to the banquet hall, which ran the length of the south wing of the house. There were fireplaces at each end of the banquet hall big enough for a tank. Under Russell's supervision a large table had been placed in front of one fireplace, among other tables and chairs arranged for the inquest.

Porter Manship, the coroner, stood beside the head table. A big, beefy man who dressed like a car salesman, he wore a cream-colored suit with flaps over the jacket pockets that buttoned and brown-and-white shoes. In that county the coroner did not need medical or legal credentials. Porter Manship had been in politics all his adult life, and he enjoyed the rewards he believed he had earned. "Sheriff!"

Earl and Wyn joined him. Earl introduced them. "Wyn's a new deputy," Earl said.

"A chip off the old block, I'd say," the coroner said. "Guess I'm talking with the future Sheriff Ainsley."

"Guess again," Earl said. "Wyn's got bigger plans, right, Wyn?"

"Sure," Wyn said. He stared at Earl, who did not look at him. "I'm the future governor."

Porter Manship smiled. "Governor Ainsley. You hear that, Earl?"

"I did," Earl said. He set the brown paper bag on the table. "Are you all set?"

Manship put his hand into his trousers pocket and pulled out a .38-caliber slug, the bullet without the casing. "Starting with the instrument of death," the coroner said.

"Yeah." Earl put his hand into his bag and took out the isinglass container, which he set on the table. "Let's go, Wyn."

They walked around the coroner's jury, six men sitting in two rows of chairs at right angles to the head table. Len Egan sat with Boyd, and behind them Wyn saw Gaby with Colin Inscott. Russell stood at the open doors of the banquet hall, watching Gaby. He had pleaded with her not to attend the inquest, but she had been adamant.

Earl led Wyn to the Tudor windows along the wall. "You told me everyone was here," Earl said.

"Everyone is here."

"She isn't," Earl said.

Wyn looked out at the banquet hall but did not see Faith. "She'll be here," he said. "She has to be here."

Bang! Porter Manship hit the table with his gavel. "Well, now," he said. "We're all assembled, so let's begin without any further delay. This isn't a trial. This isn't a hearing or an arraignment. This is a coroner's inquest. I'm the coroner. Porter Manship." He pointed with the gavel. "These six men are the coroner's jury. They're chosen by lot like any other jury. They come from the jury rolls that come from the tax rolls of the county. They're taxpayers, and they're citizens, and serving here is their Christian duty."

Facing the jury, Manship said, "You're not here to determine the cause of death. We've solved that for you." He raised his hand, showing the jury the .38-caliber slug without the casing.

Manship set down the bullet and raised the isinglass rectangle. "And this is the weapon from which the bullet was fired," he said. "But the gun doesn't help us none in terms of identification. It's registered to Kyle King Castleton. Not only that, there isn't a fingerprint on it."

Manship put the isinglass container aside. "You six men are here to decide the manner of death," he said. He raised the slug again. "How did Kyle King Castleton meet his death? Accident? Homicide? Suicide? Call Dr. Desmond Pike."

A wisp of a man with a short, nervous cough came forward. Surprised, Wyn looked at Earl. "How about that intern, that . . . Widseth?" he asked.

"Couldn't make it," Earl said flatly.

"How about subpoenas?" Wyn asked. As Earl watched the slight doctor walk toward the Coroner, Wyn grabbed his father's arm and swung him around. "How about subpoenas? Did you run out of subpoenas?"

"Me? I don't issue subpoenas," Earl said. He removed Wyn's hand from his arm. "And pipe down."

Kenneth Dordell, the court stenographer, swore in the doctor. "State your name and occupation," said the coroner.

"Desmond Pike. I am the pathologist at Castleton Community Hospital," said the physician. Under contract with the county, the hospital handled all autopsies required by the coroner.

"You performed an autopsy on the body of Kyle King Castleton?"

"I did," said the pathologist.

"Tell the jury the results of your autopsy."

"The projectile, the bullet, entered the temporal lobe of the brain," Pike said. "It passed through the temporal lobe and into and through the cerebrum, lodging in the circle of Willis." Pike coughed. "The circle of Willis provides the arterial blood supply of the brain."

"Go ahead," Manship said. "Continue."

Pike shifted in his chair. "Death was instantaneous," he said. "The bullet creates an explosion in the brain, ripping apart the anatomy."

"You've given us part of the story, Doctor," said the coroner. "What I'd like you to tell us now is how did the bullet enter the brain of the deceased. I mean, from which direction? Up, down, on a line with the deceased's head? Front or back? Tell us that, will you?"

Desmond Pike made a gun out of his thumb and forefinger. He pushed his forefinger into his skull above the right ear. "The bullet entered here," he said, and coughed. "I should say the gun was fired at close range. Very close range. A few inches."

"Point-blank?" said the coroner.

"Yes, point-blank."

"Someone held the gun to the deceased's head and pulled the trigger," Manship said.

The pathologist turned to face the coroner. "I didn't say that. Those are your words, not my words," he said, coughing.

"Correct," Manship said. "Those are my words. Someone held the gun to the deceased's head and pulled the trigger. I said that."

"Exactly."

"So we can continue," Manship said. "Could Kyle King Castleton have met death in that way? Could someone have shot him? Put a gun up against his head and shot him?"

"Yes . . . I suppose," said the pathologist.

"You've been a big help here, Doctor," Manship said. "That's all. Excused. Sheriff Ainsley. Earl Ainsley."

Kenneth Dordell waited. Earl repeated the oath and took the witness chair.

"Now, Sheriff, you were at the hospital with the deceased the night of September fifth," said the coroner.

"I was."

"You tell us what you saw and did, Sheriff," Manship said.

"First thing I saw, I saw the deceased, saw Kyle Castleton," Earl said. "I made a positive identification. I saw the wound, the cause of death. The death was not a natural death, so I took responsibility for the remains."

"Explain that, Sheriff."

"I quarantined the remains," Earl said. "I took charge until you could take charge, until the coroner assumed responsibility under the laws of this county and this state."

Wyn could see on the table in front of the coroner the gun in the isinglass container, the nickel-plated barrel gleaming and sending out spears of light. The Highway Patrol laboratory in Raleigh had not found a single fingerprint on the gun.

The coroner excused Earl and looked out into the banquet hall. "Boyd Fredericks."

"Hey, that's you," Len Egan said.

Boyd refused to acknowledge him. He rose, and walking forward, he didn't hurry. He kept his head high so no one would think he was afraid, but he was afraid; he shook inside.

When Boyd sat down in the witness chair, Manship said, "You were present at the time the deceased met his death."

"No, not at the time of death," Boyd said. "Not when he killed himself."

Bang! "Correction!" Manship said, his voice booming. "Correction, Mr. Fredericks. Boyd Fredericks. If you weren't there in the sleeping porch, you can't sit here and say the deceased met death by his own hand. Correct?"

"Yes. Yes, I wasn't there in the sleeping porch when he—when it happened."

"Thank you," Manship said. "Nobody knows how the deceased met his death, which is why I've convened this inquest. Stick to the facts, Mr. Fredericks. When I say you were present, I mean, were you at the scene? Yes or no?"

"Yes. Kyle asked me to sleep over," Boyd said. "I went to call my mother and tell her I'd be staying at the Castle." He rubbed his hands on his thighs. He had to be very careful now. "I had just finished calling when I heard a bang, a loud bang upstairs. A shot. And I knew something terrible had happened."

"How did you know? You stick to what you saw."

Boyd hated him. Boyd wished he would die, right there in his chair. "What I saw," Boyd said, speaking slowly. He couldn't make any mistakes now. "I ran up the stairs and saw Faith . . . Mrs. Castleton in the hall in front of their room across from the sleeping porch. She must have come out of their room when she heard—"

Bang! Manship hit the table with the gavel. "Now, you—"

"—the shot," Boyd said.

Bang! Manship shook the gavel at Boyd. "I told you, stick to what you saw. Did you *see* Mrs. Castleton come out of the bedroom?"

"I didn't *see* her, but she was—" Boyd said before Manship interrupted.

"You're excused," the coroner said.

"—in her stockings," Boyd continued. "She must have taken off her shoes and—"

Bang! "You're excused!" Manship said loudly.

Boyd started to rise, but he fell back into the chair as he remembered the Bible. He swung around to face the coroner. "I just remembered something," Boyd said.

Bang! "I said you're excused! You're finished testifying!" Manship waved the gavel.

Boyd thought the coroner would hit him with the gavel. He almost ducked. But he gripped the arms of the chair, holding on. He had to stay, for Faith. "Kyle always talked about dying," Boyd said.

"He wasn't afraid of dying like most people. I think he liked it, liked the idea of dying."

Bang! "You think!" Manship shouted. "Get out of that chair!" He looked across the banquet hall at Earl, needing help, but Earl shook his head.

So the coroner set down the gavel and folded his hands on the table, lacing his fingers. "We're listening."

"Well . . ." Boyd paused, shifting in the chair to face everyone in the banquet hall. "All his life Kyle behaved like he could die anytime. He would say, 'I won't live to a ripe old age.' I must have heard him say those words a hundred times. He even wrote about it in the Bible." Boyd leaned forward. "Coleman!"

The black man left the open doors. "Need something, Mist' Boyd?"

Bang! "Now you listen to me," Manship said before he saw Earl nod. "All right, do it then," Manship said.

"Coleman, bring me the Bible from the library," Boyd said. "It's on the desk near the doors."

As the black man left the banquet hall, Boyd said, "It's the family Bible, the old King James Bible Sam Castleton kept and used. It's full of family dates."

When Coleman returned, the coroner extended his hand. "Here, let me have that," he said, but the black man gave the Bible to Boyd.

"I'll find it for you," Boyd said, opening the heavy volume.

He put his forefinger on a page and read aloud: "Kyle King Castleton. Born October 20, 1910. Died shortly thereafter." Boyd raised the Bible, his finger on the page. "Kyle wrote those words," Boyd said. "It's his handwriting."

"I see it," Manship said. He took the Bible from Boyd. "Anything else? Are you finished now?" Bang! "Thank you. Call Russell Vance."

Russell's testimony was brief. He spoke of hearing the shot, of finding Faith and Boyd in the sleeping porch with Coleman, and of driving to the hospital.

"Thanks for your help," said the coroner. "I hope I haven't ruffled any of *your* feathers. Call Wyngard Ainsley."

"Up and at 'em," Earl said.

Wyn slipped past him, moved around the jury, and stopped in front of Kenneth Dordell. After Wyn had been sworn and sat in the witness chair, Manship said, "Now tell us who you are and what you do."

Wyn replied, and Manship said, "You were in the sleeping porch the night of September fifth?"

"Yes, sir."

"You examined the premises?" the coroner said.

"Only the sleeping porch," Wyn said.

"Did you find any evidence of foul play?"

"Foul play? No," Wyn said.

"Any sign of a struggle?" asked the coroner.

"No," Wyn said. "Everything looked okay, looked . . . neat."

"You didn't see anything unusual in the sleeping porch that night?"

"Well . . . yes, I did," Wyn said. "I saw blood on the bed, on the bedcovers, and on the carpet on the floor."

"Sounds unusual to me," Manship said. "Anything else, Deputy Ainsley?"

"Well . . . the gun," Wyn said. "I found a gun."

"Correct," Manship said. "A gun." He raised the isinglass box. "This gun?"

"That one, yes," Wyn said.

"Tell the jury about it," Manship said.

"I found it on the floor by the bed," Wyn said. "I felt something with my foot." He gestured. "The light caught the barrel."

"Thank you, Deputy Ainsley," said the coroner. "You've been a big help to us here."

As Wyn left the witness chair, the coroner said, "Call Mrs. Faith Venable Castleton."

Wyn didn't see her. Where the hell was she? She knew she had to testify. For a moment Wyn thought she had run, had escaped, and in the next instant he cursed himself for believing she had any reason to flee.

"Call Mrs. Faith Venable Castleton."

"I'll get her," Wyn said, on his way, moving fast. He couldn't let someone else go after her, someone like his pop or someone else his pop would send.

Wyn couldn't find her. She wasn't in her room; she wasn't in the library or the music room. He tried not to worry. She *had* to be in the house. Wyn turned back to the banquet hall to ask Russell for help, then stopped and ran to the entrance.

He left the Castle running, on his way to the gazebo beneath a pair of old sycamore trees at the crest of the knoll. Celeste Castleton, Branch's wife, had ordered the gazebo and supervised its construction, furnishing it with chairs and sofas covered in primary colors. The Frenchwoman had liked to sit in the gazebo on summer afternoons. She often took a writing kit with her, writing to her family in France. Wyn had often seen Faith on her way to or from the gazebo.

At the foot of the gazebo steps, Wyn stopped as though he had hit a gate. Faith lay on a sofa, curled up, her eyes closed, using her clasped hands for a pillow. She wore a white shift and had a white band across her hair. Her arms were bare, and the tips of her shoulders were pink from the sun. Wyn stole into the gazebo. He felt as though he had come home. And he wanted to lock them in, lock everyone out. "Mrs. Castleton?"

When she didn't move, Wyn bent. He extended his hand like someone after a butterfly. "Mrs. Castleton."

She opened her eyes. Wyn came erect. "It's me, Wyn Ainsley, Deputy Ainsley," he said all in a rush. "I'm . . ." he said, pointing. "They want you in the Castle, ma'am. In— At the inquest."

Faith sat up and bent forward. He backed away as she slipped on her shoes. She said, rising, "Thank you."

Wyn stepped aside so Faith could precede him. He followed her out of the gazebo and walked beside her down the long slope of the knoll. He felt her leg brush against his, but this time he did not move aside. Every step was a gift; every minute alone with her, a gift. Although he looked straight ahead, looked down at the Castle, Wyn could see her, see her clearly, see her pink shoulder, burned by the sun, see the tendrils of hair escaping from the coiled mass at the back of her neck. And he could see her face, see her eyes, like no one's eyes ever.

Wyn wanted to take her away. She hadn't killed Kyle. She hadn't killed anyone. The sight of Coleman in the Castle entrance ended Wyn's reverie. The black man waved his arm.

Russell joined him, and as Faith and Wyn reached the entrance, he said, "Are you all right, Mrs. Castleton?"

"I fell asleep," Faith said.

Wyn joined his father in front of the windows. "Welcome back," Earl said. "I thought you'd gone on vacation."

With Len Egan beside him, Boyd watched Faith raise her right hand and repeat the oath. Everything depended on what she said now. He had done all he could do.

Porter Manship said, "Now, Mrs. Castleton, I'm not here to make this any harder for you than it is already. You just tell us in your own words what happened here the night of September fifth."

Faith turned to him, her eyes wide, as though only he could save her from great peril. "Where shall I start?"

"You decide that, Mrs. Castleton," said the coroner. "Whatever you decide. Your own story."

Faith said, "Kyle and I said good night and—"

Manship interrupted. "In the hall?"

"In the hall," Faith said. "I went into the bedroom and sat down to take off my shoes." She stopped, turning her head as though she had come upon a sight she could not endure.

Then she looked out at the banquet hall, forcing herself to face everyone directly. They frightened her, and because she was afraid, she fought desperately to overcome the fear. They were hicks, down here in the boondocks, and Faith had only contempt for them. She refused to let her fear triumph. She had never betrayed her true feelings, and she would not begin now.

"Mrs. Castleton?"

She did not respond.

Manship rose halfway out of his chair, leaning across the table. "Mrs. Castleton, are you all right? Would you like something, some water?" When she did not answer, Manship touched her shoulder. Faith turned to face the coroner. "Would you like some water, Mrs. Castleton?" Faith shook her head. "Can you go on now?" When she nodded, the coroner sat back in his chair. "Please go on, Mrs. Castleton."

Faith looked out at the banquet hall once more, facing the enemy. They were just a bunch of hayseeds, all of them. She couldn't let a bunch of hayseeds defeat her. She had always seen a finish line ahead, and she saw it now, far, far in the distance, beckoning.

"I heard a shot," Faith said. "It terrified me. I couldn't move. Then I heard Coleman calling, 'Mr. Kyle, Mr. Kyle,' like someone in great pain, in agony. Somehow I reached the corridor, but I could not go on. I could not. I thought I would collapse. I felt myself slipping away. Boyd saved me. He reached me and saved me."

"Boyd Fredericks," Manship said.

"He kept me on my feet," Faith said. "Together we followed Coleman into the sleeping porch."

Boyd wanted to jump up and applaud. To himself he said, "She's perfect."

At the table Manship held the isinglass container. "Thank you, Mrs. Castleton. You've helped a whole lot," he said. "I'll keep you just a little bit longer. I just have a few more questions. Now, Mrs. Castleton, to start with, you and the deceased were married not too long ago, am I correct?"

"Yes, you are correct," Faith said.

"Less than a year ago, if my memory serves," Manship said. He moved the container from side to side.

"We were married last November," Faith said.

"Less than a year," Manship said. "How long did you and the deceased know each other before you were married?"

"I can't say," Faith answered. "I can't remember, really."

The barrel of the gun sparkled in the light from the chandeliers. "Months?" Manship asked. "Weeks?"

"No, not weeks," Faith said. "More than weeks. Is this important?"

"Could be," said the coroner.

Faith faced Manship squarely. "How? What does the . . . past have to do with this terrible tragedy? I've lost my husband."

Manship pushed the container aside. "You've got everyone's sympathy for your loss, Mrs. Castleton," he said. "But your husband met a violent death. It's the reason for this inquest. You're here to answer questions, Mrs. Castleton, not ask them. You say you and the deceased knew each other a few months before you were married." Manship made a sweeping gesture with the gavel. "Did you ever see this place before your marriage to the deceased?"

"I did not."

"Did you ever hear of the deceased's family?"

"Yes, I heard of the family," Faith said.

"Heard how important they are?"

"I had heard the name Castleton."

"One of the most important families in America," Manship said. "And after you knew the deceased a few months, the two of you were married. After what they call a whirlwind courtship. Correct?"

"Kyle proposed," Faith said. "I accepted."

"Correct," said the coroner. "Correct. You met Kyle Castleton, and you married him. Last November, less than a year ago. Most folks would say you were newlyweds." He watched Faith. "Mrs. Castleton?"

"What is it?"

"I guess you didn't hear me. I said folks would consider you and the deceased newlyweds, you being married less than a year," Manship said. "And on the night when the deceased met his death, you were in one room, on one side of the corridor, and the deceased was on the other side in another room, in the sleeping porch. Sleeping in different rooms. Did that happen often, Mrs. Castleton?"

Wyn knew instantly who had tutored Porter Manship. He shoved his elbow into his father's ribs. "I wonder why he decided to ask that question."

Earl looked up at the kid. "Beats me."

At the table the coroner said, "Mrs. Castleton, did you hear me this time?"

"I heard you," Faith said. "Your question is an insult."

"It's not my intent or meaning," Manship said. "But I still expect an answer, Mrs. Castleton." When Faith did not reply, he said, "Should I repeat the question?"

"You would probably enjoy it," Faith said. "I heard the question. Kyle— My husband liked the sleeping porch," Faith said. "I did not."

"Did you do that much?"

"That?" Faith said. "What is *that?*"

"Did you sleep apart much?"

"You filthy man," Faith said. "You filthy-minded man."

Bang! "Answer the question!" Bang! "Answer the question!"

"Kyle and I were together most of the time," Faith said.

"All right, then," Manship said. "Since you were together most of the time, did you fight much?"

"Fight? Fight?"

"Did you argue?" asked the coroner.

"We were in love," Faith said. "My husband and I were very much in love. We did not argue. We did not fight. Do you have any other filthy questions?"

"I do, and I won't be swayed by any sensational statements from the witness," Manship said. "I've got a job to do here, and nothing and no one will stop me from doing it. Now, uh, as far as you could tell, had the deceased been behaving normally lately?"

"Nothing had changed," Faith said.

"Did the deceased show any signs of being unhappy?" Manship asked.

"He did not," Faith said.

"Did he seem worried?"

"My husband did not worry," Faith said.

"No further questions." Bang! "This ends the testimony," Manship said. He waited until Faith left the witness chair and then faced the six men of the jury. "You've heard the testimony of all those connected with the death of the deceased, Kyle King Castleton. Now it's up to you to decide how the deceased met his death."

Earl nudged Wyn. "Let's get some air. Place smells like wet cement."

They left the Castle, and walking to his car, Earl fanned himself with his hat. "Goddamn heat." He opened the car door and sat down sideways, his feet on the running board. Wyn leaned against the hood. He saw Arver Long coming, fingering his shiny mustache.

"This thing over?" asked Long.

"The jury is deciding."

"Deciding what? No witnesses and no fingerprints on the gun," Long said. "Where's the evidence?" No one spoke. Long looked around him. "Right, Sheriff?"

"You're right, Arver," Earl said. "You can't get anywhere without evidence."

Long grinned. "Case closed," he said. "Okay with you, Sheriff, if I get out of the sun?" As he walked around the black-and-white, Wyn saw Russell come out of the Castle, waving.

Gesturing, Wyn said, "Pop, the jury has decided, I guess."

In the banquet hall the coroner sat at his table, and the six jurors were in their chairs. Bang! "Come to order," Manship said. "Has the jury reached a verdict?"

Benjamin Briggs, the oldest of the jurors, rose. "Yes, we have, Your Honor."

"I'm not Your Honor," Manship said. "I'm not a judge. Just give us your verdict."

"We all voted that the deceased, Kyle King Castleton, died at the hands of a person or persons unknown."

"At the hands of a person or persons unknown," Manship said. Bang!

"The jury is excused. You men are free to leave."

Boyd came out of his chair and looked down at Len Egan. "Am I free to leave?"

Len said, "Beats me." He was reaching for his hat on the seat beside him when he noticed Boyd hurrying away. "Maybe . . . hey!"

"Sheriff!" Boyd hurried after Earl. "Sheriff!"

Earl stopped. He raised his hand and waved in great arcs. "Bye. Say hello to your mother."

Leaving the banquet hall with his father, Wyn said, "How about me?" He had packed his clothes after his shower that morning.

"On your way," Earl said. "You're back in your own bed, and you're off tomorrow, so get some rest. They're burying Kyle the day after."

"Me again," Wyn said. "I'm not the only deputy you've got, Pop."

"They'll all be there," Earl said. He stopped at the Castle entrance. He thought of raising his hat and letting out a cheer. He had moved as fast as he could, making as little trouble for anyone as he could. He had done all he could to spare the Castletons a bigger mess. He could shut the door on this one at the cemetery. "Anyway, this one is over, and nobody got hurt," Earl said, allowing himself that much backslapping. He pulled his hatbrim down over his eyes, squinting as he looked up at Wyn. "Come on out and visit your mother while she can still recognize you. The twins been asking too."

"Maybe tomorrow," Wyn said. He didn't see Faith. As Earl left the Castle, Wyn went to the music room. She wasn't in the music room. She wasn't in the library.

He had to see her once more. She didn't know him from Adam, but Wyn couldn't leave without seeing her one last time.

Wyn returned to the banquet hall. Coleman and two other black men were moving chairs. "Coleman, have you seen Mrs. Castleton?"

"No, sir," Coleman said. "Not since she's been here, I haven't."

Wyn climbed the stairs to the upper floor. He knocked on her bedroom door but had no response. On a hunch he crossed the corridor and opened the door to the sleeping porch. It was deserted.

Wyn hurried down the stairs and left the Castle. He climbed the knoll to the gazebo. She had not returned. He looked at the sofa where he had found her asleep. He remembered her eyes when she woke, when she sat up and reached for her shoes. "Cinderella," he said aloud, leaving the gazebo, on his way to the kitchen entrance to collect his suitcase.

———◦◉◦———

A SINGLE DIRT ROAD ran through the Flats, twisting and turning, with no sidewalks and no street signs, no numbers on the sagging shacks and the few stores. The road ahead teemed with life, with men and women and children and, everywhere, babies and with animals: dogs and cats, chickens, ducks, and goats.

At the far end of the Flats a row of sycamores lined the road. The trees hid a white clapboard church with a steeple, a replica of the churches of colonial New England.

The church seemed out of place in the Flats. Unlike the shacks and the stores, the wooden building sparkled in the sunlight. The ground around the church was raked clean, and a border of petunias lay along each side of the entrance.

The Resurrection Baptist Church was the mainstay of the population in the Flats, and the Reverend Millard Spencer Fitch was the community's bellwether. At his altar the Reverend Fitch promised his persecuted flock their wretched existence would one day be replaced by a splendid new world of everlasting freedom and happiness.

Millard Fitch's study lay behind the altar. There, on the day after the coroner's inquest, he sat at his rolltop desk beneath an autographed photograph of Paul Robeson. Holding his Panama hat, Dan

Cohen sat beside him and facing them, in matching wooden chairs, were Coleman and Willy Floyd, the married young black man whom Dan had rescued from jail on Labor Day.

The reverend had called Dan Cohen because he needed the white man's presence to lend authority to the meeting. And he had summoned Coleman since the elderly black man, kind and gentle, was the acknowledged patriarch of the community.

In his chair Willy Floyd could not be still. He fidgeted, twisting and turning, rubbing his head, crumpling his cap in his hands, crossing his ankles and then uncrossing them and pulling up his legs.

Millard Fitch let him fidget. The handsome fellow had become the bane of the reverend's life. He turned to Dan. "Thank you for coming today. I'm very grateful to you," the reverend said, and to Willy Floyd: "You know Mr. Cohen, Willy Floyd."

"Yes, sir, Reverend," said Willy Floyd. He nodded several times. "I know him. How're you, Mr. Cohen? What for you ask me here, Reverend?"

"I think you know," said Millard Fitch, and then, unable to check his annoyance, he said, "Of course you know. I am afraid of bloodshed in our community."

Willy Floyd sat up, staring at the reverend in astonishment. *"Blood!"* He looked at Coleman, looked at Dan, spreading his hands. "Why you bring me here to talk about blood, Reverend?"

Coleman took Willy Floyd's arm. "You listen and you'll find out."

"I got nothing to do with any kind of trouble that comes to blood spillin'," said Willy Floyd. He shook his head hard. "No, sir, Reverend, not me. You've got the wrong man this time." He looked at Dan. "I'm the wrong man for this kind of trouble, Mr. Cohen."

"Stop!" said the reverend, fighting his anger. "Jasper Weems came to me, Willy Floyd. I heard everything from Jasper Weems."

"Jasper Weems?" Willy Floyd was outraged. "What for that lyin' man came to you, Reverend? What for?"

"He did not lie," said Millard Fitch.

"He lied!" said Willy Floyd. He wrung his cap into a tube. "Jasper Weems lied!"

"Lied about what? I haven't told you what Jasper told me," said Millard Fitch.

"There's no truth in anything you heard from Jasper Weems," said Willy Floyd.

"You are committing adultery with Jasper's wife," the reverend said. "With Violet Weems."

"Not me." Willy Floyd looked down at the floor, shaking his head. "Not me, Reverend, no, sir," he said, and sprung to his feet, towering over the others and shaking his head. "Me and Violet?" he said, astonished. He began to pace, walking from wall to wall in the small study. "Not me, no, sir. I barely know Violet Weems, barely recognize that woman if she pass me in the Flats."

Millard Fitch looked at Dan, waiting for his help. Dan had been uncomfortable since the reverend's telephone call. Talk of infidelity distressed him. He avoided locker room braggadocio. "Dan," said the reverend.

"Willy Floyd, you are in great danger," Dan said, hoping he could frighten the young man. "Sleeping with another man's wife is called adultery. It is a serious matter," Dan said. "Adultery is a crime both in the Bible and under the laws of this county and state. If you are convicted of adultery, you will go to prison, Willy Floyd. I could not help you. No one could help you."

"If you *live* long enough," said Millard Fitch.

Willy Floyd stopped pacing, standing in front of Dan and the reverend. "I been with *no* woman," he said. "Not me, no, sir, no woman except M'lissa, my wife. I been with her, and that's all. That's *all*, Reverend."

"And you will stay away from Violet Weems," said Millard Fitch.

"I *been* away from her," said Willy Floyd.

"Promise," said the reverend. "Swear you will not come between Jasper Weems and Violet Weems. Swear, Willy Floyd."

"I swear, I swear."

"You are giving your solemn oath to Mr. Cohen as well as to me," said the reverend.

"Right, that's right, Mr. Cohen," Willy Floyd said, sidling toward the door. "I'm giving my oath, that's right," he said, extending his hand. He found the doorknob and was gone in a flash.

As Willy Floyd left, Millard Fitch turned to Dan. "You tipped the scales in our favor. Thank you . . . again," the reverend said.

"Let us hope," Dan said. Coleman left his chair.

"I'm sure of it," the reverend said. "You put the fear of God in him. Didn't he, Coleman?"

"Yes, sir, Reverend," Coleman said. "Yes, sir, he did. I'll be moving along."

The reverend rose. "And thank you, Coleman."

"All I did was sit," Coleman said. "Good-bye, Mr. Cohen."

Coleman came out of the study. He closed the door and turned away from the church. He raised his hand to shield his eyes and then put two fingers in his mouth. A piercing whistle cut through the still day. He whistled again and hurried ahead. Coleman raised his hand once more, cupping his mouth. "Willy Floyd!"

Willy Floyd stopped, looking back as Coleman approached. "What do *you* want, Coleman? I'm busy. I'm late now. You hear me?"

Coleman pulled out his handkerchief and patted his head as he waddled down the dusty street. When he reached Willy Floyd, he said, "I hear you. Let's us get out of this sun."

They stopped beneath a sycamore. Coleman pushed his handkerchief into his pocket. Willy Floyd said, "I told you I'm busy."

"You are," Coleman said. "You're too busy, Willy Floyd." He gestured. "You can fool them in there, but you don't fool Coleman." He moved slightly until he felt the sycamore tree against his back.

"What're you talking about? Fool? You're the fool, Coleman, stopping me on the street and—"

Willy Floyd broke off as Coleman's arms encircled him, embracing the young man in a bear hug. Coleman laced his fingers, pushing his knuckles into the small of Willy Floyd's back.

Coleman had the sycamore tree against him and used it for leverage, his big arms and forearms tightening his grip. Willy Floyd said, "Cole—" in a kind of hoarse croak and could not continue. His eyes widened, and his body became limp, and at last Coleman released him.

Willy Floyd wobbled and staggered and almost fell. Coleman kept him erect, holding the younger man's arms. "Next time maybe I won't stop," Coleman said. "Maybe next time will be the last time for you."

He released Willy Floyd, reaching for his handkerchief to mop his face. Willy Floyd fell against the sycamore, holding on to the tree with both hands. Coleman turned to face him. "Now I'm on my way to visit with Jasper Weems," Coleman said. "I'll tell him Violet loves him and nobody else but him and she don't look at no other man."

Patting his head with the handkerchief, Coleman left Willy Floyd at the sycamore. After he saw Jasper Weems, he had to stop in on Honeychild's mother. Coleman always saw Honeychild's mother when he came to the Flats.

＝＞•◉•＜＝

THE LAKE AND THE LAKE HOUSE lay in a hollow near the northern edge of the estate. A hill rose from the northern shore of the lake. The far side of the hill faced another hollow and, beyond, a county road and another hill.

Sam Castleton had built his mausoleum in the hollow, facing the county road, making his monument visible to the public. He laid out the family cemetery.

Gates like those at the Castle provided access to the cemetery. Early in the morning two days after the coroner's inquest, sheriff's cars and state Highway Patrol cars lined both sides of the road around the open cemetery gates. A black Lincoln limousine stood in front of Earl's car, and he could see Serena and Frank Burris beside a mound of dirt at an open grave. Burris looked at his wristwatch. "Almost eight-thirty."

"I am in agony," Serena said. She had dressed herself in black.

"It's the heat. Why don't you move out of the sun? You can wait in the car," Burris said.

"I'll survive," she said.

They both were on edge, both uncomfortable in their mourning dress. Burris disliked black, disliked all dull colors. He looked out at the road. "Russell said eight o'clock."

"I suppose eight o'clock is the middle of the night for people in the theater," Serena said.

"Why blame her?"

Serena faced him. "Why argue?"

Burris's face twisted in anger, in hatred, and in self-hatred and disgust. And in pain. He said, "I am not—" and stopped, surrendering, again, walking around the grave to get away from her. He went through the gates and stopped beside the Lincoln, *her* Lincoln.

He could see Serena near the grave, see his nemesis, the slim, slender piranha who had imprisoned him. They had been combatants for a lifetime.

Burris did not escape into self-deception. He had learned long before, on the clay public courts of Pensacola, that he had only one asset, one trading chip: tennis. And he seized upon his single asset, determined to exploit it. He knew tennis would be his only open sesame, his only key to the good life, his chance for the good life.

He was attractive physically, but he saw handsome men everywhere. So he made himself something more than handsome. He developed a persona, working hard to improve himself. At Duke he cultivated bright, congenial people, men as well as women, students and faculty. He learned from them. And on the tennis circuit, among the rich and famous, he cultivated those who began by cultivating him. He had a natural flair for social intercourse. Burris was a naturally cheerful, buoyant sort. Men liked him, and he discovered early that women were attracted to him.

He became successful with women long before Serena, and many were rich and many were young and unmarried. But none compared with Serena and her fortune. None had the company's dazzling wealth, the company's incomparable power. And Serena seemed to ensure a life of fairy-tale splendor. She promised him everything, promised him the moon. Burris would be president of the company, and Serena would be beside him. They would rule together, rule supreme. And they would reign in the Castle. They would make the Castle world-renowned. The Prince of Wales and others like him would come to stay in the Castle.

He learned quickly, almost immediately, that he had married an uncrowned queen. Serena neither charmed nor persuaded. She commanded servants, tradesmen, public officials of all degrees of rank and power. She commanded everyone everywhere, commanded Frank Burris. He discovered quickly that if he became president, she would command him. She would lead the company and not from a distance, her home or her bedroom, but from company headquarters downtown.

Facing him from the grave, Serena blamed Burris for the flare-up, blamed his pitiable attempts at independence. After every episode, minor or major, Serena flaunted her scorn, her contempt. She had expected a conspirator who would join her, someone with a grand vision, capable of leading a coup that would annihilate her enemies, Holt and Kyle and Gaby . . . and Lucius. She expected Burris to provide something more than his arms and body naked against her nakedness. But she had been forced to settle for his gifts in the bedroom, the single arena where he did not disappoint her.

Kyle's death brought back the past. As Serena watched Burris chatting with the dumpy little sheriff, she remembered their first meeting, her first glimpse of the slender, tanned collegian who had been invited to the Castle for the weekend of a Labor Day Picnic long, long ago.

Sam Castleton brought down people from New York and Atlanta that year. To entertain them, he sent for some of the best tennis players in the world: Bill Tilden and Ellsworth Vines and the Frenchmen René Lacoste and Jean Borotra, in the country at the time. And to please his friends at home, Castleton delivered the entire Duke tennis team, headed by Frank Burris, the captain and star.

On the court the first afternoon Serena saw only Burris. That night she could not fall asleep. She had never been with a man, but she wanted Frank Burris.

After the Labor Day weekend Serena had to see him again. She offered Sam Castleton a defensible excuse to visit Duke. Her father sent her to Durham in a company car with a company guard as chauffeur. But Burris had left the campus for home that weekend. When she returned to the Castle, Serena wrote, inviting him to the Harvest Festival.

She kept him to herself at the festival. Driving back to the Castle that night, Serena turned off the road. "What's wrong?" Burris asked. He peered at her in the darkness. "Serena?"

They were in the trees, and she could hardly see him. "Do you have anyone? A girl?" She could barely talk. She felt strange, felt warm and sticky.

"Right now, it's you," Burris said. "You're my girl."

"I'm your date," Serena said. "Do you have someone somewhere else?" Serena asked with a flash of jealousy.

"Nowhere else," he said. "No girl, Serena. Not right now anyway."

"Frank." She turned in the seat to face him. "Frank, you have to look at me." She reached out and tugged at him.

"I am," he said, puzzled. Her hand on his was warm, was hot. "I'm looking."

"Do you think I'm pretty?"

"I do." He didn't dare smile, because he did not want to hurt her. He didn't understand why she cared. She had all that money, more money than anyone. "You're very pretty."

"Beautiful? Do you think I'm beautiful?"

"You *are* beautiful," Burris said.

"You're lying," Serena said, and withdrew her hand. "I am not beautiful. And I'm not pretty. When you're not pretty, it's the first thing you learn, before you learn anything else." She watched him. "Is that why you haven't kissed me?"

Burris was off-balance. The young, uncomplicated collegian had not encountered anyone like her, anyone as rich, and as powerful, and as confident. And as demanding. She asked more questions than a lawyer. "Is it?"

"What?"

"You're pretending you don't understand," Serena said. "Be honest with me. Always be honest with me. Everything is easier if you're honest. Why haven't you kissed me?"

Burris muttered, "Oh, hell." Leaning forward, using both hands to scoop her up and bring her away from the steering wheel, he kissed her.

Her lips were soft and pliant, parting slightly as he kissed her. He heard her sigh, and she raised her arms to clutch him. "Kiss me again," she said greedily. He kissed her again. And again. And again. And when she thought she would faint with pleasure and with longing, she released him and moved back until she could see him. "I love you," she said. "I love you. I think we should get married."

Burris said, *"Married?"* as though she had announced they would climb Mount Everest.

"Soon," Serena said. "I don't want to wait," she said. "Why should we wait? You will need to sign a prenuptial agreement. Do you know what a prenuptial agreement is? It's about money, but I promise, you won't have to think about money ever."

"Hey, I'm in college," Burris said. "I haven't even graduated—" he said before Serena interrupted.

"You're a senior," she said. "You'll graduate in June. We can be married then. Will you kiss me again?" Serena moved across the seat and pinned Burris against the door. "Kiss me."

For a little while Burris did not respond. But he was young, they were young, and he surrendered. He could have had Serena that night, in her car in the trees, but he had often thought of marriage, and he intended to claim his bride on their wedding night, in June.

Behind him in the road Earl stood with Wyn. "Why in hell am I always waiting for Len Egan? I told him what I told everyone else. 'Go to bed early.' "

"Here he comes," Wyn said, hoping. He could not identify the approaching car.

"Here *they* come," Earl said. Wyn saw the headlights on the car. "Goddamn that kid." Wyn swore he would warn Len Egan. Unless he changed, one of these days Len would go out the door of the courthouse and not be allowed back in.

A hearse led the funeral procession, followed by three cars, and behind the cars a stake body truck filled with black men in overalls and straw hats. Colin drove the Stutz behind the hearse with Gaby beside him, and in the rear Faith sat with Coleman. Russell drove the second car, a Buick sedan filled with Castle servants. A company car driven by a guard in uniform followed the Buick. Wyn recognized the old man in the rear, Lucius Peete.

A deputy pointed at the black men climbing down from the truck. "Where did all those niggers come from? What're they doing here?"

"They're from the farms," Earl said. "And button your goddamn shirt collar and straighten your tie."

At the grave Burris said, "Here comes the widow."

"The grieving widow," Serena said. "She doesn't look like she's grieving. She looks like she is celebrating." Here, beside Kyle's grave, Serena saw Faith for the first time, saw a great, great beauty. Serena had been all her life a connoisseur of beauty, foremost of feminine beauty. Faith's flawless features, framed by her thick, lustrous black hair, and her eyes, her haunting gray eyes, made her seem unreal, theatrical.

"We should offer our condolences," Burris said. "Serena?" He looked at her. "We should say something."

"We can tell her to confess," Serena said, hating Faith for her physical perfection. "Person or persons unknown," she said, her voice filled with venom. "Not to me."

Burris watched Faith, with Gaby and Colin near the gates. "She seems to have convinced Gaby," he said.

"Gaby has nothing but air between her ears," Serena said. "She was a young fool, and now she's an older fool. The widow doesn't fool me, and she won't fool Holt. Not Holt."

The men in overalls and all the Castle servants except Coleman stood in a group several yards clear of the white people. Those from the farms held their straw hats in their hands, and none, man or woman, spoke a single word.

"Wyn . . ." Earl gestured at the company car. Wyn saw the guard waiting at the open door for the old man and ran into the road.

"Give you a hand?" Wyn asked.

"We're okay, Sheriff," the guard said. He helped Lucius Peete out of the car, and a minister followed them. The minister carried a Bible, and at the grave he went first to Faith. He spoke to each person in the group. Then he spoke to Coleman, and the black man began to weep.

"That nigger sure can cry," Earl said.

"Holy—" Wyn pointed. "Pop, look up there!"

On the hill facing the cemetery, in a line along the crest, stood a column of figures, men in white robes and white conical hats with masks. "It's the Klan!" Wyn said. "With rifles!"

"I'm not blind. Pipe down," Earl said.

"This is a funeral!" Wyn said. "Those bastards!"

"Pipe down, I said. Do you see the Highway Patrol chasing them? Like hell," Earl said. "There's eight . . . nine, ten . . . there's twelve up there. Clete Harlow could be up there. The Mayor. Orville Clement came in for the Labor Day Picnic. He could still be in town. He could be up there. Senator Clement."

"Then he's a bastard too," Wyn said.

"Hey, you . . ." Earl swung Wyn around so they faced each other. "Shut up," Earl said. "Come over here." Earl took Wyn away from the other deputies. "Where in hell did you come from? Did you just drop out of the sky? That's the Klan up there on the hill," Earl said. "The *Klan*. They're not your enemy."

"I'm supposed to *like* them?" Wyn looked at the hill and spit.

On the hill the Klansman at the left end of the line said loudly, "Shoulder . . . arms!" He and the eleven others brought their rifles to their shoulders. He said, "Ready . . ." and pushed the stock of his rifle into his shoulder, the barrel pointed at the sky. The others raised their rifles. "Aim . . . fire!"

A roar of gunfire reverberated across the cemetery below. "Ready . . ."

The second volley was followed by a third. "Shoulder arms!" the leader barked. "Right face!" Having paid homage to Kyle, the men in white followed their leader, who limped as he led them down the hill and out of sight.

Below, the driver of the hearse joined Earl. "Can we borrow four of your men, Sheriff?"

"Done and done," Earl said. "Wyn, you and Arver Long. And here comes Len Egan finally. Fetch Egan. Move."

"That's three," said the driver. "We need four."

"You've got four," Earl said. "I'm four."

The driver's assistant waited at the rear of the hearse. Each took one end of the casket, and the driver coached them. "Take it slow," said the driver. "The secret is slow and easy."

Wyn saw Faith as he approached with the casket. Although she stood beside Russell, she seemed to be alone, seemed to be a stranger among the others. Faith's self-control, her implacable poise combined to make her appear invulnerable.

"Hold it," said the driver when they were over the grave. "We're a few inches short," the driver said. The men shuffled forward. "Stop! Good. Hold it right there." They held the casket directly over the two broad canvas belts that lay across the grave. "Now we'll lower it," the driver said. "Slow. Slow. That's it, but slow."

Coleman began to sob. Serena looked at Lucius Peete. "Can no one stop that nigger?"

When Earl released the coffin, he moved to one side, standing clear of the mourners. "Wyn," he said, beckoning him to stand apart as well.

Behind him the minister went to the head of the grave. "I did not have the privilege of knowing Kyle King Castleton," the minister said. "Yet I join those near and dear to him in mourning the tragic passing of one so young and vibrant, so anxious and eager for adventure, so determined to see beyond the horizon."

Boyd, standing nearby, could barely listen. You could say the same about anyone, a man or a woman. If Kyle could hear the minister, he would be making faces and laughing. Everything the minister said was bull. God, why didn't he stop?

Soon the minister did stop. He looked down at the casket and, after a pause, raised his head. "The Lord is my shepherd," he said, beginning the Twenty-third Psalm.

Boyd had to leave before he broke down crying in front of everyone. He started for the gates, moving fast, his head down, biting his lip as hard as he could and blinking hard. As he reached the gates, his eyes filled, and weeping, he ran into the road.

———⸘⬦⸙———

L UCIUS PEETE STILL WENT to his office in company headquarters every day even though he would be seventy-eight years old on his next birthday, and Sue Ann Glover, his secretary, was almost as old as he. Lucius Peete had always been slender, and now he was stooped, and his hands shook. But the day after the funeral he helped Sue Ann carry extra chairs into his office. "Six," he said. "We need six chairs altogether."

"Six? I only count five," Sue Ann said.

"And Russell Vance," Lucius Peete said.

"Russell?"

"Put one chair at the windows," he said. "Serena likes to be in the sun."

Just before ten o'clock Sue Ann came to the door. "Miss Serena is here," she said, and stepped aside as Serena entered ahead of Burris.

"Serena," Lucius said, rising. "Frank."

"Have you heard from Holt?" Serena asked, heading directly to the chair at the window.

"This morning," Lucius said. Burris carried a chair across the office to sit beside her. "He sent a cable." He removed a cablegram from an envelope with a blue border and held a monocle in a gold rim to his right eye. " 'Heartbroken,' " he read aloud. " 'Homeward soonest.' " He held up the cablegram. "Would you like to read it, Serena?"

"I believe you," she said. "How's business?" she asked, and added louder: "On the ship?"

Three years earlier, after Mardi Gras, Holt Castleton had remained in New Orleans and bought a freighter. Everyone put it down to another lark and waited for him to come home. He hadn't come home yet. He had hired a ship's architect, asking for personal quarters on the freighter. He had lived aboard the ship while it was being refitted, and he remained when the ship put out to sea with its first cargo. One morning several months later Lucius received a cable: AM LEARNING A TRADE.

Holt operated the freighter for profit, and in the first year and each succeeding year the ship earned money. After the first year Holt cabled Lucius Peete: BALANCE SHEET FOLLOWS. PAY ME.

So Lucius learned why Holt had gone to sea. Sam Castleton's will contained a clause offering any descendant two dollars for every dollar the heir earned. Holt had accepted his grandfather's challenge.

In his office Lucius said, "He continues to show a profit, Serena. Ah, Gaby," he said as she paused in the doorway.

Behind her Colin said, "I say, Lucius, you've found the fountain of youth. Share your secret, old sport."

Faith arrived with Russell, and when everyone was seated, Lucius said, "We are here to learn the contents of Kyle King Castleton's last will and testament." He displayed a sheaf of legal-size paper.

"Stop," Serena said. "You told me you were asking the family to hear Kyle's will. Just the family."

Russell rose. "I'm sorry. I'll leave."

Gaby looked down at the floor. She had run from confrontations all her life. The constant conflicts between her father and grandfather, and after her father's death, between Sam Castleton and Holt, had made Gaby ill. She had fled to avoid the unending fights.

Lucius turned to Serena. "Russell is very much involved with the family. I talk with Russell more often, about more matters than I do to anyone in the family."

"Russell can stay," Gaby said, trembling inside and out as she dared confront her aunt. Gaby had never spoken out. All her life she had surrendered to whomever she faced, succumbing meekly to authority. And hating herself after each defeat. Now she discovered, in astonishment, that she wanted to smile. She could not remember being as happy. She faced Serena directly, hoping her aunt would challenge her, and when the older woman remained silent, Gaby looked up at Russell. "Come back."

Russell returned to his chair, and Lucius took the monocle from his vest pocket. "Kyle completed a new will after he married," he said.

At his right Colin said, "I say, it's handwritten. Is that legal?"

"Kyle wrote it," Lucius said. He raised the will so all could see. "It is his handwriting."

"You're certain of that, are you?" Colin asked.

"He wrote it here, at this desk," Lucius said. "He sat here in front of me while he wrote it. Sue Ann and I were witnesses."

"No offense, old boy," Colin said. "Carry on."

Lucius adjusted his monocle and read aloud: " 'I, Kyle King Castleton, being of sound mind and body, so far as I myself can judge, set down my last will and testament.

" 'I've been very lucky in my life. I've had everything a man, a boy and a man, could want, everything anyone could dream of having. I've also been very lucky in the people I've met and known. I want to thank a few of those people. Reading this over so far, I see there are a lot of I's in this will. I, I, I, I. Well, it's my will.

" 'First and foremost, ever since I can remember, one person has always been there, taking care of me. Most of my life he was the first person I saw in the morning and the last at night. And if I ever needed anything during the night, he was there too. He seemed to know when I needed something even before I knew I needed it. I guess he knows me better than anyone else in this world, certainly longer than anyone in this world. It's Coleman, of course.

" 'Dear, dependable, loyal, loving Coleman. He never judged, never grudged, never pouted, never shouted, never scowled, never growled, never scolded, never punished, never absent, always present.

" 'But he isn't just Coleman. Like Hercules, or Hannibal, or

Samson, or Caesar. He is Coleman Something. And can't tell me Coleman who. He doesn't know who. I had to discover who. This I did.

" 'Coleman Beaudine. The Reverend Millard Fitch of the Resurrection Baptist Church provided the information. Reverend Fitch and Coleman came into this world at the same time in the same place, right here in the Flats. Reverend Fitch remembers Coleman's mother, and he remembers the identity of Coleman's father, the Vanishing American. Beaudine. To Coleman Beaudine I bequeath fifty thousand dollars.' "

Serena said in outrage, "Fifty thousand!" and Burris, at her side, said, "How much?" and Gaby, leaning forward, said, "Fifty thousand!" and Colin, rising, said, "No offense, old chap. Are you certain of the figure?"

He took a step toward the desk, craning his neck, trying to read the will. "Fifty thousand? Not five? Five hundred? Five thousand?"

"Richest nigger in North Carolina," Serena said.

"In the South," Burris said. "North and South."

"Hold on," Colin said. "Lucius, did you know Kyle would do this?"

"I witnessed his signature," Lucius said.

"And you didn't talk to him?" Colin asked.

"I did," Lucius said. "We argued for a long time. He said, 'Is fifty thousand enough?' "

"Stop enjoying this so much, Lucius," Serena snapped.

Colin said, "Bully," and took his seat again. He looked at Gaby, blaming her. "That's just splendid."

At the window Serena said, "I always suspected Kyle of being an abolitionist."

"How dare you?" Gaby came out of her chair, facing Serena, her face red and blotchy with emotion. "Kyle is dead, and you're making cracks about him. You didn't know Kyle. You didn't care about him. You sit in your house wishing we all were dead so that you could have the Castle. You'll never have the Castle. *You'll* die— you'll—" Gaby stopped. She discovered herself standing amid all the others. The tiny figure seemed to shrink, and Gaby dropped down into her chair as though she had been punished.

The puny little whisper of a woman bored Serena. "I only meant to praise Kyle." She turned to Faith. "I said what I did to praise your husband, Mrs. Castleton."

Burris leaned forward, his arms resting on his thighs, looking down at the floor. "Can we finish this?"

"We can," Lucius said, fitting the monocle into his eye and continuing to read. " 'I have someone else who is always there when I need him. Boyd Fredericks is my best friend, and to him I bequeath my most precious possession, my baby, the finest aircraft in the world, my Waco. I also bequeath Boyd Fredericks my flying gear since we both wear the same size.

" 'The balance of my estate I bequeath to my beloved wife, Faith. Adios, darling.' " Lucius set down the sheaf of papers and took the monocle from his eye.

"Hold on," Colin said. "Balance of my estate?" He gestured to Gaby. "You've skipped Gaby and Holt. My dear fellow, you simply can't cut next of kin out of a will."

"Next of kin is arguable," Lucius said. "I warned Kyle of this possibility, so Kyle added a rider to his will." He shuffled through the papers. "Rider A," Lucius said. "To my beloved sister, Gaby, and my beloved brother, Holt, I leave the sum of one dollar each."

"Good grief!" Colin scowled at Gaby. "One dollar! What kind of joke is he playing?"

Gaby did not look at him, and she did not respond. "Rider A completes Kyle's will," Lucius said. "In my opinion, the will is incontrovertible. Contesting this will would be an act of futility, an expensive, profitless act."

Serena, who had not expected a penny from Kyle, said, "You've made your case, Lucius. The meeting is adjourned."

Burris started to rise when Lucius said, "There is the B Stock."

"You're talking of another will," Serena said. "My father's will, not my nephew's."

"Thank you, Serena," said the aged lawyer, and looked at Faith. "Mrs. Castleton, did Kyle ever speak to you of the B Stock?"

Faith said, "B Stock? What is B Stock?"

"The B Stock controls the company," Lucius said. "It is not ordinary stock. The public cannot purchase B Stock. It cannot be bought or sold. All holders of B Stock sit on the company's board of directors. Their votes make up a clear majority of all company stock, common and preferred.

"Under the terms of Sam Castleton's will, all B Stock remains in the family forevermore. Sam Castleton willed all B Stock to his children, Serena and Branch, and to their children and their children's children, and so on. If Kyle had left a child, the child would have inherited his B Stock. Since he did not and there is no heir, his B Stock will go, in equal amounts to his siblings, to Gaby and Holt."

Colin said, whispering, "Gaby . . ." and she said, "Stop."

His face began to fill with color. He said, "Listen here—" and broke off as she turned her head. Colin took her wrist and yanked her arm, hurting her.

"I never heard of this B Stock," Colin said. "Why didn't anyone tell me about it?"

"You're hurting me," she said, glaring at him. She pulled her arm free.

At his desk Lucius said, "Can I continue? Gaby? Can I continue?"

Gaby nodded. "I'm sorry."

Lucius said, "Do you have any questions, Mrs. Castleton?"

"No . . ." Faith said. She rose from the chair. "Thank you."

"Can you give me another moment, Mrs. Castleton? There are and will be documents for you to read and endorse during probate," Lucius said. "It is a long, tedious process. I am at your service. As your counsel I can smooth the path for you, act for you as I act for the family. You may not think so at the moment, but as time passes, you will have needs that require the assistance of an attorney."

Faith faced them all, the roomful of enemies to whom she said a silent good-bye. She would never again have to look at any of their faces. "I need nothing for myself," she said. "I've already lost what I wanted above all else in this world." She turned her back to them and walked to the door.

———————

O NE MORNING LATER in the week Faith found Russell in his office in the Castle. "I'm leaving today," she said. "This afternoon."

"For New York?"

"Of course, New York," Faith said.

"Are you sure? This is your home," Russell said. "No one can force you from the Castle."

"Dear Russell," she said, "*I* am forcing me. And I need help. The newspapermen. The army at the gates. And at the depot probably. I can't face them, Russell."

"You won't," he said. "I'll drive you."

"They'll stop you," Faith said. "I've watched them. They stop everyone. They stop the milkman, the deliverymen, begging for gossip, for dirt. Dirt," Faith said. "Those vultures." She paused, collecting herself. "I thought maybe that deputy . . . Wyn. Isn't his name Wyn?"

"Wyn Ainsley."

"Do you think he would help?"

Russell quickly made the call and settled the matter with Earl. "Tell him to come around to the kitchen, Sheriff, will you do that?"

"Done," Earl said. He left his office, hitching up his pants.

Two deputies were on the sick list that day, and Wyn was covering for one. He stood behind the counter reading the sports pages as Earl joined him. "Grab an early lunch. You're going out to the Castle at three o'clock."

Wyn closed the newspaper. "The *Castle?*"

"The lady is leaving," Earl said. "Heading for New York on the Flamingo. She needs a lift, someone who will keep away the reporters."

An uneasy feeling crept up Wyn's spine. He didn't want to see her, didn't want to see the Castle. "Why me?"

Earl grinned. "She asked for you."

"Asked?" Wyn leaned against the counter, fighting a weird mix of joy and dismay.

"According to Russell Vance," Earl said. "She asked him if you would help." Earl could barely see over the long counter. He raised the hinged portion to join Wyn. "When do you want lunch?"

"Pop, do me a favor," Wyn said. "Send Arver Long, will you?"

"She didn't ask for Arver Long," Earl said, peering at Wyn curiously. "What the hell is the matter with you?"

Wyn straightened the newspaper. "Send Arver."

"Hey!" Earl grabbed him. "I'm talking to you. What the hell is the matter with you?"

"I'm sick of the Castle."

"You're sick—" Earl was dumbfounded. Everything he hoped would happen was starting to happen. Faith Venable, the Broadway star, Kyle Castleton's widow, asking for Wyn Ainsley. Nobody could duck the reporters forever. And Wyn would be with her. "You're going," Earl said. "Park behind the kitchen."

Around three o'clock Wyn drove down Millionaires Row. He could see the Castle. He could feel his heart pounding. The closer he got, the faster his heart beat. He had forgotten his reluctance at Sheriff's Headquarters. Wyn had never been alone with Faith, had never had her to himself. He squirmed in the seat, unable to get comfortable. Then he said aloud, "All you're doing is saying good-bye."

When he turned into the Castle drive, Wyn headed straight for the massed newspapermen. He put his hand on the horn, picking up speed. The solid wall of reporters and photographers split, making room for the sheriff's car.

Wyn found Russell and Coleman beside the suitcases stacked on the lower kitchen steps. "We'll hide everything in the trunk," Wyn said. He took the biggest suitcase and, reaching for another, saw Faith descending the stairs. A sudden gust of wind plastered her dress against her thigh and leg.

Wyn took another suitcase and followed Russell and Coleman to his car. He loaded the trunk and reached for the trunk lid. When he closed it, he found Faith beside him.

"Thank you for coming," she said.

He said, "Well . . ." and found himself tongue-tied, feeling dumber than dumb. "Anyway, if those reporters see you, they'll chase you—us." He opened the door of the sheriff's car and reached across the front seat for his raincoat. "Let's fix it so they don't see you. If they see you, they'll follow us, and we'll have a mob at the depot."

"I'll do whatever you say." She offered Russell her hand. "Good-bye. Thank you for your kindness," Faith said. At last she was rid of that toady, bowing his way through life.

She turned to Coleman to finish her farewells and be on her way, be on her way! Coleman took out his handkerchief and dabbed at his eyes. "Now you're leaving too."

Wyn said, "We've got a long way to go, ma'am."

"I'm ready," Faith said. She had packed the night before, making certain to leave no trace of herself behind. She had watched the clock all through the day.

"Here's what I want you to do," Wyn said. "I want you to curl up on the backseat." He raised his raincoat. "I'll drop this over you. Okay?"

"Okay."

Wyn took her arm, helping her into the car. Faith lay down on the backseat, and he covered her with the raincoat. "Are you all right?"

"I'm fine," Faith said. She would never need to see the Castle again. She closed her eyes, leaving behind the horror she had lived through.

Wyn dropped into the driver's seat and locked the doors. As they started, he picked up speed rapidly, shifting quickly through the gears, and when he passed the garage, he pushed the accelerator into the floorboard, racing toward the newspapermen and scattering them. He swung out into Millionaires Row, picking up more speed. Leaving the Castle behind, Wyn said, "You can sit up now. We're in the clear."

He could see her in the rearview mirror. He wanted to turn the wheel, drive away from the depot, away from Winston-Salem, wanted to keep going. "Wake up," he said to himself. "You're dreaming. Stop dreaming."

Once downtown, Wyn drove past the depot entrance. He turned onto a concrete ramp used only by post office trucks delivering and collecting bags of mail for the trains. The ramp descended to the train concourse. Wyn stopped, lowering the window to yell at a redcap, "The Flamingo Express?"

"Track seven, sir. You're not allowed down here, sir," said the redcap. But Wyn was already shooting past him.

"What car do you want, Mrs. Castleton?" Wyn asked. "Mrs. Castleton?"

"Oh, wait." Faith opened her purse for her ticket. "It's—I'm sorry . . . Drawing room A in car eleven."

"Right." Wyn reached track seven and turned into the platform between seven and eight. He passed the last car, with the open observation deck at the rear. The platform was crowded with passengers and their families saying good-bye, with train conductors and redcaps and porters in white jackets. Wyn had to slow to a crawl. A conductor said, "You can't—" as Wyn passed him. Another conductor ran straight at the car. Wyn stopped, and as the conductor leaned into the window, Wyn grabbed the man's blue jacket with the brass buttons and twisted. "Step on the running board and get me to car eleven on the Flamingo."

On the running board the conductor said, "Slow, go slow. Go slow! This is crazy! Stop! *Stop!* Here's eleven."

"Bring some redcaps," Wyn ordered. He got out of the car and opened the trunk. "Everything in here is for drawing room A. Where are those redcaps?"

"They're coming," said the conductor, waving both arms. "You can't leave your car—" he said, but Wyn had already turned to open the rear door of the sheriff's car. Extending his hand, he said, "We're here." He felt her slender, warm fingers curling around his and nearly jumped at the shock of pleasure it gave him.

He stepped up into the vestibule and stood against the door so she could enter the sleeping car. He saw a metal C on the door at his elbow and a D across the aisle. "You're at the other end," he said.

At her drawing room Faith said, smiling, "You saved me a great deal of trouble."

She stopped him cold every time, leaving him stupid and speechless. He managed to say, "Saved?" shaking his head, feeling his face flush like some pimply teacher's pet. He looked over his shoulder. "I'll light a fire under those redcaps," Wyn said. He had no sooner turned than he saw one approaching, arms loaded. "Down here," he said, gesturing. "Here. Drawing room A." He turned back to Faith. "You'd better get inside before some reporter shows up. I'll handle the redcaps."

Wyn waited in the corridor, guarding the drawing room door while the redcaps stacked the luggage. He tipped them and joined Faith, closing the door in case reporters came. As she stood among the suitcases, she seemed more beautiful than ever. Anyway, this was the end. The train would pull out, and she would disappear. He could go back to his own life again. Wyn tried not to look at her. "All set," he said.

"I owe you for the redcaps," Faith said.

"That's— No, you don't," he said. "No," he said, shaking his head. He couldn't take money from her. "You'll be okay now. Lock up after me." He opened the door slightly, blocking it with his body. "Ready?"

Faith nodded, then said quickly, "No!" She crossed the drawing room and rose on tiptoe to kiss him on the cheek. "Ready," she said.

Wyn backed out into the corridor. He tested the door to be certain she had locked it. He went into the vestibule and down the steps to the platform. He walked the length of the railroad car to his black-and-white. He opened the car door but remained on the platform, raising his hand and brushing his face with his fingers. Wyn could still feel her lips, and he said softly, "Among my souvenirs."

Wyn drove back to the courthouse. He left the key in the ignition of the car for his relief. He returned to headquarters so he could sign out. Len Egan was sitting at a typewriter, using two fingers to finish a report on a stolen car. "Hey, Wyn!"

Wyn said, "Hi," going to the counter and opening the duty roster book. He looked up at the clock and set down his name and the time.

"Hey, I'll be through here in a minute," Len said. "What're you doing tonight?"

"Nothing. Hitting the hay," Wyn said.

"How about supper? Out in the country somewhere? Get out of this heat," Len said.

Wyn had a flashing thought of Faith in the drawing room. Soon the porter would be making up her berth.

"Wyn?"

"Yeah, sure," Wyn said.

"Go home and shower and change, and I'll pick you up," Len said. "Six o'clock, around there."

"Sure, all right," Wyn said. But then he changed his mind. He walked to a desk facing Len and leaned against it. "Actually, I'm not hungry."

"Huh?" Len stopped typing. "Who the hell is? Christ, it's four o'clock. I'm talking about supper."

"This heat—"

"I said the country. We'll drive out in the country somewhere," Len said.

Wyn could not sit in a booth with Len Egan, listening to him rattle on for an hour or more. "Guess I'll skip it."

"Hell, let's make it later," Len said. "Seven, seven-thirty."

"No, forget it," Wyn said. He started for the door at the rear of the office.

"Jesus, you'd think I asked you for a loan. I only said—" Len stopped because he was alone.

Wyn left the courthouse and walked to his car in the row behind the sheriff's cars. He drove out of the parking area into the late-afternoon traffic. She wouldn't be back. Wyn would bet anyone she wouldn't be back. Why should she come back? Why in hell should you *care?* Christ, man, grow up. Will you grow *up?* She's a million miles out of your reach. A trillion. Okay! *Okay!* But she was right there in the car with him. He could still see her. Hell, he could smell her perfume. Come on-n-n-n-n! Her *perfume!* Goddammit, after all those days in the Castle he knew her perfume when he smelled it. So what? She's gone. And she was never here anyway, not for you, not for a rookie deputy sheriff. Where do you get off even thinking— "All right!" he shouted, stopping for a red light. He leaned across the seat to roll down the passenger window to be rid of her perfume, of *her,* and saw the street sign. He was driving in the opposite direction from his way home.

A car horn behind him made Wyn realize the light had changed. In a rush he shifted before he had depressed the clutch, and the screeching protest of the gears brought another blast from the angry driver in the rear. Wyn was ready to explode. He pulled back the emergency brake, trying to pull it loose. He opened the car door, kicked it wide open with his foot, turned in the seat to leap out of the car. And stopped cold. He slammed the door closed. Picking fights in *uniform?* He shifted gears, forgetting the emergency brake, then remembering the brake as the car bucked. Dropping the brake, he zoomed across the intersection, continuing the wrong way until he could make a left turn three blocks beyond.

Wyn crawled through the streets. Nothing in his life had prepared him for a sudden infatuation with a woman. Lucky for him she was gone. Wyn stuck his head out of the window, hoping for a breeze, and remembered the gust of wind which had caught Faith's dress on the kitchen steps. He remembered the line of her thigh and leg. He groaned, wounded and helpless. "Hell . . ."

Home for Wyn was a large bedroom and bathroom upstairs in which his landlady had installed a shower over the tub with a curtain on a track. Mrs. Metcalfe changed the sheets every week and provided more towels than Wyn could use. And although Wyn locked his door when he left, he found endless surprises on the night table beside his bed: cookies, two peaches, a wedge of banana cake, Mrs. Metcalfe's favorite, lemonade in a pitcher with cracked ice. Sometimes his landlady left a note inviting him to come downstairs for ice cream or pie.

Mrs. Metcalfe's daughter, Mary Ellen, was married and lived in Mobile, Mrs. Metcalfe had told Wyn, and when her husband died, she could not face living alone. She wanted a roomer, a man. She would feel safe at night with a man.

When Wyn got there, Mrs. Metcalfe was sitting on the porch. "Isn't this heat awful? You must be plain worn out," she said.

Wyn had learned to keep moving. "I guess."

"You need to get into something cool."

"I will, ma'am." He went up the stairs two at a time.

He stood under the shower in the bathtub until he began to shiver from the sting of the cold water. After he had rubbed himself dry, Wyn dropped, naked, into the bed. Where was Faith now? he wondered. She was probably in the dining car.

Wyn turned on his side so hard the bed squeaked. He was enraged at himself again. He just had to forget all about her. He jumped up and took some clothes out of his dresser, throwing everything on the bed so he could get dressed.

He pulled on a white T-shirt and a pair of faded, shapeless cotton trousers. He shoved his bare feet into worn leather moccasins. "Not sitting around here," he muttered aloud. Wyn picked up the telephone and carried it to the bed. "Kay? Hi."

"Wyn . . . hello," she said.

"Are you in the middle of dinner?"

"No, no."

"Sure?"

"No . . . I mean, yes," Kay said. "Yes, I'm sure. We haven't even thought of food."

"It's the heat," Wyn said, trying to relax. He pushed off his moccasins, raised his legs onto the bed, and fell back against the pillows. "So I'm not busting in on anything."

"You're not."

"Listen, Kay, I was thinking . . . you haven't eaten yet, and neither have I. We could drive out for some chicken."

"Wyn, I—" she said before he interrupted.

"Or anything else," he said. "It doesn't have to be chicken. Whatever you decide is okay with me."

"Can you hold on for a moment?" Kay said.

"For you?" He grinned. "All night."

"I'll be right back," Kay said. She set the receiver down beside the phone. She crossed the room quickly to shut the door so her mother wouldn't hear. Kay hurried back to the telephone. "Wyn?"

"I'm here."

"Wyn, I can't," Kay said. "It's Mother. She's sick. She was out all day in this heat. I called the doctor, and he told me what to do. He said she'll be all right. Can you hear me?"

"Sure. I can hear you."

"I've kept my voice down," Kay said. "If Mother hears me, she'll say she's fine and I should go. And I can't, Wyn. If something happened—"

"How about tomorrow night?" he said, feeling condemned. He had to get out of this place.

"I'm sure she'll be fine by then."

"I'll see you tomorrow then," Wyn said. "And remember me to your mother, Kay."

Wyn got out of bed with the telephone. He had forgotten Len Egan's phone number. Wyn called the courthouse to get it.

Len Egan's brother said he had just left. "Came home to change clothes, which is all he ever does around here except sleep."

Wyn set down the telephone, pushing his bare feet into his moccasins. Okay, he'd go out on his own.

Below, on the porch, Mrs. Metcalfe said, "Person doesn't even feel like eating in this kind of weather."

He said, moving fast, "You're right." He added, "Night, Mrs. Metcalfe," in case she had some ideas about dinner.

Wyn drove three blocks to the diner where he usually ate breakfasts and many of his dinners. He parked across the street. A man in filthy overalls sat on a stool in the diner, slurping coffee, and another man, in a booth, tore a slice of white bread apart and shoveled the pieces into his mouth as if he were in a race. Wyn turned the ignition key, starting the engine. He drove three miles to a hamburger shop where they made good hamburgers. Outside, a gang of kids, boys and girls, were squirting soda pop at each other. Wyn didn't stop.

He decided to splurge and drove to Schoonover's, an old downtown restaurant that catered to everyone from lawyers and doctors to cops.

Wyn parked a block from the restaurant. Now, in the last hours of daylight, the heat had lessened. Two couples in front of him entered the restaurant, and Wyn held the door. He waited while they decided where to sit. Ceiling fans whirred overhead, and the currents of moving air they created were sensuous after the heat of the day.

"Wyn! Over here!" Len Egan sat in a booth, holding a fork over his head, shaking his head at Wyn's appearance and grinning. "Can't eat in the heat," he said loudly as Wyn walked toward him.

To himself Wyn said, "Goddamn idiot has to tell everyone," but he managed to smile.

"Miss," Len said to a passing waitress, "set another place for my friend, here, will ya? Thanks, honey." Len fell back into the booth. "Take a load off, Wyn."

"You were going to go driving out in the country," Wyn said as he slid into the bench facing Len.

"Alone?" Len shook his head. "Not alone. I decided to treat myself. Haven't been in Schoonover's in a coon's age." He pointed at his plate. "Chicken pie is real good."

Wyn chose a cold plate. When the food came and he began to eat, he discovered he was hungry. He remembered he had not eaten lunch, had eaten only two doughnuts for breakfast. After his father had told him he would be going to the Castle for Faith, he had not thought of eating. "Maybe things will quiet down now with the Castleton woman gone, huh, Wyn?" Len said.

"I guess." Wyn thought of the Flamingo Express racing along the tracks. She would be in New York tomorrow. Wyn wanted to run, as though he could leave Faith behind. But he knew he could not escape. She had imprisoned him. He began to bolt his food.

He and Len each paid his own check, but they joined in a tip for the waitress. Wyn said, "Okay . . ." sitting back and stretching, extending his arms horizontally.

"Hey, what's your hurry? Where you going?" Len said. "You can't sleep. It's too hot to sleep. Hang around." He grinned. "I got an idea." He held out his hand. "Gimme a dollar. C'mon, gimme." Wyn took out his wallet and removed a dollar. Len tapped the deputy's badge inside and winked. "Brings me luck."

When he had Wyn's dollar, Len slid out of the booth. "Be right back." Wyn watched him walk through the swinging doors to the kitchen.

When their waitress saw the goof go into the kitchen, she picked up the pot of coffee and crossed the restaurant to stop beside Wyn. "Refill, hon?"

"I've had enough, thanks," Wyn said.

She looked down at him, her free hand on her hip. "Let me know if you change your mind, hon."

"Sure," Wyn said, a million miles away. He was wondering if Faith would sleep on the train. Lots of people couldn't sleep on a train.

"Let's go," Len said, waving at Wyn as he left the kitchen and headed for the door. Len carried a small brown paper bag. Wyn slid out of the booth and paused to hitch up his pants, unconsciously aping his father's habit.

Wyn grabbed Len in front of the restaurant, pulling him away from the doors. "You bought some whiskey? I just ate," Wyn said. "I don't want any whiskey."

"It's not for you," Len said. He pulled his arm free. "C'mon. We'll take my car."

Len drove fast. Beside him, Wyn said, "Where to? Where are you heading?"

"Cut it out, huh? What else you got to do anyway?"

"Where are we going, Len?"

"Maybe we'll get laid," Len said. He turned to Wyn, grinning. "How'd you like that, huh?"

"Laid?" Wyn's voice rose. "Now? Who with? Where?" Then he fell back into the seat, ready for anything that might provide an escape from Faith.

Len drove down Pleasant Avenue through downtown into what had once been the city's first upper-class residential area. The houses that remained were neglected and dilapidated. "Where are these women?" Wyn asked.

"See for yourself," Len said. He drove into an alley behind a block of sagging frame houses. Waning daylight left the alley in shadows. Len swung into a littered yard. "C'mon."

"Where?" They walked through the yard. Len opened a door at the rear of the house. Inside, a narrow hallway lit by a single naked bulb high overhead ended in a staircase that had once been used by servants. "C'mon." Len took the stairs two and three at a time.

Wyn heard him knocking on a door. When Wyn reached the head of the stairs, he saw Len facing a woman in a bright blue, stained kimono, a plump woman with bleached blond hair. She scowled at Len. "What the hell do you want?"

"Guess." Len raised his arm. "C'mere, Wyn," he said. "Peaches, this is my pal, Wyn. He's a deputy like me."

"Beat it," she said. "Both of you. Get lost."

"You bet," Len said, and pushed her back into the door so he could pass. "C'mon, Wyn." Inside, he looked back. "C'mon, I said."

Wyn joined them in a large room filled with furniture: sofas, love seats, overstuffed chairs, a table with dishes and the remains of a meal, a large upright phonograph, and lamps with elaborate shades. The room opened to a tiny kitchen, and on the other side a Chinese screen shielded a bed.

Peaches walked around Len, using both hands to pat her hair into place. "I can't now," she said. "I'm working now." A large embroidered red dragon covered the back of her kimono. "I'm working."

"You are?" Len took three long steps to reach the Chinese screen. He stood on tiptoe. "I don't see anyone."

"You bastard," she said. "Rotten bastard. You're supposed to come in daytime."

"I got lonesome for you," Len said. He took the brown paper bag from his pocket and removed a pint bottle of bootleg whiskey. He went to the table and reached for a glass. "Brought you something, Peaches."

"Not when I'm working," Peaches said. "I'm working. And you hold your horses." She disappeared behind the screen.

Len poured whiskey into a glass. "Wyn?"

"I'm going."

"Going? Are you nuts?" Len drank most of the whiskey in the

glass and set it down. He pointed. "She's great. Peaches Klem. We've got this arrangement. I kind of look out for her."

"In the city? She's inside the city limits," Wyn said. "The cops handle her."

Len grinned. "I told her lots of my friends are cops."

Peaches said, "All right, you." She stood beside the Chinese screen, naked except for high-heeled shoes.

"Now, that's what I like." Len leaped to his feet, arms spread, and pulled her to the bed behind the screen.

Wyn looked around uncomfortably as he heard the thud, thud of Len's shoes hitting the floor. He heard Len say, "Do what you do while I'm undressing." And he heard Peaches say, "Hold your horses." Wyn walked toward the door. He was not a prude, but the squalor, the idea of having sex in a crowd, drove him out. Wyn went down the stairs slowly. He had to wait for Len to drive him back to his car near Schoonover's.

———— ···(·)··· ————

A T THE LAKE HOUSE Gaby made her way down to the water and out onto the dock. The boats tied to the dock rose and fell, and the water slapped against the pilings, breaking the silence. Gaby held on to one of the pilings that rose above the dock. The lake shimmered in the sunlight. The sound of the water beneath the dock, the sounds of birds in the trees, the fluttering leaves all made Gaby feel at home. Safe here where she had once been happy, she leaned against the piling.

After a while she went to the end of the dock to look down at the dark water. Then she heard a car. She came up the path and saw Russell. "At last," he said. "I've been here every night since you came back."

"Every night?"

"Are you surprised?" Russell asked. "Did you think I'd forget? Or change? Gaby, was that a game you played on the terrace the night you arrived?"

"I've wanted to be here too," Gaby said. She looked up at him. "Every night," she said. "All through the night."

"Darling," Russell said, taking her in his arms. "My darling," he said, and kissed her.

"Harder," she said, clinging to him, and when he kissed her again, said, "Yes. Harder. Harder." She pressed herself against him, pulling at his shirt and slipping her hands under it, her hot hands against his hot skin. "At last," she murmured. "I'm with you at last."

"I love you," Russell said. "I've loved you from the start. I'll always love you."

"Darling." She took his face in her hands, peering up at him. "I love you," she said. "Only you, darling. Even when I was . . . with him, it was you." She brought his head down, her mouth against his fiercely. "I've thought of this every night," she whispered.

When it began, years earlier, they used to play a game. In the corridor at the head of the stairs Russell would say, "Close your eyes," and Gaby would obey. "No peeking. Promise."

"Promise," Gaby would say, and chant, "Eeny meeny . . . ," pointing in all directions as she continued, and when she finished, they would go to the last room at which she pointed.

Inside, the entryway took up the width of the house and rose to the rafters. A massive fieldstone fireplace stood in the center with sofas and chairs grouped around the hearth. As Gaby and Russell walked to the staircase, he felt her stiffen and stop. "Gaby? What is it?"

She did not really hear him. She felt as if the ghost of her grandfather had joined them. Gaby felt as though he were sitting at the fireplace, facing them.

Sam Castleton had been sitting at the fireplace four years earlier on that Saturday afternoon in May when they burst into the lake house, chasing each other, unable to wait. They always came in separate cars and from separate directions. "Welcome," Sam Castleton said.

They stopped dead, frozen. Sam Castleton waved his cane. "Shut the door and come on in."

As he beckoned them forward, he said, "You're wondering how I got here, eh? Coleman brought me. I sent him away so you wouldn't be warned off. Pull up some chairs."

Sam Castleton watched the pair. "I could have waited upstairs, but you don't deserve such treatment. You deserve better," he said. "Sit down. Sit down, little girl."

Gaby sat on the edge of a chair, and Russell, his face white with shock, stood before Sam Castleton like a plebe. "Stop this, both of you," Castleton said. "I'm not a police officer, and I'm not a judge. Strange as it seems, I was young once. You folks haven't done anything wrong. Haven't done much of anything right either. Sneaking around like common criminals. Someone saw you all the way over in the north end of the county. Driving more than a hundred miles back and forth just for dinner. We've got some pretty good restaurants right here in town. There's pretty good grub at my own table, if I say so myself. You're always welcome. The Castle has always been open to your friends, little girl."

Neither of the two lovers offered a word.

"Well, I'm just listening to myself talk," Castleton said. "Doesn't entertain me much, and I'm making you two more miserable every minute." Using his cane, Castleton rose slowly. A very tall man, he seemed almost cadaverous. He towered over Russell, but he looked weak, almost fragile.

"Russell, call Coleman, that's a good lad," said Castleton. "Tell him to come fetch me." Castleton pointed with the cane. "And you two ought to make yourselves scarce. Coleman was young once too. If he sees you, every nigger in North Carolina will know what's been happening here by the time they leave church next Sunday." He waved the cane. "You can find your way home, little girl. Scat."

Every night of his life, even ill, even alone, Sam Castleton dined in the stately banquet hall he had sketched for his architect. Just before seven, Coleman came for Gaby. "Dinner, Miss Gaby. Mist' Sam, he's there."

The banquet hall blazed with lights. "Thanks for coming, little girl," Sam Castleton said. "You look pretty as a picture."

Gaby was ready for him. "You had us followed!" she said accusingly. "Are you proud of yourself?"

"Always have been," Castleton said. "Too late to change now."

"I'm not a . . . little girl! I'm over twenty-one!"

"Sure are," Castleton said. "You're of age. You've got your own money, more money than any girl in the United States, in the world maybe. You can start spending some of your trust. It's the interest, but that's enough to live like a king, queen. Take a trip. Get on a boat. You should see the world. You ought to know something about the world. So far all you know is what you learned in the lake house from my estate manager. You could have got that from anyone old enough."

She bit her lip, refusing to let him make her cry. "You're cruel."

"Probably am," Castleton said. "The truth is always cruel. That's something you can learn from me, right here, tonight. Won't cost a cent."

"I love Russell!"

"I love you," Castleton said.

"*Your* kind of love," Gaby said, then became frightened. She had never spoken rudely to him.

"Only kind I know," Castleton said.

"Can we end this?" Gaby said.

"Sure," Castleton said. "I can't talk to myself. Only want to say the fellow you picked is a hired hand."

Gaby refused to cry, refused to let him win. "Russell is a fine, decent man, the nicest person I've ever known!"

"For a fact," said Sam Castleton. "He earns every dollar I pay him. Fact is, little girl, you haven't been around many people, have you?"

"You always win," Gaby said. "Not this time. You won't win this time!"

In the morning Gaby learned her grandfather had sent Russell to Texas to a series of cattle auctions. Russell had orders to buy new stock for the farms. Sam Castleton managed to be at Gaby's side all through the day and the days which followed.

Later in the week Gaby boarded a train for New York. A school chum, Peggy Hunicutt, told Gaby she would be at Pennsylvania Station. She said Gaby could stay with the Hunicutts until she found her own house for the summer.

Gaby would have preferred staying with Peggy, sharing a bedroom. She dreaded being alone after the torment of her last days in the Castle, but she could not impose on Peggy, and she could not burden anyone with the grief and sorrow she carried.

Gaby had met Peggy Hunicutt at the school in Virginia where she lived through a miserable year in her teens, homesick and lonely, cowering among her jolly, babbling classmates from New York and Chicago and Atlanta. Gaby went to chapel, attended classes, changed for gym, cleaned her plate in the dining hall, and wrote home dutifully, lying weekly.

Peggy Hunicutt had made her a friend, a confidante. Peggy's

room became a haven for Gaby, and when Sam Castleton sent Russell away, Gaby could not remain in the Castle, submitting to his watchful gaze.

Peggy Hunicutt's family lived in Quogue, and Peggy found a house in East Hampton for Gaby. The house was owned by a family that kept a shooting lodge in Scotland and would be gone for the summer.

Gaby wanted to flee even before she unpacked. The East Hampton house could have been an enormous inn. Gaby took the staff with the house, but they were quartered behind the rose garden, leaving her alone through the long, long, lonely nights. But she could not go home, could not bow to her grandfather's iron will.

Peggy Hunicutt came to the rescue once more. "Give a party!"

"A *party?* Peggy! You're the only person I know!"

"I'll furnish the guest list and the guests," Peggy said. "You furnish the whiskey. You can use Daddy's bootlegger."

Peggy filled the house with young men and women for the party. She stood at the door, greeting the guests and introducing Gaby. Peggy suggested the games and led the contestants. The party became Peggy's. No one spoke of leaving. Much later Gaby stood on the veranda looking down on a young man turning cartwheels in the sand. Someone said, "Nothing left in his pockets. Enough to make a chap a beachcomber." At her elbow a man in a white dinner jacket bowed his head. "Hullo. We met earlier. I'm Colin Inscott." He remained at Gaby's side for the rest of the evening. Colin knew everyone, and he made Gaby laugh.

He telephoned the following morning, thanking her. "I say, you must be exhausted after last night."

"I'm not," she said. "I didn't do anything."

"In that case let's do something today."

Colin took Gaby to lunch; he took her to dinner that night. He came for her the following day and drove her to the stables where he kept his horses. He introduced her to the horses, moving slowly from animal to animal. "They've taken to you," he announced.

He brought her back the next day. Gaby had grown up with horses but had avoided any contact with them, obeying her mother, who was frightened of the animals. "I've picked your mount," Colin said. "Come, say hello to Sally."

When Gaby protested, Colin said, "Give her a chance." He took Gaby's hand. "Give me a chance."

Later that week Colin put Gaby on the mare. A solicitous, patient teacher, he rode beside her.

Colin filled her days and nights. He showed her Long Island. He asked her to join him for a week on a friend's yacht. They sailed to Rhode Island and on to Martha's Vineyard and Nantucket.

One morning late in August, Peggy Hunicutt arrived, uninvited. "Outside," she said. "Away from the help." They went to the garage, and Peggy came right to the point. "It's time to shed Colin Inscott, my dear."

Gaby walked toward the dunes, and Peggy followed her. "Gaby, he's after your money. Colin Inscott has one reason for waking up in the morning: to find a rich woman. You are a very rich woman."

"You're the only one talking about marriage," Gaby said.

"Actions speak louder than words. Gaby, go home. Run for your life. You're not listening."

"I can hear you."

"Hear, yes," Peggy said. "Believe, no. Run, Gaby. I know this sucker. I love you, Gaby. He doesn't."

And Peggy had been right. And Sam Castleton had stolen Gaby's chance at happiness.

Now, at the fireplace in the lake house Gaby held on to Russell, held him close. "I thought I saw Grandpa sitting there."

"We're alone," Russell said. He took her chin, raising her head. "We're alone."

"Come on, then," she said, pulling him toward the staircase. "Come on," she said, unable to wait any longer.

———◦◉◦———

IN NEW YORK CITY IN 1932, where men lived in shacks, in Hoovervilles, named for the president, reporters were dispatched by their city editors to cover the arrival of a beautiful Broadway star, now the major heir to one of America's great fortunes. Kyle's death made Faith the most important running story of the year.

She had to endure the reporters and photographers at Pennsylvania Station, and she faced another horde at her apartment building on Fifth Avenue.

The doorman, the superintendent, and all three elevator operators rescued her. In the lobby the doorman removed his gaudy garrison cap. "I'm awful sorry for your loss, Miss Venable. If there's anything. Anything."

"Thank you, Malcolm."

On the ninth floor the elevator operator said, "I'll come back for your luggage, Miss Venable."

Faith left the elevator and stopped. "My keys! I packed them . . . somewhere."

"Simple," said the operator. "I'll let you in."

He unlocked the door and opened it wide, and Faith entered her apartment for the first time in nearly a year. She crossed the expansive foyer, the large living room. She drew back the thick drapes and opened the windows. She could hear faintly the sounds from the city street.

Kyle had insisted that Faith keep her apartment. "It will be our hideaway," he said. "Besides, I like the view." The apartment faced the Metropolitan Museum of Art. Faith stood at the windows for a little while, looking past the Metropolitan to the towers of Central Park West. She heard the doorbell and turned, pausing to kick off her shoes.

The elevator operator carried her luggage into the master bedroom on the Fifth Avenue side of the apartment. Faith followed him out to the foyer. When he closed the door, she threw the safety bolt she had had installed after taking possession. She retrieved her shoes, looking around her, safe for the first time in months. "Home sweet home," she murmured. Faith loved the apartment. She had taken almost a year to furnish it alone, choosing everything herself.

Yet nothing in it reflected Faith, her physical presence or her personality. The foyer and the living room were less appealing than the rooms of some hotels. The expensive furniture was monochromatic, as were the walls everywhere but in her bedroom.

Faith had changed her bedroom into a gallery in which she was the only subject. She covered the long wall facing her bed with three sheets, those large posters that ring theater entrances with the titles of the shows and the names of the stars. Everywhere Faith's name ran across the top. Framed photographs and newspaper reviews with photographs covered the other walls, with the largest hanging over Faith's headboard.

When she returned to the bedroom, she stopped near the door, taking an inventory of her collection. Then she opened a large suitcase, collected three dresses, and hung them in the closet. As she went back for more clothes, she veered to one side, raising both hands and carefully aligning a photograph of herself taken onstage, facing the audience, in front of the entire cast of *Which Way to Paris?*

———◦◉◦———

A ROUND TEN O'CLOCK the next morning, on the north side of Eighty-second Street, midway between Fifth Avenue and Madison, solid iron doors set flush with the sidewalk opened and rose slowly. The warning bell that accompanied the ascent of the service elevator remained silent. The elevator rose from the basement of Faith's building, and she stood on it with Malcolm, the doorman, who had brought her down into the basement from the ninth floor. "Them reporters must be camping out," Malcolm said. "They were out front when I came to work."

"You've saved me, Malcolm," Faith said.

"This isn't much," he said. "You can get back in the same way, Miss Venable." He pointed. "That enamel buzzer in the wall. The super will come for you." He took Faith to a taxi on the other side of the street. "The flag's down, Miss Venable. He wouldn't stay without the meter running." Malcolm helped her into the cab.

On Sixty-fourth Street, east of Third Avenue, the driver stopped at a row of brownstone houses. Beside the bright red door of one house, a brass plaque read M. B. ABRAMS, M.D.

Dr. Mortimer Benjamin Abrams worked and lived in the four-story house, and he used his basement for his butterflies. He had been a lepidopterist since boyhood. He lived on the top floor, his mother, a retired dentist, lived on the floor below, and he practiced medicine in the first and second stories. In the reception room Hilda, his nurse, said, "I'll tell Doctor you're here, Miss Venable," and then added: "Miss Venable, I'm awfully sorry."

Morty Abrams followed the nurse out of his office, his arms

spread wide. "Faith." He was in his middle forties, a solid man with a barrel chest and big forearms. He had played tackle on the Columbia College football team before medical school.

She held him close. "Morty, Morty. Now I know I'm home." Morty Abrams was the show business doctor. Everyone on Broadway came to Morty.

Back in his office at his desk Morty picked up his cigar. "You're all right? You're sleeping? Eating?"

She nodded. "It's not that, Morty . . ." He was silent, blowing smoke at the ceiling. "I've missed my last two periods."

Morty set the cigar into the ashtray and looked up thoughtfully. "Have you ever missed periods?" Faith shook her head. He pressed a buzzer on his desk. Hilda joined them, and Morty said, "Hilda, help Miss Venable. I want to do a pelvic."

Faith and the nurse went into the examining room. Morty smoked until he heard Hilda say, "Ready, Doctor."

Faith lay on the examining table in a white gown, her legs apart and her feet in metal stirrups attached to the table. Hilda waited with rubber gloves.

When he finished, Morty said, "I think so." He took Faith's feet out of the stirrups. "Sit up." Morty peeled off the gloves. "It's early, but let me look at your breasts."

He cupped a breast with each hand. "It's too early for me to tell. Hilda, help Miss Venable dress."

In his office Morty waited patiently, smoking, until Faith and the nurse entered. Faith said, "Thanks, Hilda."

"If there's anything I can do, Miss Venable," Hilda said.

"You're sweet," Faith said.

The nurse left them, and Morty said, "I'm sending you to the best obstetrician in America, maybe in the world. Denis Claxton at Cornell. Absolutely the best. The Rockefellers' obstetrician. I'll make an appointment."

"I want you," Faith said.

"You've got me," Morty said. "Me you've got. Faith?" He picked up his cigar stub and struck a match. "What happened down there? What happened?"

Faith said almost inaudibly, "You too, Morty?" She came out of her chair.

Morty stopped her. "I'm sorry," he said, his arm around her. "Faith, I'm sorry." He led her back to the chair. He couldn't let her out of his sight. He had to keep her there until she quieted down. "Dr. Abrams, the yenta," he said. "Sit down for a minute, Faith. Catch your breath."

Morty went back to his desk. Although her chair faced his, Faith looked off into nowhere. "You can't understand what it's like down there," she said. "It's like having a king, having an emperor. On the street people wait until you pass, shrink back against the wall, taking off their hats, waiting until you pass. Not just the Negroes. Everyone. Everyone is afraid. The police are afraid. The sheriff. They do everything but bow when they see a Castleton coming."

Hilda opened the door, and Morty said, "Not now." When the door closed, Morty picked up his cigar butt, looked at what remained, and dropped it into the ashtray.

Faith said, "I'm keeping the other patients waiting."

"I'm with a patient," Morty said.

She looked away. Morty watched her. He seemed to be holding his breath. Faith said, "Kyle was sadistic. Every hour of every day. If I said, 'Let's have a picnic,' he'd agree. And he would come to the picnic and make it a punishment for everyone else. He would make you want to run away to escape him.

"Kyle had a thousand ways to be mean," Faith said. "He would stop eating to be mean, to make everyone sick with worry—me, Coleman, Kyle's servant. Kyle would sit watching me eat until I couldn't bear to eat any longer. I would stop coming to the table, would eat in my room, our room.

"Sometimes I would wake and know he was watching me in the dark," Faith said. "I would turn up the light and see him, eyes open, smiling, what he called smiling. And I would say, 'What is it, Kyle? What's wrong?' And he would say, still smiling, 'Not wrong. Right.' That was his way of talking. Two words. Three. He used words like a knife, jabbing them into you.

"Sometimes he would leave in the morning, and I wouldn't see him until the next day," Faith said. "He would walk into the bedroom in his flying jacket and change clothes, acting like he had come out of the bathroom, like he hadn't been away.

"And everyone behaved as though Kyle were the most wonder-

ful person on earth. Everyone behaved as though they were lucky to
be with him. And they *knew* him inside and out."

Faith wrung her hands. "He burned flies," she said. "He would
sneak up on a fly, he moved like a ghost, and touch it with a match.
He sneaked up on everyone. I would turn and there was Kyle. And
he would say, he would *purr,* 'I love you,' and make it sound like 'I
hate you.' "

She shook her head. "But he didn't hate," Faith said. "He was
too . . . lifeless for hate. He didn't *care.* That's it," she said, her voice
stronger. "That's really it: He didn't *care,*" Faith said, as though she
had made a great discovery. "Kyle didn't care about anything on
earth, most of all himself. He was meanest to himself. He would tell
me how useless he was, what a total failure he had made of his life."

Morty said, "He was some fella, this Mr. Castleton."

"Some fellow," Faith said. She rose, pushing her purse under
her arm, composed and confident once more. "Are there any special
instructions for me?"

"You're a healthy woman. You'll deliver a healthy child and
be a healthy mother," Morty said. He went to her side, taking her
arm and leading her across the office. "I want you to see Denis
Claxton. Hilda will make the appointment." He opened the office
door. "Hilda, make an appointment with Claxton and call Miss—
Mrs. Castleton." Morty gave Faith's shoulder a reassuring pat. "I'll
get you a cab."

Minutes later she was driving north on Lexington Avenue. The
cabdriver looked up into the rearview mirror. "I saw you in *Bermuda
Bangles,* Miss Venable," he said. "The missus and me, on her birthday. She picked it, and I'm glad she did. You were great, Miss Venable. We both thought you were great."

"That's the nicest compliment I've ever had," Faith said. As the
driver turned into Eighty-second Street, she said, "Please go slowly
after Madison."

Faith left the taxi, head down with her face averted. She
pressed the buzzer set into the building wall. When the iron doors
opened and the elevator appeared, Faith saw the building superintendent. "I kinda had a hunch you were up here, Miss Venable, so I
killed the bell."

In the super's office in the basement Faith called Malcolm.

"Please ask the press to come into the lobby." She smiled at the super. "I can't hide forever."

The service elevator brought Faith to the far end of the lobby facing Fifth Avenue. She walked toward the crowd of newspapermen, and as they saw her, she stopped beside a broad ficus that towered over her. The photographers began to shoot. Faith raised her hand, and when she could be heard, she said, "I have an announcement to make. I am going to have a baby."

IN A FRAME HOUSE IN REGO PARK, Queens, across the East River from Manhattan, Clara Siegenthaler and her daughter Marge were at the table in the kitchen. Two New York tabloids lay on the table, and a coffeepot flanked the newspapers, beside a plate of toast and jam. The front page of each tabloid carried a large photograph of Faith. One headline read:

FAITH VENABLE PREGNANT
CASTLETON WIDOW TO BEAR DEAD HUSBAND'S CHILD

The other headline read: HEIRESS CARRIES DEAD HUSBAND'S CHILD.

Clara Siegenthaler raised one of the newspapers. "Helen with a baby," she said. "I'd hate to be in that kid's shoes."

"Think so?" Marge tapped the photograph on the other tabloid. "They'll be gold shoes, Mama. Gold."

Behind them the door to the back porch stood open. A rotating fan on the kitchen cabinets faced the table. Clara Siegenthaler, a thin woman with gray hair and gray skin, fanned herself with the newspaper. "God, not even nine o'clock, and it's boiling already," she said. "It'll be roasting out there."

"Out there? It's roasting in here," Marge said. She raised the other newspaper. A big, heavy woman, she had dark circles under her eyes. "What show is that picture from, Mama?"

Clara looked at the photograph of Faith onstage, standing at a bar between two sailors. "How would I know? You talk like I had front-row seats," Clara said. "I'm *still* waiting for Helen to invite me.

Pa 'n' me." She snarled. "No, I wouldn't give her the satisfaction," Clara said. "If she wants me to see her on the stage, let her put two tickets in an envelope."

"Don't hold your breath."

"Wait a minute, you!" Clara swung around, flinging the newspaper down on the table. "You're talking to your mother. You don't talk to your mother that way."

Marge held up her hands. "I apologize. Okay?" She spread jam on a slice of toast and said moodily, "I'll end up the fat lady in the circus if I don't watch out."

"Anyway, you'd be working."

"Who's being cute now? Mama?"

"I didn't mean nothing," Clara said.

"Neither did I," Marge said. She bit into the toast. "Honest to God, I get so scared sometimes I shake all over. What's going to happen to us? It's thirteen months since Walt got laid off."

"It's terrible, Marge," Clara said.

"It's bad enough during the day," Marge said. "Walt sitting there till I chase him out. I tell him to go over to the union hall, but he hates it over there. 'Misery loves company, in a pig's ear,' Walt says."

"We're used to being alone during the day," Clara said.

"Nights are the worst," Marge said. "I fear the nights, honest to God. I fear heading up the stairs. Walt hasn't made a day's wages in more than a year, but at night, you know—he—"

"Stop right there," Clara said. "I don't want to hear anything like that from a daughter of mine."

"Hear what?"

"You know what," Clara said. "What you are saying. You can't talk to your mother about those things."

"Those things! Leaping Lena! I'm thirty-eight years old," Marge said. "I've been married almost eighteen years. I've got two grown kids and I can't say what's on my mind?"

"Not to my face."

"Okay, turn around," Marge said, and laughed. Her breasts rose and fell, and she shook her head and hit the table with her hands. Clara began to laugh. They pointed at each other, laughing.

"Just what we needed," Clara said. She wiped her eyes with the back of her hand.

"Say, let's go to the movies," Clara said. There were matinees on Queens Boulevard.

"The movies! It's not even nine o'clock," Marge said.

"I can tell time," Clara said. "I mean, later. They start at eleven-thirty. Come on, Marge. Get you out of the house. I'm paying."

"I can't."

"What? You just said—"

Marge interrupted. "I changed my mind," Marge said. Sitting in a movie house having a good time seemed like a kind of sin. What was she supposed to tell Walt? "Mama, I can't. I can't."

More than three hours later Marge emerged from the subway station at Lexington Avenue and Eighty-sixth Street. The sun lay directly overhead. From a church nearby she heard bells tolling twelve o'clock. "God, this heat," Marge said.

She wore a girdle, pulled so tight she could hardly breathe. She wore stockings and high heels for the first time in six months. She had worn the shoes last when Walt's brother Cliff's kid got married. Another brainstorm, getting married in the middle of a depression.

Marge went into a doorway and, in the shade, opened her purse for her hand mirror. Jesus, she could see the sweat on her forehead. She took her handkerchief and patted her face.

She headed across Eighty-sixth, then down Fifth. At Eighty-second she saw a doorman under an awning, cool as a cucumber in a blue outfit with white stripes along the seams of his pants.

Malcolm noticed the big woman, walking like someone on stilts, all dolled up for a night out. He stepped back into the doorway, raising his garrison cap to use his handkerchief, patting his face and forehead, and when he replaced the cap, Malcolm almost jabbed her with his elbow. She said, "'Scuse me, I'd like to see Faith Venable."

"Who?"

"Faith Venable. She lives here," Marge said. "I know she lives here."

"This is a private building," Malcolm said. "Strangers aren't allowed in this building."

"I'm no stranger," Marge said. "I'm her sister. I'm Hel— Faith's sister."

"You're—" Malcolm said, and stopped. You never could tell.

"Her sister, Marge. Just tell her it's Marge Kreychek. You can do that much, can't you?"

Malcolm didn't take chances. He said, "Wait," opening one of the double glass doors. He stepped inside and turned, opening the door wider. "It's cooler in the lobby."

"Thanks," Marge said. "It's murder out here."

Malcolm took her to a long marble bench beneath a tapestry. Marge held her purse in her lap, her ankles crossed, watching the doorman until he disappeared.

Marge wasn't asking for herself. She didn't care about herself. She had come for the kids, for the kids and for Walt too. So he could stop looking as if he were heading for the hangman. If she could come home with a few hundred bucks. If they could just catch their breath for a little while, just sleep easy for a little while.

Above, in Faith's apartment, the sofas and the coffee table had been pushed away from the fireplace, almost to the walls, and the carpet had been rolled up. Ward Kirby, a young man, so thin he seemed all bones, faced Faith. He was naked to the waist and barefoot. Faith wore a leotard, and she too was barefoot.

Ward Kirby, a dancer, a chorus line gypsy, had been in three shows with Faith. He was amusing and asked nothing of her. "I'm worried," he said. "Shouldn't Morty be told? Shouldn't you have your doctor's permission?"

"Morty says it's the best thing I can do, for me and for the baby," Faith said. "He says physical activity is important. I don't intend to blow up like a sow."

"Perish the thought, angel," Ward said. "We should have an exercise bar, but no matter. I can't make a ballerina out of you anyway."

"You're not here to teach me ballet," Faith said. "I've always wanted to learn some basic dance steps. Let's begin."

"Agreed," Ward said. "How long since you've exercised? Years, of course. We'll start with exercise. A week, two weeks should give you some muscle tone. Now, with me."

Ward extended both arms, raised his arms over his head, held them horizontal, and dropped his arms to his side. Faith followed his lead. "Good. Again," Ward said. They heard the house phone. "Let me."

He went through the living room to the phone in the wall in the foyer. *"Bonjour."*

In his office off the lobby Malcolm recognized the fairy's voice. "This is Malcolm. There's a woman here to see Miss Venable. Marge Kreychek." Remembering names was Malcolm's job. "Says she's Miss Venable's sister."

"Her *sister!*"

"That's what she said."

"One moment." Ward returned to the living room. "It's Malcolm. He has a woman who wants to see you," Ward said. "Your sister."

Faith raised her arms high. "I have no sister." She spread her arms wide.

"Why would someone—" Ward stopped. "Malcolm wants you."

Faith continued exercising. "You can tell him."

Ward returned to the foyer, and when he rejoined Faith, he said, "She must be a crazy lady."

"It happens all the time," Faith said. "Sisters, brothers, aunts, uncles." She put her hands over her belly. "This is my only living relative."

———※◇※———

IN NORTH CAROLINA around noon that day Wyn picked up Kay at her house. "Where to?"

Beside him Kay said, "Anywhere. Somewhere cool." She put her hand over Wyn's hand on the gearshift between them. "Let's keep going until we know we'll be all alone."

"Sounds right," Wyn said. "I know a hill."

Kay pushed her hair back from her forehead and raised her head. "I thought a picnic would be fun. I hope you like what I made."

He smiled at her. "I like everything you do," Wyn said, and added quickly, "And I'm not teasing."

Kay pushed her fingers through his. "I don't mind when you tease."

"Well, you should," Wyn said. "You're too . . . good." He glanced at her. "You are, Kay."

Kay shook her head, flushing and looking away, and then, to extricate herself, she said, "Isn't it strange about Faith Venable? Kyle Castleton's widow?"

Wyn almost drove off the road. "What's strange?"

"Didn't you see the paper?"

"I skipped the diner and came straight to your house," Wyn said. He had to know. *Now.* "What about her?"

"She's two months pregnant," Kay said. "She's having a baby."

Wyn's hand slipped off the gearshift, and Kay's hand fell. "I feel so sorry for her," she said. "She's all alone. A woman should have her husband with her when she's pregnant." Kay looked at Wyn. "What is she like?"

He didn't want to answer, didn't want to think about her. She was in New York, where she belonged, and he was where he belonged, a deputy sheriff learning his trade, just another hick from hicksville.

"Wyn?"

He said, "Huh?" like someone waking up, and berated himself for abandoning Kay to wallow in never-never land with Faith Venable.

"What is she like?"

Could he not escape this subject? He said innocently, "Well . . . she's beautiful . . . like you—"

"No, I'm not," Kay said, shaking her head.

"Like you," Wyn repeated. "And she is . . ." He paused and then said, "Mysterious. She's not like us, Kay. She's different."

"How?" Kay waited. "Wyn?" She touched him. "How is she different?"

"I can't tell you," Wyn said honestly. He shifted in the seat, moving his hands up on the steering wheel and picking up speed, in a rush to leave Faith behind, to embrace Kay, with whom he told himself he belonged. "I can tell you how you're different," he said. "You're good, you're fair, you're honest, you're friendly, you like people, you trust people, you're . . . I'll think of more in a minute."

Kay looked out the window, staring at the fields. "I'm not," she said, and stopped and took a deep breath. "Golly!"

She saved them. Wyn laughed as Kay laughed, and they were, finally, alone in the car.

"Kay? Are you getting hungry?"

"You are," she said. "You skipped the diner, so you haven't had breakfast or anything." She turned and took a large brown paper bag from the backseat.

"Hey, I can wait," Wyn said.

She set the bag in her lap and opened it. She extended a napkin and looked down into the bag. "You have a choice," she said. "What would you like?"

"You pick it for me," Wyn said.

Kay chose an egg salad sandwich and unwrapped it carefully. The sandwich was cut at an angle, and she held out half. "Tell me if you like it," she said. "You must be honest."

Wyn raised the sandwich. "Scout's honor," he said.

As he bit into the sandwich, Kay watched him closely. Wyn could see her out the corner of his eye, her eyes wide, her face solemn, waiting for his verdict. So he had to be as solemn. Wyn bit into the sandwich of egg salad. He would have been rapturous if she had given him paste, but he wolfed down the egg salad and extended his hand. "Great! More!"

He wolfed down the other half. Kay had another sandwich. "Here's something different."

"We're on a picnic," Wyn said. "I can't spoil the picnic."

"You won't," Kay said. She wanted to feed him, wanted to watch him as she fed him.

"I'll wait," Wyn said. "Besides . . ." he said, and pointed. In the distance, to the left, Kay saw a hill rising from the fields.

Minutes later Wyn turned, crossed the road, and drove into a narrow, rutted lane. They rode through the fields, and Wyn stopped at the foot of the hill. "On the other side there are some trees about halfway up." He faced Kay. "Are you game?"

"Sure," she said, nodding.

"Good girl." Wyn patted her arm. "Give me that," he said, taking the paper bag. "And the blanket."

Kay left the car to reach into the rear for the blanket she had selected. "I can take something."

Beside her Wyn said, "Gimme," snatching the blanket out of her hands. "You've done everything so far."

They left the car and walked into the fields, skirting the base of the hill. "Everything is so fresh," Kay said. She lifted her arms to the sky. "So clean." She stopped to remove her sandals. "I feel . . . silly," she said.

Wyn watched her. She wore a sky blue summer cotton dress that buttoned down the front, and she was bare-legged. She moved with a natural grace, and Wyn, himself an athlete, liked watching her, liked the pure animal pleasure Kay took from her gamboling.

They spread the blanket beneath some trees and sat side by side, cross-legged, in the shade. In addition to the egg salad, Kay had made sandwiches of ham and cheese and bologna, all thick with mustard. She had brought cookies and fruit and her own lemonade in a large thermos bottle and coffee for Wyn in a small thermos bottle.

"Dig right in," she said.

Afterward, protected from the heat by the trees and sated and lazy, Kay said, "The cars seem far, far away."

"They are far away," Wyn said. "Everything is far away from up here. It's just us."

"Just us . . ." Kay said. She raised her cup. "Would you like some lemonade?"

"Mmm," Wyn said, and drank from her cup. "Would you like some coffee?"

"Mmm," Kay said, and drank from his cup, and when she raised her head, Wyn kissed her, a kind of casual good-night kiss.

"Mmm," he said, and took her cup of lemonade. He set it aside, off the blanket, with his cup, and turned back to her. She faced him, wide-eyed, her breasts rising and falling. Wyn looked at the lovely, sweet, trusting, and decent young woman who had chosen him, and he put his arms around her.

As Wyn kissed her this time, Kay's arms tightened around him, and she straightened her legs, dropping onto the blanket and bringing him with her. And although their kiss ended and they looked into each other's eyes, they were already together. She murmured, "Wyn, Wyn," as she kissed him, clutching him fiercely.

Wyn could feel her young, slim body against him, her hot, active body against him, one leg entwined in his leg and her breasts rising and falling. He brought her closer, kissing, kissing, lips and face and throat, lower and lower until his face lay in her breasts.

He raised his head, and as Kay watched him, he unfastened the top button of her dress. He unfastened the second. He undid the third, and his hand stole into her dress to push the bra aside. She said, "Don't," but he did not stop. "No, Wyn. Not—" She put her hand over his hand, pressed his hand into her breast. She whispered, "Darling . . . ," holding his hand against her, and then she felt his tongue between her breasts and sighed, helpless. And, helpless, raised her bra to free her breasts.

Wyn opened the dress more fully, looking down at the prize she offered, and Kay cupped her breast for him.

He came to her gently and with something like reverence. He felt her hips stir beneath him. "Darling, darling."

She moved one hand over her breast, making a V with her fingers, circling his lips, and with her other hand in his hair, she kept him captive although she had already surrendered more than she had ever offered, ventured far, far beyond the limits of safety. "Do that. Do that, darling. Like that, like that . . . oh, darling," she said, and her legs parted to admit him.

"Don't stop yet," she said, keeping him at her breast. "Don't stop."

She felt his hand on her dress on her thigh, felt him slowly raising her dress, felt his bare hand on her thigh, felt his hand moving slowly, gently, his fingers hot along her thigh.

And he felt her stirring beneath him, felt her hot mouth kissing. They had never been so near the edge. Kay had kept him off-balance, staying well clear of danger. Now she seemed to be an eager, demanding, frenzied accomplice. "Oh, Wyn-n-n."

His hand covered her treasure, lay ever so gently atop her treasure. She had admitted Wyn to the deepest, most zealously guarded of her secrets. And Wyn knew she had chosen him, only him. And told himself he must retreat. He could not, could not. He was *there.*

His fingers slipped across her panties, onto her belly. He found the hem of her panties and ever so slowly pulled them down from her belly, pulled them down and down until she blocked him, her hand over his, stopping him. "I can't."

Wyn paused, waiting to recoup. And Kay did not forsake him. She held him with as much passion, as strong a need. "I can't," she repeated. "I want to. With you. Only with you, darling. But—not now, not yet. Edith didn't. She waited, she and Jim waited. And Lucille didn't. She waited," Kay said, enlisting her sisters as allies. "Wyn?"

She felt his body slacken. He quit; he refused to corrupt the innocent, trusting girl he held in his arms. And deep within he discovered he was trying to prove something, trying, in a lunatic way, to show Faith the kind of man she had ignored. "You're angry," Kay said.

"I'm not," Wyn said. He raised his head, looking down at her. "Honest. I'm really not."

She had really done him a favor, done them both a favor, Wyn decided. He wasn't ready for anything solid, anything long-term. He sat upright. "Let's go," he said. "Want to go?"

"If you do."

"How about you?" he asked, annoyed, and immediately, quietly added: "It'll be cooling off in town by now." He pushed himself erect. "And let me help," he said. He extended both hands, and Kay held on to him as though he had saved her life.

"I'll take the blanket," Kay said. They started down the hill, and halfway down, she found Wyn's hand. "I liked the picnic. Thank you."

"Me too."

Below, at the car, Kay set the blanket and the bag in the rear of the car. "Wyn?" He stood beside the driver's door, and they faced each other on either side of the car. "You're supposed to say it first, and I'm supposed to wait," Kay said. "But I can't. I love you, Wyn. I've never loved anyone before. Ever. I've never even had a crush on anyone." She waited for him to reply, and when he didn't, she pushed her hair back from her forehead. "We can go now."

Wyn had to say something. He watched Kay open the car door. "Kay?" She looked across the roof of the car. "Let's go out to my folks' place," Wyn said. "There's a new litter out there. Cleo, the basset, has a new litter."

<hr>

EARLY THE SAME DAY Frank Burris followed his regular schedule, showering and shaving and dressing before going downstairs to breakfast.

Serena always had a tray and the newspaper in bed, leaving Burris alone at the table with *his* paper. He subscribed to his newspaper and insisted on paying for it. He had long ago tired of waiting for Serena to surrender hers. "Morning, Mist' Burris."

"Morning, Laura." The maid poured his coffee as Burris reached the table. He moved his chair back and said, "Holy Moses!" staring at the huge headline beside his plate. Burris snatched up the newspaper with the photograph of Faith on the front page. He whirled around. "Bitch," he said, cursing Serena. "You bitch," he said, leaving the table.

Serena lay on two pillows set lengthwise against the headboard. She wore white linen gloves to protect her hands from the newsprint. "Serena!" She could hear his footsteps as she dropped the newspaper across the gossamer bedcovers she used in the sustained heat. "Serena!"

Burris charged into the room, waving his newspaper. "You read this a half hour ago," he said, and pointed. "I was in there shaving. Couldn't you have said something?"

"I have been thinking," Serena said.

"You could have yelled," he said. "You could have sent Honeychild."

They had been enemies for so long both had forgotten any other way of life. They were sustained by their bile, their vendetta broken only by their encounters in the bedroom, where even their couplings, in mute savagery, were acts of war.

Burris stood over the bed. "Faith is pregnant!" he said. "She's having a baby! He—it will inherit Kyle's stock. Holy Mother of God, this changes everything! We've got a chance! We've got a chance!"

"All I've thought of since Honeychild brought me the newspaper is how I can make you president of the company," Serena said smoothly, winning the day's battle.

Burris dropped onto the bed. "Faith will be voting Kyle's B Stock," he said. "So it's simple. If she votes with Gaby and Holt, nothing changes. If she doesn't . . . if she comes in with us . . ." Burris stopped, feeling young, feeling like a kid again. He remembered the days and nights before a big match, at Sea Bright or at Forest Hills. "Serena . . . it could really happen. I could really be president of the company." Burris jumped up from the bed. "Let's go to New York and see her," he said. "Come on, Serena. Let's go to New York. Right now." He waited. "Why not? For God's sake, say something! Why the hell not?" He waited. "You go. Alone. You're right. I shouldn't go. I'm not the diplomat around here. You go, Serena. I'll get Honeychild," he said, turning to summon the maid, but Serena said, "No, Frank."

"Why not?" He came back to the bed. When she didn't reply, he said, "Holt will be back any day. He could be back already." Burris pointed. "He could be over there in the Castle, but he won't stay." Burris leaned over the bed to take his newspaper and slap the front page. "Not after he sees this."

"Holt won't be welcome in New York," Serena said. "Nor will I be welcome. Faith Venable does not love the Castletons." Serena looked up at Burris. "You saw her when Lucius read Kyle's will. Once she heard she had Kyle's money, she couldn't wait to get away. The trollop!"

"The trollop will be voting the stock," Burris said. "At the first meeting after her kid is born she must vote the stock."

"Or choose a proxy," Serena said.

"It's the same thing," Burris said. "She's the ball game, Serena. She calls the shot. It's you and me or it's Gaby and Holt."

"At last," Serena said. She stared ahead. Burris had told her nothing she hadn't known since reading her newspaper. She had dismissed Burris, her mind racing as she plotted, devising strategy and tactics for the campaign that lay ahead. "At last."

"We can't just sit here hoping," Burris said.

"I'll be late for my swim," she said.

"Late for your swim," Burris said, hating her. "You're only punishing me for intruding on Your Majesty. What are you going to do?"

"We have seven months," Serena said.

Burris walked to the door, the newspaper dangling from his hand, and as he crossed the bedroom, he used his other hand to push it under his arm.

Serena left the bed and drew back the drapes, facing the Castle, which rose from the morning ground fog. Although Serena was the firstborn, Sam Castleton believed in primogeniture, and when Serena was old enough to understand, he told her Branch would succeed him, at the company and in the Castle. Sam Castleton's will, establishing the foundation and the disbursement of the B Stock, effectively banished Serena from control.

Serena turned her back, pulling off her linen gloves as she walked to her dressing room. The Castle no longer meant anything.

She had long ago lost interest in it. The company remained her only goal. Serena dropped the gloves. "Honeychild!"

"I'm here."

Serena whirled around to face the light-skinned maid, who had passed Burris in the corridor. "I'm here," Honeychild repeated, and in her fashion remonstrating with her mistress for shouting.

"Don't gloat," Serena said. "I'm going for my swim." As she pulled her nightgown over her head, Honeychild raised the bathing suit she held. Serena snatched it out of her hand. Honeychild held the robe for her mistress. She knelt to slip on Serena's espadrilles. She gave Serena a folded thick towel.

Honeychild watched from the windows in Serena's bedroom as her mistress went through the gate into Castle property on her way to the lake. When she could no longer see the tall, slim figure, Honeychild began to undress. She enjoyed Serena's shower in the morning.

Serena had not eaten lunch since her teens, and when she returned from her swim, she dressed quickly, but remained bare-legged. She chose a purse, which she filled with what she needed, and carried it to her bed.

She telephoned Lucius Peete, and when Sue Ann answered, she said, "I need some information. Give it to me before you tell Lucius I'm calling and why."

In the white Cord convertible she had chosen, Serena roared downtown. She stopped along the yellow curb in a bus stop, and walked back to the florist with BLISS FLOWERS painted on the awning.

Inside, a young man in a gray jacket said, "Help you, ma'am?" just as Cameron Bliss, in the rear, saw Serena.

"I'll handle it!" Bliss almost ran through the shop. "Mrs. Burris! Welcome, welcome." He stopped several feet from his clerk so she could not couple them in her mind. "How can we serve you? You should have telephoned in this beastly weather. We could have spared you the drive into the city. Our delivery truck is refrigerated, Mrs. Burris."

When he paused, Serena said, "I wish to send some roses to New York."

"Telegraph? Certainly, Mrs. Burris. Of course. Long-stemmed American beauties. We'll—" he said as Serena interrupted.

"No." She disliked red roses. "Yellow roses," she said. "Send . . . two dozen, no, three."

"Certainly," Bliss said. "Three dozen, Mrs. Burris." He bowed, extending his left arm, inviting Serena to precede him.

At the wrapping counter Bliss opened an order book. "Now, then, who is the lucky recipient, Mrs. Burris?"

"You must choose the best florist in New York," Serena said. "Do you have the name of the best?"

"I do, Mrs. Burris. Trust me," he said. "I shall not fail you."

"The flowers go to Faith Venable Castleton," Serena said. She repeated the address Sue Ann had given her. "And there will be a card." She watched him writing. "Are you ready?"

"Ready, Mrs. Burris. I'm ready."

"Take this down very carefully," she said. "The card must read, 'You are not alone. Serena.' "

Writing, Cameron Bliss said, slowly, "You . . . are . . . not . . . alone . . . Serena." He finished the *a* in Serena's name with an extended downward serif.

Serena said, "Good," and for the first time since learning of Kyle's death, she smiled.

------◦◉◦------

E VERY SUNDAY MORNING, following Russell's orders, a stake body truck loaded with unmarried blacks who worked and slept on the farms came to the Castle to take the servants to church.

On Sunday in the week of Kyle's death Coleman missed church. He left the Castle before the cooks were in the kitchen, climbed the knoll, took the shortcut to the lake and beyond, to the cemetery in the glen below the hill. Coleman went to Kyle's fresh grave in the cemetery, where he stood over the grave and talked to his little lost boy and wept.

Everyone in the Castle learned of Coleman's inheritance almost as soon as he did, and some before he was told. Cora Lou, an upstairs maid, heard Colin Inscott when he and Gaby returned from hearing the will in Lucius Peete's office. "Leaving fifty thousand dollars to a servant, a black servant. I'll wager Coleman can't even count to fifty!" Cora Lou vanished to spread the word.

The following Sunday Coleman dressed in one of Sam Castleton's dark suits that Kyle had chosen for him. "You'll look better than your preacher," Kyle had said.

When the truck from the farms stopped at the Castle smokehouse, Coleman followed the others down the kitchen steps. The men standing in the rear of the truck saw him coming. Someone said, "Here comes the millionaire." Someone else said, "Now Coleman gonna have his own place on Millionaires Row." One man pushed his hand between two stakes. "How's about lending me a few bucks, Coleman?" Others raised stakes from the slots in the truck bed, making room for Coleman, and others bent far forward to help him although Russell insisted the truck carry a solid stepladder for the women from the Castle.

At the Flats beside the Resurrection Baptist Church, other parishioners joined the men from the farms, pleading with Coleman for money. He tried to escape and could not. Women as well as men surrounded him. Then an elderly man in a purple gown fastened at his neck and falling to the ground raised his hand as he approached the crowd. "Coleman." The others gave way, and Coleman recognized Arnold Tally, the choirmaster. "Reverend says for you to wait after church, Coleman."

"Can't wait," Coleman said. "I'm serving Sunday dinner."

"Well, you wait, understand? I am delivering a message from the reverend," said Arnold Tally. "Come with me."

So Willy Floyd and the rest relinquished Coleman to his last captor. The choirmaster brought Coleman into the church and led the bewildered black man to a pew. "Sit here where Reverend can see you."

The choirmaster left Coleman on the rack. He forgot the mob that pursued him, in agony because he might not return to the Castle in time to serve dinner. For Coleman the prayers and the hymns were endless. And the sermon was still to come.

In front of the open doors after the service, the minister greeted his parishioners, chatting with all who paused. He said, "Brother Coleman, be patient. I'll join you under the trees."

"The truck is leaving," Coleman said.

"Brother Tally will drive you," said the Reverend Fitch. "He'll take you in my car."

So Coleman stood under the trees, in despair, watching the parishioners clustering around their pastor, watching the flatbed truck filled with farm hands and servants from the Castle pass by, raising dust.

"Here you are, Brother Coleman," said Reverend Fitch. "Walk with me."

They walked toward the church. The open doors sagged, hanging like limp rags. The church had been built by amateurs, and the doors were not plumb. "Closed doors keep out the heat," said the reverend. "Help me, Brother Coleman. Lift it first. Like this." Coleman obeyed. "Good." They closed the doors.

Reverend Fitch steered Coleman away from the entrance to the rear of the church. The minister stopped at a window, ran his hand along the windowsill, brushed aside the flaking paint, exposing rotting wood. "Look, Brother Coleman. We need a new window here. We need new windows everywhere." Reverend Fitch put his hand on the rung of a ladder. "This paint only hides the rot and decay. The house of the Lord is collapsing. We must have a new house." The reverend brushed his hands. "You can make this a reality, Brother Coleman. You can save our community."

"Me?" The black man tried to understand and could not.

"Your inheritance," said Reverend Fitch. "Kyle Castleton left you fifty thousand dollars! Think of it, Brother Coleman! A church will rise here that will be the glory of our community, of the entire state!" Reverend Fitch stood before Coleman, his eyes glowing and his face radiant. "You are the instrument of our rebirth!"

The minister frightened Coleman. Since Lucius Peete's appearance at the Castle telling him of his inheritance, everything and everyone frightened Coleman.

"Look here!" said Reverend Fitch. "A new church will rise here, Brother Coleman," said the reverend. "A shining house of the Lord!" The reverend shook the big black man. "Claim your inheritance, Coleman! You will erect a splendid monument, a home for our people!"

Coleman could think only of Sunday dinner. " 'Scuse me, Reverend Fitch," he said. "You say you'll take me back to the Castle. They're waiting for Coleman."

Reverend Fitch said, *"They're* waiting—" and stopped. He said, "We'll talk again, Brother Coleman. Come along."

They reached the church entrance. "There is Brother Tally," said the reverend. The choirmaster had removed his gown and sat behind the wheel of an old, boxy Durant sedan with yellowing, foggy windows. "We'll talk again, Brother Coleman."

At the Castle Cora Lou, who helped Coleman serve, said, "Miss Gaby wants Sunday dinner on the music room terrace."

Coleman heard Cora Lou, but she seemed far away. Only Miss Gaby mattered to Coleman. Miss Gaby would save him. Coleman marched back into the kitchen, buttoning his fresh white jacket.

There were three for dinner on the terrace. Gaby sat between Colin and Russell.

Coleman always ate with the cooks and the others. They always ate after he had served the dessert and poured the coffee out front. But this Sunday he did not return to the kitchen. He remained in the music room, hidden, and when he saw Gaby set down her napkin, he could wait no longer. He came to the open terrace doors. "Miss Gaby? Can you come?"

She said, "Of course, Coleman. What is it?"

Looking up, Gaby saw something desperate in the black man's face and rose.

In the music room Coleman said, "Miss Gaby, you got to take Mist' Kyle's money."

"No, Coleman. Kyle wanted you—" she said, and he interrupted.

"You got to help me, Miss Gaby," Coleman said, pleading. "You got to take Mist' Kyle's money."

Gaby looked back, hoping Colin had not heard the black man. She said, "Not here." She led Coleman out of the music room. She listened patiently to his tale of woe as she walked him to the kitchen. "Eat your dinner," she said, leaving him with the other servants.

Later, when she could slip away from Colin, Gaby brought Coleman to Russell. "We must help Coleman," Gaby said. "Everyone is after his inheritance. Even his *minister.*"

"You take it, Miss Gaby," Coleman said.

"Stop!" she said, her patience spent. The black man, who towered over her, seemed to shrink, hanging his head. Gaby faced Russell. "He'll lose it all unless we do something!"

Russell said, "Gaby . . . *Mrs. Inscott,* I—" He could hear Serena in Lucius Peete's office. "Richest nigger in North Carolina." He could hear Frank Burris that day. "I have the man," Russell said. "I'll call him in the morning."

DAN COHEN HAD TO BE in court on Monday morning, repre-senting a family whose landlord hoped to evict them for not paying the rent. The father had been gassed in the Argonne in the World War, and the mother, pregnant and in her third trimester with her fourth child, earned money for food working as a seam-stress. So Russell did not talk with Dan Cohen until early afternoon. "A lot of money is involved," Russell said on the phone.

"I think Lucius Peete still represents the Castletons," Dan said.

"This person is not a Castleton," Russell said. "When can we see you?"

"Would you like to come now?" Dan said.

The three buildings Dan had inherited from his mother were decrepit and run-down, and Dan could afford neither repairs nor maintenance. His office, on the second floor of the middle building, lay over a cut-rate barbershop.

Russell and Coleman sat side by side facing Dan. "I suggest a retirement fund," Dan said. "The money can go into government bonds. You and I can act as trustees, Mr. Vance."

"That makes sense," Russell said. "There ... uh ..." He glanced at Coleman. "There could be a balance, a big balance."

"Well ... scholarships?" Dan sat back, excited by his sug-gestion. "A scholarship trust confined to children in the Flats. We could administer it, Mr. Vance. I'm sorry. I shouldn't speak for you."

"Dan?" Sarah's voice, distant yet demanding, reached them. "Dan? It's me."

Dan rose and Russell looked back as Sarah came out of the dark outer office. She wore a shapeless blouse and had a big purse slung over her shoulder.

She raised her hand, holding crumpled money, some singles and a five. "Eureka!" She charged forward. "Portman paid!" She waved the money. "At last. He's only two months behind." She looked at Russell. "Forgive the exuberance. Rent money."

"Sarah, this is Russell Vance," Dan said. "And Coleman," he said as the black man came to his feet.

"Sorry, didn't know you were busy," Sarah said, and Russell knew she always said it.

"Well . . . we are," Dan said.

"I'm going," Sarah said. "On my way." She pecked her husband's cheek and left.

Russell said, "We've settled everything, haven't we?"

"We have," Dan said. He would have to decide on a fee. He would talk with Sarah. "I'll get to work on the details."

"I'm counting on everything being kept in strict confidence," Russell said.

"It cannot be otherwise, Mr. Vance."

Russell said to Coleman, "Your worries are over. You *won't* have any money. We'll have your money."

"Not really . . ." Dan said.

"Not really," Russell said, and beckoned Coleman. "We're leaving now."

⸺ ⦾ ⸺

AT NOON, fifteen days after Kyle's death, Lucius Peete's secretary, Sue Ann, brought him a tray with half a cantaloupe, which he favored for lunch. She set the tray on the desk before him. "Better enjoy these while you can," Sue Ann said. "These are the last."

"I'll do my best." Lucius Peete took his napkin and spread it across his knees.

"Another week or two, and you'll be back to baked apples," said Sue Ann. She disliked the apples, which she had to bake in a small electric oven in the supply room behind her office.

As Lucius raised a monogrammed sterling silver spoon, they heard the door in Sue Ann's office. "Sue Ann? Lucius?"

And then a man walked briskly through Sue Ann's office as though he were late, pulling at the knot in his tie to loosen it, pulling the tie out of the shirt collar and crumpling it into a ball in one hand like a sheet of scratch paper. He stuffed the tie into a jacket pocket before pulling off the jacket and dropping it onto a chair.

He was a compact man just above middle height, and burned by the sun. His face and hands were a deep reddish brown. Lucius leaned forward, peering at the man as he fumbled for his monocle. "Holt?"

Sue Ann clapped her hands. "Mr. Holt! Wherever did you come from?"

Walking to the desk, Holt Castleton rolled back his shirt-sleeves halfway to the elbow. Although he had small hands with stubby fingers, his forearms were oversize and thick with muscles, and he moved with a ferocious intensity, like a prizefighter stalking his opponent. He seemed to be holding himself in check, keeping back an explosion.

"My ship docked in Miami yesterday," said Holt. "I left the freighter in Cape Town and got a ship there for Miami." He stopped in front of the aged woman, taking both her hands in his hands. "Hello, Miss Sue Ann," he said, and kissed her as he had kissed her since the days when Sue Ann would bend so the boy could reach her. Behind them Lucius held on to the arms of his chair to come erect slowly.

"Oh, Mr. Holt," she said, "we were so worried." Her eyes were wet, and a tear fell from her left eye.

"Shshshshsh," he murmured, raising his hand and touching the tear with his forefinger. "I'm fine, Sue Ann. You can see that, can't you?" She nodded obediently. "So you mustn't worry."

She shook her head. "I won't."

"This is September, Lucius, not the middle of winter," Holt said. He walked over and opened a window wide, opened another. "The newspapers say you are having a heat wave."

"You didn't telephone," Lucius said.

"I'm here, Lucius."

"Let me look at you," Lucius said. He tilted the lampshade near his desk and raised his monocle.

"Moment," Holt said. He opened the bathroom door and, inside, bent over the sink, turning the cold-water tap. Holt cupped his hands under the water, splashing his face. "Ahh." He ran his wet fingers through his hair and filled his hands with water once more to bathe his face. He came out of the bathroom licking his lips with his tongue like a jungle cat.

Lucius gestured. "There are towels."

"I've been away from civilization," Holt said. Crossing the office, he ran his fingers through his hair in the gesture Serena used. His hair was russet-colored like Serena's, and he resembled her, with the same almost Roman nose and the sharp, clean angles in his face. But Holt was an especially attractive man. His energy, his intensity were magnetic. He could not be ignored anywhere. He stopped in front of Lucius. "Here I am."

Lucius set the monocle into his eye. He took Holt's forearms, bending forward slightly to study the younger man. Lucius Peete had been present in the hospital on the day of Holt's birth. After the boy's parents were killed, Lucius became a kind of parent, appearing at the Castle several times a week on his way to or from his office. "You look like an island native," Lucius said. "How old are you?"

"I am thirty," Holt said. "Is your memory failing? I hope not, Lucius. I depend on you."

"My memory is not fading," Lucius said. He released Holt, who began to move around the office, circling chairs and lamps. "You were born on July twenty-sixth," Lucius said, and returned to his chair. "George Bernard Shaw's birthday."

Holt made the old lawyer uncomfortable and wary. Holt's appearance opened a stuffed, jumbled memory chest. Lucius lived chiefly with memories, particularly when he returned to his empty house. But he tried to choose pleasant episodes that would allow him to fall asleep and, most important, remain asleep through the long, lonely nights. He watched Holt circling the office. "You look older," Lucius said.

"The sea can age you. It *can* be your enemy. The sea can hurt you. Even a calm sea. Still, I love it. It's me alone at sea, and the wind and the sun." Holt stopped moving. "And I suppose Kyle's death aged me. Dead at twenty-two. Sue Ann, order me a car and a driver. My bags are with the guard at the door. Tell him to put my bags in the car."

Sue Ann hurried out of the office, and Holt began to pace once more. "I've been away twenty-seven months, Lucius," Holt said. "Tell me everything."

"You get the company's annual financial statement," Lucius said. "And I've sent you the quarterly reports. You have the second quarter."

"So everything is normal," Holt said. "Nothing has changed." He stopped beside an armoire. "Am I right, Lucius?"

"Sales are up," Lucius said. "If you've read the reports, you know sales are up even though the Depression continues."

"Sales are always up," Holt said. He began to move once more.

Sue Ann came to the door. "Your car is on the way, Holt."

He smiled at her. 'Thank you, Sue Ann." When she was gone, he eyed Lucius narrowly. "You haven't mentioned the widow."

Lucius frowned and said, "The widow . . ." and paused. "She is gone, Holt. She has returned to New York. We won't see her again," said the old man.

Holt walked to the desk. "You think not?"

"It's a permanent move," said the old man. "She was not happy here. I spoke with Russell, and he agreed. I believe even if Kyle had lived, they would have left."

"The widow is pregnant," Holt said. "She is carrying Kyle's child, Lucius."

"I know."

"So the child gets Kyle's B Stock," Holt said. "And the widow has the child. Has that fact crossed your mind?"

"It has crossed my mind," said the old man. He pushed himself up in his chair, holding the chair arms.

"So you could be wrong," Holt said. "We could be seeing the widow here. I can feel her coming back already. The widow is a loose cannon. Kyle voted with Gaby and me. But we can't say how the widow will vote. She could vote with Serena, and Serena and her stud would have the company." Holt came to the desk, facing the old man. "You haven't mentioned the chance of such a turn either, Lucius." Looking down at the old man, tiny in the big leather chair, Holt felt a burning flash of rage. He held on to the desk with both hands. Lucius could be allied with them, with Serena and the scheming whore.

"I do not expect a change in the voting," Lucius said. "Kyle's wife was devoted to him. She gave up her career for him. I expect her to vote as Kyle voted."

Holt didn't believe him. In Miami the day before, the newspapers had carried Faith's photograph, and the headlines spoke of Kyle's baby. Holt took the newspapers aboard the train. He had been awake most of the night.

—◦◦◦—

L ESS THAN A MILE AWAY, in the courthouse, Wyn stood beside the door from the cellblock with a clipboard. Every weekday
morning the men and women arrested the day before were taken to
the municipal court, where they were tried for charges brought
against them. Most of the prisoners were drunks and derelicts, and
many were both. All these prisoners always pleaded guilty and many
welcomed a stay of thirty or sixty or ninety days or even six months
in the county workhouse. They could bathe and were deloused. They
were issued clean clothes and fed decent food, and they slept in
clean cells.

"Wyn! Here they come!"

A deputy opened the cellblock door, and behind him, another
led a row of prisoners, including two middle-aged, scabrous women
in filthy clothes. The names of all the prisoners were on a roster on
the clipboard. "Last names first!" Wyn said, loud.

The deputy with the prisoners shouted, "Line up!"

The first prisoner reached Wyn. "Ernest, Walter."

Wyn checked off his name. "Over there, Walter." Wyn gestured at Ben Miller, the deputy who would lead the prisoners to the
court, on the far side of the courthouse.

"Corliss, Oscar," said the next prisoner.

Wyn checked him off. "On your way," he said.

There were nine prisoners on the roster, and when they were
lined up with Ben Miller, Wyn gave him the clipboard.

Wyn walked through Sheriff's Headquarters and out into the
parking area. The prisoners always made him feel dirty, and he welcomed the outdoors and the sun, despite the heat. He found a shady
corner of the courthouse and stretched. Wyn was on duty inside that
day, and after a few moments he started back to headquarters.
"Sheriff!"

Wyn saw a guy who looked like an Indian striding toward the
courthouse, rolling down his shirtsleeves and getting into his jacket.
"I'm a deputy," Wyn said. "Wyn Ainsley."

"Holt Castleton," the guy said, and in saying it, he changed. He
no longer looked like an Indian. And they were alone outside the

courthouse. Wyn didn't see anyone except Holt. No one else counted. "Can I follow you to the sheriff's office?"

"Sheriff's . . . Sure," Wyn said. "Around this way," he said, gesturing and discovering the clipboard in his hand.

Holt said, "Wyn . . . You must be awfully tired of people trying to make jokes with your name."

Wyn grinned. "Sure am." In a crazy way he wanted to thank the guy for being . . . okay. They walked past a sheriff's car, and Wyn pointed. "Over here. We're in the basement."

Inside, as Earl bent over the water fountain, he heard Wyn say, "In here, Mr. Castleton." So Earl discovered Holt had returned. Earl drank as though he had been dropped into a desert.

Wyn said, "Sheriff?"

Earl left the water fountain. "Well, this is a real honor, Mr. Castleton."

"It's the other way around, Sheriff," Holt said. "Especially since I'm busting in on you without notice."

"Forget about notice, Mr. Castleton," Earl said. "We're here to serve. It's in the oath."

Holt smiled. "The welcome I've had already can't be in the oath."

"We appreciate your kind words, Mr. Castleton," Earl said. "I'd like to say, and this is for both of us, we're awful sorry for your loss."

"Thank you," Holt said, and pointed. "Can I share the water fountain?"

Earl jumped back. "Sure thing," he said. "Help yourself, Mr. Castleton." Holt bent over the fountain. "When did you get back, Mr. Castleton?"

"An hour ago," Holt said. Earl glanced at Wyn and saw that Castleton had spooked the kid. Holt came erect, rubbing his mouth with the back of his hand. "I've come to see that justice is done, Sheriff."

"Justice . . ." Earl said before he knew it, before he could even begin to think. "We can talk in my office, Mr. Castleton," he said, gesturing.

"I have no secrets, Sheriff," Holt said, leaving the water fountain. Earl and Wyn followed him to the long booking counter.

Earl said, "Well, now . . . being as you were gone, were away on your ship, you probably haven't heard about the coroner's inquest."

"I have not," Holt said. "Will you oblige me, Sheriff?" In fact, he had read every detail of the inquest.

"It happened right there in the Castle," Earl said. "In front of a coroner's jury. And the coroner didn't leave anything out of his investigation, Mr. Castleton. When it was over, the jury brought in its verdict. Person or persons unknown."

Holt said, "I disagree."

"You—" Earl began, and stopped.

"I disagree, Sheriff," Holt said. "The jury is wrong."

"Wrong?"

"The persons who killed Kyle are not unknown," Holt said. "They are known to me."

Wyn said, hushed, "Known . . ." and Holt turned to him as though they were allies.

"My brother was murdered," Holt said, and Wyn *knew* Faith would be in it. And he would be in it. He could not escape.

Earl figured he had to protect himself and do it fast. "Hold it, Mr. Castleton," he said. He raised his hand. "Hold it right there. Now I want to hear what you've got to say, every word. It'll be the first order of business in this headquarters, you can depend on me. But if you go on now, go on telling me what you've come to tell me, you'll only need to say it all over again to the county attorney." Earl nodded. "Max Isbell. The only place you get justice is in a court of law, and the only man who can get it for you around here is the county attorney."

Earl stepped aside. "Gene!" Gene Hovde, the deputy behind the booking counter, jumped to his feet. "Gene, call them upstairs in Max Isbell's office. Tell them we're on the way. And Mr. Holt Castleton is with us," Earl said. "Over this way, Mr. Castleton." Earl raised the hinged section of the booking counter. "Come on, Wyn."

After they had ridden up on the elevator to the third floor and walked toward the county attorney's office, they found Max Isbell waiting in the corridor, his hand extended. "Hello, Mr. Castleton," said Isbell as Holt reached for his hand. The county attorney clasped Holt's arm with his other hand.

Max Isbell was a thin man with a prominent Adam's apple who wore white suits all summer. One of the best wing shots in North Carolina, he hunted every weekend in season. "Come in, come in,"

Max Isbell said, holding on to Holt as though he had been reunited with a lifelong friend.

Inside his office Isbell said, "I want to express my condolences, Mr. Castleton. I speak for Mrs. Isbell as well. Your . . . tragedy struck us hard, harder than most, Mr. Castleton. You see, awhile back, Mrs. Isbell lost a younger sister."

"I'm awfully sorry," Holt said. "It's a terrible, terrible blow. All of a sudden someone who has been with you for as long as you can remember is gone. Gone." Holt raised his hand and snapped his fingers with a ringing click. "Vanished. Taken away from you."

"Exactly, Mr. Castleton," Isbell said. "You've put it exactly right."

"Your sister . . . sister-in-law," Holt said. "How did she die?"

"Tuberculosis," Isbell said. "We had her in a TB sanitarium, but she did not improve."

"You have my condolences," Holt said. "Please convey my sentiments to your wife."

"Thank you, Mr. Castleton," Isbell said. "I'll do that." He moved a chair closer to his desk and stood behind it. "Mr. Castleton," he said, as he went around his desk to his own chair, where he waited for Holt to sit down.

But Holt walked across the office. "We were not prepared," he said, like someone dictating. "And my brother died unnaturally," he said. "Kyle was murdered."

Isbell said, "Murdered!" and looked at Earl.

Holt stopped beside a mounted globe of the world. "I told the sheriff," Holt said. "He brought me here to tell you."

Earl had been stretched out on the rack long enough. "There's more," he said. "Mr. Castleton says he knows who killed his brother."

"Right, Sheriff," Holt said, now walking toward the desk. "His wife killed him. His wife and—" he said, before Isbell interrupted.

"His *wife!*"

"—and his best friend," Holt said. "Kyle's wife and Boyd Fredericks." Holt looked from Isbell to Earl and Wyn. And Wyn felt like someone in chains, unable to leap across the office and seize Holt by the collar and yell, "She didn't! She couldn't!"

Holt said, "You're all surprised. Shocked. You're looking for a reason, for a motive. The motive is greed—greed, and jealousy, and hate. And the mastermind is Kyle's wife, his widow, Faith Venable, the Broadway star, the toast of Broadway. Faith Venable came out of nowhere, a mystery woman who made it to the top, zip-zip, like that. Every year from every corner of the country women pour into New York carrying a suitcase and a dream. Broadway. And every year they disappear. Not Faith Venable. Out of nowhere to stardom. She has everything: fame, fortune, the world at her feet. Is it enough? It should be enough, but not for Faith Venable. One night Kyle Castleton comes through the stage door, and Faith Venable finds her greatest role. She plays her greatest part. She becomes the loving wife. It's good-bye, Broadway. Faith Venable becomes Mrs. Kyle Castleton, one of the richest women on the planet Earth."

Holt skirted the globe. "But not rich enough for Faith Venable," he said. "She discovers a mother lode, a specific Castleton stock which is handed down from parent to child." Holt whirled around to face his audience. *"Only* from parent to child," he said. "She needed Kyle's child in her belly, and when she had it, she needed someone to help her. Boyd Fredericks. He hated Kyle."

Everyone was listening intently as Holt circled the office. "Boyd is poor, and Kyle was rich. Faith Venable promised to make Boyd rich. Boyd was easy for Faith, easier than Kyle had been. Hate is always easier to harness than love."

Isbell came out from behind the desk. "Hold it, Mr. Castleton. You've made—you've dropped a bombshell. You have accused two people of murder."

"I expect you to convict them of murder," Holt said. "I want them put in the electric chair."

Wyn didn't believe what he had just heard. Wyn wanted to grab Holt and demand proof, wanted Holt to admit that everything he had said was a lie. But he could only stand mute as Isbell said, "Mr. Castleton, I am a prosecutor. I need evidence of a crime when I go into court. I suppose you have evidence to corroborate your statement."

Holt put his hand on the county attorney's shoulder. "With what I've given you, the evidence should not be hard to uncover," Holt said. "You have the sheriff here and his deputy and your own staff. You're all partners in this building." Holt released Isbell. "I'll leave so you can go to work."

Earl was fast to accommodate. "We'll take you to your car, Mr. Castleton. C'mon, Wyn."

"Sheriff!" Isbell's cry could be heard by his secretaries in the outer office. "I'm sure Mr. Castleton can find his way out of the building. Can't you, Mr. Castleton?"

"I'm willing to try," Holt said. He opened the door. "Remember, gentlemen. I am at your service," he said, and left them.

When he was out of earshot, Isbell pulled off his jacket. "That son of a bitch!" Isbell said, throwing his jacket into a chair. "Did you hear that son of a bitch!" Isbell said. "He's insane! They're all insane! The electric chair!"

Isbell strode to the window. He pulled aside the drapes and looked down at the statue below his office. "Fuck you!" he said. He turned to face Earl and Wyn, his chest heaving, and said quietly, "It's the B Stock." He looked at Earl. "The wife is pregnant. Her kid will get Kyle's B Stock."

"Not while Holt is breathing," Earl said.

"What is B Stock?" Wyn asked.

Isbell scowled. "Where have *you* been?"

Earl came to the desk to stand between Wyn and Isbell. "Sam Castleton fixed it so there would always be more B Stock than the shares the public buys over the counter," Earl said. "So the owners of B Stock really own the company. And only Castletons can own it, parent to child."

"If you're finished, maybe you ought to go to work," Isbell said. "You heard Holt same as I did. Bring me some kind of evidence."

Wyn stared at his father and the county attorney incredulously. "You just said he's insane. You said he's a lunatic." Wyn whirled around, facing his father. "What the hell is going on here?"

Earl said, "Hold it, huh?" He felt like giving the kid a swift kick in the behind. Wyn acted as if he were a stranger in town. The kid had grown up with the Castletons and still didn't understand the first thing about them and the power they had.

Wyn walked to the desk, facing Isbell. "You said the guy is crazy. He sure as hell sounds crazy. Now you're asking for *evidence?*"

"Get him out of here," Isbell said.

"Try it," Wyn said. He took two long steps and was on Isbell's side of the desk.

"Will you get him out of here?" Isbell shouted. "Get him out of my office!"

"Wyn!" Earl came after him. "I'll see you outside. In my car. My *car!*"

Wyn looked across the desk at Isbell. "You . . . hero," he said, and turned. He passed Earl on his way to the door.

When the door closed, Isbell dropped into his chair. "Why don't you tell that son of yours to grow up? For God's sake he's carrying a gun," Isbell said.

"You put on a bigger show than he did."

"And I've seen enough of you for one day," Isbell said. "You're the investigating officer in this county. You'd better start earning your money."

"Picking a fight with me won't make you feel better," Earl said. "You're stuck with Holt Castleton same as I am."

In the corridor Wyn passed the elevators, walking to the stair well. He went down the stairs slowly, cursing himself for his outburst in the county attorney's office. Holt's accusation of murder had left Wyn spinning. All that had happened since his first glimpse of Kyle Castleton, stretched out and bloody in the hospital, came down on Wyn, names and faces, episodes and events rumbling through his mind. His life had changed forever that night.

Wyn reached the first floor and opened the stairwell door. He crossed the corridor and left the courthouse, heading for the parking area.

And stopped, standing in the midday heat. What if Holt turned out to be right? Wyn walked across the parking area. She hadn't killed Kyle, he told himself. How do you know she hadn't? Because she hadn't. She couldn't. Wyn stopped beside Earl's car, opened the car door, and dropped into the passenger seat. "You drive," Earl said. He stood over Wyn, holding the open car door.

Wyn crawled over the gearshift, and his father sat down beside him. "Goddamn heat," he said. "That was quite a show you put on upstairs."

Wyn opened the driver's door. "I've had enough for one day."

"Bullshit," Earl said. "Isbell is a grade A horse's ass. Does that mean you have to copy him?" Earl pushed his hat down over his eyes. "Let's get out of here."

"Where are we going?"

"Just go," Earl said. "Go, go. And don't talk to me. I gotta think."

———◉———

O LIVE FREDERICKS CAME HOME, AFTER A LONG, hot day of piano lessons, with a headache. Boyd heard the Ford coming, and he stood at the open door. "Aren't you late?"

"Late, hot, and tired," Olive said. "Louise Ostergren decided she wouldn't pay me. She would pay me next week." Harriett Oster-gren had been Olive's last pupil. "Louise waved a ten-dollar bill in my face. 'It's all I've got, hon.' Bitch."

"Mother."

"That's what she is," Olive said. "Don't tell me about Louise Ostergren. 'Ten dollars is more than I've got,' I told her. 'Send Har-riett to the store for change,' I said. 'I can't send her out in this heat,' Louise said. 'Send me,' I said. 'I'll go. Or I'll stay because I'm not leaving without my money.' " Olive removed her hat. "I've got to get out of these clothes. I'm soaked clear through."

"Before you do," Boyd said, walking to the grand piano. He took an envelope from the music rack.

"Registered," Olive said. The word stamped across the envelope frightened her. " 'Return Receipt Requested . . .' It's to you!" She raised the envelope. "Lucius Peete," she said, finding the lawyer's name and address in the upper corner. "Why is Lucius Peete writing you?"

"Why don't you read the letter?"

"Stop playing games with me, young man," Olive said.

"I am not playing games," Boyd said. "The letter is about Kyle's will."

"Kyle's will?" Olive pushed the envelope against her breasts, staring at Boyd, her eyes widening. "Boyd!" she said, smiling, the heat forgotten, her long, tedious day forgotten. She could kiss her students good-bye. All the unbearable years of poverty, of haggling with tradesmen, of holding off and evading creditors, of borrowing and repaying, of standing over a succession of inept, reluctant, pim-ply children crowded in on Olive in her sticky, airless parlor and then vanished, poof, as though dispersed by a genie who had come to rescue her from her life of misery. The Castletons had millions. She held up the envelope as though she could see the letter inside. "What does it say?"

Boyd sat down on the piano stool. "Read it."

Olive pulled the letter from the envelope and read aloud. "Dear Mr. Fredericks: I am the executor of the estate of Kyle King Castleton, deceased. You have been named a legatee in the last will and testament of Kyle King Castleton. I quote from the document.

" 'To Boyd Fredericks I bequeath my most precious possession, my baby, the finest aircraft in the world, my Waco. I also bequeath Boyd Fredericks my flying gear since we both wear the same size.'

" 'Mr. Castleton's will—' " Olive stopped. She could not go on. She wanted to cry. "You were his best friend, his only friend," she said, her voice a defeated monotone. "All that money," she said. "He could have saved us." She let the letter and envelope slip from her fingers. She stepped back and dropped onto the sofa.

"I hated the plane," Boyd said. He moved around the piano on the way to his bedroom.

"Boyd." Olive pushed herself out of the sofa and picked up her hat. "We may as well examine your inheritance," she said.

"It's an airplane, Mother." He glared at her.

Olive did not respond. She put on her hat. Boyd gave her his daggers look but followed her through the kitchen and into the yard.

They crossed the yard in silence to the Model T parked in front of the garage. Olive backed out into the street. They rode in silence until she said, "You're probably dying of the heat. Open the door," thus making the conciliatory gesture to end the hostilities. In hot weather Boyd often rode with his door ajar, his right foot on the running board. "How far is the airport?"

"You turn on Old Kettle Road, and it's two miles ahead."

At the city limits Olive said, "I don't see an airport."

"We'll be coming to a gas station," Boyd said. "Turn left past the gas station." Olive made the turn onto a narrow, rutted road. "There," Boyd said, pointing.

In the distance Olive saw a mound rising above the flatland. "It looks like a haystack," she said. The hangar had a rounded roof. Closer, Olive could see a small building huddled against the hangar. High above, a wind sock hung limply from a pole.

A shiny black Packard sedan was parked behind the small building, and in front of it, next to a screen door, a man sat in a captain's chair tilted against the wall. As Olive stopped, the chair dropped, and a gangly man rose. Dressed like no one she had ever seen, he wore a pearl gray hat and a darker gray shirt. The buttons were mother-of-pearl. Painted airplanes covered his necktie, and a tiny diamond on a stickpin protruded from the engine of one plane. "Who's that?"

"Stan Jessup," Boyd said. "He owns the airport."

"Hey, Boyd!" Jessup saluted.

"Hello, Stan." Boyd got out of the car. Olive followed, shading her eyes with her hand. Jessup removed his hat.

When Boyd introduced him, Jessup said, "It's a pleasure, ma'am." He pushed his fist into Boyd's ribs. "You're the lucky guy. Come to see your plane, I guess."

"How do you know about the airplane?" Olive asked.

"I've been notified, ma'am," Jessup said. "Kyle's lawyer sent me a lawyer's letter. Have a look, ma'am."

They walked to the hangar. A black man sitting on the ground in the shade pushed himself to his feet. "That you, Mist' Boyd? Sure is. Sure is a treat seein' you."

"How are you, Jordan?"

"Jordan the same," said the black man. "He don' change."

Jordan followed them into the hangar. Olive saw two airplanes near the entrance. Behind them, facing the airfield, stood Kyle's orange Waco. "Here she is, Boyd," Jessup said.

"Mr. . . . Jessup?" Olive squinted, shading her eyes. "How much does this airplane cost?" she asked.

"New? Delivered?" Jessup rubbed the varnished wood propeller. "Just over ten thousand," he said. "Make it ten and a half with the leather trim Kyle specified for the cockpit."

"How about this airplane?" Olive asked. "It looks new, but I suppose you'd call it used, like a used car. How much is this airplane worth?"

"Right around eight thousand is my guess."

Olive wanted to shout, wanted to hug Boyd. Eight thousand! She could paint the house inside and out and have thousands left. She could junk her car and buy a new one. And she could pay the bills. "Boyd, did you hear Mr. Jessup? Eight thousand dollars."

"If you had a buyer," Jessup said. "People aren't buying airplanes, ma'am. There's a Depression in this country, which can't be news to you."

He had ruined her fleeting glimpse of something better in life. Olive swung around, grabbing the wing. "Someone bought this!"

"Kyle Castleton," Jessup said. "There's only one Kyle Castleton, ma'am. Was."

"Are you trying to tell me there is no one in this entire country who could be looking for an airplane to buy?" Olive asked.

"I'm not in the forty-eight states," Jessup said. "I'm right here in one little corner of North Carolina. So if you find any customers, you bring them right out here, ma'am. I've got some planes to sell myself. And anything else they're willing to buy. I'm ready to move on. Long past ready." Jessup rubbed the propeller. "Rent is fifty dollars a month," he said. "Starting the first of the month, you'll be responsible, Boyd. Fifty smacks. Due and payable on the first of the month. Jordan!"

The black man came out of the shadows from a corner of the hangar. Jessup said, "Jordan, I'm leaving. You lock up, hear?"

"Yes, sir, Mist' Jessup," Jordan said.

"And, Boyd, you come back soon," Jessup said. "Don't you be a stranger now." He raised his hat and bowed slightly. "Very happy to have made your acquaintance, Mrs. Fredericks."

———=◁◉▷=———

I N   H I S   C A R at Castleton Community Hospital Earl looked at the rearview mirror, watching Arthur Widseth come out of the emergency entrance. The intern wore a suit and a white shirt with a tie. "Hop in, Doc."

Widseth said, "It's very nice of you to come for me, Sheriff."

"Can't take too much credit," Earl said. "The hospital is right on my way," he said, lying. "Fact is, you should have your own car, Doc. You'll need to be making house calls soon's you finish here. How can you make house calls without a car?"

"I'm a long way from having my own practice," said the intern.

He played with the knot of his tie. "I've never been called . . . sub-poenaed before."

"Relax," Earl said. "You're a witness. The grand jury isn't after you." Earl grinned. "Doc, you're not a bad-looking fellow when you're all decked out."

"This is my graduation suit," Widseth said. "My college gradua-tion, not medical school. It's a little tight."

Earl drove through a red light. "You should be thin as a rail the way they work you fellows. Ought to have more than one suit too. Guess that's out on what they pay you."

"Interns don't get paid," Widseth said.

"Nothing? They don't pay you *any* money? News to me," Earl said, lying.

"Room and board," said the intern. "And our laundry. The hospital does our laundry."

"Christ, around here they treat niggers better," Earl said. "Well, it's only a year. Then you can hang up your shingle."

"You need money to open an office," Widseth said. "There was a time when the banks would lend you the money. The Depression ended that."

"Hell, I forgot the Depression," Earl said. "Goddamn banks are closing, lots of them."

"So are doctors," said the intern. "The journals used to be full of offers for interns. Now all you see are ads by doctors who want to sell their practices. There aren't any buyers, so those doctors close their offices. Patients can't pay their bills. We were warned about all this in medical school."

"Tough," Earl said. "Nice kid like you. It isn't fair. I never thought I'd live to see the day a *doctor* couldn't work. Hell, the only worry a doctor ever had was *overwork*. This goddamn Depression."

"Why should we be special?"

"Why? Because you *are* special," Earl said. "You're a healer, Doc. You're a lifesaver, that's why. You fellows save lives. Damn!" He hit the steering wheel with his fist and drove through another red light.

"Sheriff?" Widseth gestured. "Red light."

"Yeah, well, I'm mad." Earl scowled. "Here's a nice kid like you, a smart young fellow, goes to school all those years for one reason: to help people. Now he can't even do that. Can't buy a car. Can't even buy a *suit*. Damn!"

Earl slumped down into the seat. Neither spoke until Earl drove through the open gates of the courthouse. "Here we are, Doc."

Earl stopped in the space reserved for him. He opened his door, then turned to face the intern. "Wait a minute!" Earl said. "Maybe you can stay right here where you are, Doc. Go to work right there at Castleton. Think that would suit you?"

"Suit me?" The intern swung around in the seat, coming alive. "I've stopped hoping. Half the interns in North Carolina are aiming at Castleton."

"Yeah, but you're closer to the mark," Earl said. "Hell, you're right on top of it, Doc. You're here. You haven't heard any complaints about your work, have you?" Earl grinned. "I mean, except from me, but that's buried and forgotten." He looked at the intern. "So you'd like it, right, Doc?"

"It would be like a dream come true," Widseth said.

Earl shoved his fist into the intern's ribs. "Wake up. I know some people, and they can talk to other people. Important people."

Widseth said, "I've been afraid even to think I could stay."

"Start thinking," Earl said, and jabbed the intern once more. "Up and at 'em, Doc." As Widseth opened the car door, Earl leaned across the gearstick separating them. "You'll be alone in there, Doc," Earl said. "Understand? Sure you do. Just answer the questions. No guessing." Earl looked directly at the intern. "No guessing. Understand?"

The intern nodded.

"Say it, Doc," Earl said.

"I understand."

Earl patted the intern's shoulder. "We're ready."

———◦《◉》◦———

INSIDE, on the third floor, Wyn and Jim Anderson stood against the railing along the stairs. The high school coach had come to the sheriff's office looking for Wyn. "Where do I go for the grand jury? I can't even remember what a grand jury does," Jim said. "Why should they pick me?"

"You're an upstanding citizen," Wyn said. "Let's go. I'm a witness myself."

Since the day with Holt in Isbell's office, Wyn had lived on a roller coaster of emotions. He thought constantly of quitting. He thought of warning Faith, telling her to run. He didn't even know where she lived, but he could find out. He thought of Boyd Fredericks, the poor sap.

Wyn hated the nights now. All his life Wyn had been a sound sleeper. Now he woke in the night, woke with the piercing conviction Faith would be electrocuted. And when the night ended, when daylight crept beneath the window shades, Wyn hated the long, endless day as well.

At the stairwell Jim Anderson said, "Football practice starts in two weeks. How long will this last?"

"You'll be okay," Wyn said. "You're hearing one case."

"I've been around kids so long I don't belong anywhere else," Jim said.

Behind them Earl and the intern came out of the elevator. "There's Wyn," Earl said. "You remember him, Doc. My boy, Wyn. He was there that night at the hospital." Earl saw Jim Anderson. "That you, Coach?"

"Sorry to say," Jim said.

"What're you doing up here? Still trying to duck your property taxes?"

Jim frowned. "Huh?"

"He's trying to be funny," Wyn said.

"Seriously," Earl said, "there's talk you've been molesting the girls during gym classes. Finally nabbed you, I guess."

Wyn came away from the railing, keeping Jim behind him. "Cut it out," Wyn said to his father.

"Sure," Earl said, and wagged his finger at Jim. "Stay clear of the jail bait, Coach. Come on, Doc."

Jim pushed Wyn into the railing and faced Earl. "You foul-mouthed little pig," Jim said. "If you were anywhere near the size of a man, I'd bust you in half."

"Don't let the size stop you," Earl said. "Or the uniform. Or the place."

"No, you don't," Wyn said, slipping between them. He pushed Jim away. "Beat it. Down to the end of the corridor and turn left. You too, Doc." He shoved the intern, watching his father carefully. "I said, go!"

Wyn stood over Earl, ready to stop him if he moved. Wyn watched Jim and Widseth walking down the corridor until they were out of sight before facing his father. "Proud of yourself?" Earl thought the kid would take a swing at him. "Jim Anderson is a nice guy," Wyn said. "Maybe the nicest guy in this town. Why did you pick on him?"

Earl moved sideways along the railing. "If you'll give me room to breathe, I might tell you." He hitched up his pants. "I can't tell you. I like Jim Anderson, like him as much as I like anyone."

"He didn't have it coming."

"Neither do I," Earl said. "I didn't have it coming either. Max Isbell is convening a grand jury to hear evidence of a murder. *Murder!* Because Holt Castleton says so. Holt Castleton, that—" Earl stopped. "Now I don't even trust you. C'mon. We're subpoenaed too, in case you forgot."

On the far side of the courthouse Jim Anderson entered a kind of amphitheater, a large, oval room with a high ceiling. The door closed, leaving him in shadows. The amphitheater was dimly lit, and Jim felt as though he were standing in an empty church.

He faced three tiers of large chairs rising steeply from the floor. The rows of chairs flanked both sides of a large, stepped aisle. Jim squinted in the dim light. Several chairs were occupied, and he saw a woman among the men. Jim cleared his throat and walked to the aisle. Despite the darkness, he recognized Carter Goodrich, who sat beside another man in the first row. Carter Goodrich owned the Farmers and Merchants Bank, the most important in the city. Jim climbed the steps to the last row and took one of the chairs on the aisle.

The chairs were large, with seats and arms of padded leather. Jim leaned forward, his legs apart, his elbows on his knees, sitting as he did on the bench during a baseball or football game. A woman said, "Is that you, Mr. Anderson?" Then he saw a woman in the second row raise her arm. "Over here. It's Grace Lathrop."

He said hello. Grace Lathrop was president of the Washington High School Alumni Association.

"We're sharing a new adventure," said Grace Lathrop. "Isn't it exciting?"

"I guess." Two men entered, separated at the steps, and took chairs in separate rows. Jim counted the chairs. Twenty-three.

A woman entered and sat in the first row. Another woman arrived, and behind her three men followed in single file. Now the door opened steadily. A man took the chair across the aisle from Jim. The third row began to fill, and then the amphitheater became bright as daylight.

In the first row the man beside Carter Goodrich turned, and Jim recognized Seward Hall, president of the Cumberland and Gulf Railroad.

Below, a long wooden table faced the grand jury. To one side stood a waist-high lectern. Jim saw a man in a white suit enter. "Max Isbell," said the juror across the aisle. "County attorney."

Edgar Damon, the clerk of the grand jury, and Charlotte Ennis, a court stenographer, followed Isbell, who said, "Let's get started."

Edgar Damon went to the aisle in the center of the amphitheater. "Please rise and raise your right hands," Damon said. As the jurors obeyed, Damon held up his right hand. "Repeat after me," he said. "I swear by Almighty God . . ."

"I swear by Almighty God . . ."

"That I will faithfully discharge my duties and obligations . . ."

After the grand jury had been sworn, Isbell left the table. "My name is Max Isbell. I am the county attorney," he said. "Some of you know me; some of you do not. Some of you have served on other grand juries. For the benefit of newcomers, I'll start by saying a few words about the grand jury process and its functions.

"A grand jury is chosen by the presiding judge of the highest state court, in this state the district court of this county."

Isbell saw every man and woman looking down at him, and he pushed his hands into his pants pockets. "You are here to determine whether a crime has been committed and by whom. In this instance the crime is murder. It is the most heinous of all crimes and is called a capital crime." Isbell turned and walked back to the table. He opened a file folder and flipped back several sheets of paper. "On the night of September fifth, 1932, less than a month ago, Kyle King Castleton died at his home. He died a violent death, death by gunshot. He was killed by a single bullet to his right temple, to his head.

"Kyle Castleton was twenty-two years old, a young man with his entire life ahead of him," Isbell said. "He had been blessed by the fates. The Castleton family is known to all of you. It's probably fair to say the Castleton family is the most well known in the entire South," Isbell said. "Can any young man have wished for a happier future than Kyle Castleton?" Shaking his head, Isbell walked around the table, behind the clerk and Charlotte Ennis, taking down the county attorney's words in her stenographer's notebook.

"A coroner's inquest followed the death of Kyle Castleton," Isbell said. He raised the bound transcript, which had a green cover. "The inquest is a matter of public record. Each of you will be given a copy."

Isbell opened the transcript. "The coroner's jury found that Kyle King Castleton met his death at the hands of a person or persons unknown." Isbell looked up at the grand jury. "Met his death at the hands of a person or persons unknown," he said. "The state has sufficient cause to believe this person or these persons can be searched out and identified.

"I will carefully examine this death with you," Isbell said. "We will proceed step by step, moment by moment through the evening of five September, Labor Day evening. We will examine the evidence." Isbell stepped aside, pointing at the lectern. "We will listen to witnesses who are intimate with the tragic events of the night Kyle Castleton met his violent death.

"I will question the witnesses," Isbell said. "If any of you have a question, you can submit it, in writing, to the marshal, and I'll try to provide an answer. You all have paper and pencils."

Jim found a rectangular wooden sleeve attached to the seat of the chair. A legal pad protruded, and in the sleeve he felt a pencil compartment with pencils.

Isbell waited for their attention to return. "When we have concluded, you will decide whether a crime has been committed and whether a particular person or persons should be tried for the crime. This is not a courtroom, and you are not sitting in a jury box. A unanimous vote is not asked of you. A majority of fourteen members of the grand jury is needed for an indictment."

In a narrow anteroom flanking the amphitheater Wyn leaned against the wall, facing Earl, who sat between the intern and Russell Vance. "Is there no end to this nightmare?" Russell asked. "Sheriff?"

"I've been subpoenaed, same as you," Earl said as the door opened.

A marshal in uniform said, "Russell Vance."

Earl rose. "The doc here has to get back to the hospital."

"He called Russell Vance," the marshal said dourly.

Earl dropped back into his chair, facing Wyn and gesturing. "Take a load off."

Wyn did not reply, but after a time he sat down beside Widseth.

No one spoke. They seemed to be in a vacuum. The intern turned and twisted in his chair. "I said I'd be back by eleven," Widseth said.

"You can't fight a subpoena, Doc. You or anyone else," Earl said. "Right, Wyn?"

Wyn looked at the door. "Right."

For the intern, hours crawled by until the door opened and Russell emerged. Behind him the marshal said, "Dr. Arthur Widseth."

The intern rose, looking down at Earl and Wyn. "Wish me luck."

"All you need's the truth, Doc," Earl said.

"At least that's over," Russell said. "I've put that miserable business behind me. Good-bye, gentlemen."

When Russell left and they were alone, Wyn said, "What did you promise the doc?"

Earl crossed his legs, his face blank. "You say something?"

"Don't try your old tricks with me," Wyn said. "I've watched you too long. And I see you're branching out."

"Me? News to me," Earl said. "I've got a full-time job right here in the courthouse."

Wyn felt as though he were choking. He could think only of the electric chair in Raleigh, could see Faith in the chair, see the straps, see a man, cadaverous and in black, at a switch. "You're running a chauffeur service these days?" Wyn said. "You're the sheriff, and there are deputies in cars all over the county, but you had to pick up the doc personally. You had to have him to yourself for a while, for a kind of rehearsal before you gave him to Max Isbell."

"The doc is under oath in there," Earl said.

"Right. What does he get for lying?"

Earl came out of the chair. "All right, you—"

Wyn leaped up, though he never challenged his father. "Come on," Wyn said. "Say it. Cat got your tongue?"

"Nope." Earl shook his head. He had never laid a hand on Wyn, and he could not allow the boy to hit him. Nothing between them would ever be the same if the boy hit him.

"You're my kid, so you win another chance. If you stop all this now. Besides, you've got no argument with me. If you're really out for trouble, Holt Castleton is your man. But look before you leap, kid. Or even I won't be able to save you."

Inside, Widseth stood in the witness box, and after he had been sworn, Isbell said, "We're aware of your schedule, Doctor. We'll try not to keep you long. Doctor, have you ever testified before a grand jury?"

"No, sir, I have not."

Isbell said, "To begin with, Doctor, you're not on trial. No one is on trial. We've asked you to testify here because we need your help. Now, Doctor, you were on duty at Castleton Community Hospital on the night of September fifth."

"On call, yes," said the intern.

"On call," said the county attorney. "Did you see Kyle Castleton the night of September fifth?"

"Yes, I did."

"We're all laymen here, Doctor," Isbell said. "Please keep that in mind, will you? Now tell us in lay terms what happened. Tell us everything you remember of that night."

"Well, the first thing that happened, a man ran into the emergency room, very upset, saying, yelling, 'There's been an accident! There's been a terrible accident!' " The intern looked at Isbell. "Should I use their names? I didn't know their names until later."

"Yes, identify them," Isbell said.

"The man was Russell Vance," Widseth said.

"The estate manager at the Castle?"

"The estate manager, yes."

"Go on, Doctor," Isbell said.

"Well, Russell Vance ran in, and he held the door, yelling into the parking lot, 'Hurry! For God's sake, hurry!' I started to run," the intern said. "I don't like having injured people moved. But a nigg— a Negro came in carrying Kyle Castleton. Russell Vance said, 'He's been shot. It's Kyle Castleton. He's been shot in the head.' "

"Go on, Doctor," Isbell said.

"I could see the wound," Widseth said. "We got him onto the examining table. I tried to get a pulse, but he had no pulse."

"You didn't feel a pulsebeat, a heartbeat?" said Isbell.

"No," said the intern. "I did not. His heart had stopped beating. His eyes were open and the pupils were fixed. I used my flashlight. He was dead."

"And the cause of death?"

"He had been shot," said the intern.

"Now, Doctor, besides Russell Vance and Coleman, the Negro, was anyone else from the castle in the emergency room?" Isbell asked.

"Two others. Mrs. Castleton and—" said the intern before Isbell interrupted.

"Mrs. Kyle Castleton? The wife of the deceased?"

"Yes," said the intern. "I recognized her from her pictures in the paper, and Russell Vance told me."

"And the other person?"

"Boyd Fredericks."

"Thank you, Doctor," said the county attorney. "You've been very helpful to us. You're excused, Doctor."

When the intern came out of the amphitheater, Earl grinned. "Wasn't so bad, was it, Doc?"

Behind Widseth, the marshal said, "Wyngard Ainsley."

Earl came out of his chair. "How about rank? I'm the sheriff?"

"You're next, Sheriff," said the marshal.

"Swell," Earl said. "Hang around, Doc. I'll run you back to the hospital."

"Thanks," Widseth said. "Sheriff?" Earl dropped into the chair. "Thanks for everything."

"You're among friends, Doc."

In the witness box in the amphitheater Wyn raised his right hand, and the clerk said, "Repeat after me. I do solemnly swear . . ."

As Wyn finished the oath, the clerk said, "State your name and occupation."

"Wyn Ain—Wyngard Ainsley. I'm twenty-five."

A ripple of laughter swept the amphitheater. "I mean . . . deputy sheriff," Wyn said.

Isbell flipped through the transcript of the coroner's inquest. He had read it often enough to quote from many pages of the document. He carried the transcript to the witness box. "Nice of you to come in," Isbell said. He needed the boy. "First time before the grand jury?"

"First time."

"You're here among neighbors. They're on a serious mission, a mission of life and death. They need your help." Wyn remembered Isbell in his office after Holt Castleton left, remembered the brief geyser of obscenity before the county attorney wilted in defeat. Wyn wanted to punch him in the mouth.

Isbell leaned on the witness box. "On the night of September fifth you were on duty when Kyle Castleton was killed—met his death."

"Correct."

"And you were at the Castle that night?"

"Correct."

"Did you visit the sleeping porch in the Castle the night of September sixth?"

"Correct."

"Were you alone?"

"Correct."

Isbell stepped back, facing Wyn. The county attorney had learned long before to identify unfriendly witnesses. He would receive no help from Earl Ainsley's snotty son. "So you were the first person to reach the scene of the crime," Isbell said.

Behind him, in the second tier of chairs, Grace Lathrop said, "You are premature, Mr. Isbell. We are here to discover whether or not a crime has been committed."

On the other side of the aisle Zoe Kellerman said, "Took the words right out of my mouth." Zoe Kellerman, a tall woman who wore dark dresses with long sleeves all through the year, carried a parasol to shield her from the sun, whatever the season. "*We* decide if there's a crime."

"You ladies are correct," Isbell said. "I stand corrected. Since you and only you members of the grand jury are empowered to vote an indictment, my mistake is not irreparable. But I'll remind you that I and only I conduct the business of the grand jury. I've said earlier that if any juror has a question, has a comment, that juror will write it out, present it to the marshal, and he will deliver it to me. And I will try to furnish the juror with a satisfactory reply. Please do not interrupt again."

In the first row Carter Goodrich looked over his shoulder at Zoe Kellerman. She fought an impulse to put her thumbs in her ears, wiggle her fingers, and stick out her tongue. She was a self-reliant, determined woman. Ten years earlier, when her husband, Gregory, became incapacitated with a failing heart, Zoe Kellerman moved into his real estate office and maintained it, supporting the family.

Below, beside the witness box, Isbell said, "We were discussing your entrance in the sleeping porch. Please describe it."

"It's a . . . sleeping porch," Wyn said. "It's a big, square room with screens. A bedroom. There's a bed, and tables, and lamps. There's a chest of drawers, a big chest; everything is big."

"Describe the condition of the sleeping porch."

"I just did," Wyn said.

"No, you did not. Listen to the question. And remember, you are under oath."

Wyn almost went over the rail of the witness box. "I'm not a liar. I don't need an oath to tell the truth. I—" he said before Isbell interrupted.

"Listen to the question!"

"—tell the truth!" Wyn said.

"I'm warning you . . ." Isbell said, and stopped. He couldn't play the little bastard's game, acting the dope in front of Carter Goodrich and Seward Hall. "The stenographer will read the question."

Charlotte Ennis read from her notebook: "Describe the condition of the sleeping porch."

"Describe the condition of the sleeping porch," Isbell said. "Not what it contained. You've already done that. The condition."

"The bed was rumpled, like someone had been on it, down near the foot of the bed," Wyn said. "And there were wet, sticky spots on the bed and on the floor in front of the bed."

"Could these spots have been blood?"

"They were blood," Wyn said. "Tests proved they were."

"Did you see anything else unusual?"

"A gun," Wyn said. He wanted to stop, but he couldn't. He had to stay, had to help Isbell put Faith into the electric chair. Wyn lowered his head, as though he could hide.

"A gun," Isbell said. He walked to the table and took the .38-caliber revolver he had brought from his office. He returned to the witness box, raising the gun, the nickel-plated barrel gleaming in the bright lights. "This gun?"

"Correct."

"Where did you find this gun?"

"On the floor in front of the bed," Wyn said.

"Continue."

"I picked it up with my handkerchief," Wyn said.

Isbell turned the gun over and back, over and back, and long arrows of light danced along the barrel. "At the coroner's inquest Sheriff Earl Ainsley testified this gun, which you picked up with your handkerchief, was sent to Highway Patrol headquarters in Raleigh, where it was tested for fingerprints. Tests proved there were no fingerprints," Isbell said. "Kyle King Castleton was killed by a bullet fired from this gun. He was found lying across the bed. He was not wearing gloves. If he killed himself, he had to remove his fingerprints after pulling the trigger and sending a bullet into his brain." Isbell lowered the gun and faced Wyn. "As a law enforcement officer, experienced in such matters, do you believe a man can kill himself and remove his fingerprints?"

"Someone else could have removed the fingerprints," said Jim Anderson.

Wyn said, "Yeah." The remark had rescued him from the paralysis of despair. "You're right!"

"Order!" Isbell said. "Let's have order here!"

Zoe Kellerman looked back at Jim. "I didn't think of that. Good for you."

Isbell berated himself for choosing Jim Anderson. "I've warned the panel to follow the rules," said the county attorney. "Remember your paper and pencil, right there in your chair. One, write out the question. Two, pass it to the marshal, who will deliver the question to me."

Jim had been giving orders for eighteen years, commanding hordes of young athletes. "As long as we've started, let's finish this one and put it on the record," Jim said. "Couldn't any person have wiped the gun clean?"

Isbell carried the gun to the table, set it down, and faced the witness box. "Answer him."

"Sure," Wyn said. "Anyone could have wiped off the prints easy. And here's something else. If someone killed Kyle Castleton, why leave the gun?"

Isbell strode to the witness box. "You're here to answer questions, not ask them."

"But we should ask the question. Why leave the gun at the scene of the crime? Here's another question. Is killing yourself a crime?"

"One more word and you'll be charged with contempt."

Wyn almost laughed. "I'm no lawyer, but if you think you can hold me in contempt for what I just said, neither are you."

"You're excused! You're excused!"

Wyn came out of the witness box. He paused to look up at Jim Anderson, silently thanking the coach for saving him.

———— ◎ ————

TWO DAYS LATER Isbell telephoned Earl. "They voted an indictment, twenty for, three against," Isbell said.

"What'ya know?"

"Weisenheimer," Isbell said. "I'm going to trial, and I have no case."

"You'll think of something," Earl said. "I'll pick up Boyd Fredericks."

"Not without an arrest warrant," Isbell said. "I'll be in court tomorrow morning. You can pick up the warrant there."

"How about the newspapers?"

"I've just come from the reporters," Isbell said.

———— ◎ ————

COLIN INSCOTT had not been told that B Stock could be transferred only to the children of Sam Castleton's heirs. He believed he had been betrayed by the Castletons and their omnipresent lawyers. Before his marriage he had been summoned to New York from East Hampton, to William Street in the financial district. He had been surrounded by lawyers as though they had a common criminal on their hands. Colin could still hear them. "Now you understand you cannot . . . you may not . . . under no circumstances."

Mounds of paper were thrust at him that afternoon in William Street. "Signify your agreement by signing here . . . and here . . ." Not a hint of the B Stock; not a word.

At the Castle Colin carried on as always. He dressed with care, turning a cheerful face to the world, greeting one and all with his usual urbanity and élan. He lived a lie, waiting for nightfall.

At times Colin believed Gaby had made a pact with Lucius Peete. She became evasive after Lucius read them Kyle's will. When Colin tried to embrace her, she said, "I can't," even though he tried night after night.

One morning Colin suggested a drive in the country. "I say, old girl, we've been living in a crowd ever since we arrived." Colin put his arm around Gaby. "I'd like to become reacquainted with my wife."

His arm repelled her. She ached for Russell's arms. But Colin had trapped her. Gaby could not escape. He took her away from the Castle, driving far out into the countryside to a country inn for lunch. He talked all through lunch, of East Hampton, of their plans for renovating the second floor of the house, and as he continued to babble, Gaby stopped listening. She wanted Russell, needed Russell.

Driving back to the Castle, Colin stopped beside a field. "Moment." He left her to gather wildflowers, returning with a large bouquet. "Your Majesty."

She could not be cruel. "How sweet," Gaby said. "They're beautiful."

Gaby did not see Russell when they returned, but she did manage to get Coleman alone. "Mist' Russell, he gone to the farms, Miss Gaby." Russell did not return for dinner, and Holt did not appear, leaving her alone with Colin once more.

In her bedroom that night Gaby sat at the dressing table, caught up in sweet days of her early childhood. She remembered her father holding her high in the air before holding her close to ask, "How's my Raggedy Ann?" In the mirror she saw Colin enter and raised her hairbrush to begin her nightly ritual.

Colin found the wildflowers in two vases, one on a table, the other on Gaby's chest of drawers. So Colin knew he had been reprieved at last. He pulled the scarf from his neck. "Be with you in two shakes."

When Gaby was an infant, Celeste Castleton furnished the room with twin beds so her only daughter could keep a friend beside her overnight. Colin came out of the dressing room wearing white pajamas with red piping. He stretched out atop the covers of his bed. "I say, I'm lucky to have you, old girl."

"You're sweet."

"Honest is closer to the mark," Colin said. "You *are* a handsome woman, Gaby."

He saw her try to smile. "Thank you."

"I'd rather put it the other way around," Colin said. "I'd like a painting of you as you are now, brushing your hair."

She set down the brush. "Thank you, Colin."

"Meant every word, old girl. Honor bright."

Colin's clipped locutions, his pathetic parody of an English gentleman, had irked her from the beginning. Since their arrival at the Castle, his speech seemed to have become even more theatrical. As she walked toward the beds, Colin said, "You look very fetching in your negligee."

"Nightgown," she said, pulling her robe across her breasts.

"Nightgown, right," Colin said. "Fetching in your nightgown." He moved aside, patting his bed. "Room for one more."

She passed him, eyes averted, on her way to the far side of her bed. She could not be unfaithful to Russell. "I'm tired," Gaby said, removing her robe. "More than tired," she said. "Worn out." She slipped into the bed, pulling up the covers.

Colin turned to her, propped on his elbow, cradling his chin in his hand. "I say, I've the specific cure for what ails you."

She had to stop him, had to finish the evening so she could slip into the safety of the darkness. "Colin, honestly . . ." she said, and stopped, and tried again. "I'm worn out. I'm—" Gaby broke off, raising her arm to turn down the light on the night table between the beds.

The light came up. She said, "Why did you—" stopping as Colin swung his legs over the bed and rose, smiling down on her.

"Misery loves company," he said.

She shook her head, like a child stubbornly defying orders. "No, Colin. No." She held the covers under her chin with both hands. She wanted to scream at him. "Not tonight," she said. "I don't feel— Not tonight."

"Whatever you say, my dear." Colin stood between the beds. He couldn't quit again, before he even began. "Lonely over here, all by my lonesome," Colin said, thinking she would change her mind once they were together under the covers. "Lights out, you say." He reached for the lamp cord, but Gaby was faster, brushing his hand aside.

"Colin, I'm tired," she said. "I need to sleep."

"Exactly. You and I both, old girl," Colin said. "Sleep it is. Two peas in a pod."

"Let's just go to bed, Colin. You go to bed, to your bed," Gaby said.

"Tonight and last night and the night before and the night before and the night before," Colin said, standing over her.

"I know I haven't been . . . responsive," she said. "It's the Castle. Being here brings back memories, brings back bad times I thought I had forgotten."

Colin wanted to slap her. "I'll help you forget, old girl. Two heads are better than one."

She looked up at him. "I can't," she said, pleading.

He sat down on the bed, facing her. "Gaby, I am not Jack the Ripper," he said. "Really, I am not."

She could not bear to face him, to be alone with him. "I'm to blame," Gaby said. "Can't we leave it at that? This . . . situation is my fault, all my fault."

"You're talking rot."

"I suppose I am," she said. "Can we both please stop?"

"Do I have a choice? Look at us," he said. "We're strangers. Ships that pass in the night."

She turned her back to him. "Good night, Colin."

He switched off the light. She heard him getting into his bed. "Hail the Virgin Queen," Colin said.

Gaby flung aside the covers. She knew every inch of her bedroom and reached the door before Colin said, "What the devil . . .

Gaby?" He pawed for the lamp, banging his knuckles on the night table.

Below, passing the staircase, Russell saw lights in the corridor above him. He stopped, wondering if Coleman had forgotten his last task of the day.

In the corridor Colin said, "Gaby, stop! Have you gone bonkers?"

He caught up with her as she reached the sleeping porch. Gaby said, "I think we shouldn't be together tonight." At the foot of the staircase Russell could hear them clearly.

"Rubbish!" Colin pulled the door out of her hand and slammed it shut.

"Please go back to your room, my room," Gaby said.

"I've had enough," Colin said. "More than enough. Why are you avoiding me, Gaby? Be honest, just this once."

"Honest?" Gaby stared at him. "I wouldn't throw stones if I were you."

"Hold on," Colin said. "I've been honest with you from the beginning."

"Have you?" She despised him. "You're not even honest with yourself," Gaby said. "The English gentleman, the squire, lord of the manor, using that silly language you've picked up at your horse shows." Her face clouded with anger. "You've cheated from the beginning. You and your waitresses, and tarts, and—and . . . every woman you meet. Bringing home lipstick on your clothes. Liar!" Her face clouded with anger. "Go away," she said, opening the door of the sleeping porch.

Colin grabbed her. "We're not finished."

She looked squarely at him. "We are, Colin." She pulled away from him and entered the sleeping porch. She shut the door in his face.

Colin might have quit for the night, but when he heard the key turn in the lock, he became enraged. He raised his fist and hit the door. "Gaby!" Colin hit the door again, feeling a spear of pain shooting up along his arm. "Gaby! Open this door!" He hit it again. "I am warning you!"

Gaby said, "No," as though he could hear her. "Go away."

She heard him hit the door. "Gaby!"

Gaby went to the door. She admitted him and discovered she was not afraid. This . . . beggar was in her house. He ate her food and wore her clothes. Gaby had paid for his pajamas. "You warned me. Now I'll warn you," she said. "Go away and stay away. Stay away, Colin."

"Be careful, Gaby," he said. "I advise you as a friend."

"Friend!" She wanted to spit on him. "You're my enemy."

"I'm your husband," he said. "I am your loving, devoted husband."

"Stop!" Gaby said. "Stop, you fool." She lunged away to escape, but Colin trapped her.

She fought him, using her fists, striking him in his left eye. She almost fought free, but Colin lifted her off the floor and threw her onto the bed. All he needed was a child to be safe forever. She had cheated him of the chance long enough.

"Let me go!" On the bed Gaby rolled from side to side but couldn't escape. Colin fell atop her, pulling up her nightgown and fumbling with his pajama pants.

Gaby screamed, then screamed again, fighting him. Colin put his hand over her mouth. Gaby bit him, closing her jaws over his hand, biting with all her strength.

"Ai-i-i-i-e-e-e!" Colin cried out, and as Gaby released him, he fell away. She pushed her hands into his chest, kicking and squirming until she managed to wriggle out from under him.

"Oh, no!" Colin fell forward, taking a handful of her hair and twisting. Gaby screamed once more as Colin pulled her down beside him, and the door swung open.

"My God!" Russell stood in the swath of light from the corridor with Coleman behind him. "You . . ." Russell leaped at the bed.

Colin moved faster, moved like a snake, grabbing the footboard for leverage and vaulting over the bed.

"Animal!" Russell said, raising his arm and swinging wildly. Colin crouched and drove his fist into Russell's belly.

Russell staggered, grunting, his mouth open, fighting for breath as Colin hit him in the face. Russell's head snapped back, and Colin hit him again.

Gaby came out of the bed and leaped at Colin. He bent almost double and threw her aside. She fell hard, and Colin went at Russell, swinging with both fists.

Coleman stood by, watching them in agony. He wanted to lunge forward, scoop up Colin, and throw him out of the sleeping porch, but he could not move on a white man, could not touch the white man. He could only cry out, "Stop, you're killing him. You're killing Mist' Russell," he repeated as Holt, running, shoved him into the door.

Russell's legs buckled, and as he swayed from side to side, Holt grabbed Colin from behind and threw him onto the bed.

Colin sprang to his feet, raising his fists. "You want some too?" he barked, his British accent abandoned. "Come on," he said.

Holt ignored him, turning instead to Gaby, who stood beside Russell. "Now what? He's your husband."

"He tried to rape me," Gaby said.

Colin's arms fell. "That's a lie!"

But Holt could clearly see it wasn't. "I'll testify for her," Holt said. "Russell will testify. Coleman, pack his clothes." The black man left the sleeping porch.

"You," Holt said, facing Colin. "Get out of my sight. Go now while I'm still friendly. You can wait for your bags but not in the Castle. Let me hear you slam the door."

"You can't get away with this," Colin said.

"You just made the worst mistake of your life," Holt said.

———※《◎》※———

EARLY THE NEXT MORNING Earl walked out of the courthouse toward the line of black-and-white cars. "Why in hell can't I ever find Len Egan? I swear, one of these days . . ." Behind him Arver Long caught Wyn's eye and moved his forefinger across his throat. "Wyn, you ride with me," Earl said. "Okay, Arver, don't try setting a world's record, hear."

"Not me, Sheriff."

"Not much," Earl said. "Goddamn that Len Egan." He stopped at his car. "You drive, Wyn."

In the Ford coupe twelve miles to the south Olive reached the city limits. A bulging canvas bag lay on the seat between her and Boyd. He sat with his knees drawn up, his feet on a suitcase. More luggage was jammed into the trunk of the Model T. He had been awakened by Olive's cries. She burst into his room, raising the newspaper and holding it across her chest so Boyd could see the headline.

KYLE CASTLETON MURDERED GRAND JURY DECIDES
WIFE AND BEST FRIEND INDICTED

"Hurry!" Olive had cried. She pulled him from the bed. "Take only what you absolutely need!"

Now, in the coupe, Boyd said, "They're crazy. I loved Kyle."

"Max Isbell," Olive said. "That toad. I remember Max Isbell. Hiding near the gym during girls' gym class, waiting to cop feels."

Boyd leaned forward, his hands against the windshield. "The bridge is closed!"

Ahead, wooden sawhorses blocked the entrance to the bridge over the railroad tracks. "Mother, stop!"

"I can see," Olive said. She made a U-turn. "I'll take the Ashland Pike." She put her arm out the window. "Look there. Free as the birds." In the distance an airplane rose, the wings rocking as the aircraft gained altitude.

"Do you want to fly?" Boyd said. "We own a plane in case you forgot."

"Another victory," Olive said.

"I can pilot the plane," Boyd said. Even here in the coupe, the memory of Kyle's antics left Boyd hollow inside and quaking. Often, high, high up, with the engine roaring and the wind like a hurricane, he would feel Kyle tapping him on the shoulder and see Kyle's hands in the air, beginning another lesson. Kyle would keep his hands in the air, forcing Boyd to grab the stick. And Boyd would become the terrified pilot, holding the aircraft on a steady course until, without warning, Kyle would take over, sending the plane into a dive or, pointing the nose at the sun, climbing straight up. Boyd would shut his eyes, squeezing his eyelids, waiting for the airplane to fall over on its back, swallowing again and again and again so he wouldn't be sick. "Mother!"

Two black-and-whites, parked bumper to bumper, blocked the road. Olive drove onto the shoulder. "Mother, stop!"

"Who says they're waiting for us? They're probably waiting for an escaped criminal." Olive made a complete turn and looked into the rearview mirror. "I told you," she said. "They're not moving. A person can't be unlucky all the time."

As the Model T passed a roadside vegetable stand, Wyn drove out from behind it, and Arver Long's black-and-white followed. Sitting beside Wyn, Earl said, "Hit it."

When Arver Long heard the siren, he turned up his own. The shrill, piercing screams shattered the peace of the countryside. The two sheriff's cars boxed in the Ford, forcing Olive to stop.

"Park in front of her," Earl said.

"She isn't going anywhere," Wyn said.

"Not anymore." Earl opened his door. "If I'd waited for Max Isbell, that biddy would have been in Cuba by the time I had the warrant. C'mon."

Earl opened Boyd's door. The boy was as pale as a waxworks. "Son, I'm arresting you on suspicion of murder."

"He didn't do it!" Olive said as Boyd got out of the car. She opened her own door, hitting Arver, who was partially blocking it. "Let me out!"

"Let her out," Earl said wearily.

Olive stepped down from the Model T. "I'm going with him," she said. "I'm his mother. His only next of kin."

"You can't go with him, lady," Earl said. "Wyn!"

They took Boyd to Earl's car. "Get in, son," Earl said. He gestured, and Wyn followed him to the car trunk.

"I'll go back with Arver," Earl said. "When you get to the courthouse, use the handcuffs, Wyn. One on you, one on him."

"He's not going anywhere."

"Do it anyway," Earl said, and winked. "For the newspaper photographers. Makes a better picture." He left Wyn and spread his arms wide as he walked toward Olive. "Go on home and behave yourself," Earl said. He stopped beside Arver Long's car, reached inside for the radio microphone. "One-zero-one to dispatcher. One-zero-one to Dispatcher."

"Come in, sheriff."

"Did you ever find Len Egan?"

"He's back in service right now, Sheriff," said the dispatcher.

"Yeah, finally," Earl said. "Send him out to County Road A, out to the bridge. Tell him to pick up those sawhorses and deliver them."

"Those sawhorses are Public Works' job, Sheriff," said the dispatcher.

"Exactly what Len Egan will tell you," Earl said. "And you say it's an order. Say, 'Guess who?' "

Ahead Wyn swung Earl's car onto the road, shoving the accelerator into the floorboard, tires spewing gravel as the car rocked from side to side. Boyd fell against him and fell back into the door, holding on to the door handle as Wyn sped down the center of the road.

Boyd wanted him to go faster, so fast they crashed. At that moment Boyd wanted to die. Everything would be settled if he died. His mother could stop worrying about her worthless son, could stop telling him how he had wasted his talent. And Faith would stop worrying. She could stop being afraid he would blab, would tell someone everything he had seen. If he died, they wouldn't be able to prove anything.

Wyn drove along, trying to forget the waiting photographers. He didn't care if they sat in the courthouse until noon, or noon tomorrow. He didn't want to see another photographer. When Wyn had come for Kay one night the week before, she said she had a surprise for him. Kay took him into the sunroom and made him sit in one of the wicker chairs under a floor lamp. Kay put a scrapbook in his lap. "It's for you, Wyn."

Inside, he found page after page of news stories with his name, many with his photograph. "Do you like it?"

He could not be mad at Kay, could not say the scrapbook made him feel like a dope. "Kay, I haven't done anything special," Wyn said. "I haven't done anything at all. I've just *been* there, like a—a doorman."

"You've done your job," Kay said.

He did not fight her and refused to say or do anything that would hurt her. She knelt beside the wicker chair, her hands on the chair arm touching his arm. "It's something to look back on, Wyn."

Now, with Boyd beside him in his father's black-and-white, Wyn followed a large bus. Soon Wyn turned onto a dirt road. Boyd looked around. "Where are you taking me?" He watched his captor. "I've got a right to know where you're taking me."

"We're on a detour," Wyn said. He had to avoid his father, avoid any deputies in the area. In less than five minutes he saw an enormous billboard in the distance on his right. The billboard stood on wooden poles, and a trellis rose from the ground to the sign. Wyn slowed to a crawl. He left the road and stopped behind the huge sign.

Boyd shrank back against the door. Wyn's long silence, his sudden stop miles from the city left Boyd terrified. "Why did you come here? What are you doing here?"

"We can talk here," Wyn said. He had to settle everything once and for all, had to be absolutely sure of Faith, had to appease the demons that tormented him in the long, sleepless nights. "There's no one around. You can tell me the truth, tell me what really happened."

"Happened?"

Wyn said loudly, "Don't play games with me or I'll—" and stopped. Boyd looked almost paralyzed with fear already. Wyn dropped back in his seat, his left arm across the steering wheel. He had to switch tactics, try to be an old pal facing a pal. "The night of Labor Day," Wyn said. "In the sleeping porch."

"I have told you everything," Boyd said. "I've told you, told the sheriff, told the coroner. I've told everyone." His lips trembled, and he held one hand in the other, pulling at his fingers in an effort to stop the shaking.

"Tell me, Boyd," Wyn said. "You heard the shot. You ran upstairs. You found Fa— Mrs. Castleton. Where?"

To himself, Boyd said, "Be careful, be careful." From the way Wyn talked he knew something.

"Boyd! Where was she?"

"In the hall."

"Where? Exactly where?"

Boyd couldn't meet his eye. "In the middle of the hall. She came out of the bedroom and stopped in the middle of the hall."

Wyn leaned forward. "Did you see her come out of her bedroom? Boyd!"

Boyd began to cry. He hung his head, crying.

"Christ," Wyn said, rising from the seat to pull his handkerchief out of his back pocket. "Here."

Boyd shook his head, raising his own handkerchief to display it. Wyn fell back into the seat. Boyd covered his face with the handkerchief, wiping his eyes, and Wyn turned the ignition key and stepped on the starter.

WHEN THEY TOOK BOYD AWAY, Olive drove straight back into the city, passing the turnoff for her house on her way downtown. She drove straight to Paul Ellerbee's office downtown, taking a chance he would be there.

When the secretary Paul Ellerbee shared with an accountant and another lawyer told him who was waiting, he came out into the reception room, his arms extended. "Olive. It's been—how long has it been, Olive?" He led her into his office and put her in a chair facing his. "I'd know you anywhere," Paul Ellerbee said.

"No, you wouldn't," Olive said. "Not what's left of me. I don't know myself anymore." She stared at the lawyer. His vest lay open, and his belly hung over the waistband of his trousers. "I wouldn't know you either," Olive said. "Look what you've done to yourself, Paulie."

"Paulie," said the lawyer. "How long since anyone has called me Paulie? Longer than either of us wants to remember, I guess." She bent forward, reaching for an open pack of Castletons on his desk. Paul Ellerbee extended a lighter. "When did you start that?"

"When you started," Olive said. "Only I did it in the girls' bathroom, and you did it in the boys'." She lit the cigarette, inhaling deeply. She waved the smoke from her face. "You know why I'm here," she said. "Boyd. What are they trying to do? They say he killed Kyle! He and that woman! *Boyd* . . . who couldn't hurt a fly, who's afraid of his own shadow." Olive shook her head slowly. "Paulie, I can't stand it. You've got to help me."

Ellerbee rubbed his chin. "I hate to tell you this, Olive, really hate it. But I won't represent Boyd. You're asking me to go against the Castletons. I can't do that. If I went into court, in a couple of months, probably less, I wouldn't have the rent for this place. Nobody would come near me. You know that. You've lived here all your life, same as I have."

Olive leaned forward, pushing her cigarette into the ashtray on the desk. "Thanks for everything."

"Wait. Just wait a minute," Ellerbee said.

"For what?"

He rubbed his chin. "For . . . because I like you. I always liked you, which should be news to you. But listen. There were three nay votes when the grand jury voted to indict your boy. Max Isbell only needs fourteen to indict, so those three nays mean nothing. But the folks who voted nay will pay for those votes, Olive. Not today and not tomorrow, but sooner or later those three will wish they'd never walked into the grand jury room."

"Thanks for your information, Paulie." Olive turned her back, on her way out.

"Olive! *Olive!*"

She didn't stop. "Will you—" He broke off, following her. Paul Ellerbee had been born with a short right foot, and although he wore a shoe with a raised sole and heel, he limped badly.

She stopped abruptly, whirled around so fast he almost bumped into her. He said, "Olive—"

"Olive, Olive, Olive," she said. "Bye, Paulie."

———

I N NEW YORK the same day Faith opened the door of her apartment around noon, and Ward Kirby entered carrying a large florist's box. "The elevator operator gave me this. Faith, they say you killed Kyle!"

Faith wore dark loose lounging pajamas with a white silk blouse, cut low. She had pinned her hair atop her head, and she looked young, girlish. She stopped in front of the stylish dancer. "Do you think I did?"

"You couldn't!" he said, almost shouting. "Not in a million years!"

"Not in a million years," Faith said. Ward walked into the apartment. He set the florist's box down on the coffee table, removed the lid of the box, and extended the small white envelope atop the mass of yellow roses.

The yellow roses infuriated Faith. She hated Serena's arrogant intrusion. Faith remembered the first card: "You are not alone." She almost tore the envelope to shreds. "Aren't you going to find out who they're from?" Ward asked.

Faith removed the card. " 'Courage, Serena.' "

"An admirer," Ward said.

"How did you guess?" Faith felt trapped by this parade of yellow roses. Serena was a stranger, a Castleton, not a friend. Faith could not trust her but could not avoid her.

"These need water," Ward said. He picked up Faith's newspaper. "Who is Boyd Fredericks?"

"Stop asking . . . stop," Faith said. The elevator operator had left her newspaper early that morning, and when Faith opened the door, she looked down at her picture and saw ACCUSED OF CASTLETON MURDER.

She bent for the newspaper and unfolded it, reading the headline:

WIDOW AND LIFELONG FRIEND
ACCUSED OF CASTLETON MURDER

Ward said, "Faith, answer my question."

"Come with me," she said, taking his arm. Leading him to the foyer, she said firmly, "Good-bye, Ward."

"You can't be alone now."

"I want you to go home."

He said, "Faith, I'll wait for your call," as the doorbell sounded.

Ward opened the door and found himself facing two men in dark suits. One took his wallet from his pocket. He said, "I'm Pat Tierney, and this is Martin Biaggi."

Ward saw the brass badge and cried, "She's innocent!"

Pat Tierney elbowed him aside. "Mrs. Castleton, we don't like this much, but we're here to take you downtown."

Faith swayed and thought she would faint. She reached out to keep from falling and felt someone take her arm. "Are you all right, Mrs. Castleton?"

Tierney was holding her. The detective looked directly into her face. "Mrs. Castleton?"

"Thank you," Faith said, and moved aside, facing the detectives. "I'm ready," she said.

"I'm sorry, Mrs. Castleton," Tierney said. "It's suspicion of murder."

"I didn't kill Kyle."

"Any fool knows you're innocent," Ward said. God, how he hated cops.

"It's *suspicion* of murder," Tierney said.

His partner said, "They gotta prove it." Martin Biaggi tried not to keep looking at her, tried not to act like a punk seeing his first dame.

"All we are are errand boys," Tierney said. "We got this call from down in Carolina."

"You'll wanna pack some clothes," Biaggi said.

"I didn't understand," Faith said. "You're arresting me. I am a criminal."

"Look at this woman," Ward said. "This . . . spectacular woman. Does this woman look like a murderer to you? Does she?"

"Hey, you, we're just doing our job," Biaggi said.

"You're in the wrong place," Ward said.

Tierney put his hand into Ward's chest. "Butt out, you. Don't make me have to tell you again."

Faith said, "I'll need—" and stopped. "My bedroom is this way."

"You go ahead, Mrs. Castleton," Tierney said. "We'll wait. Take whatever time you need."

Faith said, barely, "Thank you," and circled the coffee table as though she could avoid the florist's box with Serena's roses.

"Mrs. Castleton!" Biaggi spoke more sharply than he had intended, berating himself for his boorishness. She stopped in the entrance of the hallway. "Maybe you want to call your lawyer, Mrs. Castleton."

"That's right!" Ward spun around as gracefully as though he were onstage. He slapped his forehead with the flat of his hand. "Why didn't I think of that?" He waved his arms. "Quickly, Faith. Do it."

"All right," Faith said, walking into the hallway.

In her bedroom Faith sat down on the bed and took the telephone from the night table. And discovered she did not remember the number. The last hours, beginning with the newspaper headline across the front of page one, long hours of fighting fear, of refusing to surrender to panic, and finally the appearance of the detectives, had combined to demoralize her. She could not think. She had to think. Faith's intelligence and her will had sustained her always. She took her personal telephone book from the night table but flung it aside. She refused to be defeated. She sat holding the telephone until she remembered Bella Spitz's phone number.

Just as Morty Abrams was the show business doctor, Bella Spitz was the show business lawyer. But Morty took everyone as a patient, and Bella Spitz took no one except stars, and not all of them; she took only the biggest stars.

Faith raised the receiver and began to dial Bella's number but stopped. She slipped the telephone receiver into the cradle. Bella would drop everything to be with Faith. She would remain at Faith's side, in New York and in North Carolina. But having a northern lawyer in North Carolina would doom Faith.

Faith took a suitcase from the closet and carried it to the bed. She opened the suitcase and suddenly saw an apparition of Kyle. He rose like a genie, a towering, looming figure, his head bloody. Faith ran.

She reached the hallway and stopped. She said, "No, no," fighting her nerves as she had earlier until she returned to the bedroom and to the closet for her clothes.

When she emerged at last, Ward said, "I'll take that." He crossed the foyer, hand outstretched. "I'm going with you."

"You haven't done anything," Faith said.

"Neither have you."

"They've come for me," Faith said. She stopped beside the detectives. "I'm ready."

In the lobby Tierney said, "We'll handle the reporters, Mrs. Castleton. Don't stop for anything."

Biaggi said, "Gimme," and took the suitcase from Ward. "Now, get lost."

"Wait, please," Faith said. She gave Ward a brief kiss. "You mustn't worry."

"Oh, go, go, go, before I start crying," Ward said.

Faith saw the crowd of newspapermen, heard their voices as they spotted her. She felt Tierney's hand on her arm. "We'll keep you between us, Mrs. Castleton."

Biaggi raised Faith's suitcase, held it across his chest. "Make way," he said, moving the suitcase from side to side, ramming it into the reporters closing in. Tierney held on to Faith, and Biaggi reached the unmarked car in front of the building. He set the suitcase on the roof and opened the door.

Biaggi took Faith's hand. "In you go," he said, lowering the front seat so Faith could get into the rear. She heard a newspaperman shout, "Woman's House of Detention!"

Photographers surrounded the car. Faith put her face in her hands. She felt the car move, and Tierney swung away from the curb to make a U-turn on Fifth Avenue. Faith sat back. "Where are you taking me?"

"You heard the guy," Biaggi said. "Woman's House of Detention. You'll be staying there but not for long. They'll be moving you down to Carolina."

Faith felt a soft throbbing above her eyes. To her right people seemed blurred and Central Park shimmered in the sun. "Will you open the windows, please?"

"They're open," Biaggi said. "I'll lower yours all the way."

He reached behind her for the handle and lowered the window at her side. "How's that?"

"Thank you," Faith said.

Biaggi said, "Lower the other one, Pat."

"Right you are," Tierney said. As he lowered the window, Faith saw the Frick mansion, and then the Jewish church, Temple something . . . Emanu-El. A young man whose name she could not remember had taken Faith inside one day to show her his family's name on the wall.

They reached the Pierre, then the Sherry-Netherland and the Savoy-Plaza. The opening night party for *Bermuda Bangles* had been held at the Savoy-Plaza.

Somewhere below Thirty-fourth Street Tierney turned, driving west toward the Hudson. He turned again on Sixth Avenue, heading south. On Tenth Street Tierney stopped beside a uniformed policeman at the gate of the Women's House of Detention at the Jefferson Market. Tierney opened his wallet and held it out of the window. "Manhattan South," he said.

The patrolman glanced into the backseat. He'd seen the dame
. . . yeah! The Venable dame! "Okay."

Biaggi carried her suitcase. Another cop took them into the
building. "We'll find our way," Tierney said. He stopped beside an
elevator. "Mrs. Castleton."

They rode to the fourth floor. The elevator opened into a
square room with benches along the walls. A sergeant sat behind a
desk at the far wall, and beside the desk Faith saw a door with bars.
They stopped at the desk. "We're from Manhattan South delivering
a suspect," Tierney said. He gave the sergeant a folded sheet of paper. "Sign us out, will you?"

The sergeant signed his name. "Here you go."

Tierney removed his hat. "We leave you here, Mrs. Castleton.
Good luck."

Biaggi set down the suitcase. "Yeah, good luck."

The sergeant opened a large ledger. "State your name and address."

Faith faced the sergeant, her hands at her sides. She felt ill,
cold and ill. "Mrs. Kyle Castleton," she said, and gave her address.

"Age?"

At the elevator the two detectives watched her. Biaggi whispered, "What ya think?"

"It happens," Tierney said.

"Why? What the hell for? She had it all," Biaggi said. "More'n
she could count. Why pop him?"

"It happens," Tierney said. The elevator door slid back. "We're
out of it, in any case."

The sergeant finished and pressed a button under the desk.
"Wait."

Faith heard footsteps. The sergeant used his pen to point at the
door with bars. "In there."

A woman in a blue uniform came to the door. The officer,
Doris Manning, an obese woman with short graying hair, filled the
door. She removed a large key ring from her belt and opened the
door. "Remember your suitcase," she said.

Faith didn't move, couldn't move. Doris Manning said, "Miss
Venable?" and came forward. She bent for the suitcase and took
Faith's arm with her other hand. "Hold on to me."

Inside, Doris Manning stopped to lock the cell door and clip the key ring to her belt. "I hate what they're doing to you, Miss Venable."

They walked along the corridor to a small office with another door with bars. A desk flanked the door, and beside it stood a chest-high table. "Let's get this over with," Doris said. "I need to take your fingerprints, Miss Venable."

At the table Doris took Faith's thumb. "I'll make this quick." She pressed Faith's thumb into the ink pad. "They must be crazy down there, down South," Doris continued. "I've read every write-up since this started. Anyone can tell Kyle Castleton did himself in. Here, I'll take the ink off for you," Doris said.

"Now your purse." Faith emptied her purse, and Doris put everything into a large manila envelope. "You get all this back."

She brought Faith into another room. "You'll have to undress, and I have to witness it, Miss Venable. It's the law."

Faith removed her clothes. Doris said, "Now put everything on but this." She took a folded gray cotton smock from a cabinet. "Need some help?" Ignoring her, Faith slipped the smock over her head. "Here comes the worst of it."

Doris brought her to yet another door with bars. Faith could see the cells on either side, filled with women staring at her. "Hey, Faith! Hey, it's her, Faith Venable!"

"They'll quit," Doris said. "They're showing off, is all." She stopped at an empty cell. "You're not near any of them anyway." She turned. "Miss Venable?" Trembling and cold, Faith walked into the jail cell, and Doris locked the door behind her.

"If you want anything, Miss Venable, let me know, or tell my relief, Sylvia Doroshow. A real Yiddishe mama, Sylvia."

Faith heard the key in the lock, heard the tumblers drop. The cellblock fell silent. She went to the iron cot against the wall and lay on her side with her legs drawn up, overcome with fear. She bolted upright, pushed herself off the cot, and began to pace, fighting the enemy, the fear that threatened to paralyze her.

———※◎※———

As THEY ENTERED UNION STATION, Earl said, "Your train arrives in New York at seven-o-eight. I picked it instead of the four o'clock, so you can do the paperwork and still leave tomorrow. In and out."

"Why are you sending me? You could've sent someone else," Wyn said.

"Let's not go over this again, okay? I'm tired of the same speech, and you must be tired of hearing me make it," Earl said. "I'm sending you to New York because the eyes of the country, of the world are on this case. Which means they'll be on you."

Earl stopped Wyn beside a United States Marine Corps recruiting poster. He looked at Wyn, all decked out in a suit and tie. His kid looked better than the stud in uniform on the poster. Earl took envelopes from his pocket and extended one. "Here are your tickets, coming and going," Earl said. "Sleeper to New York, compartment coming back. I got you a lower for tonight."

"Thanks," Wyn said miserably.

"And here's a court order authorizing New York to turn over the prisoner." Earl watched Wyn slip the envelopes into an inside pocket of his jacket. "Hey!" He opened Wyn's jacket wide. "Where's your gun? Jesus, Wyn!"

Wyn grimaced. "Christ, Pop. Everyone in the depot can hear you."

"Pardon me all to hell," Earl snapped. He unbuttoned the flap of his holster. "Here." He gave Wyn his gun. "Try not to lose it."

Wyn pushed the gun into his waistband and buttoned his jacket.

"Now, don't get mad all over again," Earl said. He extended a set of handcuffs. "You're escorting a prisoner accused of murder. You lose her and you're going to get hounded right out of the state."

"Are you finished?" Wyn cursed himself for coming back home. He should have stayed in California, stayed on the beach. He could have found some kind of job out there.

"Why the hell are you so mad?" Earl asked. He couldn't understand the kid. Wyn should be the happiest guy in the world, getting a paid vacation in a sleeping car to New York and back.

"So I'm all set," Wyn said.

"I'll walk down to the train with you."

"I'm okay." Wyn shifted his suitcase from one hand to the other, starting for the gates.

"Wyn!" He looked back. Earl hitched up his pants. "I don't lay awake nights thinking up ways to make you miserable."

"See you tomorrow."

Earl grinned. "I'll be here, kid. Ready to take delivery."

On the concourse below, a conductor pointed at Wyn's Pullman car, and another punched his ticket. An elderly porter in a starched white jacket standing in the vestibule took Wyn's bag. "Welcome aboard, cap'n."

The porter showed Wyn his seat. "Back in good times we carried five, six sleeping cars for Philadelphia 'n' New York," the porter said. "Up to eight 'round Christmas. Depression ruined us. Here we are with one car, 'n' we'll be half full if we're lucky. 'Scuse me, sir." The porter knelt to push Wyn's suitcase under the seat. "Hope you enjoy a fine trip, sir."

The porter left. Wyn had no sooner sat down than he sprang to his feet. "Hey!" The porter paused as Wyn dug into his pocket. He had thirty-three cents in change. Wyn kept the pennies.

"Thank you, sir," the porter said. The boy was a nice lad, a nice, green country lad.

Wyn went back to his seat, passing a man and a woman playing checkers on a board on their knees. The porter returned with luggage, followed by a young woman with a child. Wyn heard the child asking questions. The car gave off a musty smell that reminded Wyn of a funeral parlor. He leaned out into the aisle, and as he looked in both directions, the train car jerked forward. The train rolled out of the roofed concourse, and sunlight flooded the sleeping car.

The train moved through the city, picking up speed. Wyn took the envelopes from his jacket pocket and removed the extradition papers from one. She was in a place called the Women's House of Detention. Wyn looked out the window at grubby buildings and neglected streets. Faith was in jail up there, alone if she were lucky. She could be in the tank with the whores and the beggars.

"What's your name?"

The child Wyn had seen earlier stood in the aisle, staring at him.

"Wyn. What's yours?"

"Alex."

"Hi, Alex," Wyn said. "How're you doing?"

"I'm fine, thank you," the boy said. "My full name is Alexander Osborne Elliott. I'm named for my two grandfathers."

"I think they're pretty lucky," Wyn said. "So are you, having a big name like yours."

"Do you have a little boy?"

"No, I don't, Alex."

"Do you have a little girl?"

"Nope. I'm not married," Wyn said.

"You will be. Everyone gets married."

"I'll remember you told me," Wyn said. He saw the kid's mother coming.

"There you are," she said, taking Alex's hand. "I hope he hasn't bothered you."

Wyn rose. "He's a nice little fellow."

"He's very curious about people," she said.

"Will you be in the dining car later?" Alex asked.

"Sure. I'll be there."

"Then I'll see you again," Alex said.

"It's a date."

"Good-bye," Alex said. His mother said good-bye, and Wyn dropped into his seat. For a little while Alex had rescued him, but now he had hours ahead before dinner and an endless night after that. Wyn shifted in his seat, feeling the handcuffs against his buttocks.

———⊗———

L ATE THE NEXT MORNING Faith lay on the cot in her cell, unable to escape the obscenities the inmates flung at one another. She didn't see Doris Manning arrive. "Miss Venable?"

The matron put a key in the cell door. Faith sat up on the cot as the door opened into the corridor. "There's someone here for you, a sheriff from down there," Doris said. Faith remembered the oily little man, smiling at everyone with his false smile. "I let them finish what they had to do, the transfer, before I came for you," Doris said. "I figured you're better off in your cell alone than sitting upstairs on display."

"You're very kind." Faith came to the cell door. "You've been kind ever since I came."

"I hate what they're doing to you," Doris said.

The women in the cells saw Faith, and the clamor started all over again. "Pigs," Doris said. "They're all pigs. Honest to God, they're worse than the men, and I've been with the worst of them too."

Once in her office, the matron said, "I have all your things." She bent for Faith's suitcase beside the desk. "At least you can dress in private, Miss Venable."

They returned to the room where Faith had removed all her clothes. "You'll be alone in here," Doris said. "Just knock when you're ready."

"Please stay," Faith said. "Can you stay?"

"Can and will." Doris opened the suitcase. "I put everything you were wearing in here, Miss Venable. Tight fit. Hope I didn't crease anything."

"It doesn't matter," Faith said bleakly.

In the room where Faith had been booked, Wyn stood at the desk beside the sergeant with Pat Tierney and Martin Biaggi, the New York detectives. "We're out of this now," Tierney said. "She's your prisoner, Sheriff."

Wyn had given up correcting them. Biaggi winked. "Could be worse, huh, Sheriff?"

"She's a dish, I'll give her that," Tierney said.

Wyn watched the door in the corner directly ahead of him. "Won't be long now," Biaggi said as they heard the distinctive tap-tap of high heels.

Wyn saw the fat matron carrying a suitcase. She set it down, and Faith appeared. He swallowed. His throat hurt.

Doris unlocked the door. "Good luck, Miss Venable. This will pass."

Faith bent for the suitcase. "Thank you for everything," she said, and saw Wyn. "You—" she said, as though she were facing a ghost, her voice hollow with disbelief. Here in the ugly, forbidding jail where she had been held for the most horrible night of her life, the bumbling, hesitant yokel who had always been underfoot in the Castle, clumsily trying to please her, stood waiting.

Wyn joined her. The hell with the handcuffs, the hell with Earl. "I'll handle this," Wyn said, reaching for the suitcase.

"So we're all set?" Tierney said.

In the detectives' car they were safe from the newspapermen who thronged the entrance of the sprawling sandstone building. As they left the reporters behind, Wyn said, "The stationmaster gave me directions." Earlier Wyn had gone from his train directly to the stationmaster's office, asking for private accommodations when he returned with Faith.

"We know Penn Station," Biaggi said. "North Concourse, right?"

"Trust us, Sheriff," Tierney said, thinking they made them awfully young down South. At Thirty-fourth Street he drove into an unlit entrance of the terminal and stopped beside an unmarked door. He raised his hat. "Good luck, Miss Venable. I mean it."

"That's from both of us," Biaggi said.

The door opened to a flight of metal stairs. Wyn and Faith climbed the stairs to a broad corridor sheathed in marble. "This way," he said, carrying her suitcase. He took her to a pleasant room with comfortable leather furniture and a burgundy rug. "Nobody will find us here," Wyn said.

Faith went to the windows and looked down into the streets. Wyn had an impulse to carry her off, pick her up and disappear with her. "Why don't you sit down?" he said, awkwardly polite.

Faith went to a sofa and sat at one end. "I'm glad you came," she said. "Glad it's you and not a . . . stranger."

"Can I get something for you?" he asked.

"Nothing," she said vacantly. Wyn crossed the room to a big leather chair and sat on the edge, facing her. "Do you suppose there is a powder room nearby?" Faith asked.

He nearly leaped out of the chair. "We'll find one."

"We?" she said, and immediately added, "I'm sorry."

"Why? You didn't do anything wrong." Wyn stopped beside the sofa. "You're in a terrible spot," he said. "Nothing is worse than cops. You've been free as the breeze all your life. All of a sudden you're not. You have to ask permission for the ladies' room like you were back in kindergarten. But it's not kindergarten. It's . . . awful." He paused. "We can go now, okay?"

She flashed a smile at his bumbling kindness, and he thought she became even more beautiful. "Okay."

They left the room, walked to the end of the corridor, and came out on a balcony. A broad marble staircase led to the concourse and the ticket booths and shops. "Down there, I guess," Wyn said.

At the foot of the staircase he stopped a redcap, who gave them directions. Faith kept her face averted. "May I stay close to you? Someone could recognize me," she said.

They passed a row of food stands with attendants in chef's caps behind the counters. Beyond, Wyn saw the figure of a woman on a door. "Over there."

Waiting, Wyn walked from one shop to the other, looking into the broad display windows until he heard Faith say behind him, "I could have escaped, you know."

He spun around. They were close enough to kiss. Her eyes trapped him. He felt himself sinking. "You wouldn't," he said.

"No, I wouldn't," she said. She turned her head into his shoulder. "May I use you as a shield again?"

They had just returned to the room when the stationmaster stuck his head in. "Excuse me, your train is on the tracks, Sheriff. We won't be boarding for another couple of hours, but I can take you down now. I've talked with your conductor, so if you need or want something, he'll oblige you."

Wyn turned to Faith. "Are you ready? I mean . . ."

"I'm ready."

In the corridor the stationmaster said, "I already put your bag in the compartment, Sheriff," and Wyn remembered he had left his suitcase with the train man. "In here."

They stepped into a small elevator and emerged at the rear of the concourse. "Track twenty-six," said the stationmaster. "We're operating empty trains. People can't afford to travel. Here's twenty-six." Ahead a conductor stood beside a boarding stool. "He'll look after you."

At their car the conductor said, "This way, please," and took them to the compartment. "I think you'll be comfortable," he said. "I've kept the shade drawn and the fans going." He pointed at the small, caged fans in all four corners overhead. Wyn gave him the tickets.

When they were alone, Faith sat on a long, padded bench beneath the window. "You're probably thinking about our being together all night," Wyn said. "I'll stay out of your way."

"It doesn't matter," Faith said, amused despite her predicament.

"Can I bring you anything?" Wyn asked. She seemed so helpless.

Faith said, "What I need you cannot bring me." She curled up on the bench, using her arm for a pillow, and closed her eyes.

To Wyn's left a chair, upholstered like the bench, stood beside the sink. He inched toward it and sat down slowly, as though he might break the chair, and at last he breathed easily.

Faith fell asleep quickly, exhausted by the strain she had endured since her arrest. She had not slept in her cell, had lain on her cot wide-eyed through the night.

Wyn sat watching her. When the passengers began to board, he thought she might wake, but she slept on. She slept through the first convulsive movements of the train, and when they emerged from the tunnel beneath the Hudson and the deep, extended steam whistle announcing the train's arrival in Jersey City filled the compartment, she didn't stir.

Long afterward Wyn heard a knock on the door and, as he reached it, a second knock. A dining car waiter said, "Evening. Conductor says you probably want dinner in here."

Behind him Wyn heard Faith. "Thank you. Yes, in here."

The waiter extended two large menus. "You can ring when you're ready."

Wyn said, "Wait." He closed the door and leaned against it, facing Faith. Something in his face frightened her, and she backed away into the window seat.

"What is it? What's wrong?" she asked, extending her right hand until she felt the window, as though she needed support.

"You've been hiding since we got to Pennsylvania Station," Wyn said. "You don't have to hide." He took a step toward her, took another. "You haven't done anything. You're innocent." He watched her and gently said, "You're innocent." He nodded. "Okay?"

Surrendering herself to him, she said, "Okay."

He grinned, turned completely around, reached the door in two giant steps, and opened it wide to face the waiter. "When does the dining car open?"

"First call is six," said the waiter. "Not many comes to first call, Sheriff," he said, trying to be helpful. "Might happen you'll be all alone, just you two, Sheriff."

"I'm not a sheriff," Wyn said. "Don't call me Sheriff again, understand?"

"Yes, sir." The waiter's head bobbed up and down. "Yes, sir, I understand."

Wyn saw a woman in the corridor stop and stare at him. "When does it fill up?" Wyn asked, looking at the waiter. "When is the dining car full?"

"Nowadays we're never full," the waiter said. "Seven o'clock is the time most people come. Most people like seven o'clock."

"Seven o'clock," Wyn said. "Put us down for seven o'clock."

"I come fetch you, Sher— I come fetch you," the waiter said.

"Come when everyone else is there," Wyn said. "Keep two places, and come for us last, understand?"

"Last, yes, sir," the waiter said, backing into the corridor. "Come last," he said, closing the door.

Still wound up, still steaming, forced to keep himself under a tight check, unable to explode, Wyn closed the door. "Is seven all right?" he asked.

Faith sat upright, feeling years older than Wyn, centuries older, felt ancient. "Seven is fine."

When the dining car steward led Faith and Wyn to a table, she wore a turban that covered her hair completely. The steward seated Faith and left menus beside their plates. "I can recommend the steaks," he said. "We have some prime western beef tonight."

Wyn opened the menu. The menu was à la carte, so Wyn saw a price beside each entry. A ten-ounce sirloin steak cost $1.25. Besides dinner, he had to pay for breakfast and lunch tomorrow. Wyn looked for something other than steak.

"When do we arrive tomorrow?"

Faith's question startled him. They had barely spoken in the last hour or more. Wyn lowered the menu. "Around three," he said. "I'll tell you exactly." He reached into his jacket for the tickets.

"No, no," Faith said. "Around three is close enough."

"I suppose we ought to order," Wyn said. She nodded, looking at her menu. "You're probably hungry after that place."

"I am," Faith said. "I'm starved. I haven't eaten since . . . I couldn't . . . not with them, not with those . . . whatever they are."

"They're gone," Wyn said. "You're out of there."

"Out of *there*," Faith said. She did not continue, did not need to continue. Her journey had only begun.

"And we're here," Wyn said. He could not help her, could not pretend, but he had to try. He grinned. "And we're both hungry."

Faith watched the clean, callow young man reading the menu. She needed him, needed an ally. She could not trust Serena or any Castleton. Serena's flowers only alerted Faith to danger. The boy she faced would not harm her. She was totally and helplessly alone, dragged from her world, on her way to their treacherous and powerful world. "You order for me," Faith said.

He shook his head, abashed. "I can't. Honest."

"All right. I will," she said. "How are hamburgers and french fries?"

"Sounds good," he said, and grinned. "Sounds perfect."

Faith ordered for them, and after the steward had left, she could see Wyn shifting in his chair, searching for something to say, something worldly and clever. "May I ask you a personal question?"

"You can ask me anything," Wyn said. She made him forget everything, forget his badge, and the gun, and the handcuffs, and the reason for the handcuffs, made him forget Earl and Max Isbell, waiting for them, forget Holt Castleton waiting for them.

"Why did you become a sheriff?"

"Deputy," Wyn said. "I needed a job, and jobs have just about disappeared since the Depression started. And my father is the sheriff."

Faith could not couple the sly little sheriff with this boy she faced until she remembered the house in Rego Park, remembered the kitchen and eating in the kitchen, sitting between her father and Marge. She dismissed all of them, dismissed the boy's father. "You make it sound easy," Faith said. "It can't be."

"Making probationer was easy because of Pop—my father," Wyn said. "We trained with the Highway Patrol, and they're *not* easy."

"Do you like your job?"

"Right now, no," Wyn said. "I mean, not this, not taking you . . . I mean, it's not *you* . . . Yes, it is. Bringing you in . . . I sound like the village idiot."

"You're just nervous," Faith said.

Wyn said, "Maybe we ought to change the subject."

"We can't," Faith said, facing him. "We're trapped. Both of us are trapped together."

The waiter set food before them. Both sat back, both silent, waiting for the intrusion to end.

They were the last to leave the dining car and, entering the compartment, discovered the berths made up, one on either side of the bench below the window. "I should have told you right away," Wyn said. "I'll be in my clothes." He held the door ajar. "You can change, and when you're ready, you can call me," Wyn said, leaving the compartment.

He stood in the aisle, rocking with the swaying of the car. The lights were dim. A shrill whistle sounded, long and mournful. Ahead the vestibule door opened, and a porter came down the aisle carrying two pillows, the white pillowcases shining. The porter stopped to knock on a door. A man in pajamas opened the door, took the pillows.

Wyn watched the door of the compartment. He had been standing out in the aisle an awfully long time. He couldn't remember when they had left the dining car. It seemed like an hour. How long did it take a woman to get ready for bed? He crossed the aisle, put his ear to the door. Wyn heard only the click, click, click of the wheels on the rails. He stepped back. She had been okay when they left the diner. "How do you know?" he asked himself. "She's heading back to be booked for *murder*! She's a prisoner! What if she—? Cut it out," he said to himself. "She wouldn't do anything. You're *crazy*," he said, but sprang forward and knocked on the door. "Everything all right in there?" He listened. Why didn't she answer? "Everything all right?"

She could have locked the door. But why would she lock the door? Wyn tried not to think of why. He knocked again and listened hard. He waited until he could no longer wait and turned the door handle. "When you didn't answer, I—"

Except for a shaft of moonlight, the compartment was in shadows. Faith sat on the bench at the window still dressed. She had removed her turban, and her hair fell over her shoulders. Steam covered the window like gauze. And through it, in the distance, Wyn could see a huge silver moon lying in the trees like a trapped balloon. As the car rocked and the door swung shut, Wyn saw Faith's forefinger moving down the window from top to bottom, top to bottom, making spaced lines in the steam. Wyn said, "Don't!" like someone in pain. He lunged forward. "Don't!" he said, dropping down on the bench and taking her hand. "Stop it," Wyn said.

"Isn't it beautiful?" Faith said, looking out at the moon in the distance.

"You're beautiful," Wyn said, and he kissed her. Faith's lips were soft, warm and soft, and he put his arms around her, bringing her to him.

He took Faith by surprise, but she welcomed his daring. His confidence made him all the more valuable to her. Faith let the boy lead, making herself a willing captive. She clung to him, the protector who would shield her from the enemies poised to destroy her. Faith would not release him, tilting back her head and holding him close.

"You're the most beautiful . . ." he said, kissing her once more.

Her warm lips against him, she said, "We've never used our names. Wyn. Darling Wyn." She slipped her arms inside his jacket. "Come closer," she whispered. He felt her hands, exploring, felt her body fit into his, felt her lips part against his.

Faith inflamed him, and she was as demanding as he, falling back onto the bench with him. They were unleashed, tearing at their clothes.

He looked down at Faith in the moonlight. "Is this all right for you now? Can you . . . Is it dangerous?"

"Are you afraid?"

"I'm afraid to hurt you—your condition."

"You won't hurt me," she said. "Never . . . ah," she said as she found him. "I have you," she whispered. "I have you now, lover. Now and forever." She raised her hips, her silky fingers keeping him prisoner. "Ahh, you darling." She raised her legs, crossed her ankles across his back. "Deeper," she said. "Go deeper. Go deeper, deeper!"

He felt her teeth dig into his shoulder, and he cried out, a hoarse, feral cry, a cry of discovery, of elation, of triumph, of power!

Her voice rose above his, as wild, as abandoned. "Go now!" she demanded. "Go with me now!"

Biting and clawing, she carried him away, took him higher and higher, carried him to the summit where the world exploded, flinging him into the void until he returned to discover Faith in his arms.

"I love you," Wyn said impulsively. He had never used the words, never thought of using them. "I love you," he said.

She took his face in her hands. "Do you, darling?"

"Yes, yes," he said. "I love you, Faith. I love you." She made him giddy with happiness.

"Oh, my darling," Faith said, kissing him. "Oh, my beloved darling. How I've longed for you to say those words," she said, lying. "How I prayed. I love *you* too."

Now he was hers.

———※———

JUST AFTER THREE O'CLOCK the following afternoon, Wyn sent the porter for the conductor and waited in the aisle. When the conductor appeared, Wyn said, "We'll stay until everyone is off and on. Call us just before the train is ready to pull out of the station."

He returned to the compartment. Faith sat on the bench, and when Wyn joined her, she took his hands in hers. "I'm about to lose you."

"You'll never lose me," Wyn said.

"I didn't kill him," she said.

"You're innocent," Wyn said. "They can't prove anything. They have no proof."

The train stopped abruptly, throwing Faith against Wyn. She pressed herself against him. "If only we could keep going and going," she said. The train moved forward, creeping into the depot. Faith released Wyn and rose. "I'd better get ready," she said. "How do I get ready to be tried for murder?"

On the concourse in the station Earl leaned against his car, turning his head away from the blinding locomotive light. "Here they come."

"What do you think, Sheriff? Do you think she did it, her and Boyd Fredericks?" asked Arver Long.

"Wasn't there," Earl said. "How can I say?"

"From your experience, Sheriff," Long said. "You've had a lot of experience."

"You're right about that, Arver. And I'll tell you what I've learned. The only thing I'm ever sure of is what they tell me."

"Who's they?"

"You'll find out soon's you've had enough experience," Earl said. He pushed up his hat, eyeing the passengers leaving the train. "Do you see them?"

As Long looked around the platform, Faith and Wyn left the compartment, following the conductor. In the vestibule the porter saw them coming and took their bags.

Wyn went ahead. He left the train and raised his hand to help Faith down. As she joined him on the platform, he saw the black-and-white. "They've come for us."

"For me," Faith said. "For the prisoner."

"Not for long," Wyn said.

Faith looked at the hayseed, looked at her only hope. "I'd like to believe you."

"Here they come," Earl said.

"I see them," Long said. "She is one great-looking woman."

"Tell the nigger to stow the suitcases in the trunk," Earl said. He removed his hat as his prisoner approached. "Wish I could make this easier for you, Mrs. Castleton." She utterly ignored him, entering the car. Wyn put his back to the black-and-white, taking Earl's hand and dropping the gun and the handcuffs into it before joining Faith.

At the courthouse Len Egan stood on a chair so he could look out the basement windows into the parking area. He saw them coming, then saw Wyn helping her out of the sheriff's car. She was a knockout, like they all said. Len returned to the counter to raise the hinged section. He pulled down on his shirt cuffs.

Once they were inside, Earl said, "Over here, Mrs. Castleton." He nodded at Len. "Deputy Egan, book Mrs. Castleton."

Wyn said, "I'll book her. I'm delivering Mrs. Castleton, and I'll do the booking."

Len Egan watched Earl, waiting for orders, and Wyn waited, ready for . . . anything. "You do that," Earl said. He removed his hat. "Mrs. Castleton, none of this that's happening started down here with us." Earl skirted the water fountain on the way to his office.

Behind them Arver Long walked into the door with his shoulder. He was carrying their luggage. "Leave it for me," Wyn said. "I'll handle it. Mrs. Castleton?" Wyn gestured. "Over here, please."

At the counter Wyn bent over the large open ledger, hiding it with his body. Below NAME he wrote, "Faith Venable Castleton," and on the facing page, below CHARGE, "Suspicion of murder."

Faith opened her purse, holding it upside down over the counter. "I can help," she said. "I know the ropes now. I'm a quick study."

When they were gone to the cells in back, Len Egan bounded forward as though he intended to follow them. "Is that the Promised Land or isn't it?"

Arver Long dropped into a chair, taking Len's newspaper. "You're not telling me she's better than Peaches Klem?"

"Peaches Klem! Wash out your mouth," Len said. He looked back at the door to the cellblock. "I swear to God I'd be willing to die after one night with her."

Inside, with Faith, Wyn stopped at a steel door. Faith said, "Are the cells . . . ?" and looked away.

Wyn took her chin, raised her head. As he kissed her, Faith held on to the lapels of his jacket, pulling herself toward him. "This is the last time."

"Not for us," he said. "There will never be a last time for us."

She put her fingers against his lips and then against hers. "Promise."

"Promise," he said, and opened the door.

There were ten cells in the cellblock, five on each side. "It's the last one on the right," Wyn said. "There are two windows. It's the coolest."

A single, unshaded lightbulb hung over the center of the cell-block. At the end of the short corridor Wyn opened the door with bars. He had to lock her in the cell. He looked for the right key on the key ring. His hand shook. In the cell Faith moved backward, toward the wall. As she put her fingers to her lips to send Wyn a kiss, a shrill, piercing cry rang out. "Faith!"

Boyd leaped up from the cot in the cell facing Faith's and threw himself into the door. *"Faith!"*

Wyn found the key, slipped it into the lock, and looked up, facing Faith for an instant before leaving her.

"Are you angry with me?" Boyd cried.

"No, I am not angry with you," Faith said. She sat down on a wooden stool beside the cot in her cell.

"Why are they doing this to us? I can't believe it's happening!" Boyd said. "I'm in *jail!* For *murder!* Faith!"

"Stop screaming," she said, irritated. "I'm in jail too. I'm just as miserable. I'm just as afraid."

"At least we have each other," Boyd said. "We're together again."

"Be quiet!" Faith said harshly.

"We're alone," Boyd said. "No one can hear us."

"I can hear you, and I've heard enough," she said, furious.

Len Egan came through the door, jingling the keys on the ring. When he stopped at Boyd's cell, he saw her on the stool, legs crossed like someone in a dentist's office. Just seeing her made Len Egan feel nutty. He opened Boyd's cell door. "Your ma's here."

Back in Earl's office, Wyn asked, "When is the arraignment?"

"Beats me," Earl said. "Ask Max Isbell."

"I'm asking you," Wyn said. "She's been locked up in New York, and now she's locked up here. She'll be in there with the drunks we pick up tonight." Wyn had learned early that not all drunks dropped off to sleep. Some moaned in imagined pain and agony, some wailed, some gave way to DTs, delirium tremens, and among these some inflicted minor or serious damage to themselves, bashing their heads into a wall or into a door. "In the morning they'll be in court," Wyn said. "She's entitled to the same treatment we give drunks."

"Whyn't you head for home? You couldn't have got much sleep last night," Earl said.

"Not much," Wyn said.

The telephone rang, and Earl raised the receiver. "Sheriff." Wyn turned to the door, but Earl raised his hand, beckoning him. "She's here," he said into the telephone. "Wyn brought her in a little while back. She's signed, sealed, and delivered." Earl listened. "I hear you." He looked up at Wyn. "Max Isbell wants them arraigned tomorrow."

———⊙———

BY SEVEN O'CLOCK the following morning Wyn was sipping his second cup of coffee, sitting on a stool in his usual diner, showered and shaved and wearing a fresh uniform. He had to stay away from the courthouse until his father got there in order to avoid any suspicion an early arrival would provoke.

Faith would not be given anything until the courthouse cafeteria opened at eight o'clock and a deputy brought breakfast over to the cellblock. At this thought Wyn slid off the stool. He could not carry a pot of coffee to Faith like someone from the Salvation Army, but he could no longer remain in the diner, miles away from her.

He drove slowly and, reaching the courthouse, saw his father's black-and-white. Wyn almost ran into the basement. He found Earl at the counter with Walter Messinger, a deputy working the night shift. When Messinger went to a desk with a typewriter to complete an accident report, Wyn said, "You were right yesterday. I'm beat. I thought I'd hang around today, maybe go over to municipal court for the arraignment."

"Sure, take it easy," Earl said.

"How about you? Are you coming over?"

"You can tell me the outcome," Earl said.

The municipal court, the primary county court, occupied a corner of the courthouse basement. Physically it was like no other courtroom in the building. Along the eastern wall a row of windows were level with the parking area. Along that wall ran a sloping corridor, a chute caged off from the courtroom by heavy wire. The chute reached to the street floor of the courthouse, and a marshal there guarded a door opening to the cage. Below, a thick wire mesh gate opened into the courtroom, and here another marshal stood guard. As each case was called, he brought the prisoner to the bench.

The municipal court ruled on offenses up to but not including felonies and could impose fines of up to a thousand dollars and penal terms, in the city jail or the county workhouse, of up to but not exceeding one year. It could also bind over for trial prisoners charged with serious crimes, its gravest responsibility. And the municipal court judge could fix bail.

In a corridor in the basement Wyn met Orville Platt, an assistant county attorney. "It's a madhouse," said Platt. "Old Judge Fletcher likes his name in the papers. He filled the place with reporters. He gave passes to every reporter he could find."

They had to fight their way into the courtroom. At the gate at the bar someone tugged at Wyn's arm. He looked down at Olive sitting in the first row on the left side of the courtroom. She held a handkerchief, and her eyes were red. "Are you happy now? Are you all happy?"

Wyn said, "Mrs. Fredericks, I'm not—" but broke off to follow Platt through the gate. Beyond were identical wooden counsel tables, one on each side of the aisle. Max Isbell sat on the right, near the cage. Wyn walked past him to the wall beneath the windows.

He could see Faith, halfway up the cage, standing among the dregs of the night, her white face like alabaster. He tried not to look at her, but couldn't stop looking. He felt useless, felt like a coward. Once more, without warning, Wyn imagined Faith in the electric chair, saw the straps binding her, and he closed his eyes in torment.

"All rise!"

The marshal's voice boomed through the courtroom. Judge Abner Fletcher, a pudgy, pasty man with a few strands of gray hair combed carefully across his head, climbed the steps to the bench.

Judge Fletcher, the sitting judge in the municipal court, had been expelled from a small Georgia college after a black cleaning woman had escaped from his dormitory room one night and run, beaten and bleeding, her clothes torn, onto the campus, where she collapsed.

Abner Fletcher had come home to read the law with his uncle, Cord Madison, the senior partner in one of the two most important firms in the state. When Fletcher failed the state bar examination the third time, he asked his uncle for help. After Fletcher had been admitted to the bar, Cord Madison found a job for him in the Statehouse in Raleigh. Ten years later, after Fletcher's wife had taken their two children and left him, left Raleigh and the South, he came home, and Cord Madison managed the appointment to the municipal court.

Fletcher took his place and, when the courtroom quieted, struck the bench with his gavel. "We have a full docket here today. Clerk, call the first case."

At his desk below the bench the clerk said, "Call Harlan Sims Fox."

In the chute a man said, "Make way." He wore filthy overalls, and his face was blotchy and covered with sores, his nose swollen and crimson from years of bad moonshine. "Make way."

At the counsel table Max Isbell turned a pencil over and over and over. "That son of a bitch Fletcher is going to keep us here all day," he muttered.

The hapless drunk crossed the courtroom. He stopped between the counsel tables and faced the bench. "Harlan Sims Fox," the judge said. "Back so soon, Harlan? Not a very smart fox, are you, Harlan?"

"No, sir, Your Honor."

"No, sir," Fletcher said. "Drunk and disorderly, Harlan. How do you plead?"

"Guilty, Your Honor," the drunk said.

Fletcher leaned forward, folding his arms across the bench, an avuncular patron. "Whatever will I do with you?"

"Guess it's the workhouse for me, Your Honor," said the drunk.

"Guess again, Harlan," the judge said. "We're not issuing you another free ticket for another sixty days of clean sheets and three meals a day. Get out of my court."

A ripple of laughter swept through the courtroom as the drunk turned, swaying, and made his way to the gate. He almost fell over the bar as he tried to free himself. Olive left her seat to open the gate for the alcoholic, and on the bench Fletcher said, "Next."

Another drunk came out of the cage, another foil for Fletcher's bullying and amusement. The judge repeated his performance, tormenting the wretch below the bench before sending him, too, back into the streets.

Fletcher continued slowly, sparing none of the prisoners. The laughter in the courtroom brought a smug, pleased smile to his face, assuring the victim he faced of more ridicule.

At exactly eleven o'clock, two hours after Abner Fletcher had entered the courtroom, the clerk said, "Faith Venable Castleton." He paused. "Boyd Fredericks."

The courtroom fell silent. The wire door swung open, metal rasping against metal. Boyd followed Faith down the chute into the courtroom, searching for his mother. Boyd saw her and raised his hand before turning to stop beside Faith, facing the bench. Fletcher looked up. "Are the People present?"

Isbell stood up at the counsel table. "The People are present, Your Honor."

"Is the accused represented by counsel? Mrs. Castleton?"

Faith said slowly and distinctly, "I am innocent."

"Mrs. Castleton, in our system of justice, everyone is innocent until proved guilty," the judge said. "The right to counsel is guaranteed every defendant. If the defendant does not have the means to retain counsel, the court will provide counsel for the defendant."

"I did not kill Kyle Castleton," Faith said.

Fletcher banged the gavel. "The defendant will speak only when she is spoken to. Let's have a clear understanding about procedure in my court." He banged the gavel. "Mrs. Castleton, do you wish to be provided with counsel?"

"I do not need a lawyer to say I am innocent."

"So be it," said the judge. "Boyd Fredericks, do you wish to be provided with counsel?"

"I am innocent," Boyd said.

Fletcher banged the gavel. "Clerk will read the charge."

"Faith Venable Castleton," said the clerk. "Conspiracy to commit murder."

"How do you plead?" asked the judge.

"I'm innocent!"

"The defendants having entered a plea of innocent, it is my duty to hold you for trial," Fletcher said. "I'll set bail at twenty-five thousand dollars."

"I'll give you a check," Faith said.

Fletcher leaned over the bench, making a face. "A *check?*"

"My check," Faith said. "For fifty thousand dollars. For Mr. Fredericks as well as myself."

Behind her, Olive began to weep once more, pressing the handkerchief to her eyes, head bowed and her shoulders shaking.

"A fifty-thousand-dollar *check!*"

"I have never harmed another person," Faith said, "but I was taken from my home, taken to jail, taken a thousand miles to another jail. I have been locked up, *caged,* like an animal." She took a checkbook from her purse. "I want this . . . torture to end." She raised the checkbook. "My bank is the Stuyvesant National in New York. The bank will transfer funds to my checking account. A check for fifty thousand dollars. To whom?"

"Quite a speech, Mrs. Castleton," the judge said. "You're pretty good at it too. I guess you should be. It's part of your business. Now my business is presiding over my court. In my court the accused posts a bail bond. The bail bond comes from a bail bondsman licensed by the state. The court can furnish you with the names of some bail bondsmen and—"

"Your Honor," Isbell said, on his feet.

"—you can take your pick, how's that?" The judge looked at Isbell. "All right, Mr. Isbell."

"May I approach the bench, Your Honor?"

Fletcher nodded. Isbell crossed the well, and the judge leaned forward. "I'm listening."

"I have a suggestion," Isbell said, so quietly not even the clerk at his elbow could hear him. "I suggest the court appoint someone to telephone Mrs. Castleton's bank in New York. She must have fifty thousand dollars in her account, or she wouldn't say she did. As of the telephone call, that money will belong to the court. The money will be as good as here."

"No, it won't," said the judge. "It will be in New York, in her bank, in some Jew's hands. You're telling me to trust some Jew in New York?"

Isbell looked up at the judge. "You can't mean that."

Fletcher pointed with the gavel. "There's half a dozen bail bondsmen across the street."

"Let's continue in your chambers," Isbell said.

"In my—? Who the hell are you? . . . Telling *me* we're going to my chambers!"

Isbell stepped back from the bench. "I'll see you in your chambers, Your Honor," Isbell said, and this time the clerk and everyone in the courtroom heard him.

Fletcher glared down at the lean county attorney in the white suit but finally banged the gavel. "Five-minute recess."

Isbell went ahead of the judge, through the door and down the narrow corridor behind the bench. He stood at Fletcher's desk until the judge entered. "Let's get one thing straight, Isbell." Fletcher plopped down into his chair. "You don't scare me. I can cite you for contempt same as I would any snot-nosed little shit starting out."

"Shut up." Isbell pointed at the wall. "We've got a courtroom full of reporters out there. You brought them in here, Abner. By tomorrow morning everyone in America will read Faith Venable got thrown back in the cooler because the rednecks wouldn't take her check for bail." Isbell shook his head. "Not a chance, Abner."

"I don't give a good hoot in—"

"Shut up. People are expecting me to try a murder case," Isbell said. "I'm carrying eighteen different kinds of trouble on my back already, and you are not adding to the stack."

"You don't scare me, Mr. County Attorney."

"You're lying," Isbell said. "I sure hope you're lying." He sat on a corner of Fletcher's desk. "If you're not, if Earl Ainsley puts her back in the cooler, I resign. I call Lucius Peete today with the news. The straw that broke the camel's back. Let the old man tell the Castletons, starting with Holt. Hell, my house is paid up, and the cabin is clear. I can feed my family on what I shoot. And I'm *not* lying, Abner. And then you will wish you had never been born." Isbell raised the telephone and set it in the center of the desk. "Do you call the bank in New York, or do I?"

Eight minutes after Max Isbell's ultimatum in the judge's chambers, Faith took her checkbook from her purse. As Wyn saw her open it and begin to write, he swung around to fight his way to the rear of the courtroom. "Coming through," he said, trying to keep his voice down. "Coming through." He had to reach Faith before the reporters began to maul her. "Let . . . me . . . through." At the rear of the courtroom he started pushing and shoving his way to the aisle. Wyn didn't care if his father fired him.

Faith tore the check from her checkbook and offered it to the marshal who waited at her side. He carried the check to the bench.

Wyn used both elbows. "Let me through!"

On the bench Fletcher glanced at the check. "Give this to the clerk," he said, and hit the bench with the gavel. "Faith Venable Castleton," he said. "Boyd Fredericks. Bail in the amount of twenty-five thousand dollars having been posted for each of you, you are herewith released."

Behind them Olive rose and opened the gate to reach Boyd. The newspapermen leaped up en masse to fight their way to the aisles, trapping Wyn. "Let me through!" he cried.

Bang! Bang! Bang! Bang! "Order! Order! Marshals!" A row of three marshals advanced on the reporters. The courtroom became quiet. The judge said, "The prisoners are warned they remain under the jurisdiction of this court and are forbidden to leave the county." Bang! "This court is now adjourned." Fletcher held on to the gavel, waiting for the photographers.

Trapped in the aisle, Wyn put his hands on the shoulders of two men, used them as poles to vault onto a bench, and stepped over it to the bench ahead.

A photographer raising his big camera knocked Olive into Boyd, almost toppling both. "Over here, Mrs. Castleton!" he yelled.

Faith saw a wall of faces, heard a babble of voices calling out her name. She could not escape. She had come to the limit of her endurance. The courtroom grew dark, grew darker.

"I've got you," Wyn said, his arm around her. "Hold on to me," he said, "and don't let go." His arm tightened around her, and he extended his free hand and used it like a fullback, stiff-arming newspapermen. "Coming through!" Wyn said. "Coming through!" He shoved his hand into a reporter's face. "One side! One side!"

Wyn swung to his left, almost losing Faith as he grabbed a marshal. "Give me a hand!" Wyn held on to him, using the marshal for interference, his left arm around Faith as they kept moving toward the cage in the corner of the courtroom.

One photographer jumped up on a chair at the counsel tables. Another stepped from another chair to the tables, aiming his camera at Faith and calling to her.

Holding a handful of Wyn's shirt like a toddler with a parent, Faith came back from the pit. The courtroom brightened, and a rising tide of anger welled up in her. She released Wyn. "I'm all right."

He held on to her. "Almost there," he said, and to the marshal he said, "Open up! Open up!"

The marshal unlocked the door with bars, and Wyn pushed him into the cage, following with Faith. "Lock it, man!" As Wyn brought Faith up the ramp, he looked back at the marshal. "Get the door up here open for me."

"It's open now," the marshal said.

Wyn glanced at Faith. "We're almost in the clear."

She did not reply. They came through the upper door of the cage onto the first floor of the courthouse. Wyn used a shortcut. He took Faith through the boiler room, and seconds later they were in the parking lot. "The reporters will head for the sheriff's cars," Wyn said. "We'll use mine."

"Where are you taking me?"

Wyn hugged the courthouse wall until they were a few feet from his car. "Keep your head down," he said. They ran to his car. Wyn opened the door. "Come on."

Faith didn't move. "Where are you taking me?"

"Gee . . . I didn't think of anything except getting you out of the courtroom." He gestured, looking for newspapermen. "Get in the car."

Faith didn't move. "I'm still a prisoner," she said. She turned slightly, looking at the courthouse as though she faced an enemy. "I can't leave the county. I need someplace to stay. A hotel."

"Okay, okay," he said, looking for reporters. "Just get in."

He took her elbow, but Faith shrugged off his hand. All of a sudden Wyn faced a stranger. "All I have are the clothes on my back," Faith said. "I need my luggage."

"I'll bring it," Wyn said. He held the car door. "Get in, okay? Faith?"

"I won't leave without my luggage." She looked at Wyn. "I will not run. I won't run."

She sent a shiver of awe and admiration down Wyn's back. "I'll fetch your luggage," Wyn said. "Just get in the car. If the reporters see you, we'll be here all day. Faith?" He didn't come near her, didn't make a move lest she bolt and he lose her. "Will you wait in the car?"

She stepped up onto the running board and dropped into the seat. Wyn shut the door. He wanted her to stretch out on the seat and hide as she had when he had driven her from the Castle to her train, but he knew she would defy him. "Try not to look toward the front of the courthouse," Wyn said.

Inside, Wyn saw Earl at a corner of the counter, listening to a farmer accusing a neighbor of poaching. Wyn stopped in the center of the counter, facing Clem Carpenter, a deputy standing behind the booking ledger. "Let's have the key to the property room."

"Yeah, for what?"

"Give me the key," Wyn said. "I'm in a rush." He bent over the desk and yanked open the top drawer.

"Hey, I need you to sign—" said Clem Carpenter.

"Later," Wyn said, striding past his father. In the corridor, alone, he began to run.

When he came back, carrying Faith's luggage, her vanity case under one arm, the farmer had gone, and Earl stood alone at the counter. "Mrs. Castleton posted bail," Wyn said. "For Boyd Fredericks too."

"I heard."

"I'm taking her to a hotel," Wyn said.

Clem Carpenter jumped up from a desk, holding a clipboard. "You gotta sign for that stuff."

"I'll be back," Wyn said.

"Gimme the keys to the property room," Carpenter said. Wyn stopped, set down a suitcase, and tossed the key ring at the counter. Earl caught it.

"Much obliged," he said.

Wyn expected to be trapped by newspapermen when he came out of the courthouse. But he was alone, and he found Faith alone. "We'll be out of here in two shakes," he said.

Driving into the street, Wyn said, "The best hotel in town is the Piedmont Plaza, but it's kind of expensive." He turned at the corner.

Faith thought, insanely, she might laugh. Her young champion had managed to provide a moment's respite from the day's agony, the agony of all the days and nights of constant, abiding fear, which crept into her body like a freezing wind. "I'll manage," she said.

"I want to be able to see you," Wyn said. "Somewhere. Not in the hotel. The hotel is out, I guess, for us."

"We can't meet."

"We could meet somewhere," Wyn said desperately.

"It's too risky," Faith said. "For you as well as for me. Especially for you. Sworn to uphold the law."

"Faith." Wyn looked at her, and when she turned, he said, "We haven't broken the law."

"I'm afraid," she said.

"I wouldn't do anything to hurt you," he said. "There are places . . . no one would see us."

"I want to," she said, always the actress. "But for now it's impossible. We cannot risk being seen."

"You can trust me," he said. Wyn gestured. "Piedmont Plaza. Up there in the next block." Wyn wanted to keep going, wanted to disappear with her. "I can't even touch you."

Faith put her hand on his thigh. "You'll touch me," she said. "And I'll touch you." He could feel her searching fingers as she whispered. "You belong to me. All of you belongs to me."

Wyn turned in toward the curb, and a uniformed doorman came out from under the marquee, his face wrinkling with distaste at the jalopy.

Faith said, "This is good-bye . . . for now." Wyn got out of the car, took the luggage from the backseat, and set it down on the curb. He came erect, facing Faith. "Thank you," she said, "for everything."

Wyn touched the brim of his campaign hat with the tips of his fingers. "Yes, ma'am."

He had to get back in the car, had to drive away from the hotel. He looked in the rearview mirror, but she had already gone inside, and Wyn drove to the courthouse as though he were in a funeral cortege.

At headquarters Clem Carpenter said, "Didn't expect you back this quick. Where's the lady from murder one?"

Wyn went to the counter, reaching for the morning newspaper. "She escaped."

"Not from me she wouldn't," Carpenter said. "She's a looker, that one. Think she killed him?"

"Why don't you go to lunch or something?"

"I bring my lunch," Carpenter said. "Do you? Think she killed him?"

Wyn couldn't run. He had to listen, had to take it from the idiot. "Do you?"

"Beats me," Carpenter said, and made a face, hitting the desk with his fist. "Damn! Sheriff said to see him when you— Here's Wyn, Sheriff," Carpenter said as Earl came through the door to the cellblock.

Earl went to the counter, facing Wyn like a prisoner being booked. "Your girlfriend called."

The newspaper's sports section slipped from Wyn's fingers. He had just left her. "Called?"

"Yeah . . . Kay," Earl said. "Said to tell you. She left her number. Christ, don't you even have your girl's number?"

"She's not my girl," Wyn said. "We've had a few dates. And I have her number."

"She said you should call her."

"Okay . . . thanks." Wyn bent to pick up the sports section, but Earl didn't move. Taking the hint at last, Wyn went to Len Egan's favorite desk in a corner. He set the telephone directly in front of him and hid it with his body as he dialed Kay. He could see his father pretending not to listen. "Hello, it's Wyn."

In the front hallway beside the staircase in her house, Kay said, "Hello," and smiled, and sat down slowly, all warm and fluttery.

"You called," Wyn said. "Is something wrong? Are you okay?"

The sound of his voice made her okay. "I'm fine," Kay said. Morning after morning she had wakened certain he would call, convincing herself she would see him that night. When he did not call, especially after the picnic on the hill, she tried and failed to dismiss him from her mind, to dislike him, to be angry. She tried to fill her days. She met with girlfriends, played tennis, went to movies with her mother, went on walks. And always and everywhere she missed Wyn, even in church, in the pew with her mother listening to the minister. She had never called a boy, never heard of a girl calling except for something special, a party at someone's house or a hay ride. A girl needed a reason, and Kay finally had one.

"Is it your mother?" Wyn asked.

"My mother is fine."

"Well . . . good. That's good," Wyn said. He could not get comfortable. Christ, he hadn't even spoken to her since the picnic. Why hadn't he called? "Kay I've been awfully busy around here. I even went to New York."

"I read about it," she said. Kay had cut out the newspaper accounts and pasted them in the scrapbook.

"Anyway . . ."

"Wyn? Did you hear about Jim?"

Suddenly Wyn didn't want to hear. "What about him?"

"They didn't renew his contract," Kay said. "The school board—"

"They *what?*" Wyn's voice carried across the big room. Clem Carpenter looked up, holding a thermos bottle and a cup, and at the counter Earl watched Wyn.

"The school board didn't renew his contract," Kay said. "They—"

"Those bastards," Wyn said. "Why not?" Wyn looked over at his father, suddenly realizing why. "Jim Anderson is the best coach in town. Kay?"

"They didn't give him a reason," Kay said. "They sent back the contract. Wyn, he signed it months ago. School starts next week."

"Those bastards. I'm sorry, Kay, I shouldn't be talking this way."

"You're angry," Kay said, "and so am I. They're so unfair, Wyn. They're rotten."

"How is Jim handling this . . . mess?"

"He won't show his feelings," Kay said. "He's always the same way. He thinks only of Edith, how she is feeling."

"Like he acts with everyone," Wyn said. "How is Edith?"

"Just awful," Kay said. "She's so mad. She keeps reading the letter from the school board aloud."

Wyn had to see Jim and Edith. And he couldn't go without asking Kay to come with him. "I'm going over there," Wyn said. "I mean, after work. Do you want to come with me?"

"I'll be there," Kay said. "Edith is on her way to get me."

"Okay, I'll see you there," Wyn said.

When he hung up, Kay stayed in the chair, her face burning. She put both hands against her face, feeling the heat. She had to change. Kay decided to wear the dress she had worn on the picnic.

Wyn left the corner desk and stopped in front of his father. "Jim Anderson is out. The school board wouldn't renew him."

"I could've told you that."

"*You* could've?"

"Jim Anderson voted against the murder indictment," Earl said. "So it became only a matter of time before he got rewarded for his heroic stand."

"Did they have to fire him? There isn't a better coach anywhere," Wyn said. "Do you know how long he's been coaching at Washington High? It's the only place he ever worked. Christ, he graduated from Washington. He was born here."

"Will you grow up?" Earl said. "And keep your voice down, huh? Now listen and you'll learn something. I sure as hell hope you'll learn something. You don't try very hard." Earl raised his right hand with three fingers raised. "Three jurors voted against the indictment, three out of twenty-three. You need only fourteen to indict, so those three didn't mean a good goddamn. And Holt Castleton doesn't give a good goddamn 'cause Max Isbell delivered the indictment. But someone on the school board, maybe more than one, learned how Jim Anderson voted, and now he's joined the great army of the unemployed. The other two votes came from women. Sooner or later it'll cost them or someone near them. People don't want to be around anyone who argues with the Castletons." Earl frowned. "Christ, where the hell have you been all your life?"

Wyn watched the clock all afternoon. At five o'clock, after roll call, he ran out of the courthouse to his car. He drove directly to a gasoline station two blocks from the courthouse. He parked in front of the telephone booth and called the Piedmont Plaza. "Mrs. Faith Castleton," Wyn said. "This is New York calling."

"Room eight-nineteen," said the hotel operator. "I'm ringing."

"Hello . . ."

He could almost feel her beside him. "Hi . . . hello," Wyn said. "How are you?"

"I'm all right," Faith said. "Tired. I'm bone tired." She sat down on the bed.

"Is this okay? Calling you?"

"How can I say? How can I tell you?" She had drawn the curtains and turned up the lights, and now, on the bed, she wanted to darken the lights, wanted to be in the dark, as though she could shut out the enemy host that threatened her.

"I told the operator I'm calling from New York," Wyn said. When she did not reply, he added, "I wish I could help."

"You're sweet," she said.

"Do you need anything? Can I do anything?"

"Can you? No," she said. Faith wanted the silly dreamer to go away, to stop mooning over her.

"I wish—" he began, and stopped. "All I'm trying to say . . . you know what I'm trying to say." Wyn listened. "Hello? Hello?"

"I'm here," Faith said.

"I'm here." He wanted to hold her. "Get some rest," he said, cringing because he sounded like a sap. What else could she do? "I mean . . ."

When he paused, Faith said, "Thank you for calling."

"I'll check in tomorrow," Wyn said. "I'll keep in touch, okay?"

"Okay," Faith said, and replaced the receiver. She left her hand on the telephone, facing an amateur's painting of the Rialto Bridge in Venice on the wall. The traveling clock she had used since her first road tour stood beside the telephone. She murmured, "I may as well," and raised the receiver to ask for a room-service menu from which she could order dinner. But as the hotel operator responded, Faith set down the telephone. She removed her dress. Hiding here in her room would be like giving up, would be the end for her. Faith pulled off her clothes like someone racing the clock, leaving her dress, bra, panties, stockings on the bed and the floor. She crossed the bedroom for a shower.

Wyn went home to shower and change clothes, in a hurry to see Jim Anderson. When he reached the coach's house, Wyn saw lights in the open garage.

He found the older man looking through a drawer in his work-bench. "Hey, Jim."

Jim saw the big kid coming and knew why he had come. The coach wanted to hug him and, astonished by the depth of his emotions, turned his head. Jim took a stack of road maps from the work-bench drawer, shuffled through them without reading anything until he could trust himself. "Hey, yourself."

Wyn stood in the entrance. "I just heard what the school board did," he said. "It stinks, Jim. It really does."

Jim forced a smile. "You're right, Wyn."

"I can't believe they did this," Wyn said. Being with his old coach ignited a mounting anger Wyn could barely control. "It's god-damn unbelievable! They fired you! After what you've done for Washington. Honest to Christ!" Wyn could not continue, so great was the rage that engulfed him.

He made Jim smile. The coach pulled the light cord dangling from the rafters, darkening the garage. "Everyone knows the reason for the letter," Wyn said. "Those bastards. Those gutless wonders." They walked toward the house.

For Jim, the outrage of his friends and neighbors, the sympathy he heard wherever he went, the endless questions, the repetition of the empty threats to punish the board members became agonizing.

Like Wyn, they all were his champions, and they all were helpless. And he could not hide. The telephone rang all day and into the night. "They can kick us, but they can't put us down," Jim said.

Wyn stepped away. "Christ, is that all you can say? I remember you saying that in the locker room."

"I'm still saying it."

"Goddammit, get mad."

"I am mad," Jim said, knowing he could not convince Wyn. He could not convince himself. The abrupt end of his career at the high school had devastated him. Still, he had to help Edith, had to prop her up.

"What are you going to do now?" Wyn stopped beside a fake well complete with a pump handle that Edith Anderson had turned into a planter. "Just roll over and die?"

"Not quite yet," Jim said. He showed Wyn the stack of road maps. "Do you remember Ernie Dowd?" Jim slapped his leg with the maps. "No, I guess he was before your time. Ernie helped coach baseball and football here back when we could afford to pay assistant coaches. Anyway, he's down in Ocala, Florida, coaching football. We've always kept in touch. In fact, Edith and I were down there with him and Carol last summer. About two months ago he wrote asking if I could give him the name of anyone who could carry a full teaching load and also take on the baseball team." Jim put his arm around Wyn's shoulders, and they left the planter. "We're driving down tomorrow."

"How's Edith taking this?"

"Ask her," Jim said.

Wyn followed Jim into the house, and when Kay saw him, she stood up in front of her chair. "Hello, Wyn."

Wyn said, "Hello, Kay," and went to Edith, who stood over a small mound of sweaters, examining each. "I didn't hear about this until Kay told me today," Wyn said. "I'm awful sorry, Edith. Whatever good that does. They're rotten, Edith. They're rotten."

"Who? The school board? The Castletons? Who, Wyn? I can't go around hating everyone," Edith said.

"Make it easy on yourself," Jim said. "Don't hate anyone."

She whirled around, holding a sweater at the shoulders. "We can't all be perfect."

Jim stopped beside her, and Edith turned her face away as though he had meant to kiss her. "Come on now," Jim said. "You're not mad at me."

"I am! You're so perfect!"

"Far from it."

Wyn stopped beside Kay. "What they did is criminal . . . it's like a criminal act."

Edith said, "You tell him, Wyn."

"I'd like to tell *them,*" Wyn said. "Tell all of them. Tell them what they've lost." He felt Kay's fingers brushing his, and her hand slipping into his hand, trapping him.

Jim said, "I would take it most kindly if we could drop the discussion."

He could not be ignored. "You always win," Edith said, frowning, but when Jim put his arm around her, she hugged him.

Jim said, "I'm glad you came, Wyn. It means a whole lot to me. Take a load off." Jim led Edith to the sofa, and Wyn took a chair beside Kay's. For more than an hour Jim kept them talking steadily, steering the conversation from one safe subject to another, just as he had handled his youthful teams following hard losses. After an hour or more he raised both arms, stretching. "We're planning an early start." He came out of the couch. "Beat it, you kids."

Jim went to the door. "Wyn, when we come back from Florida, come on over." He kissed Kay on the cheek. "And bring Kay."

Wyn said, "Thanks," and followed her out. As they left the house, Wyn said, "He's the best."

Once they were inside the car, he felt Kay's hand on his hand on the gearshift. "Hello."

Wyn grinned, wanting to disappear. "Hello."

"I've missed you," Kay said. "I'm not supposed to tell you. You're supposed to tell me. I don't care. I've missed you."

He was not a liar, but he could not be cruel. She was so innocent. "I've missed you too."

Her hand tightened over his. "Have you, Wyn?"

"I've just been busy every day," he said. "We've all been busy. We're swamped down at the courthouse. Everything is happening at once."

"But why haven't you called? I shouldn't be asking that question, shouldn't be . . . nosy," Kay said. "There's a whole lot I shouldn't do, I guess."

"You can ask me anything," Wyn said.

"I thought after the picnic . . . after our afternoon, you would—we—I haven't seen you since that afternoon," Kay said.

"I'm sorry," Wyn said. He came to a stop sign, and as he shifted gears, Kay's hand fell away from his. "Kay, I'm really sorry."

She looked down, playing with her hands. "Is it because . . . I wouldn't?"

"No!" Wyn jammed his foot down on the brake and swung into the curb. "Kay!" He turned in the seat to face her. "The picnic, the whole afternoon, was perfect," Wyn said. "Okay?"

Kay said, nodding, "Okay."

"Okay," Wyn said, driving out from the curb. She would ask him to come in. He knew she would ask him to come in. Christ.

So he had to beat her to it. A block from her house Wyn said, "This early shift is killing me. I keep falling over myself. Well, it's only another week."

"You're telling me you have to go."

He stopped in front of her house. "It's not—" he began, and paused. Tell her! Tell her! "Kay, I haven't called . . . why I haven't called . . ." Look at her! Look at her! "I think we shouldn't see each other so often."

Kay said, "Shouldn't—" and stopped, feeling forsaken. "Why? Wyn?"

"I think . . . I can't . . . I think we shouldn't."

"What have I done?"

"*Done?* You haven't done *anything*," Wyn said. "It's me. I—" He got out of the car and came around it for Kay.

Going up the walk to her house, they were a million miles apart. "I wish you would explain . . . tell me so I can understand," Kay said.

"It's not you, nothing you've done," Wyn said. "It's . . . how I feel."

They reached the porch. "You're tired of me," Kay said.

"Don't, don't," Wyn said. "I'd better— Good night," he said, and pecked at her cheek.

She flung her arms around him.

"Kay, Kay . . ." He freed himself, stepping back. "I really— Good night," he said, retreating quickly.

She watched him return to his car and drive off, watched the taillights until they vanished. Kay unlocked the front door and, as she crossed the threshold, heard her mother. "Kay? Is that you?"

She said, hiding her agony, "I'm home, Mother." and fell back against the door. She had begged! Begged! She darted forward, scurried through the house to the sun parlor. She snatched up the scrapbook with all the clippings of Wyn. She had to tear it to pieces, had to burn it, destroy it. Then she stopped short, raised the scrapbook, and wrapped her arms around it as the tears came and she stood in the dark, weeping silently.

In the car Wyn drove furiously, hoping to blot out what he had just done. He passed the street leading to his room in Mrs. Metcalfe's house. A mile beyond, Wyn turned toward the business district, and when he saw the Piedmont Plaza, he shifted down into second gear, crawling past the hotel, saying good night to Faith before heading home.

———◦◦◦———

SITTING BESIDE FAITH AT LUNCH, Serena said, "No lawyer in this state will be loyal to you, no matter if he swears on his beloved mother's life." A liar all her life, Serena believed everyone lied. "You are the wrong Castleton." After Frank Burris left that morning, Serena ordered the cook to have a small table put out on the long terrace and set for lunch.

"One of the reasons I asked you to come is that now, at last, I can be of service," Serena said. "I have the name of a lawyer you can retain. Fields Dunning in Atlanta. He is one of the smartest lawyers in the entire South."

Serena could not be certain if Faith was listening. Seated beneath a green-and-white-striped awning, Serena saw Faith in profile. Now in early pregnancy Faith seemed luminous. Serena thought of the women in the reproductions of paintings of the Renaissance masters that she had pasted up in Miss Geraghty's art class, long, long ago. And the ravishing beauty beside her was very clever and intelligent. In Lucius Peete's office Serena had heard Lucius offer to help Faith, seen her rise and heard her decline and leave, leave with her treasure safe and snug in her belly. Faith had been born with too much, endowed with too much, like Holt. She and Holt were equals, and Serena, trailing, despised her. "May I call you Faith?"

Faith turned to her. "Yes. Of course."

"And I am Serena. And you are offering me a second chance." Serena raised her hand as though warding off an interruption. "I hated you from the night of your marriage," Serena said. "I hate all the Castletons, and when you became Kyle's wife, I included you," Serena told Mrs. Castleton. Serena told the absolute truth. She learned sitting beside her father long ago, in going after anything she wanted, to buttress lies with a careful mixture of truth.

"You came to share what belonged to me and what had been taken from me," Serena said, and she gestured at the Castle.

Faith looked across the field to the huge red mass where Kyle had tormented her. "You would like to watch it burn," Serena said. Faith turned to her, startled, and Serena smiled. "I am not clairvoyant," Serena said. "There are no lukewarm feelings over the Castle. It is always love or hate with the Castle."

So all of Faith's fears were validated by the woman she feared. Serena's yellow roses had followed Faith the morning after she checked into the Piedmont Plaza. Cameron Bliss personally came to the hotel, and he did not leave the flowers with a bellboy or the desk clerk. Bliss brought the flowers to Faith's door. He put himself at her service, offering to set the flowers in water, offering a vase or vases if these were not available. Serena telephoned the following day. "How can I help?"

In New York, behind bolted doors and protected everywhere in the building by a determined building staff, Faith felt uneasy about Serena's flowers. Here, where she was surrounded by Castletons and accused of murder, the yellow roses became spears pointed at her heart. The flowers surrounded her, holding her captive. She could not throw fresh flowers into the wastebaskets, giving chambermaids juicy news to spread through the hotel. When Serena's call included an invitation to lunch, Faith, unprepared, said, "Lunch? . . . I usually skip— When?"

"Come tomorrow." So Serena made it clear she would not be seen in public with Faith. But she trapped Faith, and cornered,

Faith needed time to prepare herself for battle. "Can we talk in the morning?"

"I'll call at ten." She could not let Faith call her, so the hotel telephone operator could announce, gleefully, that Kyle Castleton's widow, accused of murdering him, had a champion: Serena Burris.

Faith set the telephone on the night table. She did not want to see Serena, who cared nothing for her. No one cared here, no one except her young rustic, her Lochinvar, the boy controlled by his crafty, scheming father.

In the morning, when Serena telephoned, Faith said, lying, "I'm sorry. I'm not well. The doctor told me to expect such days."

Serena called the following day, and again Faith blamed her pregnancy. She thought of ending the charade, thought of being blunt, spoke aloud in front of the mirror. "You don't give a damn about me. You're trying to convince me you're my friend. You've looked me over. I am a dumb New York chorus girl who landed Kyle, and you have a plan into which I fit. Well, lady! You are a million miles— Stop!" Faith said, turning her back on the mirror, disappointed in her sophomoric indulgence. She had avoided daydreams and fatuity all her life, and her lapse only exacerbated her fears of coping with Serena. But Faith was alone, and despite her distrust and misgivings, she knew she must accept Serena's invitation. Faith had nothing to lose.

"Miss Serena?"

Faith looked up and saw the stunning black woman at the entrance to the long terrace. Honeychild said, "It's Mr. Burris calling."

"Later . . ."

"He says it's important, Miss Serena. He must talk with you," Honeychild said.

"I won't be long," Serena said. As she pushed back her chair, Honeychild disappeared. Serena had warned the black woman against mentioning her visitor to another human being.

In the shade under the striped awning Faith was left in a kind of hermetic silence. The Castle loomed over her like a mountain, and nothing moved, not a leaf. In the taxi on the way to Millionaires Row Faith had fought against hope, tried to prepare herself for disappointment. She had failed. Serena's help consisted of a name, a lawyer in Atlanta who would save her. Faith could not continue for too long without a lawyer. But he could not be Serena's lawyer.

Behind her Serena said, "I hope you will look upon this house as a place of refuge," and Faith turned to her, managing another smile, waiting to flee.

IN THE PRESIDENTIAL SUITE of the Piedmont Plaza Colin Inscott felt like a drink before lunch. But he refused to contaminate himself with the rotgut produced in southern backwoods stills. In East Hampton Colin had a bootlegger he could trust, a man capable of delivering bonded whiskey from Canada. He decided to have lunch in the suite, and as he went to call room service, the telephone rang. "Inscott here."

"This is Lucius Peete, Mr. Inscott," said the aged Castleton lawyer. "I am calling from the company."

Colin said slowly, "Of course. Lucius Peete." He caught his breath as though he had been thrust into a freezing Arctic blast.

"Mr. Inscott?"

"At your service, old chap," Colin said. He had to go slowly, slowly. Lucius Peete kept the family secrets. "At your service, sir."

"I wonder if you might come by," Lucius said.

Colin's outlook changed as he heard Lucius's request. His horizons altered, and his future glowed with limitless promise. He moved across the room, carrying the telephone to the length of the cord so he could see himself in the mirror. Lucius Peete had called for only one reason: The Castletons had come to their senses. They realized they could not deny Gaby's husband his rightful share of the B Stock. "Come by? Delighted to oblige, old boy. Name the day."

"I thought you might come now," Lucius said.

Colin grinned, a full smile of delight. He dismissed all ideas of lunch. He couldn't be sated with food, his senses dulled and his body drowsy. He needed to be alert. Lucius Peete's call made the day the most important of Colin's life. "Your servant, sir," Colin said. "We're barely a stone's throw apart. I'll pop over."

"I've sent a driver for you, Mr. Inscott," Lucius said. "He should be there anytime now."

The old goat was pretty sure of himself, Colin thought as he set down the telephone. Lucius Peete sat up there in his office waiting to make a deal. Colin walked into the bedroom to choose a blazer and an ascot. Lucius Peete was in for a little surprise. Colin had been making deals since selling his first horse. He had bought and sold and traded horses more than half his life.

Colin returned to the parlor to knot his ascot in front of the mirror. As he did, he imagined stacks of money on either side of his reflection, saw the stacks rising and rising in neat piles, and only the doorbell stopped the money's growth. "Moment!"

He opened the door and faced an enormous man in the blue uniform of the company's guards. Howard Bly had been a college fullback. "Mr. Inscott?"

"Righto." Colin flicked his wrist. "Lead on, my man, lead on."

Below, as Colin came through the revolving doors, the hotel doorman said, "Over here, Mr. Inscott." He opened the rear door of a company car.

"Good man," Colin said, looking back at the doorman. Colin liked the fellow's style. With the proper training the fellow could make a damned good houseman. Good housemen were hard to come by.

When the guard stopped a few minutes later, Colin said, "Much obliged. I'll find my way."

Above, at his desk in his office, Lucius had to push himself erect, rising so slowly and with such difficulty that Colin thought of helping the old man. "Thank you for coming, Mr. Inscott." Lucius extended his hand.

"How did you know where to find me?" The old man's hand felt like a cold towel.

"I assumed a man of your background would seek the appropriate accommodations," Lucius said. Seated, he said, "Can I offer you something cold? Sue Ann has a variety of potables in the refrigerator."

Colin could see right through the old schemer's palaver. "Look here, old boy, we're both aware of why I'm here. This is a business meeting. Why not get down to business?"

"Very well." Lucius took his monocle from a vest pocket. "To put it plainly, sir, Gaby—Mrs. Inscott has decided on a divorce."

Colin sprang from his chair. "A divorce! *She* decided! Wait a minute!" Colin slapped his chest. "How about yours truly? How about what I decide? There are two of us involved in this marriage," he said, his British patois forgotten. "Tea for two."

He didn't see Holt come out of the bathroom, running his wet hands through his hair, burned almost rosy by the sun. "Sit down," he said harshly.

Colin turned and, seeing Holt, stepped back, bumping into the chair. He lost his balance and swayed. His arms thrashed to steady himself until one hand found the chair back. Holt said, "We're just starting. Sit down."

Colin believed if he obeyed, he would lose everything. He had to defy Holt. Colin's legs wobbled, and he felt a fluttering in the calves of his legs. He hated Holt for making him afraid and hated himself for being afraid. Colin turned toward the desk to block Holt out of his sight. "I think we ought to talk about this . . . development."

"It is the reason for this meeting, sir," said Lucius.

"Where's Gaby? I'd like to see her," Colin said as Holt stopped beside Lucius Peete.

"I represent Gaby," Lucius said. "I am her counsel."

"And I am her husband," Colin said. "It's not you she's trying to divorce. It's me, and I am not planning any changes in my marital status," Colin said, fighting for his life. His ascot now felt like a noose, choking him. He tugged at it, using both hands to free himself.

Lucius said, "Mr. Inscott—" and stopped as Colin strode through the office swinging his ascot like a lariat. Colin threw back the door. Howard Bly filled the doorway.

Holt said, "Call me if you need any help, Howard," and slowly, the ascot dangling askew, Colin returned.

"To begin," Lucius said. He raised a sheaf of papers backed in a blue binding. "Mrs. Inscott will file for divorce here, in this state. The charge is mental cruelty. Should you decide to contest the divorce, Mrs. Inscott is prepared to produce witnesses who will corroborate her testimony."

Colin could see Gaby's best witness standing right beside Lucius. Holt had chased him out of the Castle, and Holt had no doubt told Gaby to divorce him. "I want to see my wife," Colin said.

"Let me continue," Lucius said. "Mrs. Inscott is neither cruel nor vindictive. You, above everyone else, are testimony to her generosity. She has instructed me to say you will be allowed to live in the home in East Hampton for the remainder of your natural life. . . ."

Colin heard "remainder of your natural life" like a death sentence he could not escape. He could not pay the household help, could not pay the monthly utility bills, could not feed the horses.

"No divorce," Colin said, fighting for his life. "I will not agree to a divorce. I will not—" he said, and stopped. He would not allow himself to cringe and cower in front of Holt. Colin raised his hands, slipped the ascot around his neck, made a simple knot with a flourish. "Nice try," he said, "but no cigar. I'm leaving now. That gorilla at the door can't stop me, and you can't stop me. I'm on my way to adopt a baby. Gaby will be a mother before you can get those divorce papers into court. And I'll be a father. And the B Stock stays in the Inscott family forever."

"It won't do," Lucius said. "You are mis—"

"Watch my smoke," Colin said, interrupting.

"—misinformed," Lucius said. "Only natural-born children of the heirs are eligible to inherit the B Stock."

Colin grimaced as though he had been struck. He heard Lucius say, "As for the Inscott family," and saw the old man put the monocle into his eye, bending over the desk. Lucius had made notes. "The Inscott family . . . here," he said, raising the legal pad.

"There is actually some question of whether or not your marriage is legal," Lucius said. "Your father was, in fact, Carlos Inasmora, a naturalized citizen. While he discarded the name in favor of Clinton Inscott, he did not legally make the change. So you are not legally Inscott, the name on your marriage certificate. Your wife is willing to ignore this element of your past. She wishes only a speedy termination of this part of her life." Lucius dropped the legal pad and took a folder from the desk. "Your authority to occupy the East Hampton house," he said. "You must sign wherever your name appears." Lucius pushed the folder across the desk. "Do you have a pen?"

———※◎※———

As COLIN HEARD LUCIUS PEETE decide his future, Zoe Kellerman, who had served on the grand jury, stood in the lobby of the Piedmont Plaza using a house phone. "I'll be at the desk," she said. She replaced the receiver and took her umbrella from the shelf beneath the telephones.

Zoe Kellerman came home around six o'clock on the day Faith and Boyd left the municipal court out on bail. She got the afternoon newspaper from the stoop and climbed the stairs to the bedroom. "How are you, hon?" She bent over the bed to kiss her husband.

"Okay, I'm okay," said Gregory Kellerman. His face and hands were gray, and his cheeks were sunken.

"Look at me." Zoe sat down in the rocker beside the bed. "How are you?"

"No complaints, Zoe."

"When did you *ever?*"

"I'm fine," he said. "How are *you?*"

"Old reliable. They're out on bail, Greg. She put up the money for him too, for Boyd Fredericks."

"Double bail," he said. "I wouldn't have expected that from her!"

"You wouldn't? What would you expect, Sherlock Holmes?"

"Search me," he said.

Zoe raised the newspaper and almost immediately lowered it, making a face. "Why didn't *I* think of that? They can't leave the county."

Zoe Kellerman called at nine o'clock the next morning, telephoning from the bedroom. "I'm calling Mrs. Faith Castleton."

"Room eight-nineteen," said the hotel operator. "I'll ring."

Zoe pushed the telephone against her breasts, nodding in triumph at her husband. "Piedmont Plaza, like I thought."

"Hello."

"Mrs. Castleton, I'm a real estate agent, although I have my own company," said Zoe Kellerman. "I'm not part of a gang that'll hound you. I thought you might like to be in something quiet during this period, something away from the madding crowd, as they say." Zoe always talked fast on the first try, trying to say everything she had rehearsed. "I thought you were probably tired of crowds, Mrs. Castleton, and would be in the mood for a short-term lease. I can show you some lovely homes, furnished, of course, ready for occupancy. I'm available to you at your convenience, available whenever—"

"Come this morning," Faith said, interrupting.

Zoe showed Faith everything she had listed. Faith rarely left the car. She said, "No," or "I'm afraid not," almost before Zoe stopped the car in front of a house. She tried two days running, and when she returned to the Piedmont Plaza late in the second afternoon, she said, "Wish I could've pleased you, Mrs. Castleton. That sounds almost snotty, but it's not meant that way. If you knew me, you'd know that."

"I know it already," Faith said.

Two days later, around noon, Zoe drove from Deer Hollow Road directly to the Piedmont Plaza. She left her car in front of the hotel, promising the doorman she would be out in five minutes. She almost ran through the lobby to the house phones.

When Faith came out of the elevator, Zoe said, "I honestly feel I have what will suit you, Mrs. Castleton. I honestly do. I drove here straight from the rental house." She walked a step ahead of Faith like a guard clearing the way. "I went through it once and decided you had to see it."

In the car Zoe said, "It's eight miles out, Mrs. Castleton. It's way out, which is what you might like, and it's wooded. It's a ritzy area, as far as I'm concerned, the ritziest. I always dreamed of living there. It isn't Millionaires Row, but you're probably pretty sick of Millionaires Row by now. I'm sorry. My big mouth.

"The way this house came up is a freak really," Zoe said. "Jane Abel—she's the owner, her father left her the house—she called me out of nowhere this morning. She's going West for a few months. Someplace called Jackson Hole. Oh, there are two domestics. In fact, the help are part of the rental, Mrs. Castleton."

Zoe didn't pause to draw breath. She delivered a biographical sketch of Jane Abel, as well as of Jane's father, who had built the house. She praised Ray Close, the realtor who had developed Deer Hollow Road, and when, mercifully, Faith saw the trees ahead, Zoe said, "I said wooded."

The developer had sold building lots of three and five acres, and the building sites were hacked out of the thick woodland. So the houses were hidden by the trees: pine and magnolia and cedar. Chinquapin bushes, dwarf chestnuts, grew in abundance, as well as pomegranates. "Someone planted a bunch of mahogany," Zoe said. "Decided to grow his own furniture. They didn't do so well."

She turned onto Deer Hollow Road and soon turned again, into a cul-de-sac, a lane topped with gravel. "Only six houses in here," Zoe said. She drove to the end, and on the right Faith saw a two-story house of fieldstone with a slate roof and leaded windows and half timbers, which were only cosmetic. Faith saw four chimneys. The builder had borrowed every architectural element developed in England for more than a millennium. "Brace yourself for the furnishings, Mrs. Castleton," Zoe said. "You'll be back in King Arthur's—"

"I'll take it," Faith said.

"Shouldn't you—? I'm glad you like the place, Mrs. Castleton. I really am," Zoe said. "I hated disappointing you earlier." She opened the car door. "You'd still better brace yourself."

Zoe walked around the car to join Faith. "Mrs. Castleton." Zoe opened the umbrella over their heads. "Before we go in, I'll just take a minute to say something. I didn't say it when we began, because you might have thought I was trying to get on your good side. What I want to say, Mrs. Castleton, I was on the grand jury. I know you're innocent. I voted against the indictment. Three of us voted against the indictment."

Faith raised her arm like someone off-balance, taking Zoe by surprise. "Something wrong? What's wrong, Mrs. Castleton?"

Faith said, "I . . ." A great rush of nausea engulfed her, rising in her throat, and a haze came down over her. She teetered and thought she would fall but felt Zoe Kellerman's hands steadying her. "I—wait," Faith said. Slowly, carefully she sat down on the running board.

"It's your condition," said Zoe. "After what you've been through, you need peace and quiet."

Faith could make out the lanky woman standing over her in the haze. Then the haze cleared, and Faith saw Zoe's extended hand. "I'll help you up. Hold on to me."

Faith took Zoe's hand, rising to her feet. "I have one condition," Faith said. "The servants can't stay." She could not keep spies in the house.

"Those two practically raised Jane Abel."

"They're being paid," Faith said. "I'm giving them a paid vacation."

When Wyn, working the night shift, called Faith around

nine o'clock, she told him she had leased the house on Deer Hollow Road.

Jane Abel wasn't leaving for Wyoming until Friday, so Faith could not take possession until Saturday morning. Zoe came for her and gave Faith an envelope. "Two sets of keys, in case you lose any," Zoe said. She didn't tell Faith she had gone to a locksmith for the extra set. "If you need anything, Mrs. Castleton. Anything."

———◦❮◦❯◦———

WYN HAD THE NIGHT SHIFT through the weekend. He couldn't go to Deer Hollow Road in daylight, couldn't risk being spotted at the Abel house. And he could not wait until Monday. He had not seen Faith since driving her from the courthouse to the Piedmont Plaza. He had to see her.

Len Egan was working nights with Wyn. Saturday morning, when Wyn returned to the courthouse, he cornered Arver Long after the day shift roll call. "I've got a big favor to ask you, Arver."

"Yeah? What?" Long asked. "My partner's waiting out there."

"Will you switch with me tonight? Work for me tonight? I'll owe you, okay?"

Long stroked his mustache. The little peckerwood had more gall than brains. Wyn said, "Pick any night, Arver. Christmas. New Year's Eve. Thanksgiving." Arver didn't seem to be listening. "Halloween!" Wyn said. They all hated Halloween.

"Yeah, but me and the wife got something doing tonight," Long said.

"I'd sure appreciate it, Arver."

Long almost walked out to the parking area. He didn't need a code book to figure out Wyn's drift. Wyn meant he would put in a good word for Arver with the old man. "You're asking me to work a double shift, work twenty hours," Long said. The little bastard nodded. "And what do I tell the wife?"

Wyn had to see Faith. "I'll give you two for one," he said. "I'll do two nights for you, Arver. Any two nights you pick."

"Yeah, well . . . Remember, any two nights I pick," Long said.

Wyn grabbed his arms. "Thanks, Arver," he said, releasing the deputy. "Thanks a lot."

That night, in the lane off Deer Hollow Road Wyn swung immediately into the grove of pine and cedar and the splendid, towering magnolia trees. He felt light-headed, and when he opened the car door, he remained behind the steering wheel, his entire body tense with anticipation. When he exited the car, he had to stop and lean against a magnolia tree. Nothing in his life had ever affected him as strongly. He said aloud, "Wow . . ." and moved forward, keeping to the trees. Far ahead he could see lights, like distant stars. He tried to spot any movement, tried to spot Faith.

As he came out of the trees, running, the lane brightened, and behind him a car entered the cul-de-sac. Wyn turned back into the grove.

He heard the unmistakable sputtering of a Model T Ford. Wyn decided the car must belong to one of the rich kids in Deer Hollow. But the Ford stopped in front of the Abel house. Someone came out of the Model T and walked to the door. A light appeared over the door, and Wyn saw Boyd Fredericks walk into the house.

Boyd Fredericks! Why had she sent for Boyd Fredericks? Maybe he had come without being asked. She couldn't have asked him when she had told Wyn, "Come after dark."

In the trees Wyn remembered Faith had paid Boyd's bail, paid twenty-five thousand dollars so he could go home to his mother. And he had driven his mother's car to Deer Hollow Road before Faith could even unpack. Wyn moved through the trees, trying to see them in the house. He moved in a slow circle, unable to remain still. He could not stay out here, in the trees in the dark, waiting. Yet he had to wait. No one, no force could have removed Wyn that Saturday night.

At the front door Boyd spread his arms wide. "Surprise!" Faith let him in and closed the door slowly, testing it to be certain it was locked. Neither spoke until he said, "You're angry, aren't you? Why, Faith? What have I done?"

"We decided we shouldn't see each other," Faith said, reminding Boyd of the promise she had extracted from him when he made his first telephone call to the Piedmont Plaza.

Boyd could feel the entire evening crumpling before it even began. "Please don't be mad, Faith." He watched her, waiting for acceptance. "Nobody knows I'm here."

When she did not respond, he turned and went down the stone steps to the snug living room, complete with wood paneling and overhead beams. Boyd said, "Faith, I love your house. I really love it."

He bounded ahead and reached the grand piano near the fireplace. "And you've got a piano!" Standing beside it, he bent to strike several keys of an airy melody. Every move he made was a plea to gain Faith's favor.

He had dressed for the evening to please her. Boyd wore white flannels and a pale blue sport jacket, Olive's gift for his last birthday.

At the piano Boyd watched Faith follow him down the stone steps. He struck another chord on the piano keys and made himself smile. "Your piano needs tuning," he said. "Mother has the best tuner in town. I'll get him for you."

Faith could barely look at the silly, stupid fool. "What did you tell your mother?"

"My *mother?*" Boyd didn't understand Faith. "I told Mother I wanted the car so I could drive out here to see you." He stared at Faith. "What's happened to you? You've . . . changed. You're different."

"I have changed," Faith said. "I am accused of murdering my husband. You are accused of murdering him. The police say we are a pair of killers. And you're offering to have my piano tuned." She stepped away from the fireplace. "Good-bye," she said. "Don't come back."

"We're alone," he pleaded. "No one knows I'm here."

"Your mother knows."

"My mother!" Boyd said. "My mother wouldn't tell anybody."

"You could have been seen by someone on Deer Hollow Road. One of the help could have seen you, recognized you. The word will spread."

"Just let me stay a little while. Is that too much to ask? I haven't done anything wrong, Faith. I came here trying to pretend everything was fine, pretend we were still having fun, the three of us, the way we always did."

"The way we always did," Faith said coldly. Then, trying to be kind so she could be rid of him, she said, "The past is the past, Boyd. It is all over and done, do you understand?" She watched him. "It is the *past*, Boyd. It is finished." She raised her arm, pressed the palm of her hand against her forehead. Her head throbbed. "Go home, Boyd. Go away and stay away."

Boyd darted forward, startling Faith, and dropped down on the piano stool. "You are cruel, Faith," he said. "You are." He nodded. "I've learned that much in my life. Being cruel is easy. Anyone can be cruel." He looked up at her. "I could tell everyone what really happened that night."

The room became absolutely still. Boyd watched her carefully until Faith said, "Everyone has been told what happened that night."

"They haven't been told the truth."

"What is the truth?"

"That day at the inquest you told the coroner you heard the shot in your bedroom. And came out into the hall." Boyd held on to the piano bench with both hands. "You didn't," he said. "I saw you come out of the *sleeping porch*. When I got to the top of the stairs, I saw you backing out of the sleeping porch. I lied for you, Faith."

"Oh, God . . ." Faith's cry rang through the house. She covered her face with her hands. "Oh, my God. . . ." She fell forward, dropped to her knees in front of the piano stool, threw her arms around Boyd's middle, and buried her head in his lap.

Boyd was terrified. He fell back against the keys, and a harsh, discordant clang rang out. "Faith! Faith!" He tried to lift her head. "I didn't mean it!" he said. "I would never say anything! Never!"

He felt her arms slacken, and she raised her head slowly, looking up at him, her eyes wide with fear. Boyd wanted to die for hurting her. "Get up, Faith. Don't . . . kneel. Don't." He helped her rise, and he rose with her.

"You were my only friend," she said, her voice barely a whisper. "I believed you would be with me even if the entire world—"

"I am!" he said, interrupting. "Faith, I am your friend. And more. More than a friend. Forever."

"Promise."

"I promise," Boyd said. "Forever."

"Now I may sleep tonight," Faith said. "Hold me," she said, leaning against him as they moved slowly to the door.

Faith opened the door slightly. She turned to Boyd and cupped his face in her hands. "We'll see each other again, Boyd. Tell me when this is over, we'll meet again."

"I promise, Faith," he said.

In the trees in the inky night Wyn saw a band of light as Faith's door opened, saw Boyd leave. Wyn heard Boyd's footsteps on the gravel, heard the heavy groans of the engine as Boyd cranked the Model T, heard the loud, tinny clatter as the engine caught.

When Boyd turned the Ford in the big half-moon arc and drove to Deer Hollow Road, Wyn came out of the trees. He remembered his first night in the Castle, in his car at the gates, watching the single lamp, her lamp. He walked along the cul-de-sac to Faith's house.

The sound of the doorbell enraged Faith. The blithering fool had come back. She climbed the stone steps ready to strike him. She stopped at the door as though she were in the wings offstage, waiting until she could handle him again.

When the door opened, Wyn felt as though he had returned from exile. He could barely keep his hands at his sides. "Hello, Faith."

In her encounter with Boyd, Faith had forgotten the boy, forgotten he would come that night. The big, rawboned rube stood facing her, smiling like a kid on his first date. Wyn wore sneakers over his bare feet, his old cotton pants, and a faded crimson skivvy shirt. She had forgotten the size of him, forgotten the flat body.

Boyd's performance had drained her. She could not accommodate two yokels one after the other without a break. She needed time to recoup, needed to gather the strength for another performance. These . . . boys demanded too much. This one stood there with his dumb grin, needing only a straw in his teeth. Faith almost slammed the door in his face. But she needed him, and she could not continue without a lawyer. "Come in."

As she closed the door, Wyn looked around him, turning slowly. "You found a real nice house."

"Another cell," Faith said. She gestured, and Wyn followed her. "Another jail cell."

"This will end," Wyn said. She stopped in front of the fireplace.

"How will it end? I'm afraid to think how it will end, and I cannot stop thinking," Faith said. "I cannot stop. I must find a lawyer.

Someone who has lived here all his life, whose family has lived here as long as the Castletons, someone who is not afraid of the Castletons. Help me," she said, without acting.

"There's one guy," Wyn said. "Dan Cohen. His family has been around forever. My pop says the Ainsleys have been around since the Indians, but so has Dan Cohen's family. I can't tell you whether or not he's afraid of the Castletons, but he can't be afraid of much. Dan Cohen is the lawyer for the coloreds."

"Oh?" Faith put her hand against her forehead. "Is there no one else?"

"I'll keep trying to think of someone," Wyn said. He wanted to hold her and kiss her. But the issue of Boyd Fredericks intruded. Wyn had to dispose of that first. "I've been here awhile."

"Here?"

"Out there," Wyn said, pointing. "In the trees. I parked in the trees."

So he had seen Boyd. "I had an uninvited guest while I waited for my invited guest," Faith said. "Boyd Fredericks."

"Why did he come out here?"

Faith hugged herself. "He is afraid he will die," she said. "So am I. I'm afraid I will die."

"Nobody's going to die!" Wyn said.

"Of course," Faith said. "I had forgotten. The county attorney will admit he made a mistake. Dan Cohen, the Negro's friend, will make the judge apologize." She spoke in a monotone. "The mayor will give me the keys to the city. And your father will furnish me with an escort to the train. And you will lead the escort."

"Cut it out!" Wyn went past the piano to take her arms. "Faith! Cut it out!"

She raised her head. "Yes, Officer."

"Wyn!" he said. "Wyn, not Officer. Not for long. I'm quitting. I don't care what my pop says." Wyn pulled his wallet out of his pocket, flipped it open to display his badge. "I can't keep this." He tossed the wallet onto a massive leather sofa facing the fireplace. "I'm no good to you wearing my monkey suit."

"You mustn't quit!" Faith said. He could not help her in sneakers.

"I can't handle it this way."

"Handle?"

"I'm a deputy sheriff, a cop," Wyn said. "A good cop would go to work tomorrow morning and file a report. 'Boyd Fredericks, one of the two defendants indicted for the murder of Kyle Castleton, came to Deer Hollow Road last night—' " Wyn stopped and made a chopping motion with his hand. "The hell with it," he said. "I'll quit."

"Wyn." Faith took his hand, leading him to the leather sofa. When they sat down, she faced him. "Promise you will not quit," she said.

When he nodded, she said, "You must leave this house. I know where to find you if I need you. You must stay away."

"I can't stay away." He could feel her legs against his. "I can't."

"Listen to me," Faith said. "Please listen." She had to be rid of this moony kid, sitting there making eyes at her. "Please listen, and believe me, I want only what is best for you. Wyn, you shouldn't be in this house. I won't let you ruin your life. I refuse to ruin your life."

"*Ruin!* You've made my life complete," Wyn said. "Ever since . . . the train, ever since that night, I—I'm different. Faith, I feel . . . brand-new. I hop out of bed in the morning ready for anything. Just knowing you're here, in the same town is . . . everything. I love you, Faith," he said, and kissed her. Wyn gathered Faith up in his arms, claiming her for himself.

She said, "Wait," but felt his lips on her throat, on her hair, felt his lips on hers. She said, "Wyn, listen," her fingers against his cheek, but he kissed her fingers, kissed her hand, pressed her hand to his face.

"I didn't expect this, didn't believe, never believed this could happen to me," Wyn said. "You make me feel like I've just started living, like I wasn't alive and now I am."

The boy carried on like the hero of a Shubert operetta. She felt his arms close around her, keeping her prisoner, felt his lips hot against her breasts beneath the blouse. She remembered Boyd groveling, remembered Kyle disappearing without a trace and returning without even a greeting, remembered Ward Kirby, all the Wards, and all the bright, sophisticated, worldly sharks of New York, the hangers-on of Broadway, the sallow, pallid dregs of Broadway, and then, despite herself, she felt the stirrings of pleasure deep within her, the first uncoiling tentacles of desire that oozed through her, promising delight, promising abandon and madness, and a respite, however brief, from the executioner's shadow. Faith fell back onto the sofa and looked up into his eyes. She could not discard the boy. He had become her only solace.

———◆———

THE FOLLOWING MORNING Faith found Dan Cohen's name in the telephone directory and summoned him to Deer Hollow Road, and before the day ended, she had retained him as her lawyer and Boyd's lawyer. She could not allow Boyd to run loose.

———◆———

GETTING OUT OF HIS CAR, Frank Burris announced, "The old homestead."

Ray Deems reached into the backseat of Burris's car for his tennis rackets. He had changed into sport clothes in his room in the Piedmont Plaza. He backed away from the parked car, looking up at the sprawling brick house. "Little crowded, aren't you?"

Burris grinned. "We make do."

"I'll bet," said Ray Deems, a slim, redheaded man twenty years younger than Burris. Like his host, Ray Deems had started on municipal clay courts, become a college star and a nationally ranked player, and a member of the Davis Cup team. Burris liked playing with younger men who could run him around, and Ray Deems, now an insurance salesman, happened to be attending a convention.

Honeychild met them at the door. She wore a bright, airy dress cut low. "You're home early, Mr. Frank."

"I am," he said. "Fetch Miss Serena."

"She's not here," Honeychild said. "She left around noon."

"Then bring us something to drink, will you?" Burris said. "Ray?" Burris took his guest's elbow.

Ray Deems looked over his shoulder. "Where did you get *that?*"

"She's my wife's maid." Burris grinned. "And don't get any ideas."

"How do I stop?"

Burris took Deems through the house to his study. The redheaded man looked around the pleasant room.

"Did you do this, Frank?"

Burris said, pleased, "I did."

Deems went to a trophy case. "These are great."

"You've got a few yourself," Burris said.

"A few." Deems moved slowly around the study. "I haven't got the pictures, though. Old Cochet," he said, stopping in front of the French master. "And Vinnie Richards."

The telephone rang, and Burris crossed the room. "Hello."

A man said, "Is this the Burris residence?"

"It is."

"Good. Miss Serena Burris, please."

"She's not in. This is her husband."

"Of course," the man said. "Mr. Burris. How are you, sir? Dennis Packard here, sir. Of Charleston." Dennis Packard had not hesitated spending the money for a long-distance call to the Castletons. He would have called them from Australia. "May I burden you with a message for Miss Burris, sir?"

"She is not my daughter . . . sir," Burris said. "She is my wife . . . sir."

"Of course, sir. To be sure," said the caller. "My apologies, sir. May I leave a message with you, Mr. Burris? I have the crib. An absolute prize if I may say so. From the hands of Charles Clement. *Charles Clement* of Glasgow. With his name and the year, 1743. Please tell Mrs. Burris her crib is on the way."

Burris said, "Her cr—" and checked himself, watching his guest examining the photographs on the walls.

"Thank you so much, sir. Au revoir."

Burris left the telephone, pulling at the knot of his tie. He rubbed his neck. The sneaky bitch. "What do you say we get going, Ray?"

They played two hard sets, each winning one. At the net after the second set, Burris said, "Want to settle it?"

"I'd be arrested for manslaughter," Deems said. "Not in this heat, Frank. Thank you anyway."

After they had showered and dressed, Burris said, "Change your mind and stay for dinner."

"I'd like nothing better," Deems said. "But I told you, this is the last night of the convention. My boss is one of the speakers. He wants to see me there. And I want him to see me."

"Fair enough," Burris said. "I'll drive you back."

"In a pig's ear," Deems said. He went to the telephone. "I'll get a taxi. The boss is paying for this one."

When Deems's taxi left, Burris returned to the study. He could not be still. He left the study and returned with an ice bucket filled with ice, beginning a daily ritual. At the safari bar beside the radio, Burris took a thick jigger that held one and a half ounces and filled it with single-malt scotch whiskey. He filled a highball glass with ice and slowly, carefully emptied the jigger of whiskey over the ice. Finally he held the glass below the nozzle of a siphon and added the merest spray of soda water. Usually Burris sat down with his highball, but now he went to the windows and there sipped his drink.

Ordinarily Burris enjoyed the single drink he allowed himself each night. He limited himself to one because more whiskey made him more hungry and could make him add weight.

He remained at the windows, without moving, until he had finished his drink. Burris returned to the bar and set down the glass and went back to the windows. He could still hear the patronizing bastard in Charleston. The bastard had cost Burris the first set in the match with Ray Deems. Burris said, "Damn!" aloud, and went back to the bar for a second drink. As he filled the highball glass with ice, he caught a glimpse of Serena's car through the windows. Burris made his drink and sat down in his chair facing the radio. He heard the door open and close and soon Honeychild's identifiable footsteps. She stopped at the entrance to the study. "Miss Serena, she home."

Whenever Serena or Burris returned, they met, however briefly. Burris joined Serena when he came home from the company each day. Now, in his chair, Burris drank from his second drink, savoring his rashness, and when Serena reached the study, he did not rise. "Come in."

Serena perched on the arm of an easy chair near the open study door. Her bare arms were dark from the sun, and her coif of russet-colored hair, rising from her forehead, gave her an imperious air. The ugly duckling dominated the study, and Burris felt the distinctive stirrings of sex, undermining his resolve. "Would you like a drink, Serena?"

She became instantly wary. "You know I don't drink," she said.

He raised his glass. "This is a celebration," he said, and sipped his drink. "I hope it's a celebration." He eyed her intently. "Are you pregnant, Serena?"

She snorted in derision. "I am not pregnant."

"Still, a crib is on the way. So sayeth the man in Charleston."

"The crib is on the way to Faith Venable," Serena said.

Burris drained the glass, feeling betrayed and overcome with disgust for caring. "Why is the crib a secret?"

"It is no longer a secret—"

"Because I found out," Burris said. "You didn't plan on telling me. I'm not smart enough to trust with your plots."

"Stop, Frank."

"Smart enough or trustworthy enough," he said. "The crib isn't a bolt from the blue, not if you're involved. How long have you been courting her, Serena?"

He rose, turning the highball glass in a small circle, jiggling the ice. "You're good at it," he said. He thought of throwing the ice in her face. "I remember how good you are."

The atmosphere in the study had turned foul with loathing. Serena stood up to leave, but she remained. She had never deceived herself. Without him she would be a middle-aged stick, a withering, solitary spinster. "Frank, the woman has the keys to the company in her hands. She has Kyle's B Stock. If I can win her over, we win. I'd line the crib with rubies if it would bring her to my side. I would prostrate myself at her feet."

The next morning in his office Burris used his private telephone to call the chief of police in Pensacola, Florida. "Hank, it's Frank Burris."

"Frank, you old goat. What brings you to town? Where are you staying?" The chief had been a tennis teammate in high school in Pensacola.

"I'm not in town," Burris said. "I need some advice."

"You sound serious as hell," said the chief. "Are you in trouble?"

"I am not in trouble," Burris said. "Settle down and listen, will you? I said I need your help."

Three days later Burris's secretary opened his door and said, "A Mr. Vincent Fahey?" His secretary spoke only in questions. "He has an appointment?"

"Send him in."

Burris came out of his chair as a slight man in a dark suit entered. He carried a gray fedora. Burris couldn't guess his age. "Come in, Mr. Fahey."

Vincent Fahey closed the door, and Burris moved a chair over. "Sit down, sit down," Burris said. He returned behind the desk, glancing at his notepad. "You're from . . . the National Information Agency."

Fahey nodded. "Miami is the home office. But I move around some."

"I'll bet," Burris said. "Your line of work, you must move around a lot." For the first time in decades Burris felt the happy tingle of excitement, a sense of the risk taking he had carried onto the court.

"I go where they send me," Fahey said.

"Well," Burris said, "I'm sure you've read about us up here, about the Kyle Castleton shooting."

"Just what the newspapers have to say."

"There's more to the story," Burris said. "One hell of a lot more. Does the term *B Stock* mean anything to you?"

Fahey crossed his legs. He wore black high-top shoes. "B Stock. Can't say it does."

So Burris offered a brief explanation. "The B Stock is the real reason I sent for you," Burris said. "Every Castleton and everyone mixed up with a Castleton wants the B Stock."

"I'm following you," Fahey said.

"I'd like to keep up with what is going on," Burris said. "Maybe you can help me. I hope you can." He took a notepad and a pen from his desk. "Here's my private number. Call me here, not at home. And you can see me here anytime," Burris said.

Fahey took the square of note paper. "Oh, where are you staying?" Burris asked. Fahey told him. "You picked a nice place, a quiet, clean hotel," Burris said.

He walked to the door with Fahey. "Good hunting," Burris said. Back at his desk, Burris pulled back his arm and swung, following through to complete a forehand drive. He no longer sat on the sidelines.

O N T U E S D A Y M O R N I N G of the following week Earl sent Wyn and Len Egan to a county in the southeastern corner of the state for a suspect wanted in a series of burglaries. Earl figured they would not be back before nine o'clock that night at the earliest. He didn't want Wyn anywhere near the courthouse that day.

An hour after the two young bucks left, Earl summoned Arver Long. "You're with me today," Earl said. "We're going out to the Castle." Long took his old black-and-white, as ordered, and the sheriff pushed his hat low over his eyes so Long could not ask any questions.

At the Castle, Coleman opened the door. The men in uniform scared him. "Morning. What can I do for you two gentlemen?"

"Mr. Castleton," Earl said. "Is he in?"

"He's in, yes, sir," Coleman said.

"Tell him it's Sheriff Ainsley," Earl said.

"Sheriff Ainsley, yes, sir."

"And, Coleman, you come back with him, hear?"

"Me? Why do you need me, Sheriff?"

"Just get Mr. Castleton," Earl said.

As Coleman left, Earl sat down in a large wooden chair, then rose immediately. "Nowhere to sit easy around here."

"A man could get used to the place," Long said, looking around.

"Guess he could at that," Earl said. He went to the music room and glanced inside. As he turned away, he saw Holt approaching. "Sorry to disturb you, Mr. Castleton."

"I suppose you're here because of Kyle's murder."

"It's our number one job nowadays," Earl said. Above them Gaby came out of the corridor, and stopped at the head of the stairs.

"And mine, Sheriff," Holt said. "I'll do anything I can to help. Bear that in mind."

"That's very helpful. It's why I'm here today. I'd like to borrow Coleman for a little while."

"Me," Coleman said. "Why did you come for me?"

Holt said, "You mind the sheriff, Coleman."

"Mist' Holt, I already told you—" Coleman said before Holt interrupted.

"Tell him," Holt said, and he said to Earl: "The Castle is yours, Sheriff. You will not be disturbed."

"I thought we would conduct this interrogation in official surroundings," Earl said.

"Coleman, you go with the sheriff," Holt said.

Coleman seemed to shrink, standing with his shoulders hunched, his arms falling across his belly, and his big hands together. "You keep after me about Mist' Kyle," he said. "Poor Mist' Kyle's dead, and poor Coleman wishes he was dead with Mist' Kyle." The black man raised his head. "All I know is I heard the shot and came into the sleeping porch. Mist' Kyle was laying across the bed bleeding. I carried him to the car, your car, Mist' Holt. And I carried him into the hospital."

Beckoning to the black man, Earl said, "Coleman."

"Where are you taking him?" Gaby demanded, hurrying down the stairs.

"Don't interfere," Holt said.

Gaby rushed past him, facing Earl. "Why are you here? Coleman isn't involved in this . . . business, this . . . dark business."

"We'd like to question him, ma'am," Earl said.

"They want to take me away, Miss Gaby," Coleman said.

"Where is your warrant, Sheriff? I'd like to see your warrant," Gaby said. "You need a warrant to drag a man out of his house."

"Now be fair, ma'am," Earl said. "We're not dragging him. And you're wrong about the warrant. I can question anyone. No offense, ma'am, but that includes you. Ma'am, the sooner we start, the sooner we finish." Earl watched her. "Ma'am?"

Earl waited until Gaby said, defeated, "How will he get back? You must bring him back."

"Ma'am, you've got my word," Earl said.

Gaby touched the black man. "I'll be here waiting, Coleman." As Coleman walked to the door between the two men in uniform, Holt followed them. Gaby watched her brother, the stranger who frightened her, frightened everyone in the Castle, frightened everyone everywhere.

When Arver Long stopped at the courthouse, Earl said, "Arver, put Coleman here in a cell."

"What for you arresting me, Sheriff?" Coleman asked, his face covered with perspiration. "I done nothing for you to arrest me, Sheriff."

Long shoved him, trying to stay clear of the nigger. "Come on, you." Long shoved him again. "*Move*, goddammit!"

Earl went to his office. He tossed his campaign hat at the coat-tree, nodding when it landed on a peg. At his desk he sat without moving, a short man with a potbelly and thinning hair, looking across the office at a blank wall, thinking. "Yeah . . . ," he said quietly, and moved the upright telephone across the desk to call Max Isbell in the county attorney's offices above him. "I got the nigger."

"Call me when you're done with him," Isbell said.

"You'll be long gone."

"Call me at home," Isbell said. "You've got my home number."

"You'll be hearing from me," Earl said, and replaced the telephone receiver. "It stinks," he muttered to himself. "It all stinks."

Leaving his office, he went to the booking counter. Arver Long sat at a desk, eating the lunch his wife had packed that morning. "Forget the nigger," Earl said. "I don't care how much noise he makes, stay away from him."

"That's easy," Long said.

Earl left the courthouse. He drove to Schoonover's and parked in front of the restaurant. Inside, he chose a table in the center, in full view of everyone. When Earl visited a public place, he liked to be seen, he did not like to be discovered. That day he took a long time deciding what to eat and a much longer time eating what he ordered.

When he returned to the courthouse, Arver Long stood at the counter, bent over the afternoon newspaper. Earl raised the hinged leaf of the counter. "How's our star boarder?"

"Haven't heard any complaints."

"Yeah . . . Arver, you hang around when your relief comes, hear?"

Long watched the day shift, his shift, go home, watched the night shift take over, wondering when he would get any supper. He wouldn't *get* any supper, he decided. He could see the shadows falling over the parking area. Goddamn nigger.

Long after the night shift left the courthouse on patrol, Earl returned. "Bring Coleman into my office, Arver."

In his office Earl took a large manila envelope from a desk drawer and removed two sheets of white paper neatly typed. He set them on his desk.

When the door opened, Earl heard Long say, "Inside."

"Over here, Coleman," Earl said, and he said to Long, "Bring Coleman a glass of cold water, and you sit, Coleman. Sit!"

At the sink in the corner Long turned the tap and filled a glass with water. He brought it to Coleman, his arm extended, keeping his distance from the black man. Coleman emptied the glass. "More."

"You heard him," Earl said.

Long brought Coleman a second glass of water and a third. Coleman drank both and afterward pressed the cold glass against his forehead, rolling it back and forth, back and forth. Earl gestured at Arver Long. "Wait at the door. Keep everyone out of here."

When Long left, Earl said, "You must be awful hungry, Coleman. When did you eat last?"

"Early, Mist' Sheriff," Coleman said. "I eat before anyone wakes up upstairs."

"Nothing since this *morning?* Big buck like you must be half starved," Earl said. "You'll be eating pretty quick, Coleman." He raised a sheet of paper. "Soon's we finish up here."

"I can't read, Mist' Sheriff," Coleman said.

"I'll do the reading," Earl said. He glanced at the paper he held. "Now, Coleman, you knew Kyle Castleton all his life, am I right?"

"Since the day Mist' Kyle was born."

"Nobody knew him better," Earl said. "Am I right?"

"I saw Mist' Kyle every day of his life except when he was gone away from the Castle," Coleman said.

"So you know he owned a gun, a thirty-eight caliber Police Positive," Earl said.

"Yes, sir," Coleman said.

"You must have seen the gun," Earl said.

"I seen it."

Earl put his gun on the desk, the muzzle pointed at Coleman's heart. "Where did you see the gun?"

"In his bedroom," Coleman said.

"You mean, *their* bedroom," Earl said. "The bedroom where Kyle and Mrs. Castleton slept. Right, Coleman?"

"Yes, sir, Mist' Sheriff."

"Where in the bedroom?" Earl asked pointedly.

"Right there on top of the bureau," Coleman said. He looked from side to side, looking for a place to set the glass.

"Put it on the desk," Earl said, and the black man obeyed. "Did you ever see the gun anywhere else?"

"I seen it in the sleeping porch, Mist' Sheriff."

"Their sleeping porch," Earl said.

"Miss Faith, she didn't care much for the sleeping porch," Coleman said.

"Just tell me where you saw the gun."

"On the table beside the bed, his side of the bed," Coleman said. "Mist' Kyle, he asked me for a scarf from the sleeping porch. His flying scarf. I found it on the table, and underneath I saw the gun."

"So he didn't hide it, did he? He left the gun laying around, like a . . . book or a cigarette lighter," Earl said.

"Mist' Kyle, he didn't smoke," Coleman said. "It's the funny part about them, makin' all them cigarettes every day and nobody in the Castle smoke."

"Coleman!"

The black man shuddered, and his eyes widened. He said, " 'Scuse me, sir, I didn't mean—"

"You saw the gun out in the open, correct?"

"Yes, sir."

"So if you saw the gun, someone else could have seen it," Earl said. "His wife could have seen it. His best friend could have seen the gun." Earl looked directly at the black man. "Coleman, do you know Boyd Fredericks very well?"

"I sure do, Mist' Sheriff," Coleman said. "I know Mist' Boyd a long time."

"How long?"

"Long's Mist' Boyd's been coming to the Castle," said the black man.

"You've known him for years, right?" Earl said. "And in all those years Boyd Fredericks could have seen that gun many times."

"You're right," Coleman said. "Although that Boyd, he's a—"

"So Kyle Castleton's best friend and Kyle Castleton's wife both saw the gun," Earl said. "One of them could have taken the gun, isn't that right?"

"Taken the gun? Why—?" Coleman stopped. A searing surge of panic engulfed him. He understood the full, deadly meaning of the trap Earl had set.

Earl said, "Boyd Fredericks or Faith Castleton, Kyle's best

friend or wife, could have taken the gun and fired it into his head, isn't that right, Coleman?"

"Please, Mist' Sheriff," Coleman said, terrified of the white man with the badge.

"I'm only repeating what you told me," Earl said. "You told me about the gun, Coleman. Anyone could have taken the gun. You proved it to me." Earl pushed his gun into the holster on his hip. He dropped the sheet of paper with the questions Isbell had prepared for him and took the second sheet. Earl leaned forward. "So all you need to do is sign . . . put your mark here, Coleman."

"Please, Mist' Sheriff." Coleman's lips were wet, and spittle dripped from a corner of his mouth onto the soiled white jacket.

Earl took his pen from his shirt pocket and unscrewed the cap. "Right here, Coleman." He came around the desk with the pen. Coleman rose, trying to get away. Earl took the sheet of paper from the desk. "Right here over your name. That's your name. Coleman Beaudine."

Earl set the sheet of paper down on the desk and took Coleman's wrist. He raised the black man's arm. "Here's the pen!" He tried to fit the pen into his hand, but Coleman's hand became a hard fist.

"Please, Mist' Sheriff."

"Make your goddamn mark!"

Earl tried to jab the pen into the black man's fist. The servant, driven beyond endurance by fear, raised his arm and threw Earl aside.

Only the coat-tree kept Earl from falling. He held on to it, regaining his balance. A nightstick, hanging by a leather thong from a peg on the coat-tree, brushed his arm, and Earl grabbed it. "Now, you . . ." he said.

As Earl raised the stick, the coat-tree toppled. It hit the floor with a loud crash. Arver Long plunged into the office, slamming the door back against the wall and reaching for his gun.

The sight of the deputy brought Earl back from the edge. His arm froze, holding the nightstick over his head, and he yelled, "No! No guns!" Earl leaped forward, tripping over the coat-tree on the floor and starting to fall.

Long grabbed him, keeping Earl on his feet. Earl pulled free and dropped the nightstick on the desk. "Get him out of here," Earl said. "Take him back to the Castle." He bent to raise the coat-tree. "I said, take him back!" Earl shouted. "Get this nigger out of my sight!"

Long said, "Come on, you." He stood clear of the black man.

Coleman turned stiffly and paused, took a step, and paused, like a toy with a mechanism that has been wound and produces movement. Earl watched Arver following the black man. "Shut the goddamn door!"

In his office Earl hung the nightstick on a peg on the coat-tree. He sat down at his desk but then discovered his hat on the floor. He bent far forward, grunting as he retrieved his hat. He examined it carefully before dropping it on the desk. He took the two sheets of white paper from the desk and aligned the sheets before tearing them into small pieces.

Arver Long followed Coleman out of the courthouse into the parking area. In the early evening a slight breeze relieved the heat of the day. Arc lights illuminated the sheriff's cars. Long pushed the black man. "Over here. Over *here,* I said."

At his black-and-white Long opened the door wide. "In the back," he said, pointing. "Over here, away from me. Stay away from me." Long couldn't stand the smell.

Coleman did not respond. He heard Long, but the voice seemed far away, seemed faint and indistinct. "Get in, I said!" Long kicked him.

Coleman lumbered forward. He bent and dropped into the backseat. He heard the faraway voice. "Black son of a bitch."

Long drove out of the parking area, his motor racing, and in the streets, reached the speed limit before he had shifted through the gears.

Behind him Coleman swayed from side to side. He began to mutter: "Gone . . . who said? . . . not now, no . . . same place . . ." The black man's speech mirrored the disorder of his mind. Coleman had, blessedly, retreated, had found refuge in chaos. He could no longer be punished. He had been battered beyond endurance. Too many men had asked too many questions; too many hate-filled faces thrust into his had made too many threats. He no longer feared their threats. The simple, gentle, trusting black man had been robbed of his faith, his trust. He had lost too much, first Mist' Kyle, whom he worshiped, and then Miss Faith, the beautiful lady whom Coleman loved. Boyd left the Castle and did not return. Mist' Holt returned instead of Mr. Boyd, and after Mist' Holt, the sheriff and his man came to take Coleman away and put him in jail, then took him out to shout at him until he sank beneath the crushing weight of his losses and the incomprehensible demands made of him.

In the rear of the black-and-white Coleman rocked from side to side. The heat, the speeding car, the glare of oncoming headlights, the long hours without water, without food produced a nausea he could not control.

In front of him, Arver Long gripped the steering wheel with both hands. The alarm clock had wakened him for the day shift at six-thirty that morning. He was still working, halfway into the night shift. He had missed supper. He had to deliver the nigger, go back downtown for his car, and drive home before he got any supper. And all because of the black son of a bitch in the backseat. Behind him Coleman began to retch.

"No, you don't!" Long yelled, turning hard into the shoulder off Millionaires Row. He jammed down the brake pedal, turned the key to kill the engine, and lunged across the front seat to open the car door. "Get the hell out of here!" He pushed down the back of the passenger seat, leaned into the rear to grab Coleman. "You're not puking all over this car!" Long yelled, pulling at the big black man. "Get out! Get out, you black son of a bitch!"

Pulling as Coleman pushed, Long got the black man out of the car. Coleman stood beside the car, hopelessly lost. "Don't see the Castle," he muttered, retching. "Where at's the Castle?" He pawed at Arver Long. "Take me to the Castle."

All of Arver Long's rage coalesced into a blinding flash that exploded, leaving him inchoate. "*Take* you . . . ." he shouted, his voice hoarse. His fingers curled into a fist, and his right hand shot out and up. He hit Coleman with all his strength, driving his fist into the black man's mouth and nose, crushing the cartilage in the nose.

Coleman made a wild, screeching sound, covering his face with his hands as blood erupted in a geyser, falling through his fingers, across his face, across his white shirt and white jacket. Blood poured from Coleman's shattered nose, splattering down on the dirt at their feet. Long sprang aside, leaving Coleman, and strode back to the car.

Inside, he slammed both doors, turned the key, and as the engine caught, released the clutch to speed off onto Millionaires Row.

Alone and in pain, sick with pain and fear, Coleman at last managed to find his handkerchief. He pressed it to his shattered nose, crying out in pain, and then wept as he began to shuffle forward.

Slowly, unsteadily Coleman continued on Millionaires Row, trying to find the Castle. Long after Arver Long had abandoned him, lights appeared in the distance. Powerful headlights approached. The lights grew brighter and brighter until Coleman heard a steady, thick drone. The sound developed into a throaty growl advancing on him. He veered across the shoulder and across Millionaires Row, but the blazing headlights frightened the black man. He turned back, crossed to the other side, and there, believing he had made another mistake, he turned back again.

In the big two-ton dump truck loaded with asphalt, the driver said, "That nigger is drunk."

"Or crazy," said his companion. "Or drunk *and* crazy."

The driver put his hand on the horn. "Get the hell—" He turned hard, using both hands, but could not avoid Coleman. The massive, reinforced bumper struck the black man, throwing him into the air and killing him.

In the truck cab the passenger said, "I think you hit the nigger."

"Hit him?"

"Sure felt like you hit him," said the passenger. "Didn't you feel a kind of thump?"

"Did you?"

"Yeah, I did," the passenger said. "Like we went through something thick and soft, like mud. Like we went through mud. Yeah, I'd say you hit him."

"Maybe I did hit him," the driver said. He took an open pack of Castleton cigarettes from the dashboard. "Gimme a light, huh?"

<hr />

BECAUSE THE FLATS LAY IN A FEN that could not be adequately drained, the heat became more oppressive as the day progressed. On the day of Coleman's funeral all the doors and windows of the Resurrection Baptist Church were wide open, and the

Reverend Millard Fitch borrowed electric fans wherever he could. He placed them facing the front pews that flanked Coleman's coffin, delivered by a white undertaker, the biggest, shiniest, most elegant coffin Millard Fitch had ever seen. The Castletons paid for the coffin, and Mr. Russell Vance, from the Castle, came the day before the funeral with a check. Millard Fitch had the check in his office trying to decide what he needed most for the church.

No white man or woman had ever sat in the church for any kind of service, but for Coleman's funeral, the reverend had three. His friend, Daniel Cohen, came, and Russell Vance came, and the reverend had a Castleton in his church, Gabrielle Castleton Inscott. Millard Fitch himself escorted all three to one of the two front pews, facing the strongest fans he had borrowed.

The white people were not going to the cemetery over at the far end of the Flats, so after the service Millard Fitch escorted them out of the church. He thanked the lady for her kindness. "I share your grief, ma'am," the reverend said. She seemed very small for a Castleton.

Dan Cohen walked to their car with Gaby and Russell. He removed his Panama. "I'm very sorry, Mrs. Inscott," Dan said. "They are all family, really, all of them."

"I loved him," Gaby said.

As Russell drove through the Flats, Gaby said, "First Kyle and now Coleman." She moved closer, resting her head against Russell's shoulder. He turned his head and kissed her hair, and Gaby snuggled against him.

They drove out of the Flats, and soon Russell turned, taking a shortcut. "Do you mind if I stop by the farms? We're coming onto the harvest, and I like to check the fields every day now."

Gaby mumbled something, like a sleepy child snug in bed. Russell kissed her hair again. "I won't be long."

"Be long," she said. Then neither spoke, and Russell thought Gaby had fallen asleep, exhausted by the emotional drain of the funeral. Millard Fitch's long eulogy, with its predictable references to the Negro's tragic history in America, including its savagery and suffering, had exhausted the mourners. Russell welcomed the end of the service, anxious to leave the Flats behind, leave Coleman's ugly death behind.

But he could not dismiss Coleman from his mind. The black man's inheritance, the fifty thousand dollars from Kyle, now imposed an endless burden. As a trustee, with Dan Cohen, Russell would be obligated to decide on investments for the principal. Russell would need to meet constantly with the others, interviewing applicants for the scholarship provided by Coleman's inheritance. All this in addition to his duties at the farms and in the Castle. "No time," he said to himself. "There's no time."

Thinking of the scholarships took Russell far, far back to his own collegiate career and his scholarship. He had won it with his high school academic work, but it provided only for his tuition. He worked for his room and board all through his four years at Chapel Hill, waiting tables, pasting up leaves for a professor in the department of botany, stoking coal in the boiler room of the School of Engineering, joining the crew cleaning the stadium on Mondays after the Saturday football games. He always found time. He hummed and whistled crossing the campus, whether to class or to work. From his first days at the University of North Carolina, Russell felt at home, indeed, felt as though he had come home. He belonged at Chapel Hill, belonged to the intellectual spirit and life of the community after the small provincial town where he had lived the first eighteen years of his life. Until he arrived on the campus, Russell had not known anyone who had ever willingly read a book. At Chapel Hill Russell made the dean's list every semester, from his freshman through his senior year. He found time for everything: classes, study, work, fun. His college years had been a wonderland from start to finish.

Gaby ended his pleasant reverie, moving away from Russell and sitting erect. "I'd like to see the sheriff," she said.

She caught Russell off guard. He said, "See the sheriff?"

Gaby watched the road. "I'd like to talk with him," she said.

Russell glanced at her. "Will that help, Gaby?"

She faced him as though he had turned on her. "Will anything help? How can I say? Coleman is dead. Nothing will help Coleman." She looked ahead. "I'd like to see him."

"All right," Russell said. "I'll call him later."

"Not later. I'd like to see him now. Where is he? His headquarters?"

"In the courthouse," Russell said. "Darling? It's been a terrible day, a terrible week. Why not wait?"

"You can take me there and leave me," Gaby said. "I can manage." She remembered the pudgy little man, fawning over Holt and preening in his uniform while Coleman had stood by, terrified. She had failed Coleman, and he had died. "You can leave."

"Gaby?" He spoke quietly. "Gaby, look at me." When she faced him, Russell said, "I'll never leave you. Never again."

She took his hand, brought it to her lips. "I left you," Gaby said. "You didn't hurt us, my love. I hurt us."

"And it's behind us," he said, holding on to her and steering with one hand. They were together. So long as they were together, Russell would have driven her to the ends of the earth.

Earl's guests, unexpected and unannounced, arrived, and when he saw the little Castleton woman with Russell Vance coming through the open doors straight at him, he thought of diving under the counter. Christ, he didn't remember her name, her married name! "Mr. Vance! How are you, Mr. Vance?" What in Christ's name was her name?

Behind his father, at a desk typing an arrest report, Wyn looked up from the typewriter as Russell Vance and Kyle Castleton's sister walked toward the counter.

Earl raised the hinged section of the counter and went out to meet the pair. They had not driven into town with an invitation to a barbecue. "Something wrong, Mr. Vance?" *Inscott!* She had married that guy Inscott from up there in New York, somewhere around New York. "Mrs. Inscott," Earl said. "Something wrong, ma'am?"

"You came to the Castle and took Coleman away," Gaby said. "Why didn't you bring him back?"

Earl gestured. "We can talk in my office, Mrs. Inscott," he said.

"I haven't come here with secrets," Gaby said. She stepped past Earl, walked to the counter, and turned to face him. "Sheriff, why didn't you bring Coleman back to the Castle?"

Earl swung around, facing Wyn. "Get Deputy Long in here," he said sharply.

Halfway through his lunch hour Arver Long sat at a table in the deputies' dressing room with his open lunch pail. He held a meat loaf sandwich in one hand and a cup with coffee in the other. He heard

Wyn through the intercom speaker high on the wall in a corner. "Arver Long. Arver Long. Report to the sheriff at the booking counter."

Long muttered, "How about my lunch hour?" He gulped down the coffee and took a huge bite of the meat loaf sandwich. He rose, set the remainder of the sandwich in the lunch pail, and screwed the plastic cup over his thermos of coffee. "How about finishing my lunch, huh?" he said aloud, alone in the dressing room. Long closed his lunch pail and carried it to his locker. He opened the big lock with a key on his key chain and set the lunch pail on a shelf. "I'm entitled to a lunch around here."

At the counter, waiting for Long and trying to move them away from Wyn, Earl said, "You folks can sit over here."

"Mrs. Inscott asked you a question," Russell said. Earl listened to the smart son of a bitch grandstanding in front of the Castleton woman. The son of a bitch wouldn't give him an inch.

"Sheriff?"

Earl looked back at Wyn. "How about Deputy Long?"

"Probably on his way," Wyn said as the door beyond the counter opened. "Here he is."

Earl said, "Deputy Long." He raised his arm as though he were standing in a crowd.

At first Arver Long didn't recognize the small dame with the sheriff, but as he got close, he remembered her from the Castle. "You want me, Sheriff?"

"This is Mrs. Inscott," Earl said. "And Russell Vance." Earl wiped his mouth slowly, so Long wiped *his* mouth, wiping it clean of catsup. Behind them Wyn leaned over the typewriter, but he did not strike the keys.

Earl faced the Castleton woman. "I sent Coleman back to the Castle with Deputy Long. Correct, Deputy?"

"Correct, Sheriff," Long said.

"Where did you take him?" Gaby asked.

"I took him to the Castle, following the sheriff's orders."

"Did you?" Russell asked. When Long stared at him, Russell added, "Did you take him to the Castle?"

"The Castle, yes, sir," Long said.

"We found Coleman's body one and three-tenths miles from the Castle," Russell said.

"One and three-tenths *miles?*" Long said. "One and three tenths?"

"I measured it," Russell said. "On the odometer in the car. Coleman's body lay in the road one and three-tenths miles from the Castle gates."

Arver Long thought his goddamn lunch would come up. "That's right!" he said, as though he remembered something important. "I had a flat." He looked at Earl, nodding. "So I had to fix the flat . . . change tires."

Wyn came out of his chair, away from the desk, and stopped in the chute made by the raised section of the counter.

"And while I'm out there changing tires, the nig—Coleman— while I'm changing tires, Coleman said, 'Think I'll walk.' "

Earl had to get them out of headquarters. "Mrs. Inscott, you've got the facts now. A flat tire. Couldn't be helped. And Coleman decided to walk."

"Correct," Long said. "He decided to walk."

Earl moved to stand between Long and the Castleton woman. "What happened after that, we can't say, ma'am. Nobody can say. Nobody except the party or parties responsible for Coleman's death."

"Thank you," Russell said. Gaby looked as if she might drop. Coleman's funeral and now this reprise of his death with its obvious evasions and half-truths had brought her to the edge of collapse. Russell took her arm, holding her firmly. "We've heard enough. Are you ready, Mrs. Inscott?"

Gaby nodded, and Earl stepped aside, watching them leave. As they turned into the corridor, Long said, "Guess I'll finish my lunch."

Wyn came through the chute in the counter like a projectile. "Arver!"

Long didn't stop. "Yeah, what?"

Wyn reached Long and used both hands to spin the big deputy around. "Hold it!"

Long said low, "Watch it." He brushed his shirt. He didn't give a good goddamn if the sheriff was the smart-ass's father. "I pay for this uniform. This uniform is my property."

Wyn wanted to punch him in his big, fat mouth. "Sure, and you had a flat," Wyn said. "You fixed the flat."

"Changed the tire," Arver said.

"Changed the tire," Wyn said. "How about the breakdown rig?" A tow truck, equipped for any emergency and manned by two master mechanics, was in service twenty-four hours a day in the Sheriff's Department garage a block from the courthouse. "Why didn't you call breakdown?"

"Smart-ass," Arver said. He wanted the sheriff to hear him. "I called breakdown, smart-ass. Breakdown didn't respond. Out on a call probably."

"You bet," Wyn said. He spun around and raced back to a telephone on a desk behind the counter. "Let's check the log."

"Wyn!" Earl went after him, stopping at the counter. "Wyn!"

Wyn snatched up a telephone. "We'll just check the log for that night!"

Finally Earl intervened. "Drop it, Wyn. I am giving you an order."

Then no one spoke and no one moved, and the only sound came from the ticking second hand on the clock above the open doors to the corridor.

"Goddammit, you act like I killed the black son of a bitch!" Long burst out at last.

"Did you?" Earl asked.

"No!" Arver said.

"I told you to take him back to the Castle," Earl said.

"He was going to throw up in the goddamn car!" Long said, shouting now. "I dropped him because he was going to puke his guts out."

Wyn said, "I stayed in the Castle almost a week. Cleanest place I ever stayed. And the cleanest people. And Coleman was the cleanest of them."

"Yeah, thanks," Earl said, and arched his back, grimacing. "Finish your lunch, Arver." Earl waved his hand. "Go on! Get the hell out of my sight! I'll let you guess what I'm going to do about your little joyride."

After Long had left, Earl dropped the hinged section of the counter and leaned on it, watching Wyn. "How about that arrest report you were doing?"

Wyn went to the desk and dropped down into the chair, staring at the wall.

"I had the nigger in for questioning," Earl said. "In case you forgot, I've got a murder case here. And so far Max Isbell has no case. Understand? You better understand. You're a deputy sheriff, a law enforcement officer." Wyn didn't even look at him. "I'm doing my job, goddammit."

———◦◉◦———

OUTSIDE, as Russell drove away from the courthouse, Gaby said, "I shouldn't have come. I should have listened to you."

He did not respond. Gaby dropped her head on his shoulder and remained close beside him until they reached the Castle gates. As Russell turned into the drive, Gaby shifted in the seat to sit near the door. "Now you're Mrs. Inscott," Russell said. "Now I lose you."

"Never again," Gaby said. "We'll be together forever. Lucius says I'll be divorced soon."

"And we'll stop hiding," he said.

"We'll stop," Gaby said, stepping out of the car. Russell came around the trunk to join her. Walking toward the Castle, she said, "I can't remember a time when Coleman didn't stand in the doorway. He seemed to sense when I came back to the Castle and when I left. 'Now you take good care of yourself, Miss Gaby,' " she said.

In the Castle, Jacob, a young black man Russell had chosen to replace Coleman, greeted them. "You got company, Miss Gaby. Your husband, he's here, Miss Gaby. He's waiting in the music room."

Russell said, "Thank you, Jacob," and said to Gaby, "I'll call the sheriff."

"The sheriff!" Gaby's endurance teetered on the breaking point. "I've had enough of the sheriff," she said.

"All right," Russell said. "I'll talk to Colin."

"No!" Gaby took Russell's arm to restrain him. "No," she said quietly. "Not you, darling. He's my . . . problem."

"Ours," Russell said. "Let me come with you. Have you forgotten the sleeping porch? He's dangerous."

"So am I," she said. "I'm dangerous too now."

Gaby skirted the staircase with a sudden rush of energy, anxious to reach the music room, to be done with him. His presence outraged her.

Colin had chosen his clothes with care, rejecting casual wear in favor of a dark worsted suit. He wore the vest of the suit as well and a white shirt with a deep blue tie flecked with small unobtrusive checks. He said, "Gaby," crossing the music room with arms extended to take her hands. "My deepest sympathies, old girl. Good old Coleman was a favorite of mine."

Gaby darted behind a Queen Anne chair, holding the wings of the chair, using it as a shield, her reflexive fear making her furious with herself as well as with Colin. "What do you want?"

"Want?" Colin stopped, and his arms fell to his sides. "Want? I came to offer condolences, Gaby. I learned of Coleman's sad passing, and popped over to pay my respects."

"Thank you," Gaby said, stepping aside, leaving the protection of the chair to face the liar squarely. "I'm tired, Colin. I've just come from Coleman's funeral. Say what you've come to say. Say it!" She could not bear him, could not bear to remember the wasted years with him.

Colin faced her in desperation. He had begun the day with great hopes. Coleman's death gave him a pretext to see her. Colin had planned the day as carefully as he dressed. In the taxi riding out to the Castle he rehearsed what he would say to her. They would chat for a time, about Coleman, about themselves. Colin thought of suggesting a drive in the country with a stop for lunch but discarded that idea immediately. All his troubles had begun after their drive in the country, after the wildflowers he picked for her.

He decided on honesty. Gaby would invite him to lunch. They would chatter away, two old friends meeting after having been apart. Colin warned himself to be careful, to steer clear of anything personal. He would bring up the past, the good times in East Hampton, the parties, the early-morning meetings at the stables in the cold months, when they would ride together, steam rising from the horses' nostrils. Not until long afterward, with the coffee, would he mention the divorce, quietly, sadly. "Are you quite sure this is what you're after, old girl? Quite sure? No, wait. Hear me out this once. We've built a good life together. Oh, I admit, I've been . . . careless along the way. And I apologize, ever so humbly. But must it end this way? Don't we deserve another chance? I say we do. I say, let's have another go at it, old dear."

"Colin? Colin!" He looked as if he had lost his way. She could no longer stand the sight of him. "I think you'd better go," she said.

"Wait!" He leaped forward. "Wait! This divorce business . . . you can't be serious, Gaby. Not after what we've meant to each other!"

"Meant . . ." she said, her face contorting in contempt. "Get out," she said firmly.

"No, no, Gaby, listen! Listen! I'm broke! Gaby, I have no money!"

"Sell the house," she said. "I gave you the house."

"Gave? You didn't—" he said before she interrupted.

"I told Lucius Peete you should have the house, so take it."

She started for the door, but Colin grabbed her arm. "Holt said— He lied to you. Gaby, listen . . . please listen," Colin said as she pulled herself free.

"Get out. Now. Get out now or I'll . . . call the sheriff," she said. "The sheriff will handle you. He'll throw you in jail."

"Gaby, they lied," Colin said. "Lucius Peete lied. He said I could live there, live in the house."

"Do it!" she said. "Live in the house. And leave. *Leave!*" Gaby came toward him. Her tiny, childlike figure had suddenly turned lethal. "You'd better go!"

In the entrance Jacob saw Colin coming and opened the heavy door, holding it with both hands, proud of his new position and smiling a big smile. "Come back soon, hear?"

Colin didn't even see the black man. Barging outside, he stopped in front of the Castle, blinking in the dazzling sunlight. He walked down the drive and, approaching Millionaires Row, saw the green Stutz phaeton, its top down, swing into the Castle grounds.

Holt noticed the man. He turned the wheel slightly and drove directly at him. As Colin heard the powerful engine and discovered the car bearing down on him, he jumped aside. Holt stopped and stood up in the car. "I warned you against showing your face anywhere near the Castle. You're trespassing. I normally shoot trespassers."

Colin lunged at the car. "You stole my house!"

Holt put his hand against his chest, fingers spread, like a Victorian lady victimized by vapors. *"I* stole. You've been living off Gaby from the day you were married."

"She gave me the house! She just told me so."

"Get out of my sight," Holt said.

"It's my house!"

Holt shifted gears. "You signed the divorce agreement," he said. The Stutz sped past, the tires spewing gravel. Colin raised his arms, shielding his face as he walked toward the road.

So he did not see the Stutz come to a stop, shuddering as Holt jammed on the brakes. Holt made a complete turn and followed Colin, inching up on the trespasser. When Colin looked back, then tried to get out of the way, Holt turned the wheel slightly, enough to nudge his quarry with the left fender. Colin jumped aside, but Holt anticipated him, nudging him again. And again. Colin ran onto Millionaires Row as Holt stopped the Stutz between the open gates. He leaned over the driver's door to say, "You've been lucky. Do not press your luck."

Colin saw the green car shoot straight back, hurtling down the drive and disappearing as Holt spun the wheel to put the phaeton into the garage. Alone and abandoned, Colin raised his hand to shield his eyes before crossing the road to the shoulder, keeping his back to the sun as he left the Castle.

He remembered, indistinctly, a crossroads commercial area near the Castle. He could find a telephone there to summon a taxi.

At the hotel the doorman said, "Guess this heat is here to stay, Mr. Inscott." The poor guy looked all done in, the doorman thought as he opened the door.

At the front desk Colin said, "My key."

The room clerk looked up and said, "Oh, Mr. Inscott. Just one moment, sir."

"Not one second," Colin said, feeling strangled by his clothes. "My key," he said, pointing at the mail rack behind the desk.

"Wait just a moment," said the room clerk, walking past the mail rack.

"Stop!" Colin said. "Give me my key, you clod!" The room clerk darted behind the mail rack. "Come back! Give me my key!" Colin looked for someone, anyone, who could help. "You!" he said, waving at a bellhop who stood at the bell captain's station. "Come here! On the double!"

Someone said, "Mr. Inscott," and on the other side of the front desk Colin saw a heavy middle-aged man with thinning black hair brushed carefully. "I am Grover Ferris, the resident manager. Can you pay your bill, Mr. Inscott? Cash, not a check."

"Bill? Cash?" Colin patted his chest, patted his jacket pockets as though he carried money everywhere. "I say, old sport, this is something of an insult. Look here, you simply—"

"Cash," said Grover Ferris, interrupting.

"—can't expect a chap to drag around scads of money, you know. I'll pay. Certainly. You needn't worry . . ." he said, as the man facing him struck the bell summoning the bellhop.

Grover Ferris looked at the room clerk. "Get him out of here."

"Out? Hold on," Colin said. The resident manager walked toward his office behind the mail rack. "I say . . ." Colin faced the room clerk. "You simply can't . . . do this. You can't . . ." he said, and stopped as the bellhop reached the desk.

"Mr. Inscott is leaving," said the room clerk, pointing. The bellhop nodded, and Colin watched him crossing the lobby. Stacked against a pillar Colin saw his luggage and, beside the luggage, his gleaming riding boots.

<hr />

IN HEADQUARTERS AT FIVE-THIRTY in the afternoon the day after Gaby's appearance, Earl said, "You can't? Why can't you?"

Wyn leaned against a desk, holding his campaign hat. He had not seen Faith in four days, and all day he had been watching the clock, counting the hours until darkness. Faith had kept him away, needing a respite from her demanding stud, and Wyn believed all her excuses. "I can't," Wyn said. "Something came up."

Earl grinned at his son, remembering his nights at Wyn's age. "I'll bet," Earl said. "You can let it go this once. Get laid tomorrow night."

Wyn turned his hat in an endless circle. "It's not that," he said, lying again. He lied constantly now, dodging dates, appointments, invitations, shunning the whole town and everyone in it to be with Faith.

"Ha-ha. Don't tell me it's not that," Earl said. "This is your father, remember? I was young once."

Wyn had to get home, had to change. "Listen, I'll make it tomorrow night."

"Tomorrow night!" Earl said, outraged. "What is this? What the hell is going on around here anyway? You run out of here every day like I've got the smallpox."

"Come on."

"Hold it!" Earl pushed his forefinger into Wyn's chest. "Don't play dumb with me. Not with me. Your mother has stopped asking me when you're coming out. The twins don't even ask." Earl pushed his campaign hat down on his head and started for the door.

"Hey! Wait! Pop. Will you wait?" Wyn watched his father leave. He pulled the chair away from the desk and dropped into it, legs extended. And leaped up, running.

As Wyn ran out of the courthouse, Earl slammed the door of his black-and-white. "Pop! Pop!"

In his car Earl watched the young stud running across the parking area. He was one hell of a good-looking kid. As Wyn reached the car, Earl said, "Talk fast. I'm awful tired of this heat."

"Go ahead," Wyn said. "I'll follow you."

"You're coming to supper?"

"I said I'll follow you."

"Sure you can spare the time?"

"Lay off, huh?" Wyn said. "I said I'm coming." He had to call Faith, had to tell her he would be late. He could stop at a telephone booth. "I've got to make a phone call," Wyn said.

Earl turned the ignition key, killing the engine. "Make it now. You can drive."

"How will I get home?"

"You can pick me up in the morning," Earl said. "Go on, make your call."

Wyn couldn't call from headquarters, where he would have an audience. "Forget it," he said, opening the car door. "Move over."

In the car, moving slowly in traffic, Earl said, "You look like you're doing time."

Wyn made a face. "That's a rotten thing to say, Pop."

"I'm rotten," Earl said.

"You just proved it," Wyn said. "Lay off, will you?"

"Do my best," Earl said. He sat back, pushing his hat down over his eyes.

At the farmhouse the dogs could identify Earl's car from the sound of the engine, and their baying, long and mournful, made Wyn smile. "You can't sneak home," he said.

Earl said glumly, "No fooling?"

The dogs alerted the twins, and they burst out of the house, running at the car as Wyn stopped near the kennels. "I forget how beautiful they are," Wyn said.

"I'll need more than the hounds to keep the boys away," Earl said. "And you're their brother. You'd better help when the time comes."

The twins made a beeline for Wyn, opening the door and pulling him out of the car, knocking off his hat, each claiming an arm, each kissing him, their voices like firecrackers exploding around the car. The girls' excitement delighted the basset hounds, darting back and forth, heads raised. Earl scowled at the twins. "Will you grow up? Sharon! Pipe down, will you? Will you pipe down, Doreen?"

The girls captivated Wyn. Their healthy teenage exuberance, their open-heartedness, their genuine, unqualified love enchanted him. He tried to answer their questions, tried to be heard, but the twins and the hounds made his efforts futile. "Let's go inside," he said.

Sharon shouted something that ended in "the litter!" and Doreen yanked his arm, pulling him toward the kennel. "You've got to see the puppies first!"

Doreen dragged him into the kennel. Sharon followed, bumping into Wyn as she closed the door. In the litter box Wyn saw Cleo lying on her side, teats exposed, and around her the newborns. And when he looked up, he saw Kay standing against the currying table, cradling a puppy in her arms. "Hello, Wyn."

So Wyn solved the mystery, one, two, three. The plot infuriated him, leaving him tongue-tied.

Kay said, "How have you been?"

He nodded and tried to smile, tried to be polite, but his anger overpowered him. His life was his life! It was *his* goddamn life, not his father's, or his father's and mother's, or Kay's.

And his guilt overpowered him. He had dumped Kay like a sack of potatoes. So long, see you around, take care of yourself, all right? He said, "Hello, Kay. How are you?"

"Fine," she said. "I'm fine. How are you? How have you been?"

"Okay, I guess," he said, wanting just to get out of there. He put his hand on the puppy's head. "Buying a dog?"

"I think so," she said. Kay held the puppy against her chest, looking down at the tiny animal. "I—I've always liked dogs."

Sharon said, "They're not ready. They need another five or six weeks with Cleo so she can nurse them." She dropped to her knees beside the litter box and put her hand over Cleo's drooling muzzle. "Hi, Cleo, old mama." She scratched the bitch's withers. "Wyn? You gotta say hello to Cleo."

Wyn said, "Right now," grateful to the twin for the reprieve, squatting beside her and patting the bitch, exhausted from nursing nine demanding pups. "How you doing, Cleo?"

They heard Earl calling, "Supper! Soup's on!"

Wyn felt Key slide down beside him as she bent with the puppy in her arms. She kissed the tiny, squirming animal and set it down in the litter box. "Can you remember which one she is?" Wyn asked.

"He!" Sharon said.

"It's a male, Wyn!" Doreen said.

Wyn stood up, helping Kay as he did. "Can you remember him?" he asked.

"He's easy," Sharon said. She touched the puppy. "He has this little spot on his withers, see?"

"Oh, sure, right," Wyn said, sliding to the door, away from Kay. "Soup's on."

As he followed Kay and the twins out of the kennel, Wyn could see his parents at the picnic table behind the house. "We're eating outside," Sharon said.

"We told Mom," Doreen said. "Because you would be here, Wyn."

"You're spoiling me," Wyn said. He had to telephone Faith.

At the picnic table Peg spread her arms. "Welcome."

Wyn kissed her. "You're my favorite mom."

"I like you too," Peg said. She put her hand against his cheek. "A lot."

Wyn kissed her hand. "I ought to wash up," he said. "Come on, Pop!" Wyn stopped beside his father. "Let's wash up."

"Yeah . . . right," Earl said.

At the kitchen door Wyn pushed his father ahead, and in the

kitchen he went to the window to see if they were being followed. Peg sat between the twins, and across the table he saw Kay, alone, waiting for him, for the guest of honor. Wyn spun around. "Hold it!"

In the hallway, at the stairs, Earl stopped. "You wanted to wash up."

Wyn said, "Sure." He crossed the kitchen. "Hold it a minute."

"We gotta move before the corn gets cold." Earl turned to the stairs, but Wyn's arm fell like a tollgate, his hand on the balustrade.

"Of all the cheap, lousy tricks," Wyn said. "I am so goddamn tired of you trying to run my life."

Earl stared at him. "Huh?"

"Don't look dumb," Wyn said. "Don't try and pull that dumb routine with me. Not tonight, Mr. Fixit. Stay out of my life, Pop. Stay the hell out."

"Let me know when you're finished," Earl said.

"Right now!" Wyn said. "And you're finished." He pointed into the kitchen. "From now on stick to the twins! Run their lives, not mine!"

"Suppose you put the last speech in plain English so I can follow you," Earl said.

"Still playing your— I'm going," Wyn said, and turned to the kitchen, but Earl came after him.

"I'll forget the corn," Earl said. "Because you and me are coming to an understanding. You are gonna make me understand what you've been trying to say. So far you're mad over something I've done to you. What? What? Say it fast before your mother comes after us and you'll sound like a bigger horse's ass than you do already."

"You bet," Wyn said. "It's all Greek to her too. She just happened to arrange a little picnic tonight, just happened to set the table for two extra. She just happened to have Kay here when I showed up."

Earl said slowly, "Yeah . . . Kay." He looked past Wyn into the kitchen as though he could see out to the picnic table. "You figured I—we— Wrong," Earl said. "Wyn? You're wrong. We didn't."

The evening stretched ahead of Wyn into infinity. "I—I thought when I saw her in the kennel, I thought—"

"She's been coming out for a while now," Earl said. "Says she loves bassets although they could've been Dobermans, I guess. Your mother invited her to supper even though she would miss the last bus. Figured you could drive her back into town. Wyn?" Earl watched the younger man. "She's a real pretty girl."

Doreen saved him, opening the kitchen door and shouting, "Mom says all the corn will be cold!"

Earl pushed his way past Wyn. "You're a real source of constant comfort to me, kid."

Wyn had to follow him through the kitchen, follow him out to the picnic table. Wyn had to sit down beside Kay, had to butter an ear of corn instead of running to Earl's car and disappearing.

Because he had coupled his mother with his father in his indictment, Wyn had to keep eating, trying to prove how much he liked her food. The constant chatter of the twins rang in Wyn's ears like a drumroll. He encouraged them, asking them endless questions, encouraged his mother.

Kay rescued him. "I have papers to correct," she said. "Do you mind, Wyn? Am I rushing you?"

Everyone left the picnic table for Earl's car. The twins hung on to Wyn. They kissed him, and his mother kissed him, and Earl said, "See you in the morning, kid."

So, alone in the car with Kay, Wyn began the worst part of an already dismal evening. He waited for her to say something, and she waited for him and after a mile of thunderous silence she said, "How have you been?"

He said almost gratefully, "Okay. Fine. I'm fine. How have you been?"

"Fine."

"How's your mother? Is your mother okay?"

"Yes, although she doesn't complain," Kay said. "I think I told you. She has arthritis."

"Right. You did tell me," Wyn said. "And school started, so you're back in the old routine."

Wyn steadily increased his speed, watching the needle as it moved across the speedometer. "Wyn?"

He glanced at her. She sat with her hands together, watching the road. "Yes?"

"You must hate me."

"*Hate* you?"

"For following you," Kay said. "I've followed you to your mother's house, hoping I would see you. I miss you. I try—I tried to . . . stop. It doesn't help. Nothing helps." Her voice broke. "Oh, God." She turned, faced the window at her side, and said harshly, "We've never had a dog."

"They're fun. Dogs are the most loyal animals. All they want to do is love you," Wyn said, and, hearing the words, tried to tear the steering wheel off the drive shaft. He almost turned up the siren so he could floor the accelerator. Instead they reached the city limits, and he had to stop for a red light.

When he shifted gears, Kay put her hand over his. "Don't be mad."

Everything she said worsened his misery and deepened his guilt. "*Mad?* Why should I be mad?"

She caressed his hand with hers, her fingers over his. "Sometimes I can still feel you next to me," she said. "Late at night when I can't sleep. Wyn?" She looked at him as the light changed to green. "Do you remember the picnic?"

"Sure I do," he said.

"I spoiled it."

"Like hell!" Her hand slipped away from his as he shifted through the gears. "Kay? Like hell you did! You didn't spoil anything," Wyn said. "I'm the one who spoiled everything, not you. You're too . . . decent. You are, Kay. You're a wonderful person."

"What difference does it make? Be honest, Wyn," she said. "If I'm so wonderful, why did I lose you?"

He didn't respond, and she did not continue. They rode in silence. At her house Wyn opened his door, but Kay said, "No. Stay." She turned to him, took his face in her hands, and kissed him on the lips. Releasing him, she said, ever so softly, "I love you," before she fled.

He sped away through the streets, turning corners at perilous angles. He couldn't drive to Deer Hollow Road, couldn't see Faith now. He couldn't see anyone. Wyn had familiarized himself with every public telephone in the area, and he headed for the nearest booth. When Wyn stopped, he discovered he had been driving with his door ajar. He got out of the black-and-white and slammed the door. He had to make an excuse to Faith. "You mean, lie," he said, aloud.

THE FOLLOWING AFTERNOON, two days after bumping Colin out through the Castle gates, Holt stood beside the Stutz with Russell, facing the green fields of Castleton Farms. "You should drive over more often," Russell said. "Especially now, coming into harvest. Look at it, Holt."

"Lovely," Holt said dully.

"It's beautiful," Russell said. "Thrilling. Nothing is more . . . rewarding than a bountiful field." He looked off, embarrassed by his outburst.

Holt said, "You have the soul of a poet."

"Not I," Russell said. "I'm a long way from poetry. I'm an estate manager, a happy manager."

Holt looked out at the field. "What are you growing?"

"Everything," Russell said. "Corn, tomatoes, carrots, celery, peas, beans, three varieties of beans, cabbage, onions, yams, potatoes, kale, beets . . . I'll quit before you begin yawning."

"That's impressive, Russell," Holt said.

"Nothing has changed, Holt. We're not experimenters, and we're not scientific," Russell said. "These are the crops you saw when you were a kid coming to the Harvest Festival."

"The Harvest Festival," Holt said. "The dear, dead, departed days of the Harvest Festival."

Russell, suddenly wary, glanced at him. "Not dead at all," Russell said. "The festival is just two weeks away." He smiled. "I'm writing my welcoming speech already, welcoming you home."

Holt turned slowly, facing Russell. "I think not."

Russell sensed a threat, and his smile vanished. "You're the oldest, Holt. And you've been away. They know you're home. They expect some word from you."

"*They,*" Holt said. "Identify *they.*"

"Our—your guests," Russell said. "The townsfolk." Holt had put him on edge, and he couldn't stop explaining. "The festival is the big event of the fall."

Holt swung around, looking at the barn. "Where's your nigger with those horses?"

Russell stepped away. He said, "I—" and stopped as a black man led two saddled horses out of the barn. "I'm sorry to hold you up."

They walked toward the horses. "Take the roan, Holt," Russell said. "I told George to saddle him for you."

The black man said, "Sure good to see you back home, Mist' Holt. You been gone a real long time."

As Holt took the reins from the black man and mounted, Russell said, "Thanks, George." He put his left foot into the stirrup and swung his right leg over the mare he preferred. Holt nudged the roan's flanks with his heels, and the horse moved forward. Russell rode beside him.

Two long bunkhouses faced the barn, and as they reached the low wooden buildings, Holt reined his horse. He stopped beside a solid three-sided fence forming a rectangle against the bunkhouse wall. Above the fence, two showerheads protruded from the bunkhouse wall. "You've made some improvements, Russell."

"The showers? This is home for the field hands," Russell said. "They need basic sanitation facilities. And they are raising food. Keeping them clean is actually my responsibility."

Holt grinned. "Is there a *white* section?" he asked, and rode forward.

Russell watched him. Holt seemed taller than anyone else. He rode as though he were leading an army returning in triumph after great victories. Holt seemed to live his days in triumph. He unnerved Russell, unnerved all those around him. Russell prodded the mare.

They rode into the fields. Sam Castleton had put an entire section, 640 acres, under cultivation. The tilled land stretched to the horizon. "You didn't mention watermelons," Holt said.

Russell grinned. "I didn't think it was necessary," he said. "Watermelon, muskmelon, casaba"—and pointing—"summer squash, acorn squash, and turnips. Lots of turnips."

"Your niggers have corrupted you," Holt said.

"Come on, Holt. You're joking," Russell said. "There's no color line when turnips reach the table. Turnips and turnip greens are a staple at the Castle too."

They rode on, keeping to the open spaces separating the different crops. As the field hands saw the approaching riders, those who were erect removed their hats, and others, bent double or on their knees, came to their feet, pulling off their hats.

Russell pointed. "Beefsteak tomatoes, Holt. We take prizes with our beefsteaks."

"A beautiful sight, Russell," Holt said. Then, without warning, Holt urged his horse into a gallop, startling the mare, which reared.

Russell had to calm his horse before he could follow. When he reached the barn, he saw George leading the roan into the barn. Holt stood in front of the Stutz, rubbing the nickeled radiator cap with his handkerchief. He watched Russell dismount. "Is something wrong, Holt? Are you all right?"

"I've been meaning to look at the farms' books. What kind of profit are we showing?"

So Russell finally learned why Holt had come to the farms. "The farms have never shown a profit. Your grandfather—"

"Mist' Russell, I'll take her now," George said.

Russell turned angrily, facing the black man. He could see the flush of terror in the farmhand's face. Russell extended the mare's reins and turned to the uninvited guest who had suddenly become his employer.

"Your grandfather did not set up the farms for profit," Russell said. "Lucius Peete told me this when he hired me. Lucius said Sam Castleton built the farms as a kind of showcase for the people of the community."

Holt pushed the handkerchief into his pocket. "You have your car. Follow me back to the Castle."

"Say what you have to say, Holt." Russell watched him walk to the Stutz. "Holt? I need another hour or more here today."

"I want to talk now," Holt said.

Russell watched the green phaeton skirt the bunkhouses and disappear behind the long avenue of sycamores Sam Castleton had planted. George came out of the barn, raising his arm to wipe his forehead with his shirtsleeve. "Makes me feel like old times around here, having Mist' Holt back."

Russell walked toward his car beside the barn. He drove slowly, taking the long way back to the Castle, past the cemetery and the lake. He loved it all, loved the farms, the cemetery, the lake, enclosed and protected by the dense growth of trees. He could see the chimney of the lake house above the trees.

At the Castle Russell went from room to room, looking for Holt. In the library he came upon Clara, one of the maids. "Where is Mr. Holt?"

"In the study, Mist' Russell," Clara said.

"Go and find Miss Gaby wherever she is," Russell said. "Tell Miss Gaby to join us."

"Join, yes, sir," said the black woman. "Join you."

Walking to the study, Russell remembered coming to the Castle directly from college with his degree in business administration. His senior adviser, Geoffrey Lyons, a professor of economics, had written his doctoral thesis on the introduction of cigarettes into the mass market. Lyons stayed a year at company headquarters during his research. He sent Russell to Lucius Peete. "You're smart, and you can think straight," Lyons said. "And you can keep your mouth shut. Lucius Peete has been looking for someone like you, someone he can trust."

Russell reached the study and stopped in the corridor. Holt was sitting behind Russell's desk. He said, "To answer your question, I am not sitting in your chair. I'm sitting in my chair. Come in, Russell."

"Why did you drive out to the farms?" Russell asked. "Why did you waste the time?"

"No waste," Holt said. "I'm feeling my way as I learn a new trade."

"You could have told me at the farms."

"You'll need to clear out your desk," Holt said. "No rush, Russell. Take the rest of the day."

Russell leaped forward, losing all control. "You vile—"

"Russell?" Gaby's interruption saved him from oblivion. Something in his face sent her directly to his side. "Tell me what's wrong," she said.

"Holt is trying to fire me," Russell said.

"Fire!" Gaby leveled her anger directly at Holt. "Fire?"

"I believe it's because he knows about us," Russell said. "And he knows that with me on the premises, he doesn't have his obedient younger sister in his pocket." Russell moved slightly, facing Holt as well. "Holt didn't tell me, but he needs your vote to get rid of me.

Yours or Faith's. You three each own one third of the Castle and the farms. And you and Faith can stop Holt, can keep me here. I believe Faith will. I had a good relationship with Faith. She learned quickly that I didn't take sides, and I didn't lie. She trusted me, and I think she still trusts me. Faith is intelligent. She must realize she is safer on my side than Holt's, Kyle's brother, who says she killed Kyle."

Gaby said, "I want to leave." She extended her hand, and Russell took it. "We'll go today, and we'll never come back to this house, this . . . evil house."

"You're running," Russell said. "I won't let you run, and I won't run with you. Holt hopes we'll run. Look at him. He can manage you, but he can't manage you with me." Russell put his arm around her. "Stop him, Gaby. I want to stay here with you. Sam Castleton said it. I've been a hired hand since the day Lucius Peete brought me to the Castle. You can rescue me, end my years of servitude."

"I will, I will!" Gaby said. "Come away now, today!"

"No!" he said, pleading with her. "I'll never leave willingly. I've been here too long. The Castle and the farms are part of me. I belong here. Keep me here with you, Gaby. I can stay only if you stay."

Holt rose, pushed back the chair, moved slowly around the desk, eyeing them as though they were on an auction block. "Poor Gaby," Holt said. "When will you learn? Haven't you had enough? You're barely rid of one leech. For God's sake, Gaby, grow up! Russell Vance is not Prince Charming. He's just another toady looking for the soft life."

Holt gestured at the windows. "There are armies of Russell Vances out there, hoping for a chance to slip through these doors. They're like prospectors, only their tools are ambition, greed, cunning. And patience. They can wait, Gaby. They have nothing to lose."

"Stop!" Gaby swung around to go, but Holt was quicker, stopping between her and the door.

"I'm almost finished," Holt said. "Russell is wrong, Gaby. I want *him* out of here, and not with my sister. You have a weakness for white trash, Gaby. First, Colin Inscott, whose father was a Wall Street swindler, although he wasn't caught. He disappeared before he was caught. But Russell's father was caught, wasn't he, Russell? A petty thief, stealing nickels and dimes from widows and orphans."

Gaby raised her arm to move Holt aside, but he stepped back, and she went past him, leaving the study.

"You're worse than I thought," Russell said. "Or maybe I had forgotten. You were gone so long. I thought the Castletons couldn't surprise me, but you did, Holt. I suppose you're right. I suppose I am white trash." Russell paused, facing Holt. "I knew you were rotten, but until today I didn't know how rotten. You're evil through and through."

"Either you clean out your desk or the niggers will," Holt said.

Russell left the study. He heard Holt say, "The niggers will do it for you." He walked through the Castle, looking for Gaby. Then he climbed the stairs and stopped at the sleeping porch.

"Gaby?" Russell opened the door. She lay on the bed, eyes open, her hands on her belly. Russell saw her shoes on the floor. He crossed the room and sat down on the bed. "I've never lied to you, but I didn't tell you about my father, about my family," Russell said. "Everything you heard in the study is true. My father was a thief, and he went to prison. He died in prison."

Russell told Gaby of his mother, of her drunkenness, of the wretched home she ruled, of his horrible childhood and youth, of his escape, winning a scholarship to college.

"And when I came to the Castle, to the farms, I had more than a job," Russell said. "I left my old life behind. I erased it. I had to prove myself, had to succeed, and I did. I did, Gaby. Then . . . you. You and I. I couldn't believe my luck." He put his hand across her ankles. "When you left, I thought I would go under. I mean, really under, like my father. But the memories of you, of the golden days we had together, saved me. And I had the Castle. I could put everything into the Castle and into the farms. I can't stop now, Gaby. This is my new life! And you've come back! Now I really belong here, belong with you. You can keep me here with you."

Gaby turned her head, facing the sunlight in the trees. "You want to rule, like Holt."

"Not like Holt," Russell said. "I'm not like Holt, and you are my witness. I want a place for myself, the place I've earned. It isn't the money, Gaby. I have enough money. It's . . . this," he said. "All of this. Gaby, look at me." She did not budge, and although Russell believed he had lost, he said, "You've lived in one Castle, but there is another. I could show you a different Castle."

Russell rose and crossed the sleeping porch, sunk in such despair that the room blurred. As he opened the door, he heard Gaby, her voice soft with infinite promise: "Stay."

———◦《◦》◦———

IN THE COURTHOUSE Boyd walked from one end of a narrow room to the other, touching the backs of chairs with his fingertips as he passed. Except for the chairs, set around a long table, the room was barren and without windows. Light came from chandeliers above the table. There were two doors, one opening to the corridor and the other, in the center of the room, to the county attorney's office.

Boyd raised his arm to glance at his wristwatch. Eleven minutes past ten. He had taken a nine o'clock bus downtown, determined to be in the courthouse long before ten o'clock, loitering in the lobby until he climbed the stairs a few minutes before the appointment.

He pulled a chair out from the table and sat down, crossing his legs. Boyd wiggled in the chair, trying to get comfortable, then rose, carefully sliding the chair back under the table. He looked up at the clock over the corridor door, and as he began to circle the table, the door opened. When Boyd saw Dan Cohen, he wanted to run across the room to greet the slim, neat man. Summoned to the lawyer's office, Boyd had met with Dan once. No one had ever been as kind.

"I apologize for my tardiness," Dan said. "We had an emergency in our house. Our cat had kittens."

"You're not really late," Boyd said, crossing the room to join Dan. "Nobody's here. Mr. Isbell said ten o'clock, but I haven't seen him. Why did he ask me to come?"

"We'll have to wait and see," Dan said.

Thirty feet away, in his office, Max Isbell stood at the windows, his hands in his trousers pockets, looking down at the statues of Lee and the two Confederate infantrymen guarding the courthouse. Now and then he glanced at the clock over his desk, which chimed on the quarter hour. As the chimes rang out at ten-thirty, Isbell turned away from the windows and left his office. He stopped in the men's room, where he washed his hands and combed his hair. Isbell returned to the county attorney's suite and walked through it to an unmarked door.

Isbell said, "Sorry I'm late, Mr. Fredericks," before he saw Dan Cohen. Nobody had told him about Dan Cohen. "I asked you to come in so we could have a little talk," Isbell said. He raised his hand, forefinger and middle finger extended to indicate two. "We."

"I've been retained by Mr. Fredericks," Dan said. "I am his counsel." He faced Isbell. "I should tell you I also represent Mrs. Castleton."

"Congratulations," Isbell said, annoyed. He moved a chair back. "Why don't we all sit down?"

Boyd pulled out a chair for Dan. "Mr. Cohen," he said, and took the chair beside Dan's.

Isbell paused for a few moments, calculating how to proceed, then said, "Seeing you close up, Mr. Fredericks, I realize I'm old enough to be your father. So I'll call you Boyd, if it's all right with you."

Boyd tried not to be scared. He had to act like a man. He had Mr. Cohen with him. Mr. Cohen would take care of him. "All right."

"Good." Isbell put his right arm on the table as though he were in his club, among friends. "Please note there is no stenographer present. Nothing we say here will be on the record, Boyd. Nothing you say can hurt you. Your lawyer, Mr. Cohen, will attest to what I've just said."

Dan turned to Boyd. "This meeting is not official," Dan said. "You may speak freely, or you may remain silent. You are free to leave now or at any time you choose. The decision is entirely yours."

Isbell said, "You heard him, Boyd. Of course I want you to stay, so I won't beat around the bush. There is only one topic of interest here, and we both know what it is." Suddenly it occurred to him that maybe he was lucky they had picked Dan Cohen. Except for getting niggers out of jail, Isbell could not remember seeing the Jew in a criminal case.

"Kyle Castleton," Isbell said. "Nothing is worse than a murder. A murder is bad for everyone. I think Mr. Cohen will back me up on that too. A murder involves everyone in the community. First the family," Isbell said. "The family demands justice. The family expects to see the murderer pay. And where does the family turn? The family turns to the criminal justice system.

"Nor are the Castletons allowed to forget," Isbell said. "The newspapers are the scorekeepers in a murder. Every day they remind the world that Kyle Castleton has been murdered. It's an ugly business, Boyd. I'm sure your counsel will agree with me."

"Why has my client been summoned?" Dan asked abruptly.

Isbell took his arm from the table and uncrossed his legs, shifting in his chair. Maybe he had been wrong about Cohen. "Invited," Isbell said. "I invited Boyd to come in for a talk." The county attorney looked at Dan. "If I may proceed."

Isbell said, "This is what I'd like you to do, Boyd. I'd like you to go back to the night of Labor Day. I'd like you to think back to everything you remember about that night. Maybe something happened that you forgot to mention, that slipped your mind. You intended to bring it up but forgot. It happens to all of us. We're only human. Maybe it's something that you didn't think was important, that you figured didn't have any bearing on the events of that night."

"I've told you everything," Boyd said, feeling a spark of panic.

"Not me," Isbell said. "You haven't told me anything. We've never talked, Boyd. It's the reason I invited you to the courthouse today. This is the first chance we've ever had to talk."

"I told them at the inquest. I told the coroner everything."

"It's been almost a month since the inquest," Isbell said. "You were in the eye of the storm, Boyd. You probably weren't thinking straight. How could you? How could anyone be thinking straight in those circumstances? You had lost your best friend." He turned in his chair to stare grimly at Boyd.

"So I'm asking you now, a month later," said the county attorney. "I know it's painful, but go back to that night. You've probably thought of that night a lot, probably wished you could stop thinking of that night, isn't that true, Boyd?"

"Yes." Boyd nodded. "Yes, it is."

"Makes sense," Isbell said. "And in all this time have you remembered anything you didn't tell the coroner at the inquest? Anything at all?"

"I didn't remember because I didn't forget," Boyd said. "How could I forget? I'll never forget. One minute Kyle was alive, and the next minute he was dead."

"Let's talk about that next minute," said the county attorney.

He watched the kid carefully. He wanted the kid to trust him. "Take it easy, Boyd. You told the coroner that when you got to the sleeping porch, you found Faith Castleton standing over the bed, over Kyle's body."

Isbell's lie terrified Boyd. "You're wrong!" he said, turning to Dan. "That's not true! I didn't say that."

"Correct me," Isbell said. "Boyd? I'm listening."

"You have the transcript of the coroner's inquest," Dan said.

"I'd like to hear it from Boyd," Isbell said. "Unless either of you object. Boyd? Do you object?"

"I said—" Boyd began, and stopped. He had to watch out now. Faith's life . . . *his* life, depended on what he said.

Isbell waited, letting the silence build. "You said?"

Boyd took a deep breath. "I said—" He stopped, raising his head to look at the county attorney. "I said when I got to the sleeping porch, Faith was there."

"So we're agreed."

"We're not!" Boyd fell back in the chair. "We're *not* agreed! You said I saw her inside, *in* the sleeping porch, at the bed. *You* said that. I didn't!"

"What did you say? What *do* you say, Boyd?"

"We met in the hall," Boyd said, and he said to Dan: "We met in the hall, Mr. Cohen. We went into the sleeping porch together."

"Together," Isbell said. "Fair enough. Where were you when you heard the shot?"

Boyd rubbed his thighs. Finally he could tell the truth. "Downstairs," he said, "calling my mother to tell her I'd be sleeping over at the Castle."

"And you heard the shot," Isbell said.

"Heard a . . . plop," Boyd said. "A flat sound, like a thud, a hard thud."

"Above," Isbell said. "The sound came from above."

"I ran," Boyd said. "I hung up, put down the receiver, and ran."

"Up the stairs and down the corridor, where you saw Faith Castleton," Isbell said. "Am I correct, Boyd? You saw Faith Castleton backing into the corridor."

"No!" Boyd sat erect, hitting the wooden arms of his chair with both hands. The county attorney was trying to trick him. *"Crossing* the corridor," Boyd said. "Coming from her room—their room, their bedroom where they usually slept. Faith didn't like the sleeping porch."

"How far would you say it is from the telephone to the sleeping porch?"

"I don't know."

"How many stairs?"

"Twenty," Boyd said. "Thirty. A whole lot. The staircase is really two flights. Halfway up you make a turn."

"How many feet of corridor from the head of the stairs to the sleeping porch?"

"I don't know," Boyd said.

"There are thirty-six steps," Isbell said. "Sheriff Ainsley measured the distance. It took him twenty-one seconds to go from the telephone up the stairs. So the question is, Could someone have come out of the sleeping porch, crossed the corridor, turned around, and come back into the corridor in that time? The answer is someone could. Faith Castleton could have done it."

"You're trying—" Boyd said, and stopped.

"Trying? Boyd, I'm trying to gather the facts. Isn't it a fact that Faith Castleton could have killed her husband, left the sleeping porch, crossed the corridor, and turned and retraced her steps before you got upstairs?"

"She didn't kill Kyle!"

"You haven't answered my question! Could she have left the sleeping porch, crossed those few feet, and turned back before you saw her?"

"Kyle killed himself!"

"The grand jury thought otherwise," Isbell said. "They voted an indictment of murder, indicting Mrs. Castleton and you for—" Isbell stopped as someone knocked on the door to the suite. "Excuse me."

When Isbell opened the door, one of his secretaries said, "I'm sorry to interrupt you, sir. It's important," she said, repeating what Isbell had instructed her to say.

"I left orders not to be disturbed," Isbell said.

"I told them," said the secretary. "They insisted. They said you would understand."

"All right." Isbell looked back at the table. "I won't be long," he said. "You have my word." He followed the secretary, closing the door. "Good girl."

After Isbell had left, Dan turned to Boyd. "This entire maneuver is an attempt to enlist your help," the lawyer said. "When he returns, he will ask you to turn state's evidence, to say Faith Castleton killed her husband."

"She didn't!"

"But you should be aware of what he is offering," Dan said. "If you testify that Faith Castleton *did* kill her husband, you will not be charged with murder. The charges against you may even be dropped."

"I can't!" Boyd said. "I could never . . . I couldn't!"

In his office Isbell stood at his desk for a suitable amount of time. When he thought the boy had simmered long enough he left his office and returned to his guests. "Sorry we were interrupted," Isbell said. "Boyd, I want you to know this. I didn't bring you in here to hurt you. I took an oath to protect the people of this county, which means all the people, every man, woman, and child, in this jurisdiction," Isbell said. "I live by my oath. I'm here to help you. But I can't help you unless you help yourself. If you're shielding someone, tell me. I'll protect you. The court will reward you. I did not become county attorney to prosecute innocent people. I want Kyle Castleton's killer."

"And I'd be set free," Boyd said.

So Isbell knew the Jew had been talking to him. "Maybe," Isbell said. "You won't be accused of murder, I can promise you that much here and now."

"Faith is innocent," Boyd said. "That's all I have to say."

"Answer one question," Isbell said. "While you were downstairs, could Faith Castleton have shot and killed her husband?"

"She didn't do it!" Boyd said, and sprang out of the chair.

"But you were downstairs," Isbell said. "How can you be so sure?"

"Faith didn't kill him!"

Isbell rose, bending over the table, his knuckles against the wood surface. "This is your last chance, mister."

Dan had had enough. "We are leaving." Rising, he took Boyd's arm. Dan faced Isbell but spoke to Boyd. "This episode is ended. The county attorney does not wish to cause you emotional anguish or distress. It was not his purpose in inviting you to meet with him."

Isbell watched them walking to the corridor door. "I enjoyed our little visit, counsel."

In the corridor Boyd whirled around, startling Dan. "You saved my life!" Boyd said. "Mr. Cohen, you saved my life!"

"No, no," Dan said, very uncomfortable and looking from side to side, grateful for the absence of witnesses to the younger man's extravagant outburst. "I am your counsel," Dan said. "I represent you, Mr. Fredericks."

"Thank God," Boyd said. "And Mr. Cohen? Please call me Boyd."

<hr>

THAT NIGHT DAN COHEN'S YOUNGER SON, Joe, who would be sixteen the day after Christmas, woke from a nightmare. For a little while, still in the never-never land between dreaming and being awake, he lay motionless, until he felt his pillow, damp with perspiration. Then he sat up, swinging his legs over the side of the bed.

Joe got out of bed, wiping his face. He decided to fill the sink with cold water and dunk his head, a practice he'd learned from David. Joe pulled on his cotton shorts and felt his way through the bedroom. Near the door he accidentally kicked a basketball, which caromed off one wall into another.

As Joe reached the open door, he heard David in the room beside his. "Joe?"

"Go back to sleep."

The upstairs hallway separated the boys from the master bedroom, which was set back from the broad veranda below. The bathroom flanked the master bedroom and had two doors, one opening into the hall.

The door was ajar, the boys' signal that it was unoccupied. Although Sarah kept a night-light burning, the bathroom seemed much brighter, as though someone were inside. "Dad?" Joe stopped. "Mom?"

He listened, then walked to the door, which he pushed wide

open. The blazing glare made him close his eyes, then open them. Blinking, he finally realized the house was on fire.

Joe leaped to the window. Below, in the ground in front of the porte cochere, Joe saw white-hooded figures with torches around a burning pole. The flames leaped into the dark night, rising like sky-rockets.

"You sonsabitches!" Joe shouted. High up, on a level with the bathroom, the flames spread on each side of the vertical pole, forming a towering cross, lighting up the street and the sky. "You sonsabitches!" Barefoot, Joe ran for the stairs.

David heard him and reached under the bed for his glasses. "Joe? What's wrong?"

Sarah sat up in the darkness. "Joe?" She nudged Dan. "Why are you yelling? Joe!" She pushed Dan. "Wake up!" Sarah turned up the light beside her. "Joe!" She scrambled out of bed. "Dan!"

Joe stopped at the head of the stairs, clawing the wall for the light switch. David came out into the hallway as Joe ran down the stairs. "Joe! What's the matter?" David ran after him.

Below, Joe slammed the screen door back against the wall of the veranda. Four hooded men in white ran down Fairview Avenue. Joe heard automobile engines, and he saw two cars in the middle of the street. Joe ran across the porch and leaped over the steps. "You lousy bastards!"

Up and down the street, on both sides of Fairview Avenue and on both sides of the Cohen house, lights went up. They were quickly extinguished. Except for the flaming cross and the lights in the Cohen house, Fairview Avenue lay in darkness.

David ran barefoot across the veranda, following his younger brother. He saw the waiting cars, saw the four men in white robes running down the street, saw Joe chasing the men. David had to get his younger brother before he got hurt.

Beside one of the cars David saw a white figure raising a rifle. "Joe!"

The *crack* of the rifle cut through the night like a thunderclap. David saw Joe dive into a neighboring lawn, saw the white figures disappear into the waiting cars, saw the rifleman leap onto a running board, heard the roar of the automobile engines as the cars sped off, and, above it all, heard his mother's screams.

Joe pushed himself up from the dewy lawn, brushing off his arms and legs, and ran back toward his mother.

David came down the steps to meet Joe. Although David was two years older, preparing to leave for his freshman year at Chapel Hill, Joe was as tall as and heavier and more solid than David. "They shot at you!" David said.

"Shut up!" Joe grabbed David's arms savagely. "Maybe Mom didn't hear it or didn't know what she heard. I hope she doesn't. I hope to God." Joe released David, facing the flaming cross. "This is bad enough. Those bastards. Those slimy cowards."

"David!" Sarah stood behind the screen door, a robe over her nightgown. "Joseph Cohen! Come in here! Both of you, into this house!"

Joe said, "We're coming!" and he whispered to David, "Let me do the talking."

"I'm calling the cops," David said.

"The cops? What the hell for? The bastards are gone," Joe said.

"Boys!" Sarah shouted. She glanced at the flaming cross. "Oh, my God." She moaned, traumatized by the fire, shaking with fear in the hot, steamy night.

As her sons reached the veranda, Sarah came out to meet them. "How could you?" David strode past her into the house. "David!" She held on to Joe and pointed at the cross. "Isn't this bad enough? Did you have to chase them, begging for more trouble?"

"I was so mad I couldn't think straight," Joe said. "Those—" he said, and stopped. Neither son used profanity in his mother's presence.

Sarah hugged him. "I almost died," she said. "Those . . . animals. Those vile creatures. You've seen what they're capable of doing." She held on to him. "Come inside," Sarah said as Joe saw a stream of water hit the burning cross.

He broke away from his mother, running. "Joe! Stop . . ." she cried.

Joe jumped off the porch, legs spread like a hurdler, jumping high to clear the thick border of hydrangeas.

Dan Cohen stood in the driveway in front of the porte cochere, holding a garden hose, directing the stream of water at the flames. He had pulled on his pants, and he wore bedroom slippers. Water dripped from the worn nozzle onto his hand and down on his trousers. Joe grabbed the hose. "Let it burn!"

"Stop!" Dan fought him for the hose, holding it with both hands. "Joe, stop, I say!"

"Give me that goddamn—" Joe said, wrestling the hose from his father. "Let it burn! Let everyone see it, see what those bastards have done!"

Joe pushed the hose under the hydrangeas and discovered he was about to cry. His rage and feeling of helplessness had driven him to tears. He whirled around, fists clenched. But then the sight of the bedraggled figure in the driveway, his V-neck underwear and trousers soaked from the struggle with the hose, sent Joe to his father's side to protect him. "Let's go in, Dad." The boy put his arm around his father's shoulder.

They heard Sarah. "Dan!"

"We're coming," Joe said.

On the veranda David joined his mother. "Where's Dad? Is he all right?"

"He's all right," Sarah said. She pulled her robe together. "Dan!" she said, and saw him with Joe on the steps, and in the glare of the fire, saw his wet clothing clinging to him. "You're soaked! Both of you! You'll both catch cold! Look at us. We're out here like gypsies, homeless gypsies!" She opened the screen door. "I want everyone inside. This minute. Get out of those clothes, Dan. You too, Joe. David, help your father."

Inside Ella, the older of the two black servants, stood beside the stairs to the bedrooms. She wore a heavy cotton robe with a thick cord around her middle. "They're gone, Ella," Dan said. "Go back to bed."

"It's not me," Ella said. "It's Corinne. She's hiding in the closet."

"Not for long," Sarah said. "Not in this heat."

"She won't move," Ella said.

Dan said, "Come on, Ella." He took her arm.

"Dan! You're soaking wet!" Sarah said.

Dan took the black woman through the hall to the rooms behind the kitchen. His first memories were of Ella. She had bathed and dressed him and fed him. "Why they come here, Mist' Dan?"

He didn't reply. "Mist' Dan?"

In the kitchen he could smell the ironed shirts in the laundry room. Ella said, "Corinne's in my room, Mist' Dan. She run into my room and straight into the closet."

In the bedroom Dan opened the closet door. Corinne stood in a corner of the shallow closet, her back to the door. "Corinne." When he touched her, she tried to flatten herself against the wall. "They're gone, Corinne," Dan said, so quietly that Ella could not hear him. "We're safe now. You can come out now. You can stay here with Ella tonight in Ella's room. Corinne." He moved forward, touching her, and finally she turned to him.

On the other side of the house Sarah watched Joe and David come down the stairs. They had changed into dry shorts, and both were still barefoot. "So far not a sign from our friendly neighbors," Sarah said. "Not one word. David!" she said as he jumped over the last steps and ran out of the house.

Joe saw the broad red band of light across the roof of the police car as it stopped. "The cops!"

"Cops? Joe, wait!" Sarah hurried after him. "Who called the police?"

The police car stopped at the curb in front of the driveway. When Clyde James, the driver, and his partner, Carl Lemke, came out of the sedan, David stood between them and the burning cross. "You must be awfully busy tonight."

"We're busy every night," said Carl Lemke.

"Your siren must be broke," David said.

Clyde James stopped in front of the snotty Jewboy. "That's right," he said.

David stepped aside. "Take a good look," he said. "Quite a sight, isn't it? This is a present from our fellow townsmen."

"Dirty shame," said Carl Lemke. He pushed back the nightstick in its sling on his hip and saw Sarah and Joe coming. "Clyde."

Clyde James saw them too. "Maybe you should've called the fire department."

"And destroy the evidence? How would you solve the crime without the evidence? You would just have our word for what happened," David said.

Clyde James had a smart Jewboy on his hands besides a snotty one. "What happened?"

"We woke and saw the flames," David said. "There were six of them out there—" he said as Joe interrupted.

"Six white sonsabitches," Joe said. "Gutless sonsabitches."

"And three cars parked in the middle of the street," David said. He paused, facing the cops. "You men must have fantastic memories."

James studied the Jewboy. "Huh?"

"I'm giving you the facts, but you've not putting anything down on paper," David said.

"Yeah," James said.

"Yeah, what?" Joe said. "What does 'yeah' mean?"

"Did you get a good look at any of them?" James asked.

"Is that supposed to be funny? In their *sheets?* They don't have the guts to show their faces," Joe said. "They're cowards, lousy, slimy cowards."

"You said there were three cars," James said. "How about the license numbers?"

"No license number," Joe said.

Carl Lemke saw an older man come out of the house. "How about the cars?" Lemke asked. "What make were they? What color? What year?"

"They shot at us—at my brother!" David said.

"*Shot!*" Sarah's voice could be heard up and down the street. "They *shot*—!"

Dan separated his sons, standing between them and the cops. "Thank you, Officers," he said. "We appreciate your concern. I'm sure you'll do everything within your power to find those who are responsible for this terrible act. I have complete faith in the police of our city." He paused. "We needn't keep you any longer."

"Check," said James. "We'll be making out our report later. This will all go into our report downtown. Carl?" The two policemen walked to their car.

Sarah raised both hands to the burning cross. "God, won't it ever burn out?" To her sons she said "Wait, boys," although neither had moved. "You're both part of this," Sarah said. "Dan?"

"Come into the house, Sarah."

"As though nothing happened here tonight," she said. "As though we came outside to enjoy the night air." She put her hands on his shoulders and turned him to face the burning cross. "They're real gentlemen here in the heart of Dixie, the land of cotton and tobacco and the happy Negro singing in the fields," Sarah said. "They put up with your silly habit of defending the Negro, although it scares me out of a good night's sleep. You and your Reverend Millard Fitch."

Dan said, "Come inside, Sarah. Boys, come into the house."

"They can burn the house like they burned the cross," Sarah said. "And they will. The cross is a warning, Dan. They've given us fair warning. You know why this happened, don't tell me otherwise."

"The Castletons," David said.

"That's right," Sarah said. "Your father is defending Faith Venable and Boyd Fredericks. But not anymore." She leaned forward, her face inches from her husband's face. "Resign from the case, Dan. Do it the first thing tomorrow morning."

"Dad, I hate this as much as you do," David said. "But Mom's right. We've been given a warning."

For Dan, the law and the oath he had taken as an officer of the court were sacred. Hoping he could avoid a confrontation, he said, "We can discuss the matter in the morning."

"Now," Sarah said. She pushed her sons apart, standing between them. "We can discuss our future, our *lives,* now."

Dan said, "Sarah, Sarah, when did you hear of them harming a white man?"

"We are your family, Dan. You owe us a little more than you owe strangers. Faith Venable and Boyd Fredericks are strangers."

The slight man in the wet clothes plastered to his legs faced his family. He searched for a way to make them understand until he said, defying them, "I'm a lawyer."

Sarah lunged forward, arm raised, pointing at the cross. "There is the law, Dan. The Castletons are the law."

"Can't we go inside, Sarah?"

Joe said, "Mom, let's go inside."

Sarah shook her head, facing Dan. "You won't do it, will you?" Joe joined his mother. He could have told her from the beginning.

"Let's go in, Mom," he said as a car turned into Fairview Avenue.

Sarah raised her hand, shielding her eyes. "My God, now what?"

The car stopped in front of the cross, parked illegally, facing oncoming traffic. Two men left the car; one held a Speed Graphic camera. "Reporters," Joe said.

"The newspaper," Dan said. "The honorable recorders of . . . ugliness."

"We'll handle it, Dad," Joe said.

"Come, Dan," Sarah said. She put her arm around him as they went to the house.

David walked into the driveway. He stood in front of the cross. "This way, gentlemen," he said. "You don't even need a flashbulb."

Joe confronted the reporter. "Who sent you? The Klan?"

"Easy, pal," said the reporter.

"Or you'll write terrible things about us," Joe said. "You're scary. Who sent you?"

"Hey, take it easy," the reporter said. "We've got a police radio in the city room. We hear all the calls the cops or the sheriff hear." The photographer took his first picture, removed the plate, and slipped another plate into the camera. "Can you think of any reason why this happened?"

Joe looked at the reporter but did not respond.

"*Can* you?" asked the reporter.

"Uh-uh," Joe said.

<hr />

ONE MORNING LATER in the week Boyd came downstairs to the kitchen almost two hours after Olive had left the house to give her monthly free concert for the blind. Boyd saw the coffeepot dismembered in the sink. Olive always made Boyd a fresh pot after finishing the first.

Although she left Boyd evidence of his punishment, he could not remember a reason. "She doesn't need a reason," he said aloud. Boyd turned the water tap, filled the coffeepot, but set it down in the sink. He left the house angrily. He stopped in the driveway. He hadn't locked the door. "God, there's nothing worth stealing," he said. No one could move the piano, and everything else belonged in the junkyard.

Boyd walked three blocks to a café. He sat in a booth facing a

photograph of Lindbergh, head and shoulders, wearing a leather flying jacket and a leather helmet, with the goggles pushed up above
his forehead, Kyle's favorite picture in the world. Kyle had framed
the picture. Boyd ordered toast and coffee.

He walked home slowly, crisscrossing the street constantly to
stay in the shade. The house retained the cool night air. Boyd lit
another Crisp, inhaling the mentholated tobacco, and dropped
into Olive's chair, the upright ashtray at his elbow. Boyd hated the
furniture, hated everything in sight except the piano. As he tapped
the cigarette on the rim of the ashtray, the telephone rang. He
rose. "Mother," he said aloud. She must be calling to tell him how
badly he had sinned. He went to the telephone beside the piano.
"Hello."

"Boyd?"

"Who's this?"

"It's Stan Jessup," said the owner of the airport. "I've been
thinking of you, Boyd. How are you making out these days?"

"Fine," Boyd said. "I'm fine."

"Haven't seen much of you," Jessup said.

"I've been kind of busy," Boyd said. Suddenly a shudder of excitement swept through him, leaving him weak. Stan Jessup had sold
the Waco! Why else would he call?

"Boyd, where's my money?"

"Your . . . *money?*"

"Fifty bucks," Jessup said. "October hangar rent. You pay in
advance around here."

Boyd wanted to hurl the telephone at the wall. "I—" he said,
stopped, and could not continue.

"Fifty clams, Boyd," Jessup said. "United States currency."

"I heard you! I heard you! I haven't got it!" Boyd said. "You'll
have to wait!"

"Not for long," Jessup said. "You owe me. Bring it in, Boyd.
Don't get me mad. I'm not a gent like your pal Kyle Castleton."

Boyd slammed down the telephone. He snuffed out his cigarette and strode into the kitchen. He moved a chair to the cabinets
flanking the sink. Boyd stepped up on the chair and reached into the
top shelf for the porcelain dwarf where his mother kept the Christmas money. He raised the dwarf's head, which moved on a brass

hinge at the back of the neck. Each bill was folded again and again, making a small square.

Boyd rode a bus downtown. He went to a theater that offered double features. Afterward he walked around, looking in store windows, and later he went to another theater, where he sat through two showings.

He stayed downtown until long after dark. Coming home, Boyd prayed his mother would be asleep, but when he returned, he saw a light in her room.

Boyd went to the Model T in the driveway. He had his own key. He set the gas and magneto levers jutting out from the drive shaft below the steering wheel. In front of the coupe he bent for the crank. "Start, please start," he said, and turned.

The engine caught. Boyd jumped into the coupe, depressed the clutch to back out into the street, the car door swinging back and forth. He turned the wheel hard, slammed the door, and raced down the street as lights blazed on in the house.

Off Deer Hollow Road, at the end of the cul-de-sac, Faith sat at a card table she had carried to the fireplace. She had brought two lamps to the fireplace, placing one on each side of her chair. Ruled paper tablets covered the card table, and pencils and pens were everywhere. A large book of Greek mythology lay open at Faith's elbow.

For a few days after leaving the hotel, Faith had gone from room to room in the empty house, staring at herself in every mirror. Then, early one morning, Faith telephoned Ward Kirby in New York, waking the dancer. "What have they done to you? Angel, it's the middle of the night!"

"Go to Brentano's and find me a book on Penelope and Ulysses," Faith said.

"Penelope and *Ulysses!*"

"Mail it to me," Faith said. "You mail it, not Brentano's, not someone who will call the newspapers with the scandalous news."

"What brings you to those two?"

"Will you do it? Tell me now," Faith said.

"Of course I'll do it," Ward said. "How are you, angel? How are you holding up under this awful nightmare?"

"I'll live," Faith said, "I hope."

"*Stop!* You send shivers through me," Ward said. "You *must* live, or I'll die! Promise!"

"I promise," Faith said.

"God, I miss you."

"I miss you," Faith said. "Do it today, Ward. Do it now."

"Brentano's isn't open now," Ward said, "or have you stopped looking at clocks?"

"When they open," Faith said. "And mail it today. I'll send you a check. Buy yourself something cute."

"I'm cute already," Ward said. "God, I love you. Faith, I love you. Faith?" He listened, but she had gone.

Faith asked Wyn to bring her ruled tablets and pencils, and she began even before the postman delivered Ward's book, jotting down ideas and scenes and even ideas for songs. Broadway librettos were froth, fairy-tale nonsense. Faith believed she could tell a better story than those in which she had played and those she had seen.

She had, periodically, thought of Penelope for the lead of a show, a musical. Faith had read little of anything in her lifetime. But she knew Penelope had been alone for years and years, waiting for Ulysses to return and warding off suitors. So Penelope became an ideal heroine for Faith, a woman alone onstage surrounded by men.

The book Ward chose confirmed all Faith hoped for in the libretto. The story consumed her. She had to separate herself from the horrors she faced, from the terrible forces arrayed against her, and she went to the card table almost immediately after waking each morning. Often, after hours hunched over the table, Faith would rise and walk through the house to ease the ache in her back before returning to her chair, to the libretto, to the future, desperately intent on keeping the present at bay.

The doorbell startled her. Wyn usually telephoned before driving out to Deer Hollow Road. So he must have forgotten or lost the key she had given him. She smiled on her way to the door to admit him. "Ulysses," she murmured.

Boyd slipped past her before she had the door completely open. He offered an awkward salute. "Surprise."

"I told you not to come back."

"I haven't been back," Boyd said. "Have I? Until tonight. I couldn't help it, Faith," he said, growing bolder. "I only want," he said, stepping down into the living room, "to talk." Faith followed him. "Why are you so angry?"

"You should not have come."

"I had to!" he said, his voice rising. "I don't have anyone else! I'm alone!" He backed into the card table and stopped. He turned to look down at the ruled paper tablets and the open book. "Penelope. I remember her. She knitted all day and unraveled all night," Boyd said, "to keep her suitors at bay. Are you writing something about her, Faith? A play?" He clapped his hands, proud of solving the mystery. "You're writing a play, and you'll be Penelope! You'd be perfect!" Boyd flipped through the book, his forefinger keeping Faith's place.

Faith pushed him aside, closed the book, and stacked her ruled tablets. She set the closed book atop the stack. Faith could not abide Boyd, but she managed to say, gently, "You should not have come."

"I'm so afraid," Boyd said. He spoke as though he had not heard her. "I'm afraid all the time, afraid when I wake and when I go to sleep."

"Boyd. Darling," Faith said. "You cannot stay."

"I won't," he said. "Just let me catch my breath. Just let me . . . *breathe*. I can breathe here," he said. "I feel . . . safe with you, Faith."

"You must leave," Faith said. "Leave now and don't come back, Boyd." She stepped toward him, and alarmed, he sprang back, back into the fireplace.

"Why are you so mean to me? You've become mean . . . and cruel," he said.

She needed all her strength of will to mask her disgust for him. "Cruel, Boyd?" she said. "As I was in the courthouse when I posted your bail, delivered twenty-five thousand dollars of *my* money, and gave your mother back her son? And now you have a lawyer. Where do you think the money for your lawyer came from?"

"I'm in danger," Boyd said. "We're in danger together."

"Dear Boyd," she said, despising him. "We cannot be together. Go back to your mother." Faith extended her hand. "Go, Boyd. Now."

"I'm not leaving," he said. "You can't send me away, Faith. You can't. Not after what happened between us."

She said "happened" so softly she could barely be heard, but the single word seemed to reverberate through the house.

"You fool," she said, abandoning all pretense. Since the fool had challenged her, she had to end the playacting. "You should not have said what you did. Now we'll settle things. Now. Tonight." She picked up a ruler, and Boyd watched it as though she had armed herself.

"Nothing happened," Faith said flatly.

"I wish you were right," he said. "I wish—"

"I am right."

"—I had gone to the races with Kyle, flown to Cleveland with Kyle instead of staying." He put both fists against his head. "I wish I could squeeze everything out of my head."

Faith almost kicked him as she would a cur. The pathetic, sniveling excuse for a man made her belly roil. "Get out of my house." She came around the card table, and Boyd backed away.

"It's my baby!" he said. "You know it's mine! We both know! The baby is ours! It's our baby!"

"What a fairy tale! Did *you* make it up all by yourself?"

"It's true," Boyd said. "You can't pretend it isn't."

"You are mistaken," Faith said. "Do you hear me? You've made a wild accusation, without any proof."

"*I'm* the proof," Boyd said. "What happened that week is the proof."

"You're lucky," she said, "I'm your only audience. I'm *giving* you another chance."

"You're trying to scare me," Boyd said. "Well, you're not."

"You should be," Faith said. "You should be scared stiff."

"Well, guess again," he said, to prove he had some guts after all the misery they had lived through. "I'm not afraid of the truth. Why should I be? You're having a baby, and it's mine," he said. "It's mine! You're having my baby!"

"You little . . . toad," Faith said, her voice low and deadly. "If you ever repeat those words, to me or to anyone else, I will go to the police. I will tell the police you killed Kyle," she said. "I'll say I have been protecting you, but I can't live with my guilt."

Boyd was terrified. The young man had lived a lifetime cowering in the shadows, but nothing and no one, anywhere, had affected him as deeply as Faith. His lips parted, but he did not respond, facing her openmouthed, struck dumb by her threat.

Faith had changed, directly in front of him, into an evil, dangerous stranger. Boyd felt as though he would collapse in a heap at her feet.

She left him at the fireplace. "Faith!" He followed her, stumbling, barely able to keep himself moving. She could be on her way to the police with her lies. She could save herself by sending him to the electric chair. "Oh, God, Faith! Please!" He started up the stone steps and fell, crying out in pain.

She stopped at the door, looking back at him as he pushed himself to his feet. "Get out! Now!" She opened the door. "If you say another word, to me or anyone, I'm calling the sheriff."

Faith took his arm, propelled him forward, and shoved him out of the house. She slammed the door and locked it. She waited until she heard the Model T rattling as he drove off. She remained until the sound of the car faded. The encounter had left her trembling, but she returned to the card table and bent over the tablet to read what she had written so she could continue. But she fell back in the chair, tossing the pencil aside, looking into the dark fireplace. Where was Wyn? Where was the rube? She needed her rube tonight.

T HE FOLLOWING MORNING, for the first time since returning from her honeymoon with measles, Serena did not slip into her bathing suit after her breakfast of juice and coffee. In bed after breakfast she looked out at the Castle. Nothing and no one moved in the Castle. Honeychild came for the breakfast tray. "You'll be late for your swim."

"Get out and stay out," Serena snapped.

Frank Burris had not been in her bedroom for nine days. Serena had not seen him after dinner since the bootlicking toad from Charleston had telephoned to crow about his crib as though he had discovered King Tut's tomb.

She could not remember one of Frank's mutinies extending for even a week. She could not count the nights when Frank entered and left her bedroom without a word from either of them. Now they were into a second week of war.

Every morning of the year Serena showered when she returned

from the lake. Now she went directly into the shower and remained, unable to resist the flow of water that had sustained and soothed her all her life.

She returned to her bed from the shower, and lay still, the towel covering her breasts and belly. She could feel the hot, dry breeze. She had barely made herself comfortable when she raised the towel and left the bed. She returned to the bathroom and dropped the towel, reaching for her bathing suit, which lay across a chair. Frank would return to her bedroom whether or not she swam. He would understand that every move she made she made for him, for his future. He would be president of the company. He, not she, would sit in her father's office atop the building.

Serena left the house, passed the open garage, and walked down to the gate in the fence. She always left the gate open on her way to the lake. When the distinctive, musky smell of the water reached her, she quickened her pace.

She left her robe and sandals in the trees and at the lake pulled on her bathing cap, pushing her hair under it. Serena walked into the lake, stopped to button the rubber chin strap under her chin, and ran until it was deep enough to dive. She went under and raised her head, starting her routine, her arms rising and falling steadily, her kicking feet leaving a delicate, rippling wake.

In the trees behind her, Holt waited until Serena was fifty or more yards from the shore before walking into the lake. He waded out until the water reached his belly, then sank below the surface.

The water swallowed him, until, yards from where he had submerged, Holt's head appeared. Only his eyes were above the surface as he swam silently, on a line with Serena, directly behind her.

When he saw her rolling to her right, he dived fast, dropping with barely a crease in the lake. Serena turned on her back to float, face raised to the sun, eyes closed. She lay in her element, no less than Holt. Sam Castleton had kept a former Olympic swimming champion on the lake eight months of the year, making the lake required attendance for his children and grandchildren, no less than school. He offered prizes for achievement, real prizes, bats and balls and dresses and dolls. All the Castletons could do anything they wanted in the water.

When Serena rolled over and began to swim again, Holt surfaced and followed. When she turned to float, he dropped. He seemed to sense when she would resume swimming, rising behind her, directly behind her, and moving closer and closer as she approached her goal, the long dock in front of the lake house.

When Serena reached the ladder against the dock, she raised a hand to the rung above her head. Just then Holt came out of the water and grasped the ladder with both hands. "Surprise."

He took her captive. She could feel Holt's arms on hers, his body against hers, and his face inches from her face. Serena had forgotten how closely Holt resembled her. And although Serena was almost thirty years older, she remained as lean, as fit as her nephew. They were like brother and sister.

Serena could not mask her astonishment. Her heart beat fast, and to her dismay, he frightened her. So Holt's advantage became his liability because her hatred for him made Serena dangerous. She could have freed herself in an instant, dropped down into the water, or lashed out with both arms, or raised her knee to drive it into his scrotum, but she would not cede Holt the victory her struggle would grant him. "I didn't see you," she said coolly.

"I followed you across," Holt said. "You're very good."

"For an old woman," Serena said.

"For a woman." Holt lowered his right hand and freed the rubber chin strap of her bathing cap. "You're a handsome woman, Serena." He pulled off her bathing cap. "A very handsome woman."

She tossed back her head and ran her hand through her hair. "Aunt Serena," she said, and looked closely at him. "You're a stranger to me. You've been away, and before you went away, you stayed away . . . from me and from Frank. And now you follow me across the lake. Are you like Kyle and Gaby? Are you a fool like those two?"

"Try me."

Serena was already tired of his assumed and unsupported superiority. She turned hard in the water and brought her left arm down across his like a sledge. Holt grimaced and released her, holding on to the ladder with his right hand. "Why did you follow me across the lake?" she asked.

"You can guess why I've come," Holt said.

"All right," she said, ready to leave. "You've come because of the B Stock. I have half, and you have a third of the other half. And Kyle's widow has a third. You're desperate. You have nothing to lose from coming to see me, and I have nothing to gain. Maybe you are a fool."

"Since we're into it already, listen to the fool," Holt said. For the first time she saw the hate in his face. "Your half makes you as desperate as I am. More." He smiled at her. "You have less time left than I, Aunt Serena." Holding on to a rung of the ladder, Holt swung from side to side like a monkey in a tree. "This is your chance, maybe your last chance."

"You've come to tell me you'll vote your stock with me," Serena said.

"We must stop the chorus girl," Holt said. "She is smart, Aunt Serena."

"If you vote with me, I will own much more than you do. What do you ask for your vote?"

"Whatever you give me," Holt said. "Frank Burris becomes president of the company. He sits in Grandpa's office. I should have something. I should have a title. Executive vice-president. Chairman of the board of directors. I'll make myself useful. I'm an experienced businessman. I've operated a merchant ship for three years. I've made a profit each year. I'll be an asset to you."

Serena could not allow herself to consider being in the same building with Holt. She and Frank would never be safe. They would be in danger, even in danger of losing their lives. Faith Venable had been free as the wind in New York until Holt returned. Serena's fear of him, a cold, penetrating emptiness, returned.

"I've made you an offer," Holt said. "Aunt Serena? What do you say?"

"You have your answer," Serena said. She tried to fasten her chin strap. "Must you hear it? The answer is no," she said. "No! No!" Serena pushed herself away from the ladder, dropped into the lake, and swam for home, the chin strap flopping up and down as she turned her head to breathe.

———✦———

THREE HOURS LATER VINCENT FAHEY, the private detective Burris had hired, called the boss in Miami. Fahey placed his calls at midday when the boss's secretary went to lunch and the boss picked up the telephone. Fahey did not call collect, did not take any chances on drawing a curious operator who might stay on the line listening. Fahey paid for the call, asking for time and charges to include in his expense account.

Andrew McAnney, the boss, a Scotsman born in Scotland, did not like telephone conversations. He asked for written reports. "Sir, it's Vincent Fahey. Something has come up, sir. A delicate matter." Fahey told the boss what he had seen on the lake.

"Go on."

"She's the man's wife, sir," Fahey said. "With her nephew. Her own flesh and blood. Am I helping the client or hurting him?"

"He's the client," said Andrew McAnney. "He hired you, and he's paying you."

"So I tell him, do I?"

"Yes, man," the boss said. "Tell him."

At day's end Burris's secretary opened his office door. "I guess I'll be leaving?" she said, making her usual question. "Unless you need me?"

"No, no," Burris said. "Good night."

He heard her leave the office, heard the steady trudge of company employees on their way to the elevators. Shadows dropped across the walls and floor of his office. "Still here, Mr. Burris?" The guard startled him. "Anything I can do for you?"

"Do?" Burris thought of several replies to the guard's question, all ugly. He rose, shaking his head. "I'm on my way." Burris wondered if the guard knew, wondered if all the guards knew. In the elevator alone Burris wondered who else knew. He left the building grateful he had not run into anyone.

In his car Burris was about to start the engine when he stopped short. He could send for his clothes. And the trophies and photographs in the study. He owned those; he had paid for everything in the study. Then Burris turned the key, starting the engine and excoriating himself. Why should he hide? What had he done? What crime had he committed? How many chances had he ignored right here in town?

Women! Women had been crowding around him since he won his tournament, before his sixteenth birthday. There wasn't a town in the country— Burris pressed the accelerator down, in a hurry to get it over with. He would pack and leave. And send for the trophies and the pictures.

The streetlights were coming up earlier now. The days were getting shorter. The heat couldn't last much longer. Another few weeks, and tennis would be over.

Like hell! He would drive down to Florida for the winter. Burris frowned, shaking his head as though he could eliminate the private detective's report. Burris had to leave it all behind, leave all the Castletons behind.

Instead of driving into the garage, Burris left his car directly in front of the front door. Honeychild heard his car and waited at the door. "Miss Serena is on the terrace."

"Come with me," Burris said.

His unprecedented request startled Honeychild. When Burris discovered she was not following, he stopped, looking back. "Come with me!"

Honeychild followed him, keeping a distance between them. In his study he took the ice bucket, and when Honeychild appeared, Burris extended it. "Bring me some ice."

At the bar, he picked up the bottle of single-malt scotch. He filled the jigger and set it down on the bar. When Honeychild returned, he filled a tumbler with ice, poured the whiskey over the cubes, and sprayed it with soda.

He sat in his favorite chair while he sipped his drink, facing the glass cases of trophies and the framed photographs and seeing only his wasted life, made truly squalid today. When he finished his drink, he did not leave his chair but remained holding the cold, comforting glass. To himself he said, "You're stalling," but denied it. He had to tell her.

"Dinner." Honeychild stood in the hallway looking into the study.

"Not tonight," Burris said, and leaped from his chair. "Not tonight!"

Honeychild retreated down the hallway, and Burris went to the bar to set down his glass. He went back to his chair but did not sit down, and soon, as he expected, Serena joined him. She wore a loose gown, which fell to the floor, and her feet, as always, were bare. "Are you ill?" she asked.

"I am not," he said, "not physically ill."

She crossed the study, peering at him. "You were late coming home, and now . . . what? Frank?"

"I'm leaving you," he said, feeling a great surge of elation.

She said, "Leaving—" and stopped, suddenly sick inside.

"I'm done here," Burris said. "I'm done." He waved. "I'll take my . . . junk. And my clothes. I paid for my clothes."

"Leaving," Serena said, her belly roiling. She watched him carefully. "Are you serious? Frank? Is there someone else?"

"Do I have someone else?" He went to the windows, welcoming the anger which engulfed him. "Not I, Serena. How about you?"

"How about—" She stopped, took a step toward him, and solved the mystery. He had followed her to the lake, hidden in the trees, watching her. "I have been with only one man in my life."

"You sound like someone in a play." Burris left the windows. " 'I have been with only one man in my life,' " he said, standing over her. "Until ten-thirty this morning."

"You've been spying on me."

"You're dead wrong," he said. "God, isn't he a little young for you?"

She slapped him, hard, and waited, sick with fear, for him to leave the study, leave her behind.

"You just proved I'm right," Burris said.

"Holt followed me today," Serena said. "He swam behind me, across the lake. I didn't even see him until I reached the dock. He offered to vote his B Stock with mine. I refused. There is the story of my other man. The entire story."

"Why didn't you phone me?"

"I expected to tell you at dinner," she said. "I would have told you the truth." And because she had learned long ago Burris did not lie, something clicked in her head. "You hired someone to spy on me."

"Someone to protect my interests," Burris said.

"From me, Frank?" They could hear the servants in the dining room. "Are you coming to dinner?"

"I am leaving you," he said, stepping past her. "Good-bye, Serena."

In the dining room Serena took her place at the table. She listened for Burris above her. The dining room was still as a tomb.

Serena took the oil from the cruet and pulled the stopper. When she replaced the bottle, she discovered Honeychild in the dining room. "Get out!"

Not once in their marriage, however ferocious their battles, had Burris spoken of leaving her. Frequently days and even weeks passed without an exchange between them, but their routines continued without a break or a change. Serena raised her fork and set it down. Food had become a punishment. She rose from her chair and climbed the stairs to her room, but she did not close the door.

In the bedroom Burris had chosen early in their marriage, he went to the closet. It resembled a haberdashery. Burris liked dressing with a flair, and Serena could not resist buying him clothes: sweaters, evening slippers, English waistcoats, cashmere scarves, Irish tweed hats, ties of regimental stripes, costly cuff links, whatever she spied on a shopping excursion.

Burris fingered his suits on the hangers, pushing them apart to look at the jackets. He'd need a truck to empty the closet, so he chose four suits: a plaid, a navy blue serge, and two gabardines, a forest green and a tan. He carried the suits to his bed. Back in the closet, he took a Harris tweed sport jacket from the rack for the chilly days ahead. He dropped that on the bed. He set two pairs of shoes on the floor beside the bed and hung some ties over the back of the chair. He took shirts and socks from drawers in the closet and set these on the chair. He remembered underwear and brought shorts and T-shirts out of the closet. "Belts," he said aloud, and hung two belts, brown and black, over the chair with the ties.

He went back to the closet for his luggage. Lulu Belle kept a white sheet over his luggage. Burris pulled the sheet aside and stepped back. A few of his old rackets, souvenirs of old glories, lay on a shelf at his side. Burris picked up one of the rackets, his fingers curling around the familiar, comfortable stem. He came out of the closet, swinging the racket, wondering if he could get a job as a pro somewhere, at some good club. He swung the racket, using his backhand. He wondered if his age would stop him. Maybe he could get a job selling insurance like Ray Deems. This thought pulled him up short. Selling insurance!

In her room Serena lay on her bed in her long gown, her bare feet crossed. As the hours passed, she heard the clock ticking but did not look at it. When she could no longer listen to the crickets, she left the bed to draw the drapes. Serena turned toward the corridor as though she expected someone. Her bedroom, the house had fallen silent. She stood listening in the silence before finally walking out into the corridor.

She stopped near Burris's bedroom. She could see his open door. She moved carefully, stealthily, pausing between each step. Serena stood against the corridor wall beside his door. And when she looked into his room, she saw Burris sleeping on his belly across the bed.

Serena slept very little that night. She heard the birds greeting the day and afterward the steady sound of running water as Burris showered. She sat up in bed to fluff the pillows and smooth the covers for her tray.

Sometimes, even in the midst of hostilities, Burris stopped in the corridor to say, "Good morning," or, "I'll be late." So Serena pushed back her hair, but when she heard him on the staircase, her fears returned more strongly. Exhausted with fear, she lay back in the pillows.

She heard Honeychild say, "No breakfast, Mr. Burris?" She heard the door open and close. She heard Burris drive off and soon Honeychild's footsteps as the black woman climbed the stairs with her tray.

"Mr. Burris left without breakfast," Honeychild said. "He went to bed last night without dinner."

"Be quiet."

Honeychild set down the tray. Serena did not look up as Honeychild left the bedroom. In her head Serena saw Burris in his car, and she followed him, down Millionaires Row, and across the county into the city. She gave Burris more time than he needed to reach the company. And still she waited, until, frightened beyond endurance, she reached for the telephone to call the captain of the company's guard unit. "This is Serena Burris."

"Yes, ma'am, Miss Serena," said the captain, who had often driven Sam Castleton. "What can I do for you?"

"Will you see if my husband's car is there? Please go yourself and come back and tell me."

"Hold on, Miss Serena. I'm going now."

She believed the car would be there. She could not believe otherwise, could not think of life continuing if the man did not see the car. She belonged with Burris; he belonged with her. She had claimed him from the start, from her first sight of him crossing the tennis court the day— "Miss Serena? He's in his usual spot," said the captain.

She said, barely, "Thank you." She set aside the telephone and moved her tray, so that she could leave the bed. Naked, stretching her neck and arching her back, she stood beside the bed.

In the bathroom Serena pulled on her bathing suit and pushed her feet into sandals. She took her bathrobe, feeling in the pocket for her bathing cap. She could plan carefully, with no reason for haste. Stage people were not like normal people. They did not go to bed at normal hours. They stayed awake all night, sleeping until all hours of the day.

———⊶⟨⊙⟩⊷———

L ATER THE SAME MORNING, Faith came out onto the veranda, her arms full of tablets and scratch pads. She dropped everything onto a round table beside a wicker chaise longue, and returned to the house for another load—more tablets and pens and the book on Penelope and Ulysses from Brentano's in New York.

Faith took two pens and her play from the table and settled into the chaise in the shade. She drew up her legs. The gloomy house, dark even with lamps burning everywhere, had driven her out into the daylight.

Faith had swiftly completed, without rereading, two acts of her play. She planned now to read what she had, reading aloud each line of dialogue, male and female. She raised the sheaf of handwritten pages but looked out into the thicket beyond the house, because the thought of Wyn had intruded.

He had been with her most of the night, slipping away just before dawn. She had wakened for a little while before he left when he kissed her gently, kissed her everywhere. "Demon," she murmured. The indefatigable boy was a marvel.

When she heard a car, Faith looked up from the page. Except for the morning and late afternoon, few cars drove in and out of the cul-de-sac. Because Jane Abel's house was at the end, Faith had not seen any of her neighbors.

Faith could not identify the rakish car but knew instantly, from its lines, the cabriolet belonged to a Castleton. A Castleton had come to call. Faith set the play down beside her on the chaise. And when she looked up, she saw Serena leaving the car and waving.

Faith rose as Serena climbed the wooden steps to the veranda. Serena had trapped her, and like a cornered animal, Faith could think only of escape.

Serena said, "I took a chance on finding you at home."

"I am always at home," Faith said. "Everyplace else is a battle-ground."

"I'm not here to fight," Serena said. She moved a wicker chair to face Faith. "Can't we sit together?" When Serena sank into the chair, Faith perched on the edge of the chaise longue.

"We're sitting," Faith said. "Why have you come?"

"To help," Serena said. "I can help you."

"All right," Faith said. "I'm ready. I want to be free. Give me my freedom."

"I cannot," Serena said. "No one can free you. No one can defeat Holt. Holt Castleton is the most powerful man in North Carolina. You've lost. Holt demands the B Stock, the B Stock your child will inherit."

Serena terrified Faith. She held on to the couch, trying to think, to think.

"You won't die," Serena said. "They won't kill a woman. They worry about the North, especially the newspapers in the North, and the Jew congressmen and senators in Washington. You'll go to prison. You may never leave prison. Holt may decide he cannot risk setting you free. Can't risk it or simply won't care enough to let you back into the world of living men and women." Serena leaned forward. "Do you believe me? You must believe me. You are hearing the truth. And the worst will follow. Holt will take your child."

Faith said, barely, "Don't—"

"You will lose the child," Serena said. "Holt will take your baby with its B Stock. Holt will have you declared an unfit mother. The courts will oblige him. And then he will become the legal guardian, everlasting and forevermore."

Faith thought she would collapse. But she sat erect, fighting for survival.

"You can stop him," Serena said. "We can stop him. Together."

"Stop him," Faith echoed.

"I will take the child," Serena said. "My husband and I are willing to adopt the child. We'll bring the child into our home. He or she will be like our own."

Faith's hate saved her. "And you will have the B Stock." She rose from the chaise. "And you came to help me." She strode past Serena, startling the older woman. Faith threw open the door, entered the house. Serena could hear a rasping series of starts and stops inside, like furniture being moved. Serena came to her feet as Faith, bent almost double, backed out of the house, dragging an ancient, massive wooden crib. "This belongs to you," Faith said.

Serena said, "No, no, it's a gift."

Faith pulled the crib to the head of the wooden steps. She reached into the crib to take an envelope and, standing erect, opened it, removed a card, and read: " 'Castleton babies have begun life here longer than I can remember. Now your baby will follow the rest. Serena.' "

Faith tore the envelope and card in half. She tore it again and again, letting bits and pieces of paper slip through her fingers, floating down into the crib and onto the porch.

"I've had enough from you," Faith said. "Your cribs and your flowers and your lies and your help. Get out! Take your crib and get out!" Faith clutched the crib with both hands and pulled with all her strength. The convulsive effort threw her off-balance, and she lost her footing. She let go of the crib as she fell back and down onto the wooden steps.

Serena stopped short, watching Faith roll from one step to the other until she lay on the ground, legs and arms askew in the dirt.

Faith lay motionless, afraid to move, afraid to breathe. A shadow fell across her and passed as Serena walked by her toward her car. Faith heard the door open and close, heard the engine start, heard the crunching sound of the tires on the gravel, heard the car rolling along Deer Hollow Road, until the world became absolutely still. Faith touched her belly, moved her fingertips slowly across her belly as though to comfort and reassure the child within her. After a time she put both hands down flat into the dirt, pushed hard to pull herself up, up, up, until she sat erect in front of the steps, her bare legs extended.

In her Overland sedan, big and black as a hearse, Zoe Kellerman noticed the low-slung car approaching and easily identified it. Serena Castleton's car. Everyone had seen Serena's car somewhere in town. Zoe Kellerman didn't care if Serena saw her, didn't care who saw her. She didn't intend to treat Faith Castleton like a leper.

Zoe caressed the pumpkin on the seat beside her. She had bought the biggest pumpkin she could carry. She couldn't come empty-handed, and she had vetoed flowers or candy. The pumpkin had hit Zoe like a brainstorm. Even though Halloween came way at the end of the month, it would give Faith something to do. She could kill some time. Zoe made a face, wrinkling her nose. "Not *kill* some time!" she said aloud, and turned into Deer Hollow Road.

High off the ground in the bulky sedan, Zoe saw nothing below the veranda of Jane Abel's house. After stopping, she took her umbrella from the backseat and opened the door.

"Help me."

Zoe could have sworn she heard someone say, "Help." She came around the rear of the sedan like a prowler and, when she saw Faith Venable in the dirt, shrieked, "Oh, no!"

Zoe leaped forward, dragging the umbrella. Zoe thanked her lucky stars for the urge that had sent her all the way out to Deer Hollow Road today, of all days.

"Please help me."

Zoe threw aside her umbrella and extended her hands. "Hold on to me." Just then Zoe remembered the baby. "Wait! Let me do all the work! I'll do the work, you just hold on," Zoe said.

Zoe took a firm grip on Faith's hands and, rising slowly, slowly, brought Faith to her feet. "Are you all right?" Zoe bent her head, peering at Faith. "I'll help you into the house."

Faith had to protect the baby, had to save the baby. *She had to save the baby!* "Please take me to the hospital," Faith said. "I'll pay you."

"Pay—oh, Miss Venable," Zoe said. "Of course I'll take you," she said, putting her arm around Faith. "Just move slowly. One step at a time." Zoe forgot her umbrella.

She opened the passenger door of the sedan and discovered the pumpkin. "Wait!" Zoe released Faith and leaned into the sedan for the pumpkin. It fell from her hands, splitting open, and Zoe pushed it aside with her foot. "Here you go, Miss Venable."

When Zoe turned out onto Deer Hollow Road, she drove like sixty. She didn't care if a cop stopped her. If a cop stopped her, he could escort them to the hospital. "Are you feeling all right, Miss Venable?"

"I'm all right," Faith said, trying to spare herself more talk. The unexpected arrival of Serena, the invasion of her privacy, the barbaric scheme Serena had proposed, the horrible future she had presented, and then the fall, her lying helpless and alone in the dust, had shattered Faith. Riding in the uncomfortable sedan in the heat, in a stranger's car with a stranger, passing through a strange flatland with trees scattered in the distance like scarecrows, like skeletons, only added to the day's misery. "How much farther?"

"We'll be there in a jiff, Miss Venable," Zoe said, praying a cop saw her. But she reached the city still passing every car in front of her with no sign of the police. "Almost there," Zoe said.

Zoe turned two blocks from the hospital so she could avoid the front entrance. She swung into the emergency entrance parking lot, stopped near the doors and glanced at Faith, who sat huddled against the door. She was about the most beautiful woman Zoe had ever seen. "I'll get some help," Zoe said.

She left Faith alone in the musty sedan. Faith had always relied on herself, had turned away offers of help, trusting her own instincts, and needing no resources but her own. She fought now to rise from the depths. "Ready?" Zoe asked, opening the car door.

Faith saw an orderly in white and the white linen surface of the wheeled stretcher. Zoe extended her hand. "Put your weight on me."

Faith nodded and took Zoe's hand and carefully, holding the door, stepped out onto the running board and from it to the ground. The orderly pushed the stretcher toward the sedan. "Lean on us, ma'am. We'll do the rest."

Faith saw the wheeled stretcher approaching, saw the lights above the hospital door, dark now, spelling "EMERGENCY." Then, when she lay on the stretcher looking up into the bright blue sky, Faith saw Kyle, saw the bright red stains across his temple and face and across his neck, and in despair she shut her eyes to blot him out.

Inside, Faith heard a man's voice. "How do you feel?" At her side someone said, "I'm Dr. Widseth," just as she saw the name on the nameplate pinned to his blouse. "I know you've had a fall. How do you feel?" The intern looked down at Faith. "Mrs. Castleton? Can you hear me?"

"I can hear you."

"Do you have any pain, Mrs. Castleton? Do you feel any discomfort, especially in the pelvic area? Do you have cramps?"

When Faith did not reply, the intern said, "I'd like to take your blood pressure."

He reached for her right arm, but Faith moved aside.

Widseth showed her the blood-pressure cuff. "Mrs. Castleton, you're pregnant. You've had a fall. I think you're all right, but I should take your blood pressure and do an abdominal examination just to be sure."

Faith looked up at the enemy. "You are Dr. Widseth," she said. "You were here Labor Day, the night of Labor Day. You saw Kyle and gave us your opinion as a doctor, gave us your diagnosis. You said Kyle shot himself, committed suicide. How did suicide become murder?"

Widseth looked down, playing with the blood-pressure cuff. Faith said, "Doctor? Can you hear me? How did suicide become murder? How *can* suicide become murder? Doctor? Damn you, Doctor!"

"The grand jury . . ." Widseth said, and paused. "The grand jury delivered the verdict."

"Did you testify?" Faith asked. Widseth did not look at her. "You testified," she said. "Did you say Kyle killed himself? Doctor?"

"The grand jury is secret, a secret body," he said.

At the telephone the orderly said, "Doctor, it's Three West."

"So you testified," Faith said. "You helped change suicide to murder. You made me the murderer."

The orderly said, "Doctor, they've called twice. A patient with acute shortness of breath."

Widseth turned to the orderly. "Tell them to get Lederholm."

"Dr. Lederholm is up on two," the orderly said. "The old guy fell out of bed again."

"Tell them I'm coming," Widseth said. He waved the blood-pressure cuff.

"I already did," the orderly said.

"Just wait," Widseth said. The intern's face had turned rosy. "Mrs. Castleton, you should be examined."

Faith put her hands over her belly. "Get away," she said.

Widseth turned completely around and strode across the room, throwing the blood-pressure cuff at the orderly, who raised both hands to catch it. Faith said, "You . . ." summoning him. "Take me upstairs, I am a patient. Take me to a room with a telephone."

"I'm coming with you, Mrs. Castleton," Zoe said. "Just in case."

⸺•◉•⸺

IN LENOX HILL HOSPITAL on Park Avenue in New York, his answering service found Morty Abrams in the clinic to which he gave one afternoon each week. "Doctor, it's someone in North Carolina. A patient. She said—"

"Give me the number," Morty said, taking his pen from his shirt pocket. He wrote the telephone number on the cuff of his white coat.

Waiting for the long-distance operator to connect him, Morty worried over a miscarriage. After everything the poor girl had suffered, a miscarriage wouldn't be a surprise. He heard a woman say, "Castleton Community Hospital."

"Faith Venable . . . *Castleton,* please."

"I'm ringing. . . ."

Alone in her room Faith said, "Hello," and heard Morty.

"Tell me everything," he said.

"I fell," Faith said. She omitted Serena and substituted a heavy chair for the crib.

"What does the doctor say?"

"You're my doctor," Faith said.

Morty came off the stool in the telephone booth and opened the door. "You haven't been *examined?*"

"I couldn't . . . can't. I can't let the doctor down here come near me," Faith said. "He lied about me to the grand jury."

Morty didn't ask questions, didn't need a hysterical woman a thousand miles away. "I'll examine you," he said. "Is there any blood?"

"I don't think so."

"I'll wait," Morty said.

After a long pause Faith said, "No, there isn't any blood."

"Good," Morty said. "You're in bed. Good. Stay in bed. I'll talk to you later."

"Promise?"

"I promise," Morty said.

At five o'clock that afternoon a nurse knocked once on the door of Faith's room and pushed it open with her shoulder. "Dinner."

The nurse carried the tray to the wheeled food table at the foot of the bed and rolled it across the bed to Faith. "Hope you're hungry," the nurse said. "Fried chicken is the cook's specialty. How're we doing? Lean forward, huh? I'll plump up those pillows. A person can't eat flat on her back."

Faith leaned forward, and the nurse punched the pillows. "How's that? Better? Good. Dig in."

When the nurse left, Faith looked at the tray. Steam rose from a bowl of soup that seemed impenetrable beneath a layer of chopped vegetables. A leg and thigh of chicken shared a plate with a large mound of mashed potatoes buried in a lake of gravy. The chicken was gray, and the batter in which it had been fried seemed encrusted with what resembled barnacles, as though the leg and thigh had been salvaged from the sea. Faith took the fork and prodded the leg, solid as a brick wall.

"Good evening."

A tall man with graying hair, carrying a folded stethoscope, closed the door. He was a handsome man and looked distinguished, like an important judge or an honored professor. He wore a tan summer suit and a light blue shirt. "I'm Lawrence Clark, Mrs. Castleton."

His clothes and the manner in which he wore his clothes reminded Faith of the young men in the audiences in Boston when she tried out for a show for Broadway.

Lawrence Clark, the son of a physician, had learned to dress in Boston. He had gone from Chapel Hill to the Harvard Medical School and afterward, as an intern, to Peter Bent Brigham Hospital. Those five years, the happiest of his professional life, had changed Lawrence Clark forever. He had been seduced by Boston, and Massachusetts, and New England. Lawrence Clark had returned to North Carolina because his father expected him to return, but he still bought his clothes from J. Press in Cambridge, and he took his vacations somewhere in New England each July.

Clark came to the bed. "I've interrupted your dinner," he said. "I'm sorry. I'll come back."

"Who are you?" Faith asked. "What are you doing in my room?"

"Good grief! I asked the charge nurse to tell you I'd come by as soon as I could leave my office. It's Dr. Clark." He raised his hand, showing Faith the stethoscope.

"I have a doctor," Faith said. "My own doctor."

"Of course," Clark said. "Dr. Abrams. He called me earlier."

Faith said, "Called—"

"He asked for the chief of staff, and the hospital gave him my telephone number." Clark gestured. "Your dinner."

Faith pushed away the table. "Exit my dinner."

Clark said, "You're sure?" and then said, "I won't be long, Mrs. Castleton. What month is this?" Faith told him. "I'd like to do an abdominal."

Clark folded back the covers and bent over Faith. When he finished, he took his stethoscope and listened to her heart. He straightened up, removing the stethoscope and smiling. "Excellent. Excellent. Let me take your blood pressure." Clark opened the drawer of the night table and removed a blood-pressure cuff. He sat down on the bed and wrapped the cuff around Faith's arm.

"I'd like to go home," she said.

"I'd rather you spent the night, Mrs. Castleton," Clark said. "I'll look in on you after breakfast." Clark smiled again. "You should be rather hungry at breakfast time."

———◦◦◦———

LESS THAN TWO MILES from the hospital Wyn climbed the steps to his apartment. He got out of his clothes and stood under the shower in the bathtub until he felt cool.

He rubbed himself dry and, wrapping the towel around his middle, went to the bedroom window. Wyn imagined driving out far past the airport to push the sun down below the horizon.

He got into clean clothes and left the apartment to have dinner. During the long day, involved in the daily work schedule, his chores occupied him. Now, alone, he could think only of Faith, of seeing her and touching her, of holding her. Wyn drove into a gasoline station. He parked at the telephone booths to call.

She didn't answer the telephone. He listened to ring after ring after ring. She had probably stepped into the shower.

Wyn drove to his diner and sat at the counter, trying not to look at the big clock on the wall directly in front of him. When he emerged, he drove directly to Deer Hollow Road. The sun had set, and in the twilight he parked in the trees, waiting for darkness.

When night fell, he left his car, sticking to the trees. Faith's house looked dark and deserted. Closer, he saw a light in the rear, in the kitchen, and another above, at what he knew was the head of the stairs. Wyn moved faster. Faith always kept the house ablaze with lights.

He came out of the trees running and, in the dark, ran up the wooden steps and banged into something hard. He grimaced, doubling over, rubbing his shins as he hobbled across the porch to grope for the doorbell. The house was *dark!* What if . . . she could have been lying there for hours. Wyn pulled out his key and opened the door, calling, "Faith! *Faith!*"

He ran through the first floor, turning on lights. "Faith!" Wyn ran back to the stairs and climbed them two and three at a time. "Faith!"

The house was empty! He came down the stairs fast and at the front door saw the crib on the porch. Wyn lunged for the telephone. Something bad had happened, and he had to know how bad.

"This is the operator."

"I'm Deputy Sheriff Ainsley," he said. "Put me through to Castleton Community Hospital." Where else could she be?

"Yes, sir." He raised his fist, beating a tattoo on the wall. She *had* to be there.

"Castleton Community Hospital."

"Is Faith Castleton there?"

"She's in three forty-seven."

He said, "Yeah . . ." slowly, turning and falling against the wall. "I'd like to talk with her, please."

When Faith said, "Hello," when Wyn heard her voice, like no other voice anywhere, he crossed his fingers on both hands. "Faith? What happened? Are you all right?"

She said, *"Wyn?"* and bit her lip hard, searching the hospital room as though someone could be there listening. Her eyes filled, and the tears slid from her eyelashes to her face. Her tears left Faith dumbfounded. "Wyn? Wait." She raised her free arm, rubbing her eyes with her forearm like a child.

"Faith? Are you okay?"

"I am . . . okay," she said. He made her smile through her tears. The big hick, the sound of his trusting, honest voice rescued her from the day's trauma. Astonished at her reaction, Faith pushed herself up against the headboard. "I'm okay," she said.

"I can't come and see you," Wyn said.

"You'll see me," Faith said. "I can leave the hospital in the morning."

"What happened? I said that. I mean, are you sure you're okay?"

"I'm sure," she said. "Wyn?"

"I'm here."

"Good," she said. She wanted to sleep. "Good."

———«()»———

I N H I S O F F I C E early Tuesday afternoon Dan called his home. "Sarah? How are you, dear?"

"In this heat? Terrible," Sarah said. "Forget me, Dan. The boys are gone, so I can walk around half naked. I worry about you. It's hotter downtown."

"I'm all right," Dan said. "Sarah, I won't be home for dinner. I'll be late. A client."

"How late?"

Long years of such exchanges kept Dan from stepping into her trap. If he set a time, Sarah would be on the veranda waiting, and if his absence lengthened, she would become frantic, hectoring her sons in her anxiety. "Not too late," Dan said.

"A client at night," Sarah said. "Why at night?"

He said, "Sarah," ending the conversation. In one of his few victories of their marriage, Dan had long ago established his independence regarding his law practice. Sarah learned only what he chose to tell her.

Around five o'clock Dan slipped into his jacket. He left the office unlocked and the doors wide open. Nearby, in Herb Anderson's drugstore, Dan sat on a stool at the soda fountain and ordered two scoops of vanilla ice cream, his lifelong addiction. As he savored the ice cream, Herb Anderson stopped at the soda fountain. "You'll ruin your dinner."

"It's too hot for dinner," Dan said.

Refreshed and keeping to the shade, Dan returned to his office. In his shirtsleeves once more he worked through the remaining daylight hours on his report to the North Carolina B'nai B'rith chapter's monthly newsletter. He finished a draft a few minutes before eight o'clock and slipped it unread into his desk drawer. Dan liked a hiatus between writing his report and reading what he had written.

He left his desk to turn up the lights in the outer office for his guest. Dan had telephoned Russell Vance the week before. "I'd like to see you, Mr. Vance. I can drive out to the Castle."

"No, not here," Russell said. "I'm—we're rather busy here now preparing for the Harvest Festival. I'm at the farms most of the day."

"I can see you at the farms," Dan said.

"No, no," Russell said. "I'll come in . . . right after the festival."

"It's important," Dan said. "I would not press you if it weren't important."

"All right," Russell said. "I'll come Tuesday. Eight o'clock Tuesday."

Taken aback, Dan said, "I can oblige you, Mr. Vance, but isn't eight o'clock early for—"

Russell interrupted, saying, "Eight p.m."

A few minutes after eight Dan went to the open windows, hoping for a breeze. Below, a man came around the corner on the other side of the street. The man proceeded purposefully, and Dan, waiting for Russell Vance, watched the street's lone occupant stride down the block until he passed a streetlamp directly across the way. "Mr. Vance!" Dan said aloud, but Russell Vance continued without a pause.

Below, Russell reached the corner and stopped and turned.

He retraced his steps, walking more slowly than he had. Dan watched him strolling along like a window shopper, although the storefronts, some vacant and all neglected, offered little to the passerby except for a single shop with a display of prosthetic devices. As Russell reached the middle of the block, he stopped, facing Dan's building. He looked in both directions, then crossed the street briskly and entered Dan's building.

Dan walked through the outer office to the corridor. He waited at the stair landing to greet his guest.

Hearing footsteps, Russell stopped on the stairs, looking up and clutching the banister. Dan said, "I startled you. Forgive me."

Russell saw the slim, neat man in shirtsleeves, wearing a tie with his shirt cuffs buttoned despite the oppressive heat. "Sorry I'm late."

"It's unimportant," Dan said, stepping aside so Russell could precede him. "Thank you for coming."

Once in the office, Russell paused. "Would you mind closing the door?" He did not tell the lawyer he had parked his car three blocks away.

"Closing— Of course." Dan gestured. "Please sit down."

Russell did not respond. He stood behind the chairs, and Dan, reaching his chair, stood facing him. "Thank you for coming," Dan said.

"I can't stay," Russell said.

His guest's behavior, his apparent fear, the furtiveness that dominated his movements, left Dan ill at ease. "Is something wrong?"

"Wrong? No, of course not," Russell said. "It's Coleman's inheritance, isn't it? The fifty thousand dollars?"

"The trust," Dan said. "The scholarship fund. With the death of Coleman Beaudine, the scholarship fund is automatically activated. As administrators it is our duty to proceed with the awarding of scholarships."

"What's the rush?"

"The fault is mine," Dan said, chiding himself for his impetuosity. When he learned of Coleman's death, Dan reread his copy of the trust he had established. Later in the day he drove to the Resurrection Baptist Church in the Flats.

"What trouble have you brought me, Dan?" asked the Reverend Millard Fitch.

"No trouble, Millard," Dan said. They walked through the church to the minister's study. "I have a surprise for you," Dan said to his old friend. He gave the minister a detailed account of the scholarship fund.

When Dan finished, Millard Fitch said quietly, "It is a miracle." He did not tell Dan how hard he had tried to get the inheritance from Coleman himself.

Dan said he would rely strongly on Millard Fitch to provide candidates for the scholarship fund. "I can give you a list long as my arm," said the minister.

On the day Dan telephoned Russell at the Castle, he had, in a file folder, material on seven candidates for the scholarship fund.

Now, in his office in the debilitating heat, Dan said, "I am to blame, Mr. Vance."

"I'm sorry," Russell said. "I have no right . . . the fact is . . ." He looked up at Dan, anxious to confide in the quiet, gentle man with the archaic courtly manner. But Russell did not continue.

When Dan telephoned the week before, Russell understood instantly why the lawyer had called. Dan's voice made the day dark, made all the days since dark. Coleman's death would activate the scholarship fund established by the trust. Soon every black man and woman would spread the word of Coleman's bounty. And Russell Vance had turned this fairy tale into fact. Russell Vance and the lawyer, Dan Cohen, had become champions of the community's blacks.

Russell listened as Dan told him of driving to the Flats and telling Millard Fitch of the scholarship fund. "I wish you had been there to see his reaction," Dan said. "He jumped for joy. I honestly think he jumped for joy."

Dan opened a desk drawer and took out the file folder with the minister's recommendations for scholarships. "He's been here almost every day since," Dan said, opening the folder. "I have seven candidates already—*we* have seven candidates. Forgive me. I become enthusiastic when I consider these lads." Dan held the folder aloft, displaying it. "Coleman is giving them their chance. One of their own." He nodded. "All we need now is the money to launch the dream." His choice of words surprised Dan and moved him. He repeated, softly, "To launch the dream."

Dan dropped the folder on his desk. "You can help," he said. "I've written Lucius Peete asking when Kyle Castleton's will clears probate. I've telephoned again and again. He does not acknowledge my letters or my calls. You know Mr. Peete. He will not ignore you."

"I can't."

"Can't?" Dan stared at the man.

"I've made a mistake," Russell said. "This . . ." he said, swinging his arms in an aimless gesture, "all this. All this with Coleman. I represent the Castletons, not their employees. *I'm* an employee. I'm only an employee, a hired hand," he said, cringing inwardly as he repeated Sam Castleton's phrase. "I'm not authorized to—" Russell came toward the desk. "I can't do this," he said. "Find someone else," he said. He waved wildly. "Remove my name. Get my name off the trust," he said, and forced himself to look at Dan. "You can find someone else," Russell said, pleading.

Dan looked down. Russell had caught him completely off guard. Dan had lived with racial bigotry and racial fear all his life, but what he considered Russell's defection left him too angry to speak. Dan took the file folder and returned it to the desk drawer. Russell waited until he realized Dan had dismissed him. "Well . . . I'll run along," Russell said. He couldn't leave with Dan. Anyone might see them. "If you don't mind, I'll go first, ahead of you."

Dan allowed himself a rare display of spleen. "I insist on it," he said. "Good night, Mr. Vance."

———※◎※———

BECAUSE LUCIUS PEETE WAS VERY OLD, Dan thought the aged lawyer no longer kept regular hours. Dan did not leave his office until ten o'clock the following morning, when he walked to the company headquarters near the railroad station. Dan carried his briefcase, in which he had put a copy of Coleman's trust.

He could not find Lucius Peete listed in the directory on the wall in the lobby. Dan asked the company guard who escorted him to the elevators. "You see Sue Ann up there," the guard said. "She'll take care of you." The guard said, "Eleven," to the elevator operator and nodded at Dan, touching the visor of his garrison cap with his fingertips.

On the eleventh floor Dan walked to 1107. When she heard the door, Sue Ann came out of the supply room. She said, "Yes?" as the stranger removed his Panama.

"My name is Daniel Cohen," he said. Sue Ann stiffened, recognizing the name. "I would like to see Mr. Peete."

"Well, he's not here," she said.

Dan stopped beside the chairs lining one wall. "When do you expect him?" He dropped his briefcase into a chair. In his office the night before, watching Russell hurry out, Dan had decided to see Lucius Peete the following day. He believed himself personally responsible for the seven boys whose names he kept in the file folder in his desk. Driving home, Dan could think only of the decisions he faced. How many scholarships should be awarded each year? How much money should be allotted to each scholarship? Should the scholarships be confined to the collegiate years? Should the funds include an education in a professional school? And whom could he find with more courage than Russell Vance?

Dan made Sue Ann very nervous. "I don't . . . he won't—" she said, and stopped, squeezing her hands.

Dan set his hat atop the briefcase in the chair. "I've written several times," he said. "I've called . . . called and called."

Sue Ann remembered the envelopes with the name, Daniel Cohen, Attorney-at-Law, and the address. She remembered the telephone calls. "He won't be here."

"I'll wait," Dan said, taking the chair beside the briefcase.

She said, "Mr. Cohen—" and stopped. She went to her desk for help. But as she bent to press the button, the door of Lucius Peete's office opened, and she straightened up. "Oh, Mr. Holt!" Sue Ann said, greeting her rescuer. "This is Mr. Daniel Cohen, come to see Mr. Peete."

Dan rose as the younger man came out of Lucius Peete's office. Dan could not remember ever meeting or seeing Holt, but he bore the unmistakable Castleton physical characteristics, hair and nose. "I hope you can help me, Mr. Castleton. I've been trying to see Mr. Peete."

"Lucius is no longer with the company," Holt said. "He left, voluntarily or involuntarily, take your pick." Holt gestured. "Sit down." Holt took a chair facing Dan and crossed his legs.

So Dan had to sit down. "I'm here about Kyle Castleton's will," he said. "The will and Coleman's inheritance."

"We haven't filed the will," Holt said.

Dan leaned forward in the chair. "Haven't—" he began, and broke off. He could think only of the names Millard Fitch had brought him. "May I ask why you have not filed the will?"

"The family is challenging the will," Holt said. "We are claiming insanity. Kyle married a murderess, which proves he was insane."

"Your brother left fifty thousand dollars to Coleman Beaudine," Dan said, "and I represent him. I expect the terms of Kyle Castleton's will to be executed."

"Executed," Holt said. He uncrossed his legs and put his hands on his thighs, and rose. "Counselor, you are not getting a dime of Castleton money." Holt walked toward Lucius Peete's office. "Not one dime."

Dan took his hat and briefcase and came out of the chair. "I'll sue," he said, walking toward the door.

"Don't," Holt said. "Counselor?" Dan stopped. "It would be a very bad idea to sue us."

That night Dan Cohen did not sleep well. He got up early. And he left for his office early. In midafternoon Dan drove to the courthouse. On behalf of the Coleman Beaudine Trust he filed suit against Lucius Peete, executor of the last will and testament of Kyle Castleton. Dan paid the filing fees out of pocket. He could not turn his back on the boys in the file folder.

≈⊷⟨◉⟩⊷≈

EARLY THE FOLLOWING MORNING, in the driveway in front of the porte cochere of the brick house on Fairview Avenue, all four Cohens were grouped around the car. Most of the backseat and the floorboards in front of the seat were stacked with battered luggage of various shapes and sizes and with athletic equipment: a basketball, a tennis racket, a condensed milk carton of old, scuffed tennis balls, a baseball catcher's mitt, a catcher's mask, two bats, a pair of baseball shoes with cleats, and two worn pairs of sneakers. A large grocery bag filled with Ella and Corinne's food had been placed in the center of the front seat. David Cohen was on his way to Chapel Hill to begin his freshman year at the University of North Carolina.

"Getting late!" Joe announced. He was accompanying his older brother and would bring back the Essex the following day.

"No speeding!" said his mother. Sarah turned to David, whom she could trust. "No speeding!"

"Promise," David said.

"Well . . ." Sarah rubbed her hands on her dress. The family had never been apart. "You've grown up, David. You're a grown man."

"No crying," Joe said.

"I am not crying, and if I do feel like crying, I shall cry," Sarah said. "How dare you!"

Dan Cohen stood in the shade provided by the porte cochere. Both his sons were bigger than their father. They had been babies, and now they were men. Dan really didn't remember how it had happened. He could remember incidents and events, measles and mumps, a Boy Scout bean feed to which David took him, a meeting with a school principal to discuss Joe's deportment. Dan remembered taking both boys to the shoe store for shoes that kept getting bigger and bigger and bigger; he remembered only David's Bar Mitzvah at the temple, not Joe's, but he remembered Joe's broken arm.

"Did you fill up with gas?" Sarah asked.

"I did," Dan said. "I filled the tank last night and checked the tires."

"Well . . ." David said. He turned to his mother, a small smile crossing his face.

Sarah took his forearms in her hands. "I'm proud of you," she said. "You're a fine, decent, honorable person, and I'm very proud of you," she said, and she kissed him.

"We gotta go," Joe said.

"Gotta, gotta, gotta," Sarah said. "Don't be in such a rush, and don't rush home tomorrow." Joe would sleep in David's dormitory room and start back in the morning.

"Promise," Joe said. He kissed his mother. "Let's ride! Come on, Dad." The boys were leaving Dan off at his office downtown. Joe opened the front passenger door. "Dad."

"I'll sit in the back," Dan said.

"You'll be squeezed into the corner," Joe said. "I'll sit in back."

"Stop this nonsense, Joe," Dan said. "I am sitting in the back, and that is final." The boys belonged together in the front seat. "Joe, excuse me." Joe stepped aside so Dan could open the rear door.

"You are not to eat in the car," Sarah said. "Not to eat and drive. Stop along the road for lunch. Stop at a picnic site. David! Promise!"

"I promise." Standing beside the car, the tall, tanned young man looked back at his mother. Sarah made herself smile. "Mom." David raised his hand, wriggling his fingers, and Sarah wriggled her fingers.

She stepped back out of the driveway and onto the lawn, brushing against the hydrangeas, watching her men. The sedan rolled out of the driveway. Sarah could see Dan's Panama in the backseat. "Some kind of milestone," Sarah said. Then her eyes filled, and angry with herself, she strode across the lawn. She had to bathe and dress. Adell Warner would be coming at ten o'clock to pick her up for the Hadassah meeting.

In the backseat of the Essex Dan sat squashed in the corner as Joe had prophesied, his left arm raised and lying across one of Sarah's old hatboxes, which held a raincoat and a pair of rubbers. Directly in front of him, Joe looked into the rearview mirror. "Are you okay, Dad?"

"Of course."

David said, "Are you sure?"

"I wish you fellows would stop this absurd worrying," Dan said. "Stop, I say."

Joe leaned across the front seat and pushed his shoulder into David's. "Stop."

"We'd better stop, I guess," David said.

"Then do it," Joe said, straight-faced.

"I have. *You* haven't."

"Now I have," Joe said.

Their teasing delighted Dan. He believed they indulged him, and he was grateful as he was whenever he saw them, at the start or the end of the day, entering or leaving a room, or passing him, or waving from a distance. They filled Dan with such happiness that he was often made giddy. He loved them with an intensity that beggared all his attempts at description. To Dan they were godlike, flawless creatures. Always, coming upon one or the other of his sons unnoticed, he would stare in worshipful homage before the lad's perfection.

In front of Dan's office the boys got out of the car with him.

Dan hugged each. "I'm proud of you," Dan said. "Proud of both of you."

"We're chips off the old block," Joe said.

"Joe's right, Dad," David said. "We take after you."

Dan watched them get back into the car, watched the car until he could no longer see it. Drained by the good-byes, he climbed the stairs slowly.

All through the day he followed the boys in his head, accompanied the Essex toward Chapel Hill. Dan quit early, locking his office and walking to the bus stop, still with his sons.

Afterward, walking home on Fairview Avenue, Dan stopped to chat with Otis Manning, a neighbor who was raking leaves. "I can't remember a heat wave like this," Manning said. "Can you?"

"It seems worse," Dan said. "We say that every year, don't we?"

"Not this long with no letup," Manning said. "And no rain!"

"It will pass," Dan said. He walked on, anxious to get out of the sun.

In the redbrick house he took off his jacket. "Dan?" Sarah came down the stairs. "Is that you whistling? Were you *whistling?*"

"I suppose I was," Dan said.

Sarah had pinned up her hair into a wild mop on her head. She wore a shapeless cotton dress, and her bare feet were in battered slippers. Her appearance made Dan smile. Sarah peered at him, cocking her head. "What's so funny?"

"I like your hair," Dan said.

She raised both hands, touching her neck, playing with tendrils of hair. "My *hair?*"

"You look younger," he said.

He knew she was pleased, and he knew she would deny it. "It's the heat," Sarah said. "It's making you addled."

He kissed her. "It seems to be an improvement."

Sarah peered at him, but she could not disguise her pleasure. "What's gotten into you?"

"I'm the same man who has shared your life all these happy years."

As he walked to the stairs, Sarah said, "Halt!" She came after him, extending his jacket. "You're as bad as the boys."

Climbing the stairs, Dan began smiling once more, and later, standing in the shower, he grinned, thinking of his encounter with Sarah. He enjoyed taking her by surprise, enjoyed flattering her. He loved her now as he had from the first days at Chapel Hill when they crossed the campus arm in arm.

After dinner Sarah said, "I feel like writing David." She went to the desk where she kept the rental records for the buildings downtown, and Dan carried the afternoon newspaper to the veranda.

The day ended, and in the quiet street the only sound remaining came from the whirring of water sprinklers on the lawns up and down the block. Inside, Sarah finished her letter, addressed it, and sealed the envelope. She held the envelope upright, looking at the address. She said softly, "David, dear David," and left the desk. She crossed the house to the screen door that led to the veranda. "I am ending herewith the longest day of my life," Sarah said. "Coming to bed?"

"Soon," he said.

Dan sat for a little while, looking into the darkness, thinking in turn of Sarah and David and Joe, and for the first time in a long, long time he thought of his mother, his kind, courageous mother. He remained on the veranda until long after dark, and when he left, he turned down the lights, leaving the newspaper scattered on the floor.

Dan woke from a dream he could not remember, but he felt safe in the big bed with Sarah. He could hear the clock ticking and, beside him, Sarah's measured breathing. Dan turned over the pillow and rubbed his face into it and then sat up, inching away from Sarah, swung his legs over the bed, and rose slowly so as not to wake her. He moved slowly but confidently in the darkness, into the hallway to the head of the stairs, where he reached for the light switch. In his pajama pants and barefoot, Dan went down the stairs and through the house to the kitchen. He pressed the light switch and got a glass from the cabinet. Dan went to the icebox for the large jug of water.

He closed the door to keep the light from the maids' rooms. Dan filled his glass and drank as he returned to the icebox and set the jug inside. He started to leave the kitchen but stopped. Sarah could wake and would welcome a cold drink. Dan took another glass from the cabinet. He poured the water, set down the glass, and as he put the jug back in the icebox, he heard heavy footsteps, heard glass shattering somewhere in the house, saw flashlight beams dancing across the kitchen walls, and heard men. "He's *here!*" and "He's right *here!*" And paralyzed with fear, he saw white-hooded figures with conical caps filling the back porch, raising rifles, and using rifle stocks to hammer the locked door. A man yelled, "Bust it open! Goddammit, bust it down!"

Dan watched two white figures back off and run into the door with their shoulders, so he didn't see two others who burst into the kitchen behind him. They were among those who had smashed the living room window to enter from the veranda. "We got the son of a bitch!"

These two had rifles, and each grabbed one of Dan's arms, holding him erect, as the back porch door was knocked out of its hinges and the kitchen filled with the Ku Klux Klanners. "Get the rope on him!"

A Klansman without a rifle, a big man with a belly the robe could not conceal, shoved others aside, using both hands. "The rope! The goddamn rope!"

Someone grabbed Dan's hands, and someone else tied a rope around his wrists.

Above, Sarah woke, hearing breaking glass and men shouting and cursing, men tramping through her house. She guessed who the intruders were instantly, and in the darkness she turned completely over in bed, arms out, searching for Dan, pawing the bed until she discovered, horrified, she was alone. "Dan!" Her cry came from the very core of her being. "Dan!"

Sarah crawled across the bed and almost fell as she left it, almost fell as she ran, barefoot, stumbling in the darkness until she reached the glow of light from the staircase.

There she saw the hooded men at the foot of the staircase, waiting for her with rifles. One said, "Get back, you bitch!"

"Where's my husband?" Sarah started down the stairs. "Dan!"

At the front door a Klansman shouted, "Shut her up!"

She kept coming. "I'm warning you, you dirty bitch!"

She kept coming. "Dan! I want my husband!"

She reached the men, swinging her little fists, kicking at them with her bare feet. They threw her back. She fell and rose, holding on to the banister, and went at them again. "Dan!"

The man from the front door reached the stairs. "Let me!" He flung the others aside and took Sarah's shoulders with both hands. He threw her aside. She fell into the banister. Her head struck the wood railing, and knocked unconscious by the blow, she dropped back onto the stairs.

In the kitchen, as his hands were tied and knotted again and again, Dan heard Sarah calling him, heard her coming, heard the warnings of the Klansmen and their threats and the sounds of struggle until a piercing scream tore through the night.

The big Klansman, the leader, said, "Get her!" as Dan saw Corinne standing in the doorway to the maids' rooms. The black woman in a nightgown, her hair braided, kept screaming, her mouth without dentures a large, gaping hole.

Behind her, hiding, holding Corinne, Dan could see Ella crouching, both of them screaming. The leader pointed. "Get those niggers! Shut them up!"

Someone stepped on Dan's bare foot, crushing it, and another hit Corinne in the head with the butt of his rifle. He hit her again, and she staggered back, back, pushing Ella into the wall as she fell.

"Corinne!" Ella dropped to her knees beside the older black woman.

The man who had hit Corinne came after them. He raised his leg to kick Ella, driving his big, high-top, thick-soled shoe deep into the black woman's ribs. She made a terrible sound, in agony, a drawn-out, dwindling gurgle, and fell forward across Corinne, her eyes open and glazed and her legs moving spasmodically as though she were trying to climb. "Shut the goddamn door!" yelled the leader.

"My wife," Dan said. "Please . . . my wife." He was afraid he would crumple. He could barely breathe, could barely stand. His legs wobbled. The rope burned into his wrists. He shook with fear.

"Get him out now!" said the big man. He stepped back, waving at the open kitchen door, moving his arm back and forth across his chest like a traffic cop. "Now! Now! Now!"

Men seized Dan. They lifted him off the floor, took him past the leader through the back porch into the driveway.

The big man followed, limping and pointing at the car in the driveway, its headlights dark. "Not in this car! Keep going!"

One of Dan's captors said, "Let the son of a bitch walk!"

Dan felt the coarse driveway surface cut into his bare feet. To himself Dan said, "Run! Run!" He twisted hard, from one side to the other, surprising his captors and freeing himself.

"Hey!" Hands dropped down on him, fingernails ripping his flesh. "Smart son of a bitch!" They dragged him along the driveway to the long rows of darkened cars that filled the street. "Try that again, you bastard!" Someone hit him in the ear.

They were in the street. One of Dan's captors yelled, "Open the goddamn door! You in the fucking Buick!"

They dragged Dan to the Buick, filled with white robes, white cones, front and back. The rear door opened, and inside, someone yelled, "Come on!" Dan's captors shoved him into the backseat, and as he stumbled, those inside seized him, and one took a handful of his hair, twisting and pulling it.

In the rear of the Buick he was thrown against the seat. He sat among Klansmen, facing three others in the front seat. His scalp burned as though someone had held a match to it. The bare soles of his feet were raw, and the pain in his left foot, squashed by the Klansman's shoe, had become unendurable.

The car in the driveway, headlights dark, roared out into the street, tires screeching, and all along the shadowed block, drivers in white robes started the engines of their cars. All were in such a rush, shifting before clutches were fully engaged, that the high-pitched screeching of the gears woke people from one corner of the block to the other.

They all were rolling at once, tailgating, many cars inches from the car ahead, and ahead, the leader in the lead car, sitting beside the driver, said, "Step on it, man. For Christ's sake, go."

Dan heard someone in the front seat say, "Look at that son of a bitch Landis go."

Beside Dan a man yelled, "You son of a bitch, I'll put a rope around *your* neck. No names, you son of a bitch!"

Everything within Dan seemed to disintegrate. He was on his way to die. These strangers had come for him to kill him. Someone had to help him. He would be executed unless someone saved him. He would never go home again, never see Sarah, never see David and Joe. "Stop! Please stop!"

"Shut up!" The man beside Dan rammed an elbow into his ribs. Dan retched, doubling over, but he was thrown back against the seat.

"You can't . . . please . . ." Dan said. Beside him the man leaned forward, turned in the seat, raised his fist, and hit Dan in the mouth. Dan's head snapped back. Spears of pain shot through his face, and blood coursed into his mouth. He began to sink, sink, sink into a black hole, and then he gagged and spit blood over the white sheets around him.

"You son of a bitch!" said the man who had hit Dan, pushing himself back, trying to keep clear of the blood.

"Fucking son of a bitch!" said the man on Dan's other side. He raised his fist and hit Dan in the face. "Fucking son of a bitch! *Son of a bitch!*" He raised both arms, the flowing white sheet flecked with bright red blood, and shook his arms, trying to shake off the blood.

To his left a Klansman grabbed a handful of hair, pulled Dan's head down until his chin dug into his collarbone and his blood flowed across his chest.

Dan started to cough. He couldn't stop. His chest rose and fell, and he began choking. He raised his bound hands, trying to paw at his throat as though he could stop the coughing. His body shook, and he fell back in the seat. "Son of a bitch is dying," said a Klansman beside him.

"Save us the trouble," said another.

In the front seat, another turned his head to look back. "Maybe we ought to tell . . ."

"No names!" The man who had hit Dan pointed at the Klansman in the front seat. "No names, you stupid son of a bitch!"

"Well, we ought to tell someone."

The man on Dan's right took Dan's hair, pulled his head back against the seat. "The son of a bitch isn't dying . . . yet."

The others watched Dan, peering at him in the darkened car. "He's a tough son of a bitch," said one.

"We'll soon see how tough he is," said another.

The driver turned the wheel, hugging the car ahead. "I'm ready," said the driver. "I'm sick of the Jew son of a bitch. The son of a bitch is getting blood all over my car."

Dan heard them from a distance, their voices faint and indistinct, like the voices of madmen muttering to themselves. He began to shiver; he could not stop. He begged for help, saying, "Please. Please. Please," to himself. He asked for miracles: the appearance of the police, the sheriff, the Highway Patrol. He wanted to scream, to summon bystanders, demanding to be saved, but he was alone, being taken to his death, his *death*. Dan tried to cry, but there were no longer tears in him. Only emptiness.

Ahead, in the lead car, the Buick, someone said, "About time," as the driver turned off the road, and the car began to buck and rock and sway, following other cars across an open field.

"Won't be long now," someone said.

"We'll be rid of this son of a bitch," someone said.

"Son of a bitch ruined my robes," said the man at Dan's right.

"Last time he will ruin *anything*," said someone in the front seat.

"The son of a bitch will probably shit himself now," said a Klansman.

"Not in my car," said the driver. He touched the brake. "Get him out of here."

When the Buick stopped, it was part of a sprawling arc of cars grouped around a cluster of oak trees. "I said, get the son of a bitch out of here!" yelled the driver of the Buick.

The Klansman beside Dan opened the rear door. "He's going."

Dan wanted to resist, but he could not. He wanted to fight them, but he was helpless. One Klansman pulled him from the car, and the other pushed and hit him, hitting him in the back with his fist. Dan wanted to run. He could not. He felt the warm earth against his bare feet, the pebbles and the rocks, the blood drying in his mouth, and he felt cold and alone, as two Klansmen flanked him, each holding an arm, and led him to a flatbed truck beneath the branches of an old oak.

The big man, the leader, waited beside the truck. A Klansman sat behind the wheel in the cab, and as the other two approached with Dan, the driver started the engine of the truck. "Come on, come on," said the leader, waving his arm.

Dan tried to pray. He could not pray. He saw the truck directly ahead, like a mountain, saw a tree rising above the truck, and he saw, dangling from a branch high overhead, a rope. He saw the noose and, closer, the longer, thick roll of knots rising from the noose. Then his legs buckled. He could no longer walk. His body sagged, and the two Klansmen almost dropped him. "Carry the son of a bitch!" the leader shouted. "Carry him, or drag him, but get him up here!"

The leader pointed at a Klansman. "You," he said, and pointed at another, "and you, and you. Give them a hand with the son of a bitch."

Men seized Dan, and as they dragged him to the truck, he said, "No." He tried to dig his bare heels into the ground, trying to stop. He shouted, "Please!" before a big hand covered his mouth.

He saw Klansmen climbing into the flatbed behind the truck cab, saw one reach for the rope, holding the noose. His pajamas slipped from his hips, and he grabbed them, pulling the thin, soft pajama pants up around his middle.

Those Klansmen holding him picked Dan up, and those in the flatbed bent, arms out, to take him. "Got the little son of a bitch."

They dragged him across the splintered wood floor of the truck. The Klansman with the noose said, "Hold him up. Will you— Okay," he said as he used both hands to lower the noose.

"Oh, please," Dan said almost in a whisper, his lips barely moving. "Please, please." His heart pounded. He was cold. "Please." His pajamas slipped, and he reached for them and missed.

Below him the leader could not stop moving, could not stop yelling. "All set? Are you set? Will you—? What the fuck is wrong up there?" He moved away from the truck, looking up, and overhead, naked and alone and dying, Dan saw the big man who limped badly, rocking as he moved.

"Paul?" Dan leaned forward, squinting, feeling the rope tighten around his neck. "Paulie?" A convulsive shudder of hope shot through Dan's body. Dan began to cry. Because the big man kept moving, kept limping, Dan was certain. Paul Ellerbee was in the white sheet, hidden by the white cone.

"Paulie!" Dan had seen him limping since the third grade. Dan had seen him in the street, leading the Masonic parade, seen him in the courthouse. "Paulie!"

Paul Ellerbee stopped, facing the truck as though the white sheets had been stripped from his body.

"Paulie, stop them! Please stop them! Please. Paulie!"

The big man lunged at the truck, his right arm raised, his forefinger twirling. "Go, go, go, go, go!"

"Paulie-e-e-e-e-e!"

"Go! Go!" Ellerbee stood over the truck cab, pounding the hood with his fist. "Go!"

"Paulie-e-e-e-e-e!"

"Go!" The driver released the clutch, and the truck jerked forward, bucked again and again, moving out and leaving the naked man hanging. Dan's body twitched once and hung limply, his head tilted against the long, tubular row of knots. Ellerbee followed the truck. He did not look back.

Someone said, "Teach that son of a bitch to mind his own business."

"Will you look at the size of the dick on that son of a bitch?" someone said.

"All the good it does him now," someone said.

"Anyway, cut him down," someone said.

"Go ahead," someone else said. "You want him down, *you* cut him down."

"Hell, he's a white man."

"Says who? Let the Jew son of a bitch hang."

———— ◈ ————

JUST AFTER EIGHT O'CLOCK, the morning after two black men found Daniel Maimonides Cohen hanging from a tree, Len Egan walked into the locker room in sheriff's headquarters and saw Wyn, stripped to the waist, shaving. "Hey, Wyn! Gotta a heavy date or something?"

"Something . . ." Wyn said. He wore his gabardine uniform trousers.

Len grinned. "Peaches don't care if you're shaved or not."

"I wouldn't poach on your territory, Len." Wyn wanted to be shaved close these days, and he lathered his face again. As he picked up his razor, he saw his father in the long mirror over the row of sinks.

"Didn't you work last night?" Earl asked.

"Just ended my tour," Wyn said.

"Thought so," Earl said. He stopped between Wyn and Len. "The only men who shave before going to sleep are married."

"Not going to sleep," Wyn said.

"Not—" Earl said, and stopped and looked at Len. "You'll miss roll call . . . *again.*"

Len walked backward. "Pardon my dust," he said, and swung around to leave the locker room.

Earl walked to the sinks. "You must have a girl who works nights, like you do."

"You and Len," Wyn said. "There is no girl." He dipped his razor into the warm water in the sink. "I thought we settled it about me and my life the other night."

"Because I found you shaving? Suppose I start calling you mister," Earl said. "Will mister satisfy you?"

"I'm going to a wake," Wyn said. He raised his chin and threw back his head as he began to shave his neck. "Whatever Jewish people call it when someone dies."

"From here?" Earl said. "Are you planning on going from here?"

"Soon as I finish shaving."

"Not in those clothes," Earl said.

Wyn looked at him in the mirror, then turned to face him. "We've gone over all this before," Wyn said. "They're my clothes. I paid for the uniform."

"Are you trying to get even with me or something?" Earl asked. "Go home and change your clothes, okay?"

Wyn tilted his head and continued shaving his neck. Earl said, "When you're wearing the uniform, you represent the department." His hardheaded son didn't respond. "So you're saying that's the general idea."

Wyn set down the razor. "He was *lynched,*" Wyn said. "They took him out of his house and *hung* him."

" 'They' probably form the tax base of this county," Earl said. " 'They' probably pay your salary."

Wyn bent over the sink to rinse off his face and remove the lather, and he suddenly sprang back. "The paper said his kids were in Chapel Hill," Wyn said. "The older one is starting his freshman year." Wyn pointed at the swinging doors. "You better leave, Pop. Fast."

"Good idea," Earl said. He walked across the locker room and through the doors.

Wyn looked down into the sink. After a time he continued rinsing his face. He took a towel and rubbed himself dry and combed his hair before carrying his shaving mug and razor to his locker.

Standing behind the booking counter with a sergeant, Earl saw Wyn come out from the locker room. Wyn raised the hinged section of the counter and dropped it behind him. "Hold it," Earl said.

Wyn didn't stop, and he didn't look back. "I'll be here for roll call this afternoon."

As Wyn left, Earl said, "Goddamn fool." The desk sergeant acted deaf, dumb, and blind. But he saw the sheriff pawing the counter for his campaign hat.

The sergeant reached out to get the hat from the desk behind Earl. "Sheriff."

"Yeah." Earl snatched his hat from the sergeant's hand.

Outside, in the parking lot, Earl yelled, "Wyn!" He put two fingers in his mouth and whistled. "Wyn!"

Wyn stopped, looked back, then continued on toward his own car. So Earl had to chase the hardhead, yelling, "Wyn! Hold it! Wyn!" The hardhead finally stopped, and Earl reached him, puffing. "I'm not riding in that old heap of yours," Earl said. "We'll take my car."

Walking back to Earl's black-and-white, he said, "Don't much like people watching me chase my deputies." He extended his keys. "This is your bright idea, so you must have the address."

In the car in the downtown traffic neither spoke. But as they left the business district behind, Wyn said, "I keep thinking of the locker room. Did you do all that on purpose back there in the locker room?"

"Do what?"

"Listen, Pop, and believe me," Wyn said. "Either I get a straight answer or I take you back to the courthouse. Your . . . pep talk in the locker room. Why did you do it?"

"Beats me."

"Goddammit!"

"It's the truth, kid," Earl said, lying. "The God's honest truth."

He tipped his hat down over his eyes and folded his arms across his belly. He couldn't let the young stud run loose out there with those people. Earl hated going where he was going. He remembered Dan Cohen's father, remembered Dan's grandfather, an elegant man with a Vandyke beard who had started every day in the barbershop in the Piedmont Plaza.

Fairview Avenue was full of cars on both sides of the street. "Guess this is the right place all right," Earl said. Wyn parked in the next block, and they walked back to the brick house with the porte cochere. Wyn saw people everywhere. "I guess we just join the crowd," Earl said.

On the porch Earl spotted a rabbi he recognized, Sidney Levin. "Wyn, stay close," Earl said, and raised his hand. "Rabbi."

Sidney Levin wore a dark suit. "How could it happen, Sheriff? Dan Cohen was a saint. A saint."

"For a fact," Earl said. "Like you to meet my son, Rabbi. Deputy Ainsley."

The rabbi touched Wyn's hand. "I'm a southerner," he said. "Born and raised. I've lived my life in the South. Dan Cohen was a white man, Sheriff. If this could happen to Dan Cohen, it could happen . . . ," he said, and stopped. "Who's next?"

"Well, I'm not here on official business," Earl said. "I'm making . . . there's been a death."

"It's mixed up with the Castletons, isn't it?" the rabbi said.

"We're here to see the family," Earl said.

"You're telling me to watch my mouth."

"You're not from around here, if I remember right," Earl said.

"I was called fourteen years ago."

Earl looked at the rabbi. "And you're a southerner," Earl said.

"You intend to scare me, Sheriff," the rabbi said. "I'm scared."

"I'm going inside," Wyn said, disgusted, and left them.

"Wyn." Earl had to move sideways to get through the crowd. "Wait up, Wyn."

In the house, standing with Joe behind their mother on the sofa, David Cohen saw the two men in uniform inching through the mob. The boys stayed with their mother, flanking her, but Joe had left the couch to stretch, and David, grateful for the opportunity, followed him.

On the night Dan Cohen was taken from his home and hanged, the boys had reached Chapel Hill late and left the car loaded. The following morning, as they finished unloading, an aunt telephoned. They had driven all day and sat beside their mother's bed most of the previous night.

Earl spotted Dan's wife sitting in the middle of the couch, all in black, her face like chalk. They had her surrounded, sitting on both sides of her, and lined up behind the couch. Earl had never seen so many of them together, up close. None of them looked like Jews.

Earl discovered he had lost Wyn and found him again, heading for the couch. "Excuse me," Earl said, pushing someone.

Wyn squatted in front of Sarah. "My name is Wyn Ainsley, ma'am. I'm awful sorry this terrible thing happened."

Sarah said, "Thank—" and could not continue. Wyn saw her face break up. She fought back the tears. David leaned over her, his hands on her shoulders, his face pressed against her face.

Earl reached Wyn. "I'm Sheriff Ainsley, ma'am. I wish I could say something that would help. Your husband was a fine man." Earl nudged Wyn to move away from the couch until he could turn, muttering, "Let's get out of here."

They had reached the entrance when they heard her scream. "Sheriff!" Wyn stopped, and he stopped his father. "Sheriff!" Wyn turned to face Sarah. "Where is he?" she screamed. She raised both arms and groped behind her for David and Joe. "My sons came to bury their father! Where is their father?"

"You going or staying?" Earl whispered, leaving Wyn.

Sarah screamed, "Sheriff!" Wyn couldn't stand it any longer. He got out to the porch and through it, leaving the house. Ahead he saw the rabbi following Earl.

"Hold on, Sheriff!" Earl stopped, and Wyn could hear the rabbi. "We'd appreciate it if you'd release the body quickly," the rabbi said. "Today."

"You're out of my territory now," Earl said. "You're in the coroner's territory." Although the woman had stopped screaming, he could still hear her. Christ, he thought, they were worse than the niggers.

"Our religion calls for quick burial, Sheriff," the rabbi said.

"Yeah . . . well, tell the coroner," Earl said, leaving the rabbi.

As he joined Earl, Wyn looked back. The rabbi stood where they had left him, watching them. "What is Porter Manship trying to do here?"

"Ask Manship," Earl said. "He's the coroner."

"I'm asking you."

"Oh . . . shut up!" Earl kicked a large brown sycamore leaf. "He's probably waiting until this mess moves off the front page," Earl said.

In the car Wyn turned back toward the heart of the city. Suddenly Earl whipped off his hat, startling Wyn, who ducked as it sailed into the backseat. "Max Isbell made him a decent deal," Earl said. "Why didn't he take it? Why did he take on Boyd Fredericks?" Earl asked. "Dan Cohen didn't come to town yesterday. His grandfather or great-grandfather or someone wrote the goddamn constitution. Why did he do it?" Earl shouted, and hit the dashboard with his fist.

He wiped his forehead with his hand. "What kind of goddamn wake is it without food? I'm hungry. Are you hungry? You must be, working all night. Let's get some breakfast."

"After the morgue," Wyn said.

"After the— Oh, no," Earl said.

"I'm going with or without you," Wyn said. "If Porter Manship won't release the body right now, I'll go from the morgue straight to Chuck Ransom." Ransom, a feature writer for the afternoon paper, also wrote a column, "Ransom Notes," for the weekend edition.

"Chuck Ransom will probably thank me," Wyn said. "So will the Klan. They like everyone to know how brave and fearless they are."

———◦◦◦———

O N MONDAY, three days after Dan Cohen's funeral, one of the largest funerals in the city's history, Chuck Ransom and Mitch Vogt, a photographer, waited for an elevator in the Piedmont Plaza. A man waved as he passed. "What's the scoop, Chuck?"

Chuck waved and said, "How're you doing, Colonel?"

"Who's he?" asked Mitch Vogt.

"Lloyd Somebody. I forget his last name," said Chuck Ransom. One of the elevator doors opened, and he preceded the photographer. "He's a lawyer. Works for the Castletons. Six," he said to the operator.

"Who the hell doesn't?"

"You and I," said Chuck Ransom. "We don't work for the Castletons."

"You bet your boots," said Vogt. "Suppose you tell me what we're doing here?"

"It's a story," Chuck said. "A good story."

"You bet," said Vogt. "We're here for the Second Coming of Christ."

"I think there's a column in her," Chuck said.

The photographer leaned against the wall of the elevator, resting his big Speed Graphic on the rail. "It's funny about the Castletons," he said. "We've got guys covering police, city hall, the courthouse. We've got a whole damn bureau in Raleigh at the State-house. But we don't need a man over at Castleton headquarters. We always know how to cover them."

"Six," said the elevator operator.

In the corridor, alone with the photographer, Chuck said, "You talk too much, Mitch. Jobs are hard to come by. In case you haven't heard, we're in a Depression around here."

Five days later, on Saturday afternoon, Faith sat at the card table in front of the fireplace with the weekend newspaper. When she finished the news section, she turned to "Ransom Notes." Settling back, she read the headline:

SISTER UNMASKS CASTLETON WIDOW

REVEALS A LIFE OF LIES

Faith looked up, shaken, as though she were facing an intruder. She pushed herself erect and, raising the newspaper, began to read:

> Faith Venable Castleton, who awaits trial for the murder of her husband, Kyle Castleton, has lived a double life, and her deceptive existence continues to this day.
>
> So says her sister, Margaret Siegenthaler Kreychek, here with her husband, Walter. "I couldn't stay away any longer," said Mrs. Kreychek. "I came to see that justice is done."

Mrs. Kreychek, called Marge by her family and friends, talked of her famous sibling, the Broadway musical comedy star, during an extended interview in her suite at the Piedmont Plaza Hotel. Mrs. Kreychek spoke with refreshing candor. "I'm not the kind who pulls my punches," she said.

As she recalled her famous sister's life, from childhood to the present, there unfolded a strange and fascinating story, a portrait of an ambitious, single-minded woman, ruthless in her determination to reach the top. No Broadway plot, however lurid and melodramatic, could match the tale told yesterday in the Piedmont Plaza.

Faith Venable Castleton was born Helen Siegenthaler in Rego Park, a section of Queens, a part of New York City separated from Manhattan by the East River.

"Helen was just about the most beautiful person I ever saw," Marge Kreychek continued. "Everything about her was perfect, all her life. She didn't grow up to become beautiful. She was born beautiful and stayed that way.

"No one could beat Helen in brains," Mrs. Kreychek said. "She always brought home all As on her report card, top to bottom. Even in gym. Even in home economics. She even cooked better than anyone else."

Marge Kreychek displayed neither envy nor bitterness while she offered the rare glimpse of her renowned sister. Instead she seemed to bask in reflected glory as she laid bare the facts of Faith Venable Castleton's life.

"What Helen loved best was music," Mrs. Kreychek remembered. "That was true in or out of school. Once her music teacher sent home a note to my mother with Helen. The teacher said something like Helen had a voice in a million. She said it would be a crime to waste the kind of talent Helen had. She said Helen should have private lessons. Private lessons! Who had that kind of money? Not the Siegenthalers of Rego Park!

"You think that stopped Helen? It did not," Marge Kreychek continued. "By the time she got to the eighth grade, Helen was singing in amateur night contests every Saturday night. Every Saturday night Helen dolled up, and what a knockout!

Off she went to Queens, Brooklyn, the Bronx, over to Manhattan, even out to Long Island some weeks.

"She won a whole lot of those amateur nights. And she kept every cent, buying tickets for Broadway shows. Single tickets. Helen was the only Siegenthaler from Rego Park who hung out on Broadway."

The aspiring actress soon looked for bigger worlds to conquer. In the summer of her sixteenth birthday she answered a newspaper advertisement and was hired to join a team of young women selling vacuum cleaners door to door in rural New England.

"I remember her boss," Mrs. Kreychek said. "He wore the loudest clothes I ever saw, and drove a La Salle the size of a hearse. He had all the girls in that car. And guess who sat up front with him. You're right. Helen."

Marge Kreychek said Helen earned more than her father that summer. "When she came home in September, my mother asked her to kick in to running the house. Helen had an answer all ready. She went upstairs, packed her clothes, and left the house, left Rego Park, left Queens.

"But my mother really missed Helen. Ma was nuts about her," Mrs. Kreychek said. "She loved me, sure, but seeing Helen gave her a lift."

With one exception the Siegenthalers had seen the last of Helen. She returned that Christmas, arriving on Christmas Day. She came with presents, stayed for Christmas dinner, and left forever before nightfall.

"Helen said she got scared in Queens at night," Mrs. Kreychek remembered. "Another lie. Nothing that walked, crawled, or ran scared Helen. Anyway, that Christmas became the last time we saw sister Helen unless we paid to see her on the stage."

As Mrs. Kreychek reminisced in the expansive suite of the Piedmont Plaza, the afternoon slipped away, as did Faith Venable Castleton's past.

"Soon as the Depression hit, my father got laid off," Mrs. Kreychek said. "He got awful sick that winter, the winter of '29. Sister Helen never laid eyes on him. I felt terrible for Papa and for Mama too. Helen really hurt them.

"So one night I dragged Walt, my husband, all the way over to the theater where Helen was playing at the time. I wanted to tell her about Papa, tell her to come out, just once anyway. We went to the stage door. Not a chance, said the guy at the door. I came ready for him, though. I gave him a note I wrote at home before we left. He came back and said she was gone, but he left it in her dressing room."

As she remembered the details of that poignant episode, Mrs. Kreychek wept. "That's my sister, Helen," she said. "All we ever knew about Helen . . . about Faith, Mrs. Castleton, is what we read in the papers, same as everyone else."

Mrs. Kreychek fought for composure. "As long as you're putting this in the paper, put this in too," she said. "I'm not the kind to hold grudges. There's no hard feelings in me. I'm ready to help if she asks, and the same goes for Walt, my husband."

(See photograph, p. 18: ED)

Faith did not turn to the photograph. She dropped the newspaper in her lap. After a while she went to the telephone and called for a taxi. Then she found the number of the Piedmont Plaza. When the hotel operator responded, Faith said, "Margaret Kreychek."

In their suite in the hotel Marge set down the receiver. "Guess who that was just called. Helen." Marge left the telephone. "Walt?"

Walt Kreychek was a stoop-shouldered man with an Adam's apple. He wore a U-shaped wire device under his shirt collar to keep the tabs down. "What?"

"That was Helen. My sister," Marge said.

"Her nibs? You're kidding. What does she want?"

Marge faced her husband. "She's coming over."

"Helen? Coming *here?*"

"Here, yes," Marge said. She ran her hands over her huge breasts. "I've got to put something on."

"You've got something on," Walt said. "It's Helen, Marge. It's not the president's wife."

"Shut up, Walt," Marge said on her way to the bedroom. He made her nervous. First Helen calling out of nowhere, and now Walt.

In the bedroom, twice as big as the one at home, Marge stopped to kick off her shoes. She loved walking in the thick carpet. The room had twin beds, and when Marge saw them the day before, she almost cheered. She would sleep in peace, free of scrawny Walt.

Marge opened her suitcase on the stand in front of her bed. Walt brought the suitcases home from the five-and-dime the day before they left Rego Park. When that man Castleton, the one who called and asked them to come, sent the railroad tickets, he put a hundred dollars cash in a separate envelope.

Marge pulled up her dress and dropped it on the bed. She looked down at the suitcase but saw only her breasts in the bra and the girdle over her belly. "Pig," she said mercilessly. "Fat pig."

When she left the bedroom, she found Walt standing over the radio, his head cocked. "How do I look?" she asked. He did not reply.

She walked toward him. "Will you please turn off that thing? Please!" Marge pointed.

Walt pushed a knob. "It's off. Now what?"

"I said, 'How do I look?' "

"Hey, what is this, Marge? She's not Queen Marie of Romania. *You* didn't kill your husband."

"Watch your mouth, mister," Marge said. "Just watch your mouth. She's innocent until proven guilty."

"Hip, hip, hooray," he said, and began to button his vest. "So let's go."

"She said alone, Walt."

"*She* said." He pulled down on his vest and walked to the chair where he had hung his jacket.

"Walt." Marge hurried after him, her purse hitting her hip. "No, Walt." As he pushed his right arm through his jacket, she grabbed it. "Off, Walt. Walt."

He pulled his arm out of the jacket. "You're afraid of her," he said.

"Maybe I am," she said. She gestured. "Maybe it's all this. Coming down here and . . . Maybe we shouldn't have come down here altogether."

"Why the hell not? When was the last time you were in a joint like this? Yeah, right. Or the last time you had a compartment on a train all to yourself. This guy . . ." Walt made a face. "I can never remember his first name."

"Holt Castleton."

"Yeah, Holt," Walt said. "Never laid eyes on us. *Still* hasn't. But all this is a hell of a lot more than you ever got from your sister, and don't forget it."

"Sure, you're right," Marge said, leaving him. She couldn't wait to get away.

Marge liked the corridor, wider than a room, with mirrors and furniture every so often. Waiting for the elevator, she ran her hand over the red velvet seat of a high-backed chair. Away from Walt she could breathe easily. Marge sat down, but the elevator door opened before she could get comfortable.

In the elevator, on her way to meet Helen, Marge felt funny. She tried to convince herself the elevator did it, going too fast, but in her heart Marge knew the prospect of seeing Helen had made a mess out of her.

In the lobby Marge watched the revolving door, and when she saw Helen, she began to wave. "Helen! Yoo-hoo!"

Faith saw the fat woman crossing the lobby like a tank. Marge stopped before her, beaming. "It's so long ago I can't even start to remember the last time I saw you," she said. "I don't even know what to do," she said. Marge pushed her purse under her arm. "Kiss or something?"

Faith could barely look at the revolting mound of fat she faced. "We're not alone," she said.

Marge didn't see what difference that made, but she said, "I guess you're right. Gee, you look wonderful. As if that's something new. When didn't you?"

"I can remember a few occasions."

"Yeah, I'll bet," Marge said. "Not you, Helen." She pointed at Faith's belly. "And you don't even show. What month are you in anyway?"

"We're in the middle of a crowd," Faith said. "Let's go over there."

As they walked to an alcove with chairs and a sofa, Marge said, "I can't get over the way you look, Helen. You look marvelous."

Faith said, "We can talk here." She moved a chair. "Take this one." Faith sat in the chair facing Marge.

"Are you having morning sickness or are you over it by now?" Marge asked.

"I'm fine," Faith said. "I am having a normal pregnancy."

"Yeah, but I read where you were in the hospital," Marge said. She dropped her hands onto the arms of the chair, grunting as she crossed her legs. "You fell or something."

"I'm fine," Faith said.

"A narrow escape, I guess."

"Now we've covered me," Faith said. She raised a folded newspaper. "I read about you, about you talking about me. You talked a lot. It seems you couldn't stop talking."

"Oh, that," Marge said, and to herself, What can she do to you? Nothing. She can't do a thing.

"You gave them quite a story," Faith said.

"Him," Marge said. "There was only one. Oh, a photographer, but he left."

"And you told your rotten little tales."

"Now, wait, Helen," Marge said. "Wait. I didn't even know I said half of what's in the paper. He kept at me, kept asking a million questions."

"And you had a million answers," Faith said. "You really hate me, Marge."

"I didn't say that!" Marge pointed at the newspaper. "Show me where it says I hate you. You can't!"

"Don't play games with me," Faith said. "You're too old, and I'm too—" She stopped and then asked: "Why did you come?"

"Like I said in the paper, Helen," Marge said, "I came to help."

"Say it again," Faith said. "Look at me, and say it again."

Marge felt weak, and she wondered if she would faint and roll off the chair. She could hardly breathe. She held on to her purse and glanced at Faith. "To help," she said, looking away. "Helen, I know you wanted to see me, but Walt would like to say hello," Marge said. "Okay? Can he?"

"Later," Faith said. "Marge?" Faith touched the fat woman's thigh. "Margaret," she said. "Marge Siegenthaler," she said, her voice soft and silky.

"Kreychek now."

"I remember Marge Siegenthaler," Faith said. "It's just the two of us here. Two sisters. No photographers. No reporters. Marge?"

The fat woman looked up. "What?"

"Do you really want to hurt me? Make more trouble for me? They say I killed Kyle. Isn't that enough trouble for one person? They're trying to put me into the electric chair. Is that why you came? To put your own sister into the electric chair?"

Marge mumbled, "Oh, God, no." She took a tiny handkerchief from her purse, crumpling it in her hand. "Don't even say that, Helen."

"How long are you staying?"

Marge rubbed her nose with the ball she had made of the handkerchief. "We just got here."

"Go home," Faith said.

"We can't just turn around—"

"How long are you staying?" Faith asked.

"I told you—"

"No, you haven't," Faith said. "You haven't told *me* anything. You've told the reporter, not me." Faith raised the folded newspaper and almost hit the fat woman in the face. "Told the world."

"Is this why you came, Helen?" Marge asked. "Did you come to scare me off?"

"Are you going home? Tomorrow?"

"I told you—" Marge said, and stopped.

"You're here to help me," Faith said. "And you're in a suite in this hotel. You couldn't buy an egg sandwich in this hotel. Holt brought you down. Holt or Serena, but it's probably Holt. Answer me!"

"You always hated me," Marge said. "You wouldn't give me the time of day, wouldn't even *look* at me. You didn't know I was alive. Here's something else you didn't know. I used to sneak into your room when you were gone to pretend we were together. I pretended we were talking, pretended you told me things about Broadway and about guys. I loved your room, loved the smell. Everything smelled like . . smelled so good."

"Now you're taking your revenge," Faith said.

"You're wrong, Helen," Marge said. She uncrossed her legs, grunting, more comfortable with both feet on the floor. All of a sudden Helen didn't scare her. "I'm not a mean person," Marge said. "Getting even isn't in my nature. I'll tell you the real reason I came. I hoped I'd stop being hurt. I swear it on Mama's life. I thought if saw you face-to-face, I'd be over it, over being hurt. God, Helen, you told the doorman in New York you have no sister."

Faith rose, unwilling to remain with the pathetic fool. Marge pushed herself out of the chair. "Are you leaving, Helen? I can still hear the doorman. " 'Mrs. Castleton has no sister.' Jesus! You could've said anything, could've said you were sick."

Faith had told the cabdriver to wait, and as she exited through the revolving doors of the hotel, he stood leaning against the taxi, smoking. He dropped the cigarette immediately, and ground it into the street before running around the back of the cab to open the door. He had drawn one hell of a fare, all right. Christ, she was really a knockout. He touched the brim of his cap. "Ma'am."

The driver held the door until she was inside and comfortable, and then he closed it softly. In the taxi, the engine running, he looked into the rearview mirror. "Ma'am?"

"Take me home," Faith said, hating the word as she said it. "Deer Park Road."

"Deer Park Road," he said, turning the wheel. "On our way, ma'am."

Faith pushed herself into a corner of the seat, her head in a whirl. Chuck Ransom's column and the encounter with Marge had left her completely spent, and she had to fight the anger that threatened her, anger at her own impotence.

She faced an army: Holt, Serena, Frank Burris, Lucius Peete, Gaby, the sheriff, the cunning little rattlesnake. And Max Isbell. And the electric chair in Raleigh.

Against this horde she stood alone. No. Wyn. She had Wyn, her . . . collie, her sweet, kind collie.

On Deer Park Road Faith sat on the edge of the seat, money in her hand, ready for the driver. As she paid him, she said, "No change. Stay where you are."

He raised his hat. "Thank you, ma'am. Thanks very much," he said.

Walking toward the house, Faith discovered the newspaper in her hand. "Marge," she said quietly. "Time to take care of her."

Inside, she stood in front of the fireplace, staring at the empty grate. She turned and dropped into the leather sofa. Long afterward clock chimed somewhere, and when the house fell silent, Faith went to the telephone. "Operator, I'm calling New York. Rego Park. It's in Queens," Faith said. She gave the operator the number, and while she waited, she opened the telephone book and found the number of the Piedmont Plaza and memorized it.

Clara Siegenthaler was in her chair at the kitchen table. The ringing telephone woke her, and she looked around half asleep and lost, until the phone rang again. She took it from the kitchen cabinet beside her, setting it on the table. " 'Lo," she said.

"Mama? It's Helen." Faith listened. "Mama?"

"Another country heard from," Clara said.

"How are you, Mama?"

"Cut the bull, Helen," Clara said. "You don't care, and I guess now I don't care if you don't care. I'm too old and too tired. And too sick."

"You're angry, and I suppose I can't blame you," Faith said.

"Thanks very much, and what's this about? About Marge probably," Clara said. "Your sister, Marge, in case you forgot. You've seen her or talked to her or something."

"I've just come from seeing her."

"You've done your good deed for the day," Clara said. "It's your own flesh and blood, Helen, in case you forgot, which I'm sure you have. You sure behave like you have."

"I haven't forgotten, Mama," Helen said. "Mama?"

"I'm right here, Helen, right where you left me. Same kitchen. Same chair. Same beautiful view from every direction."

"Mama, I called for a reason," Faith said. "How much do you owe on your mortgage? You and Papa?"

"The mortgage? As if I didn't feel bad enough," Clara said. "We're seven months behind right now. Eight on the fourteenth if we can't make the payment, and we can't, as though you cared."

"I must care," Faith said. "I called you, so I must care."

"I'll believe it when I see it."

"You'll see it," Faith said. "How about Marge?"

"How *about* Marge?"

"Is she behind too?" Faith asked.

"Where have you been anyways, Helen? Timbuktu? Everyone is behind."

"Mama, I want you to listen to me carefully," Faith said.

"I'm listening."

Faith said, "I'll pay off your mortgage, Mama."

In her kitchen Clara raised the upright telephone, turning in the chair as though she would hear more clearly.

"Oh, God, do you mean that? Helen? Don't joke with me," Clara said.

"I will pay off your mortgage," Faith said. "And I will pay off Marge's mortgage."

"Holy Jesus," Clara said. She could feel her heart going a mile a minute. Where was Paul? She craned her neck, looking into the front of the house as though she would see her husband. Whenever she needed him. "*Marge's* mortgage?"

"But you must help me out," Faith said.

"*Me?* Help *you?* So you *are* teasing me," Clara said.

"I mean everything I say, and I'll prove it," Faith said. "When we're finished talking, get your payment book and write down the bank's address. Put everything into an envelope. I'll give you my address. But before you do anything, you must call Marge."

"Marge?"

"I'll give you the number of her hotel," Faith said. "Tell her everything I've just told you. Your mortgage and her mortgage. You'll own your house free and clear. Then tell her she must go home tomorrow and never come back. There are morning and afternoon trains. If they aren't on a train tomorrow, they'll ruin everything for all of you. When Marge gets home, she can call me from your house," Faith said. "From your house so I can talk with both of you. After our talk she can put the mortgage book in with yours in your envelope. Mama?"

"I heard you," Clara said.

"Do you understand everything I've said?"

"Of course I understand. You don't think your brains came from the stork, do you, Helen? So give me the phone number of the hotel."

<hr>

DURING THE LAST WEEK IN OCTOBER everyone talked about the Harvest Festival that coming Saturday. Every day the newspapers carried some kind of story with a picture: pumpkins, squash, okra, cabbage, tomatoes, potatoes. Every year people came to the festival, came early, bringing their whole families to help fill their cars with the Castleton bounty.

At Sheriff's Headquarters everyone fit for duty reported for duty. Earl didn't like a sick list on the last Saturday in October. He always changed roll call from 8:00 A.M. to 7:00 A.M. that day. Deputies coming off the night tour stayed in uniform, getting their breakfast free at the farms later.

Saturday morning all the deputies on the night tour headed for the locker room to clean up for the Harvest Festival, and when Wyn came out, a deputy grabbed him. "Sheriff called from home, Wyn. He's on his way and said to line up everyone. I can't find Len Egan."

"Did you check the cellblock?" Len often came to headquarters from a date and slept in a cell to be sure he wouldn't be late.

"Twice. Jesus, Wyn. The sheriff has warned him and warned him. What do we do?"

Wyn wanted to punch Len in the mouth. "When my pop gets here, tell him Len is stuck with a flat tire. I went after him."

Wyn drove a black-and-white to get through traffic faster. He took a shortcut, zigzagging through downtown until he had clear sailing all the way into the alley behind Peaches Klem's place.

An ice wagon filled the alley. "Hey!" Wyn put his hand on the horn. He leaned out of the window but couldn't find the driver. Wyn parked in someone's backyard. The iceman came out from somewhere, water dripping off his rubber poncho. "Mornin'."

"Yeah, mornin'," Wyn said, running around him, around the wagon, running past the horse. Len Egan's beat-up Hupmobile, which he had bought from a convicted bootlegger, was parked under Peaches Klem's staircase.

Wyn took the steps two at a time, holding on to the two-by-four wooden railing, and at the top used it like a catapult to fling himself into Peaches Klem's place.

The whore stood at the stove in the kitchen, waiting for the water in her teakettle to boil. She wore her dragon kimono.

"Where's that—" Wyn began, breaking off as he saw Len in the bedroom beyond the parlor. *"Len!"*

Naked and on his belly on the satin covers of the big bed, Len Egan lay sleeping among stuffed dolls, stuffed hearts, stuffed brown bears with black, beady eyes.

Wyn grabbed Len's gabardine pants off a chair and threw them on the bed. Wyn threw Len's gabardine shirt at him. Len hated whiskey, but he came awake like a drunk, groggy, mumbling, thick-tongued, incoherent. As he raised his head, trying to focus, Wyn hit him in the ribs with his shoe.

"Ow!"

Wyn threw Len's other shoe and hit the naked man in the el-bow as he raised his arm to protect himself.

"What the— Wyn!"

Peaches came to the bedroom entrance, smiling with delight as Wyn, enraged, looked for more ammunition, something more to throw. He leaned over Peaches's vanity for the Kewpie doll propped against the mirror, then dropped his arm. He wasn't mad at the whore.

Behind him Len Egan scrambled off the bed on hands and knees like an infant. "What the hell is this?"

"Get your goddamn clothes on!" Wyn said. "Get dressed, you—" Wyn stopped. He almost went after Len with both fists, but the skinny naked man looked too helpless. Wyn grabbed a cheap alarm clock off the vanity and held it aloft. "Seven o'clock roll call, goddamn you! The Harvest Festival!"

"Oh, Christ." Grabbing his pants, Len began to raise his right leg and hop around the bed. At home he had set his alarm for five o'clock, to be sure, and, waking long before five, had decided he would stop and kill some time with Peaches.

Wyn heard the teakettle as the water boiled. "How's about some coffee?" Peaches asked.

Watching Len dress, Wyn said, "No, thanks."

"I'll be late," Len said. "What'll I say?"

"Sheriff thinks you had a flat," Wyn said. "You called, and I came for you."

Peaches carried her cup out of the kitchen. "You and Len are different as night and day," she said.

"Everyone is different."

"Sure, but take Len," Peaches said. "Len will drop his pants in the middle of the street in broad daylight. Not you. I'll bet you've never been with a whore."

Len grinned, buttoning his shirt. "Tell her, Wyn."

"I haven't," Wyn said.

"I would've bet on it," Peaches said. "Something about guys like you. You need the romance, need to see the woman fluttering her eyelashes. Take Kyle Castleton."

Wyn turned to her. "Kyle Castleton?"

The whore sat down at a table, crossing her legs, pleased with herself. "He'd sit right here, right across from me. I could've been his mother for all he cared about me."

"Why did he come around?" Wyn asked, amazed.

"Damned if I can tell you," Peaches said. "He'd sit around and talk."

"Talk? Talk about what?"

"Nothing," she said. "Anything. The weather. Oh, yeah . . . and the plane. His airplane. He talked a lot about it. He loved that airplane."

"And he *never*—?" Wyn broke off.

"Uh-uh." She shook her head slowly. "Never."

"Before he got married," Wyn said.

"And after—after he got married," the whore said. "Hell, he showed up two nights before he got himself killed. Same as always. First thing, he would tell me to lock up. He didn't need to say it twice, believe me Bob. He always paid me more than I could ever make if I had a line around the block."

"What d'ya know?" Wyn said uneasily.

"I lost one hell of a customer," said Peaches Klem.

"Yeah . . ." Wyn looked into the bedroom.

"Just about ready," Len said, opening his wallet to see if the whore had helped herself while he slept.

"You . . . Wyn," said the whore. "You're a cop. What do you think? Down deep? Do you think she done it? The wife? Do you think she killed him?"

"Can't say." Wyn started for the door. He had to get away, get out, get out now. "Len!"

"Almost ready," Len said.

"You'll finish in the car."

"For Pete's sake, I can't dress and drive," Len said.

"I'm driving." Wyn opened the door. "You had a flat, remember?" He came out on the landing, squinting in the sunlight, and went down the stairs fast. He saw Len's old Hupmobile but not the black-and-white. Certain the car had been stolen, Wyn stopped at the foot of the steps.

Len stopped behind him. "Where's your car?" he asked, and Wyn remembered.

They walked through the alley to the backyard where Wyn had left the sheriff's car. An old man weeding a border of geraniums slowly came erect. "This here is private property," he said.

Wyn said, "Sorry." He got into the car as Len dropped down into the seat and slammed the passenger door.

"I don't care what kind of badge you carry," the old man said, raising his arm and threatening them with a trowel.

"Crazy old coot," Len said as Wyn turned into the alley. "How'll I get my car?"

Wyn could not dismiss the thought of Kyle's leaving the Castle to come down here and sit around with a two-dollar hooker. Why would he talk to someone like Peaches?

A mile from Peaches's place Wyn had to stop for a troop of Boy Scouts, marching down the street. As he waited for them to pass, Wyn remembered Gaby in the Stutz on the way home from the depot talking about Kyle, about his being sick all the time. Len said, "I really appreciate what you did, Wyn."

Wyn didn't really hear him, and when the last Boy Scouts passed, he shot across the intersection. Len looked at him. "Jesus, can't you even talk to me?"

"Sure," Wyn said. "But not right now." He tried to forget what Peaches had said and could not. And he had Kyle with him. There were three riders in the black-and-white all the way to Sheriff's Headquarters.

At the courthouse Wyn said, "Len, listen. I'll let you out in front of the gates. You tell—"

"You can't!" Len said, interrupting. "You're supposed to bring me in because I had a flat."

"I said, *listen!* Tell my pop I'll see him at the festival," Wyn said. He leaned over Len to open the passenger door. "Get the hell out of here!" He had to make tracks before his father tried to stop him. He drove away from the courthouse, directly to Castleton Community Hospital.

Wyn parked in the emergency entrance, leaving the black-and-white where he had stopped the night of Labor Day, the night his life had started to change.

Inside he saw a young woman sitting against the wall, holding a baby. Wyn went from one examining room to another, but all were deserted. Then an orderly, in white, pushed his way through double doors, his hands cradled, carrying a load of bottles. "The doctor will be down in a few minutes, ma'am," said the orderly. "Like I told you, we're kind of shorthanded right now."

"Thank you," she said. "I certainly do appreciate your courtesy."

The orderly went into the large examining room where Wyn had seen Kyle that night, dead on the table. He bent over the table to set down the bottles, and behind him Wyn said, "Howdy."

"You heard what I told her," said the orderly. He began to stack the bottles on a shelf. A nameplate on his blouse said T. RICE. "The doctor will be down in a little while now."

"I'm not sick," Wyn said. "I'm looking for that intern, uh . . . He's about my age, about the same size, maybe a little taller." Wyn snapped his fingers. "Widseth!"

"He isn't here," said the orderly.

"Where is he?"

"He's gone. He'll be back tomorrow," said the orderly. "Eight o'clock tomorrow morning."

Wyn watched the orderly stacking the bottles. "This is kind of important. Maybe I could call him," Wyn said.

The orderly put the last two bottles on the shelf. "You'll have to come back." He turned to leave the examining room, but Wyn barred the way.

"I said it's kind of important," Wyn said. "You see my uniform. I wouldn't be here unless it was important."

"I can't help it," said the orderly. "You'll have to come back." He turned to leave, but Wyn stopped him.

"Just his phone number," Wyn said.

"Why can't you wait? You can wait," said the orderly. "He hasn't done anything. Dr. Widseth is about the most decent, honest man you'll ever meet. You can see him right here, in this room, at eight o'clock tomorrow."

Wyn had been up all night. His whole body ached. He felt a little woozy. The whore had put him on a roller coaster. He had thumbed his nose at his father. And the orderly didn't help. "T. Rice," Wyn said. "Here's a promise. I'll count to ten. If someone doesn't tell me where I can find Dr. Widseth by the time I'm finished, T. Rice will be T. Shit. One . . . two . . . three—"

"You can't—"

"—four . . . five—"

"He's been working thirty-six hours straight," said the orderly. "Dr. Kozelka's mother died and—"

"—six . . . seven . . . eight—"

"Room two-eleven," said the orderly. "There! Two-eleven! Are you satisfied?"

"Yeah." Wyn dropped his arm, turning to the door. "Yeah, I am."

Wyn went through the double doors into a long corridor. He couldn't find an elevator. "What the hell . . ." he said aloud, and saw a nurse ahead. He quickened his pace, and as she opened a door, he raised his hand. "Hey! Hold it!"

The nurse glared at him, and as he reached her, said, "Where were you raised? In a barn? This is a *hospital.*"

"Thanks. Where's the elevator? Please?"

"In front of you," she said, triumphant. Wyn saw the elevator doors across the corridor. "Try to be quiet."

On the second floor arrows on the wall pointed out the direction of room numbers. Wyn walked along the corridor to 211. He faced a large white sign with NO VISITORS in big black letters. "You bet," he said, opening the door.

Wyn stopped on the threshold, trying to see. The shades had been drawn tight, and drapes closed over the shades. Wyn opened the door wide, and light from the corridor made an aisle across the room all the way to the windows.

Arthur Widseth, in his hospital whites, lay on the covers on the nearest of two beds separated by a night table. In his exhaustion he had not removed his shoes. He slept on his side, like a cherub, his hands under his cheek. "Doc?"

The intern woke instantly. He turned to lie on his back and pushed himself up against the headboard.

"Wyn Ainsley, Doc."

Widseth turned on the light on the night table, and Wyn crossed the room to sit on the empty bed facing the intern.

"How did you find me? . . . You scared the hell out of my orderly," Widseth said, answering himself.

"Kind of," Wyn said. "And you've been moving for thirty-six hours and are dead on your feet. Me too, almost. I'll be out of here fast, that's a promise. I need some information, medical information."

"And you had to wake me? Good God, man, the place is full of doctors!" the intern said.

"You're the only one I know," Wyn said. "Take it easy. I'll be out of here in two shakes."

"You and your father—" Widseth said, and stopped. "Oh, hell. What kind of information?"

"Here's a guy our age," Wyn said. Wyn gave the intern a medical biography of Kyle, listing all the illnesses and diseases he remembered from Gaby's account. Widseth listened without interruption, a physician at work, giving Wyn his complete attention. "Okay," Wyn said. "Maybe I forgot something. Anyway, this guy was sick all his life. He got sick young, and he stayed sick until he was grown." Wyn leaned forward, putting his arms on his knees, facing the intern. "Do all these things the guy had ruin it for him with women? I mean, can he . . . do it?"

"Do it," Widseth said, so weary it took an effort to speak. "He can do it. You're referring to impotence, the inability to have an erection. Your man can have an erection. He can have sex."

"Okay!" Wyn said, rising. "I'll get out of your way, Doc. Thanks. Thanks a lot."

As he started for the door, the intern said, "But this fellow could have another problem. He could be sterile."

Wyn said, "Sterile . . ." as though he didn't want to be overheard. He stopped at the foot of Widseth's bed, looked down at the intern. "You mean, he can't have children."

"Not in every case," Widseth said. "Not always."

"So this guy could have kids," Wyn said. He nodded at the intern. "Right?"

"Not always," Widseth said. "He could or he could not." Widseth felt nauseated with fatigue and pushed himself down in the bed, closing his eyes.

Wyn wanted to stay and argue. "Thanks," he said. "Thanks, Doc."

In the corridor Wyn walked to the stairwell. On the first floor he made a wrong turn, bringing him into the lobby. He had to walk around the hospital to the emergency entrance. A wind had sprung up, scattering the carpet of fallen leaves, and the sun had disappeared. When Wyn looked up, he saw the blue sky disappearing, being covered with dark clouds moving in from the east, from the ocean. The heat had broken at last.

———◈———

A N OUTSIZE STEEL PRINCESS with a crown, her painted robes weathered and faded and needing fresh paint, hung above the entrance to the Princess Hotel downtown in a neighborhood of Army & Navy stores, the Goodwill Industries store, a Salvation Army soup kitchen, and nearby, pawnshops, flophouses, and religious missions.

While the street became seedier with each passing year of the Depression, the Princess Hotel imposed strict rules of decorum on its guests, and it maintained an antiseptic physical cleanliness in its public and private rooms. The guest rooms were furnished primitively: a metal bed, a metal lamp, a pine chest of drawers, and two area rugs, one at the door, one beside the bed. But the cleaning women scrubbed the rooms daily. Some rooms had private baths, and each bathroom was scrubbed daily with disinfectant.

The doorman at the Piedmont Plaza had sent Colin Inscott to the Princess Hotel because he knew of Colin's money troubles, and because Colin was always neat, and because of the Princess Hotel's sanitary standards. "Cleaner than this place half the time, Mr. Inscott," said the doorman. Colin stayed because of the room rates, but even the room rates at the Princess made a problem for Colin. The management demanded payment every seven days.

The morning of the Harvest Festival Colin left the Princess after his usual breakfast of coffee and sweet roll in the coffee shop in the hotel basement. He carried his riding boots. Colin stopped in front of the hotel, raising his head to welcome the breeze from the east, welcome the shadows cast by the darkening sky.

Colin walked east and at the corner waited for the traffic to lessen. A bum, unshaved and foul-smelling, joined him, extending a filthy hand. "Can you spare something for a meal, friend?"

"No, can you?" Colin stepped off the curb, crossing the street. He walked two more blocks and turned right.

Ahead, beside a ten-cent theater that showed movies from morning until midnight, a pawnbroker's three gold balls, the gilt tarnished and flaking, hung over the sidewalk.

The tinkling bell struck by the door as it opened told Leo Klezmer he had a client, but when he saw the client, recognized him, saw what the client carried, he wished the poor man would turn around and leave.

Colin threaded his way through the tall metal racks of men's and women's clothes, the showcases containing wristwatches, pocket watches, clocks, candlestick holders, candelabra, cuff links, earrings, rings, binoculars, the inventory of hundreds, of thousands of unfortunates.

Leo Klezmer stood behind the counter in the rear of the pawnshop, flanked by a safe, big enough to hold a crowd, and on the counter, a glass case, long as a coffin, filled with guns: handguns of all sizes using ammunition of all calibers, shotguns, and rifles, new and ancient.

Leo Klezmer had used several names, including part of his own, to create the name he offered in the steamship office in Antwerp when he bought the steamship tickets for America. He kept the name in America, and it appeared on his naturalization certificate issued after he and Frieda became citizens of the United States. Leo Klezmer's certificate, framed, hung over his head from the rack with binoculars and sterling and silver-plated silver.

"Oh, Mr. Inscott, it's you," Leo said. He had kept one of Mr. Inscott's suits for himself, taking it upstairs. Frieda dropped one of her bags with mothballs over the suit, and it hung in Leo's closet.

Colin set the riding boots on the counter. Leo didn't want them on the counter, didn't want the boots. The boots made Leo unhappy, made him grimace. "Mr. Inscott, I must tell you, my good sir, this is not a popular item in the area."

"They were made for me," Colin said. He ran his hand over the soft leather, discovering, to his dismay, that he wanted to throw his arms around the boots. "These boots are handmade."

"They are beautiful boots," Leo said. "Beautiful. Mr. Inscott, tell me what I should do with these boots," Leo asked, throwing himself on Colin's mercy. "In this place, all around here, whoever rides a horse has his boots, her boots. And the farmer or the colored man, if he gets on a horse, believe me, Mr. Inscott, he does not wear anything like these beautiful boots."

Colin hit the counter with his fist. "Damn it, man, stop trying to Jew me down!" he said, and immediately said, "I'm sorry. Honest to God, may I be struck dead . . . I'm awfully sorry." Colin's English accent had long since been forgotten.

"Relax, Mr. Inscott," Leo said. "You feel worse than I do. This isn't the first I heard the words, and it won't be the last." He touched the boots. "The trouble is, Mr. Inscott, these boots cost you a pretty penny, and from me you can get only pennies. Some joke."

"They've got to go," Colin said.

Leo surrendered. "So . . . they'll go," he said. "Maybe you need an umbrella, Mr. Inscott. Maybe we'll have rain, God willing."

"I didn't come in here for an umbrella," Colin said.

<hr />

O N SATURDAY, with all the kids home from school, Olive had a full day of lessons and started early. Boyd waited until she left before going downstairs. He poured coffee from the fresh pot she had made for him. Boyd sipped the coffee, set the cup on the table, and filled a bowl with cornflakes. He covered the cereal with milk, sitting at the table barefoot, legs crossed, eating slowly until he emptied the bowl. He rinsed it and the spoon, left the kitchen, and returned to his room. The curtains billowed in the gusts of wind. Boyd stretched out on the bed, trying to sleep.

When he heard a car door slam, he went to the bedroom windows, moving the curtains to look down into the street.

Below, Wyn climbed the stairs to the front porch. He rang the doorbell and stepped back. Wyn listened and rang again. After a while he knocked on the door. As his arm fell, he heard footsteps inside. Wyn waited and suddenly sprang aside. He leaped across the porch and jumped over the stairs to the neglected lawn. As he reached the driveway, he saw Boyd running toward the alley. "Hey! Hey, Boyd!"

Boyd didn't stop. He made it to the alley fence, but he had to fumble with the latch on the gate, and by the time he opened it, Wyn tackled him. "What the hell is the matter with you? Get up," Wyn said, rising, staying close in case Boyd decided to run again.

"Leave me alone!" said Boyd. He faced Wyn defiantly. "You leave me alone!"

Wyn raised his hands, palms out. "We're alone. I only want to talk."

"Well, I don't," Boyd said.

"Yeah, well, anyway . . ." Wyn said, and took Boyd's arm. Boyd tried to pull loose and could not. "Cut it out," Wyn said. "This isn't about you, okay? This is about Kyle." Wyn watched the slender young man. "Okay?"

"Let go," Boyd said. Wyn released him. "Kyle again," Boyd said. "God!" He faced Wyn. "Well? Ask your questions."

Wyn gestured and said, "Out here?" Boyd turned, and Wyn stayed beside him, walking across the yard to the back stoop.

Inside they went through the kitchen and into the living room. Boyd turned on the lamp beside the grand piano. He sat down on the piano bench, turning to face Wyn. "Well, go ahead, go ahead. Ask your damn questions."

Wyn said, "Okay . . ." but he did not know how to proceed or even where to start. "You and Kyle—you were friends all your lives, weren't you?"

"For the ten thousandth time, yes," Boyd said.

"Anyway, being together like you were, you guys must have done some tomcatting," Wyn said. "You must have tomcatted around, didn't you?"

"Is this why you came? Grabbing me on my own property? And threatening me?"

"Just answer the question, okay?"

"As though that will solve anything," Boyd said. *"What will that solve?"*

"Oh, hell," Wyn said, too tired to endure Boyd's juvenile posturing. "Let's go downtown. You'll answer questions downtown."

Boyd glared at him. "All right, then. We did. Kyle and I did."

"You got laid," Wyn said. "Right?"

"Isn't that what you asked me? Tomcatting? Yes. Sometimes. Not often. Not around here," Boyd said. "Well, almost never around here. We'd go somewhere, fly somewhere. Not for that reason. But if there were girls . . . women . . . Have I answered your question?"

"Yeah, thanks," Wyn said. He opened the door to leave, and Boyd, relieved, put his hands on the keys, striking a chord. Then Wyn looked back. "In the same room?"

"In the same *room?*"

"Were you and he in the same room?" Wyn asked. "With the dames, the women?"

"No," Boyd said. "Not in the same room. We—Kyle always booked two rooms when we traveled."

"Yeah." Wyn closed the door. So Kyle could have been in there talking, the way he talked with Peaches. Wyn went back to the piano. "You remember how sick Kyle was growing up, don't you?"

"He was sick a lot of the time," Boyd said. "Later, from about the age of thirteen or fourteen, he was all right. He was like anyone else."

Wyn leaned against the piano. "Did he worry at all?"

"Worry? Why would Kyle Castleton worry?"

"A guy who had all those diseases can end up sterile," Wyn said.

"Sterile?" Boyd held tightly on to the piano bench.

"He can end up not being able to have kids."

Boyd leaped up. "That's the craziest idea I've ever heard!"

"It's a medical fact," Wyn said. "I've just come from the hospital, from Doc Widseth. I asked him about Kyle."

"Doc Widseth!" Boyd rose. He scurried around the lamp as though trying to escape and stood behind the piano bench facing Wyn. "What would he know about Kyle?"

"He's a doctor," Wyn said. "He told me a guy who had all those diseases like mumps and measles could become sterile."

Boyd's voice rose to a shout. "Kyle's wife is having a baby!"

"Hey, quiet down," Wyn said.

"She's having a baby!" Boyd shouted. "Does she look like Kyle was sterile?"

"Will you stop yelling?" Wyn said.

"I'm sick and tired of your accusations!" Boyd shouted.

"Hey, I didn't accuse you of anything," Wyn said. "You're acting like it's your baby."

Wyn heard Boyd suck in his breath in a great gasp, saw him step back into the wall, saw him shake his head. "You're crazy," Boyd said. "You're wrong. Mine? What are you trying to do *now?* You've accused me of *murder!* Murdering my best friend! My only friend, the only friend I ever had! Isn't that enough?" Boyd leaned over the piano, his eyes wild. "Do you need to add more lies? More crimes?"

Boyd stepped back, clear of the piano, raising his head high and standing at attention. "I'm not talking to you anymore. I'm not saying another word!"

"Jesus Christ, it's yours," Wyn said. He could barely be heard. The room darkened and tilted, and Wyn's stomach revolted, and he thought he would vomit. He held on to the piano until he could think straight.

Boyd raised his arm in front of his face as though he expected Wyn to hit him. "I didn't . . ." he said. "I didn't . . . I swear."

"You swear, you—" Wyn said, and broke off.

Boyd's arm fell, and he seemed to shrink behind the piano. "It's her fault," he said. "I swear—"

"You swear," Wyn said.

"She trapped me!" Boyd said, crying out in a desperate plea to be forgiven. "Kyle flew to Cleveland for the air show. He was gone for a week, and Faith made me keep her company."

"Made you—"

"Yes. *Made* me, yes," Boyd said. "You don't know her. She can't be stopped. She can't. Every afternoon she took me to the lake house. She undressed right in front of me."

"Trapped you," Wyn said.

"You don't know her!"

"Yeah, you're right about that," Wyn said. He had been forsaken, left entirely alone, and as he turned to leave, he seemed slower, older.

"What are you going to do?" Boyd said. "It's not a crime, is it? You can't do anything to me."

Wyn opened the door and left it open. Boyd followed close behind him. He closed the door and locked it. He returned to the piano stool and sat down with his back to the keys, his hands between his knees.

Long afterward Boyd rose and headed for the kitchen but stopped in the doorway and returned to the piano. He stood over the keys for a moment, then struck a chord with his left hand. He said something unintelligible, his face twisting in disgust. He dropped the lid over the keys with a crash and went into the kitchen. He skirted the table in the center of the room. A water glass full of pencils stood beside the toaster on the kitchen cabinet. He chose a pencil, and from the drawer he took a lined paper pad.

Boyd sat down at the table and wrote, "Dear Mother . . ." He looked up, staring at the back door until he could no longer bear the calumny he hurled at himself. He said, "Oh, God . . ." in torment, and bent over the paper pad.

"By the time you read this I will be gone," he wrote. "Gone forever. It's better this way. I have bollixed up everything all my life. No one knows this better than we do, both of us. I have only been a burden to you, Mother, a helpless baby in a man's disguise, incapable of caring for himself, of earning a living, of—"

He could not go on. He wrote, "I love you, Mother, with all my heart and soul. Boyd."

As soon as he finished, he hastily rose to his feet, looking around the kitchen. "Damn!" he said aloud.

He flung aside his chair and hurried across the kitchen for the glass of pencils. He carried the glass to the table and set the paper pad upright against the pencils, facing the back door.

When Boyd left the house, heavy clouds lay low over the treetops, and the wind raised goose pimples on his bare arms beneath the short sleeves of the polo shirt he wore. Boyd thought of turning back for a sweater, but he couldn't face going back. He ran for the bus stop almost half a mile ahead.

When the bus finally appeared and he went aboard, Boyd and the driver were alone. Boyd got his transfer and slid into a seat near the rear. He watched the storefronts pass, reading the names, reading the signs on the windows, reading the gasoline prices at the gasoline stations, concentrating hard so he wouldn't think of anything. Someone said, "Got the bus to ourselves."

A man in overalls sat across the aisle beside the window. He patted the lunch pail on the seat beside him. "I like my privacy."

Boyd managed a faint smile before slowly turning his back and looking out of the window.

"Heat wave finally ended," the man said. "If this keeps up, we'll be down in the basement pretty quick, lighting the furnace." The man wouldn't quit.

Two women saved Boyd. They boarded the bus at the next stop and sat in front of the man, talking a mile a minute, keeping him quiet.

At Union Station Boyd transferred to the Green Bus. He saw a newspaper on a seat, snatched it up, and carried it to the rear. Boyd opened the newspaper all the way so he could hide behind it.

As he began to read, Olive turned into her driveway, stopped in front of the garage, left the Model T, and half ran across the yard to the back stoop. Christine Cannon's mother had canceled her daughter's lesson. "It's her first . . . you know," said Christine's mother. "She's had terrible cramps all day."

Olive wanted to cheer. "Poor child," Olive said. "Give her a kiss from me. I'll see you next week." The Cannon house was only a mile away, enough time for lunch with Boyd.

Olive flung open the kitchen door. "Boyd! I've had a cancellation." She stopped beside the kitchen cabinet, setting down her purse. "I've had a cancellation! Boyd!" She pinned back a strand of hair. "Boyd!" She had started across the kitchen to look for him when she saw the notepad set upright against the pencils in the glass at the table.

Boyd rode the bus to the end of the line. The bus driver made a U-turn before stopping, and when Boyd went down the steps, he could see, in the distance, the wind sock flying above Stan Jessup's office at the airport. Boyd turned toward the open fields.

The undergrowth reached almost to his knees, bending before the wind and slapping his shins. When Boyd reached the open space at the end of the runway, he could feel the dust in his face. When he saw the Packard sedan beside the small office, he almost turned back. All the way out from Union Station he had prayed Stan Jessup would be gone.

The wind came unchecked across the fields and across the runway. Beneath the wind sock Stan Jessup held on to his hat, watching the dude. When Boyd was close enough, Jessup said, "This must be my lucky day. Here you come bringing my hangar rent." He extended his hand, palm up. "Pay me."

"I'm sorry, Stan."

"I'll take half," Jessup said. "Twenty-five bucks, cash or check."

"I haven't any money."

Jessup's hand fell. "You came out to see old Stan," he said. "You got lonely for the sight of a friendly face."

"I thought I'd take the plane up," Boyd said.

"You thought you'd take the plane up," Jessup said. "You thought wrong."

"It's my plane," Boyd said.

"You woke up with nothing better to do, so you decided on a joyride," Jessup said. "You haven't flown the plane since Kyle died. Far as I can tell, you've never flown it."

"I've flown it," Boyd said. "I've flown it a lot."

"Not around here," Jessup said. "And not today, or any day until I'm holding fifty clams in my hand. Now get the hell out of here."

Boyd's head pounded, and he felt faint, felt as though he would fall to the ground. "You can't stop me."

"I can't stop you? I'll kick your ass all the way back to town," Jessup said.

Boyd thought only of turning and running. He could hardly breathe. "It's my plane."

Jessup took a big handkerchief out of his pocket and blew his nose. The little bastard had stirred up his hay fever. "You're a smart punk, aren't you? You're not going anywhere," Jessup said. "There's not enough gas in that airplane to fly you into the next county. And you're not getting any around here." He shoved Boyd aside. "Jordan!"

Jessup squinted, watching the hangar. When the black man emerged, Jessup said, "Jordan, I'm going to town, but I'll be back. Stay away from the gas pump. You go near the gas pump, and I'll kill you, Jordan."

"Yes, sir, Mist' Jessup."

Jessup nudged Boyd. "Come on. I'll take you into town." He walked to the Packard and opened the driver's door. "Are you coming?"

Boyd hated Jessup. He had never hated anyone as much. "No, I am not coming."

With Jordan beside him, Boyd watched the Packard turn toward the Kettle Pike. "How you gettin' home, Mist' Boyd?" Boyd didn't answer but started for the hangar. "Mist' Boyd? Where you goin' now, Mist' Boyd?"

"Let's bring out the Waco, Jordan."

The black man stopped. "Waco?" Jordan ran to catch up with Boyd. "Can't take out the Waco, Mist' Boyd."

The black man caught Boyd in the hangar. "You heard Mist' Jessup," Jordan said. "I can't come near the gas pump, 'n' there's barely any gas left in the Waco."

Boyd felt a fluttering in his thighs, and he felt cold inside. "I'm not going far."

The two-seater aircraft sat near the wall, at an angle, resting on the tiny tail wheel. Boyd said, "Jordan, help me with the chocks."

Both bent beneath the fuselage, each moving aside a beveled wooden block fitted against each wheel. "Let's take her out," Boyd said.

Jordan took the wingtip near the wall, and Boyd used both hands to hold the other wingtip and push the airplane out of the hangar. In the daylight the sleek orange biplane seemed to come alive. "Let's wind her up," Boyd said, standing on tiptoe and reaching high over his head for the propeller. He turned it three times and stepped back. He walked to the cockpit. Jordan waited for him.

"You got no jacket, no goggles," Jordan said. "You got no scarf. It's cold, Mist' Boyd. I'm cold down here. You'll freeze up there, Mist' Boyd."

Boyd put his arm around Jordan. He wanted to hold on to the black man forever. "I'll be all right."

Jordan took Boyd's hand. "You wait, Mist' Boyd. I'll fetch you Mist' Jessup's jacket 'n' his goggles. You'll be down before he's back."

"Let go, Jordan," Boyd said, and swung clear of the black man. Boyd raised his hands and grabbed the wing struts. He stepped up onto the wing and swung himself into the rear cockpit.

He was shaking. Boyd held on to the stick, trying to stop the shaking. He could hardly breathe. He felt as though he were choking.

"You all right, Mist' Boyd?"

"Start cranking, Jordan. *Wait! Wait!*" Boyd leaned forward, peering at the instrument panel to be certain the fuel tank selector was switched to the reserve tank and not the empty. Then Boyd looked to see if the throttle, an upright lever on the left side of the cockpit, was set in the idle position.

He watched Jordan skirt the wings, stop beneath the engine, away from the propeller. A crank protruded from the engine, and Jordan took it with both hands, shouting, "Switch off!"

Boyd checked the switch a third time and leaned out so Jordan could hear him. "Switch off!"

The crank turned a wheel faster and faster, building up momentum. It was, in effect, a starter. Boyd watched Jordan turn the crank until it would spin no faster. Shouting "Switch on!" he engaged the clutch, allowing the engine to absorb the movement from the wheel. The propeller began to move very slowly, then gathered speed and an instant later began to whirl as the engine seemed to explode. Jordan ran backward. He stopped several feet from the biplane and raised his hand and moved it in a circle to send Boyd out into the runway.

Boyd felt imprisoned in the barren cockpit. The airplane trembled beneath him, alive and powerful, urging him to release it, to send it into the blue skies. He said, almost whispering, "God . . ." and broke off. He saw Jordan's hand making a circle.

Boyd reached for the stick and pulled back his hand as though he had burned his fingers. *Strap!* He had forgotten the straps! Boyd buckled himself into the seat. He could hear Jordan, and he leaned out the cockpit, his hair rippling in the wash from the propeller. He made himself smile for Jordan, extending his hand and making a fist with thumb raised.

Now he knew he must go. He could stay no longer. He had used up all his time here. Jordan stood watching and waiting. "Take the stick," Boyd said, and put his hand on the stick. "The throttle," he said. He put his hand over the throttle and, moving it forward, brought the stick all the way back with his left hand.

Jordan saw the wheels turn, saw the bright orange aircraft move across the cement apron in front of the hangar. The black man grinned, raising his hand high, thumb extended.

The Waco, like all contemporary aircraft, sloped steeply from the engine to the tail. On the ground the airplane resembled a playground slide. The pilot, taxiing, could not see ahead. So he taxied in a succession of elaborate S curves, reconnoitering as he proceeded, prepared to avoid any obstacle that appeared.

Boyd took the aircraft up the runway, heading for the edge of the airfield, where he would turn into the wind. The airplane ate up the ground. The long runway, stretching forever, began to disappear. He could see the overgrown fields coming closer and closer. He wanted to turn back, but he couldn't. "You can't! Over there!" he said, seeing the end of the runway. He made a final, slow S. As he completed the circle, he moved the throttle into the idle position and stopped on the runway, facing into the wind. Boyd pushed his feet into the brakes, moved the throttle forward, and checked the magnetos. Both checked out, and he brought the throttle back to idle.

And here the full weight of his scheme struck him. Always before, confronted with danger, he had fled. Now he sat in the throbbing aircraft, imprisoned and immobilized. All his plans, the solution he had conceived and seized for himself, the final, climactic escape from the wretchedness and ignominy of his life, the shame that every passing day heaped upon him eluded Boyd. His fear paralyzed him. He had failed again. His hands fell between his legs, and his head dropped.

So he did not see the Model T stop beside Jessup's office, did not see Olive scramble out of the black coupe and run to the office door. She tried to open the door and, when she could not, began to bang on it with both fists.

Jordan came running. "Ma'am?" Olive fell upon him, grabbing the black man's shirt with both hands. "Is my son here? Have you seen him?" Boyd's note lay before Olive's eyes: "gone forever . . ." *Forever!* Olive wanted to scream. "Boyd Fredericks! Kyle Castleton's friend."

In the gleaming orange biplane at the end of the runway Boyd sat in helpless agony. He loathed himself. "Coward!" he shouted, as though he had to be heard above the engine. "Crybaby! Take the throttle!" he shouted. "Take it!" he shouted, and put his hand on the throttle. "Move it!" He could not.

"The gas!" he shouted. He would run out of gas here on the ground! He had to go! In a convulsive movement he began clawing the straps to free himself.

As the straps fell away, Boyd raised both hands. He grabbed the cowling and came out of the cockpit seat, in a frenzy to leave the airplane. He saw the engine and heard it and flopped down into the cockpit to cut the switch. There, left with only lateral vision, Boyd saw what he had seen an instant earlier, as though time had elapsed before the image reached him. He grabbed the cowling again and pulled himself above the cockpit. He stared at the Model T crossing the field to reach him. Following far behind was Jordan.

Boyd dropped back into the seat. He moved the throttle forward with his right hand and took the stick with his left. The biplane began to roll.

Olive saw the airplane rolling. "Stop!" she screamed. "Boyd!"

On the runway Boyd pushed the throttle forward for more speed. As the tail rose, the fuselage rose, and Boyd saw the engine and the dark arc of the whirling propeller, and beyond, he saw the runway and the beckoning sky. He held on to the stick, waiting for ground speed, for liftoff.

So he didn't see the Model T veer sharply, speed toward the runway at a right angle to the aircraft. In the coupe Olive saw Boyd coming, saw the runaway ahead, and knew she would cross it ahead of the airplane. She turned again, moved at an angle, pointed the Model T directly at the orange airplane.

Olive drove the coupe into the wings of the Waco. The wings rose almost vertically as the airplane slid to the left, across the runway and into the field. The airplane fell on its side, the propeller went into the ground and snapped, and Boyd, without straps, dropped out of the cockpit. He lay with one leg doubled under him, and as he pushed himself to his feet, he heard Olive call, "Boyd! Boyd!"

When she saw him, Olive said, "Why?" and ran across the runaway to claim him. With her arms around him, Olive rocked from side to side. "I would have died too," she said. "You would have left me alone to die."

Boyd heard Jordan. "Mist' Boyd! God Almighty! You all right, Mist' Boyd?"

The black man walked around the tail of the airplane. "Thank God Almighty," he said. Jordan peered at the crazy white woman. "What all you tryin' to do, ma'am? You could've killed this boy." As the black man continued and Olive held Boyd close, keeping him prisoner, he wanted to drop back down into the dirt, sink deep, deep down into the dirt.

<hr />

WHEN WYN LEFT BOYD and got into the black-and-white, he drove in a stupor. He stopped for a red light and, when it changed to green, didn't proceed until the driver behind him sounded the horn.

Wyn reached a commercial street where a large moving van had double-parked, blocking him. While he waited, Wyn craned his neck, examining himself in the rearview mirror as though he had changed in the last hour. When the van moved, crawling down the street, Wyn followed until, angry with himself, he pushed the siren switch.

The van stopped, and as Wyn swung around it, into oncoming traffic, cars going in both directions stopped. Pedestrians stopped, some covering their ears as the piercing screech of the siren tore through the street. Wyn pushed the switch, cutting the siren. Cars began to roll, and Wyn picked up speed. Since the encounter with Boyd the world had become an enemy camp.

When Wyn could see Castleton Farms, he drove into a traffic jam. The early birds had loaded their cars and were trying to get out, some planning to return for another free load, and newcomers were lined up trying to enter. Here, where he needed it, Wyn wouldn't use the siren, wouldn't add to the confusion. He drove onto the shoulder of the road.

Two deputies, Gene Hovde and Clem Carpenter, were in the middle of the highway at the entrance to the farms, directing traffic. Wyn shouted, but they didn't hear him; they were surrounded by too many cars and too many complaining drivers. Suddenly Wyn was in an awful rush. He left the black-and-white on the shoulder, walked into the road, into the traffic. Gene Hovde saw him. "Where the hell have you been?"

Wyn said, "Hi, Gene," and "Hi, Clem," as the other deputy wagged his finger, grinning.

"Naughty, naughty," said Clem Carpenter, raising his hand, halting traffic so Wyn could cross the road.

Wyn stopped the first car that turned into the farms. "How about a ride?" From the running board Wyn could see the masses of green and white pennants circling the Castleton Pavilion.

The pavilion, built by Sam Castleton and assembled once a year for the Harvest Festival, was an open, round structure with a conical roof supported by vertical wooden beams rising from a wooden floor. It stood in the center of the long rows of tables heaped with harvested crops. Starting at dawn and continuing until the last car left the farms, the black field hands pushed loaded wheelbarrows from the barns to the tables.

While he lived, Sam Castleton had arrived early for the festival, and he had brought every member of his family with him. He and his family welcomed every guest who paused at the pavilion, and he and the family remained to the end of the day. Certain conditions in Sam Castleton's will obligated his heirs to continue the practice he established.

Wyn crouched on the running board. "Drop me at the park sign, okay?"

"Sure thing, Sheriff," the driver said, and his wife smiled at Wyn.

"The Lord has blessed us with cool weather at last," she said.

"Yes, ma'am," Wyn said, and pointed at the large sign with an arrow below the word PARK. "Turn here and stop, please."

The driver obeyed, and Wyn stepped off the running board. "Many thanks," he said, and as the car drove off, he almost walked into Kay.

She said, as if her prayers had been answered, "Oh . . . Wyn." She had wakened that morning determined to hate him. She was going to the festival with Edith and Jim so she could prove to them how much she hated him. Now facing Wyn, Kay felt all her resolve melt away.

He said, "Hello, Kay," and, hearing himself, casual and distant, tried to smile. "Did you just come?"

"We're leaving," Kay said, and behind her Wyn saw Edith and Jim Anderson.

Wyn said, "Hi, Edith. Hi, Jim." He recalled their finding Kay with him at the Labor Day Picnic about a hundred years before. Wyn gestured. "None of you is carrying anything. Did you fill your car already?"

Jim said, "We didn't come out for the Castleton bounty. We've had enough of the Castleton bounty."

"Yeah . . . I guess," Wyn said, nodding, wanting to get going. "I've got to beat it."

"In a minute," Jim said. "Stay put, Wyn." He said to Edith, "Why don't you and Kay head for the car?"

Wyn said, "I've got to go, Jim. I'll see you later."

"No, you won't," Jim said. "I brought them out here with me for only one reason. You. I knew you'd be working here at the festival. I came out to see you. I wanted Kay to see you, see you and say good-bye. I've got the Florida job. We're going to Florida. And we're taking Kay and my mother-in-law with us. Understand? Kay is coming with us. We're starting fresh. All three of us, Wyn. Kay is starting fresh. And you won't spoil anything for her, Wyn. Stay away, understand?" Jim Anderson extended his hand. "Wish us luck."

Wyn took the coach's hand. "You know I do." He had a million questions, but he had to go, *now*.

At the command post Earl established each year in front of the pavilion, he saw Wyn coming. Earl had to talk himself out of putting the kid on probation, probation without pay, goddammit. He raised his hand. "Over here!"

When Wyn saw his father waving, he almost turned and ran. The little man with the belly had been a giant all of Wyn's life, had been Wyn's safety and security, understanding everything and forgiving everything. Through Wyn's childhood and the years that followed his father had not disappointed him, delivering whatever Wyn asked. "Where in the name of Christ have you been? Today, of all days?"

"I told Vern—" Wyn said, and Earl interrupted.

"Vernon Chapman isn't the sheriff of this county. Next time tell me. *Ask* me. Going off to hell and gone because Len Egan had a flat. I don't give a good hoot in hell if Len Egan had a flat. I expected *you* here, not Len Egan. And where have you been *since* Len Egan showed up? Tell me later." Earl gestured. "Frank Burris is over there, stocking up with the common people. I sent Ben Miller to help him because I couldn't find you. Get over there quick, and send Miller back to me." Earl slapped Wyn's behind. "Move it, kid."

"I can't."

"Can't? Get over there!"

"I can't. I, uh, gotta see Holt Castleton."

Earl said slowly, "Holt Castleton? Why do you need to see him?"

"It's—" Wyn said, and stopped. He couldn't tell his father, couldn't tell anyone. Wyn couldn't trust anyone.

"Okay, let's put an end to this," Earl said. "Find Ben Miller and Burris. Relieve Miller. My advice to you is, obey." He waited for Wyn to move.

"I'm going in there," Wyn said. "Don't try to stop me, Pop."

As Earl said, "Are you—?" Wyn shoved him aside, almost knocking the little man off his feet. Earl said, "No, Wyn, no!" but the kid was gone, and straightening his hat, Earl followed.

When Wyn entered the pavilion, the array of Castletons, of the power he faced, struck him with almost physical force. Wyn identified Serena Burris with her hair like a lion's mane. He recognized Gaby, Holt's sister, and he saw Russell Vance, who stood beside her. Then Wyn spotted Holt Castleton all by himself. And Wyn heard his father behind him.

"Sorry, folks. Excuse us for this intrusion, this interruption. Deputy!" Earl said. "I'll see you out front, Deputy!"

So Wyn ran out of time before he could even begin. "Mr. Castleton?" Wyn went directly to Holt. "I'm Wyn Ainsley. I've got a trade to offer you."

Worried sick, Earl reached them. Wyn's rash behavior scared him. "I'm ordering you out of here," Earl said. "I'm giving you a direct order to leave."

"In a minute," Wyn said, and turned to Holt. "My trade is for Kyle's B Stock."

"Kyle's B Stock?" Holt took Wyn's arm roughly. "What do you mean?"

Wyn clamped his hand over Holt's and freed himself. "Not that way," Wyn said. "You're headed for trouble that way."

Earl realized he had a lunatic on his hands. His own kid had gone crazy. "He's not talking for the Sheriff's Department," Earl said. "He doesn't represent the department."

Wyn grabbed the badge on his shirt with both hands but couldn't manage to loosen the clasp. In a kind of frenzy he pulled at the badge and tore it loose, leaving a jagged gash in the shirt. Wyn took his father's hand and slapped the badge into it. "You beat me to it," Wyn said. The world narrowed, leaving him alone with Holt.

"I don't need a badge," Wyn said. "I can do what I came here to do naked. You can have Kyle's B Stock."

For a little while the only sound in the pavilion came from the crowd outside. Then Holt said, incredulous, "You . . ." He looked at Earl. "Sheriff? Did you—?" Holt looked at Wyn. "Who told you about the B Stock? Who?"

He didn't see Serena coming closer to be certain she heard every word. Holt didn't see Russell put his arm around Gaby.

Wyn's announcement made Russell dizzy. The sheriff's son could be crazy. He acted crazy. He had just ripped off his badge. Russell wanted to interrupt, but he had to wait, had to listen. Gaby nestled against him, putting her hand over his. His hand felt like ice in hers.

Holt watched Wyn. "Cat got your tongue?"

"You've been trying to get Kyle's B Stock," Wyn said. "Trying everything you can think of doing to get the B Stock." Behind him Burris entered the pavilion. "You can have it."

Serena almost cried out, barely able to contain herself. She looked at Russell, holding Gaby close, clutching his ticket to power, his key to the money vaults. She admired Russell, waiting quietly, listening, waiting to trade, to do business. Russell was no ally of Holt's. Holt had no allies. From this day forward Holt would live among enemies. Burris joined her. "Serena?"

Holt said sarcastically, "I can have the B Stock." He extended his hand, palm up. "Give it to me."

"After you let Kyle's wife free," Wyn said. "She is innocent. Let her go."

"I'm not holding her," Holt said. "The county attorney and the court are holding her."

"Maybe you don't want the stock," Wyn said. "Say so and stop wasting my time."

Holt saw Serena and Burris watching, saw Russell with Gaby. "I want it," he said.

"After the murder charge is dropped," Wyn said. "After she is free, you'll have the B Stock."

"Half," Russell said. "Half to Holt and half to his sister as established by the Sam Castleton Foundation."

"Let's finish this," Wyn said.

"We'll finish," Holt said. "The widow must sign a document on behalf of herself and her descendants into perpetuity."

"She'll sign," Wyn said.

"So you say. What does the lady say?" Holt said. "Let her tell me what you've told me."

"She'll do it," Wyn said. "And you'd better do it. You'd better let her loose. Let her go, or I'll come after you." He walked forward until he and Holt were only inches apart. "I'll come after you, and if I do, there will be only one of us left."

Wyn backed off, backed into Burris, who moved aside. As Wyn turned, Earl turned, staying close, ready to grab him if he tried to get away.

They came out into the mob. "Wyn? You and that woman . . . it's you and that woman, isn't it?" Jesus Christ, he had put them together, had sent his own kid up to New York for her.

"I've got to go," Wyn said.

Earl held on to him. "No, Wyn, wait till this is over, and I'll go with you."

"To bed? I'm going to bed," Wyn said. "I haven't had any sleep. I've got to get some sleep."

Earl could not release him. "Swear."

"I swear."

"Wyn, listen. This dame . . ." Earl shook his head. "She's not for you. She's not for anyone. She's evil, Wyn. Believe me. She'll do you in, just like she did Kyle Castleton in. Wyn? Will you listen to me?" The little man looked up at the young buck, the young, honest, innocent buck. "Listen to what I say," Earl said, and then, for the first time ever, added: "Please."

"Can I go now?"

"You forgot something," Earl said, and released him to take

Wyn's badge from his pocket. He offered it to Wyn. "You can put in for a new shirt," Earl said. "Line of duty."

Neither moved. Earl waited until the badge weighed about a ton in his hand, and he had almost given up when Wyn took it. Earl said, "You're going to sleep, right? Back to your place to sleep, right?"

"After I switch cars," Wyn said. "I'll switch cars on the way home."

Earl watched him moving through the crowd. Wyn walked like a prince, as if he owned everything around him. Earl remembered his big plans for the kid: Mayor Ainsley, Congressman Ainsley. To himself, Earl said, "It didn't work this time, but it'll happen. It'll happen."

He decided then and there to get the kid off the street, get him out of uniform. Earl decided to make him a deke, a detective second class. Why should the sheriff's own kid be wrestling drunks? Wyn could wear a suit and drive an unmarked car. As Earl pulled down his hatbrim, he spotted the dude with a dotted scarf around his neck walking straight into the pavilion. "Hey, you!"

The guy didn't stop. "Hey!" Earl yelled, and went after him. And heard Holt's sister say, "Get out!"

Colin didn't stop, didn't see her. He didn't see anyone but Holt.

"You heard her," Holt said. "Get out." Holt waved to Earl as he entered the pavilion. "Sheriff!"

"He won't help you," Colin said. "Nobody can help you now. You're not in your Castle now."

"You little runt," Holt said. "I don't need help to handle you. I step on runts like you." He took a step toward Colin and stopped dead, and in the crowd around the open pavilion a woman screamed.

"He's got a gun!"

The woman spun around to escape, swinging her arms to get away, turning the crowd into a mob.

When Russell saw the gun, he shouted, "No! No!" and threw himself at Gaby. He knocked her to the wooden floor, fell on her, and covered her body with his body.

Burris shouted, "He has a gun!" Turning fast, he wrapped his arms around Serena, shielding her.

Earl said, "Drop it," his gun in his hand. He was moving in a wide arc to get clear of everyone but the goof facing Holt. "Drop it," Earl said, dreading what he had to do. Jesus Christ, he had never shot at a man.

Facing Colin, who held the Colt revolver he had purchased with his riding boots, Holt lunged to his right for a wooden folding chair to shield himself. "You little son of a bitch," he said as Colin raised the gun. Holt threw the chair, but he was too late. Colin shot him in the belly and kept firing.

Earl jumped clear of the chair Holt had thrown. As Holt crumpled and dropped, Earl raised his gun and pulled the trigger. He killed Colin instantly.

Colin's arms flew up, and the gun fell, and he fell across Holt's legs, and their blood flowed together on the bare wooden floor. Beyond the pavilion women screamed and men shouted, all trying to escape.

By that time the pavilion was full of deputies, all with guns in their hands. "What the hell!" Len Egan said. "What the goddamn hell!" He and Arver Long and Ben Miller surrounded Earl.

"It's over," Earl said. Jesus Christ, he had a goddamn massacre on his hands, a goddamn massacre. He pushed his gun into the holster on his hip. "It's over," he said, knowing everything was starting again, the reporters and the photographers turning the courthouse into a circus again. He rubbed his eyes. He had just killed a man. He pointed at Len Egan. "Get the coroner," Earl said. "Arver, go with him. Bring the coroner back with you. Arver!" Earl's voice cracked like a whip. "I don't care if he's in the bathtub. You bring him."

"I hear you, Sheriff," Arver Long said.

Earl could see the mob around the pavilion. The circus had started already. He shoved Ben Miller. "Find something to cover the bodies. Do it," he said, shoving Ben Miller again.

Earl saw Frank Burris with Serena, and he saw Russell Vance with Holt's sister, half the size of the twins, of Sharon and Doreen. The tiny woman had it all now, all the B Stock, Kyle's and Holt's and hers. And Russell Vance had her. And three men were dead. The Castleton men were dead, gone forever, unless the widow had one in her belly. And nothing had changed.

Serena had her half of the B Stock, and the half-pint with Russell Vance would collect the other half. "Why don't you folks go on home? Let us handle this," Earl said. "Mr. Burris? Mr. Vance? Let us handle this." Earl couldn't wait to be rid of them. He could think of nothing but getting Wyn back.

Wyn left the black-and-white at the courthouse and drove home in his car. He loosened his tie as he climbed the stairs. He didn't even see Mrs. Metcalfe in her chair on the porch, didn't even hear her say, "Will it rain?" and, gasping, "Your shirt!"

In his bedroom Wyn pulled off his tie and began to unbutton his shirt but stopped. He sat down on the bed and fell back, closing his eyes. And opened his eyes, sitting erect. Deep inside he had known sleep was impossible even when he assured his father he would go to bed. He had to finish what he had started, and the worst part of the day was still to come. Wyn had been stalling ever since leaving Boyd Fredericks. He rose and buttoned his shirt as he left the bedroom.

———◉———

EARLIER IN THE DAY, as the house on Deer Hollow Road had cooled precipitously, Faith left her play about Penelope and Ulysses at the card table in front of the fireplace and lay down on the leather sofa. She slept almost immediately, and when she woke, she heard window shades flapping in the wind. Thick, heavy rain was splattering on the roof, almost rhythmic in its constancy. She hurried up the stairs to close the windows everywhere, going from room to room, and as she reached the head of the stairs, on her way to close the windows below, she heard the door below. It opened with a morbid creaking.

The sound of the door stopped her. Only she and Wyn had keys. Faith heard heavy footsteps, a man's footsteps, and although badly frightened, she started down the stairs. Below, Wyn saw her coming and stopped, and Faith saw him and stopped. He wore his uniform. He had never come to Deer Hollow Road in his uniform. And he had never come in daylight. And his shirt was torn. An icy tidal wave of fear engulfed her.

She came down the stairs slowly. Wyn always greeted her as though they had been apart for years, gathering her up in his arms and kissing her and kissing her. He didn't move. "All I can see is the electric chair," Faith said.

"You'll never see the electric chair."

Faith stopped on the stairs, leaning against the banister, her hands atop it, fingers spread as though she hung from a precipice. The only sound came from the persistent rain on the roof, like an ominous drumroll. "Say that again."

"You'll never see the electric chair," Wyn said.

On the stairs, looking down at Wyn, Faith said, "I'm afraid to believe you."

"It's all over," Wyn said. "You'll walk out of here free." Each time he saw her he discovered her mesmerizing beauty anew. "It's all over."

Faith started down the stairs slowly, pausing between each stair and watching Wyn all the time. "Is it true? Wyn?" She nodded. "It's true. You wouldn't lie, not you. Or guess. You wouldn't guess."

"I'm giving you facts," he said.

"Oh, God . . . merciful God," she said. "Oh, merciful God," she said. She reached the foot of the staircase and, catching Wyn unprepared, sprang at him. "How did this happen? Tell me everything. Everything! Wait!" Faith took his hand, pulling him. "In here, where I can see you," she said. "I can barely see you. I want to see you when you tell me." She brought him to the fireplace. Faith could hear the rain, louder at the open windows, soaking the windowsill and the floor below the windows, but she no longer cared. "Now tell me."

"I made a trade."

She watched him. "A trade . . ."

"Right," Wyn said. "With Holt Castleton. I traded him your B Stock, Kyle's B Stock for your . . . freedom. He'll talk to them at the courthouse. They'll drop all charges." Wyn took his hand from hers. He had to be clear of her, clear to think straight. "Case closed."

Faith said, carefully, "You gave away my B Stock."

"Traded . . ." Wyn said.

"Traded," she said. "You can't. It's mine. Sam Castleton's foundation says the stock is mine. Only his heirs and the children of his heirs can own the B Stock. Kyle's belongs to my child."

"You can prove that," Wyn said.

"Prove?" Faith frowned. "Sam Castleton set down the terms.

He left the B Stock, set up the B Stock, so his heirs would always control the company."

"You're talking about the foundation," Wyn said. "I'm talking about the baby."

She said, "My baby."

"Whose?"

"Mine?" Faith said.

"And . . ."

Her overpowering fear returned, even more deadly. "Why are you questioning me? Wyn?"

Wyn said, to stop the game, "It's Boyd's. Right, Faith?"

Her lips parted, and Wyn waited for her to answer, but she could not. "You must have been after the B Stock right from the start," Wyn said. "You needed a baby in your belly fast, fast. And when Kyle couldn't make a baby, you found someone who could. You wanted that stock so bad, you'd fuck for it, fuck anyone, even Boyd Fredericks, that poor simp."

When she managed to say, barely, "No . . ." Wyn wanted to hit her. And he wanted to kiss her. He loathed her, but he still loved her. "I felt sorry for Boyd," Faith said.

"Sure . . ."

"I swear. It's the truth!" Faith said. "Kyle had gone to the air races, and Boyd . . . he was so unhappy. I let him put his arms around me."

"You're still lying," Wyn said. "Why keep lying? To me? The yokel. I'm just another yokel. Try the truth, Faith. You killed Kyle."

"I didn't. Wyn, I didn't." She shook her head.

"You're safe, Faith," he said, delivering his great gift. "Holt won't do anything. Nobody will do anything."

"I didn't kill him."

"Come on. I've just given you back your freedom," Wyn said. "Tell the truth . . . for once. Kyle must have found out you were having a baby. It had to be Boyd's baby. So you had to kill him."

"I didn't!" She threw herself at Wyn and took his wrists in her hands. "I did not kill him," Faith said. "Yes, he learned I was pregnant. Yes, he guessed it was Boyd. But I did not kill him. I could not. I am not a killer. Wyn!" She released him and moved away. "I could not kill anyone! I could not, could not!"

"I told you, you're in the clear."

"He killed himself!" Faith cried. "He left me in the bedroom, and I followed him to the sleeping porch. I opened the door and saw him beside the bed holding the gun against his head. He said, 'Hello again and good-bye,' and pulled the trigger. And there you have the truth, Wyn. You say I'm free. Am I really free?"

"Free as the breeze," Wyn said.

"Then why should I lie?"

"Kyle was bare-handed," Wyn said. "And there were no finger-prints."

"I didn't touch the gun," Faith said. "Kyle fell, and the gun fell . . . dropped. I saw the gun drop."

"You're still lying," Wyn said.

"I'm not—"

"You . . . Oh, hell . . ." Wyn said, and turned away.

She watched him walk toward the stone steps on his way to the door, on his way out. And discovered she wanted him to stay. He suited her. The big, strong stud who didn't ask for anything, didn't expect anything suited her. She could get a bigger apartment. But later. First they would go somewhere. They would take a long trip. Broadway could wait. Penelope could wait. They could go to Greece. . . .

"Wyn!" She ran after him. "Wyn, you can't go!" She caught him at the door. "You can't leave me."

Wyn looked at the beautiful woman, looked into her gray eyes, her bewitching eyes. "You're still acting," he said.

"I'm not!" she said, lying. "Don't go, Wyn!"

"We're finished," he said.

"Not us," she said. "Not you and I."

"I'm going," Wyn said. "If I stay now, I'll stay forever or until you're tired of me. I'd rather die," he said.

Suddenly he pushed her hard and left the house. He crossed the veranda and walked into the rain, heading for his car as though he had weights on his legs.

"Wyn!"

He reached his car and went around it to the driver's door. He opened the door and hesitated, standing in the rain. He had given Kyle's gun, wrapped in his handkerchief, to his father. His father had sent the gun to Raleigh. "Waste of stamps," Wyn whispered. His father was no different from the coroner and Max Isbell and all the rest. His father had protected the Castletons.

Wyn dug into his pocket for the badge. He pulled it out and threw it into the trees. Wyn looked back at the house. Faith stood in the open doorway in the light. For a moment they faced each other, and then Wyn got into the car and closed the car door. He turned the ignition key, and the engine caught. He had to go, and he had nowhere to go.

Wyn turned the wheel and drove slowly around the circle at the end of the cul-de-sac, heading for Deer Hollow Road, heading out.

Alone.

• A NOTE ON THE TYPE •

The typeface used in this book, Transitional, is a digitized version of Fairfield, designed in 1937–40 by artist Rudolph Ruzicka (1883–1978), on a commission from Linotype. The assignment was the occasion for a well-known essay in the form of a letter from W. A. Dwiggins to Ruzicka, in response to the latter's request for advice. Dwiggins, who had recently designed Electra and Caledonia, relates that he would start by making very large scale drawings (10 and 64 times the size you are reading) and having test cuttings made, which were used to print on a variety of papers. "By looking at all these for two or three days I get an idea of how to go forward—or, if the result is a dud, how to start over again." At this stage he took *parts* of letters that satisfied him and made cardboard cutouts, which he then used to assemble other letters. This "template" method anticipated one that many contemporary computer type designers use.